ICE MAGIC
FIRE MAGIC

SHAUNA ROBERTS

ICE MAGIC, FIRE MAGIC

Cover Art & Design © Tom Vandenberg
Edited by Terri-Lynne DeFino & Eric T. Reynolds

ISBN-13   978-0-9892631-8-4

Published simultaneously in the United States of America and the United Kingdom by

Hadley Rille Books
Eric T. Reynolds, Publisher
PO Box 25466
Overland Park, KS 66225 USA
www.hrbpress.com
contact@hadleyrillebooks.com

Dedicated to my husband, David A. Malueg,
the rock under my feet and the sun who lights my days.

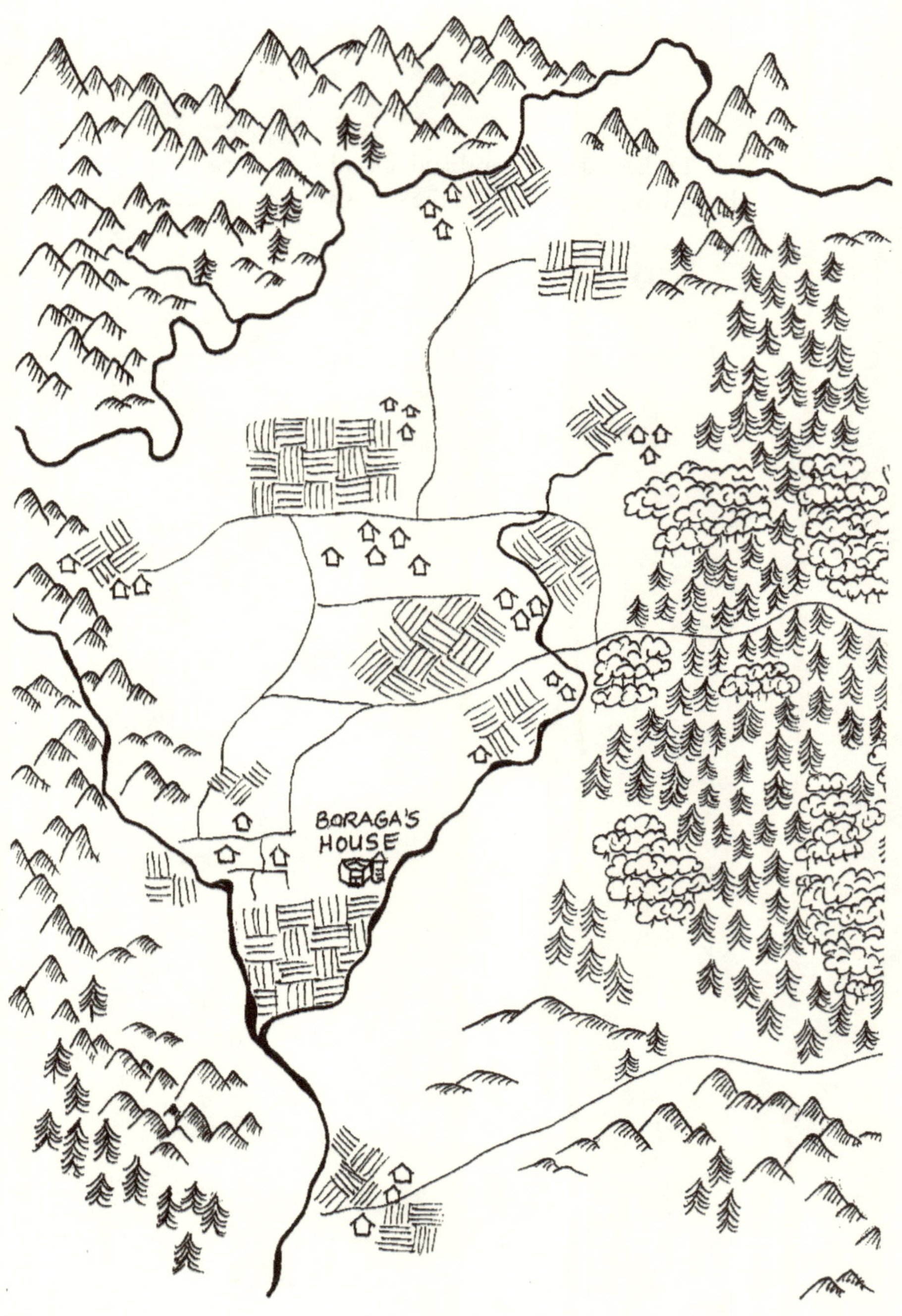

BORAGA'S
HOUSE

Dedicated to my husband, David A. Malueg,
the rock under my feet and the sun who lights my days.

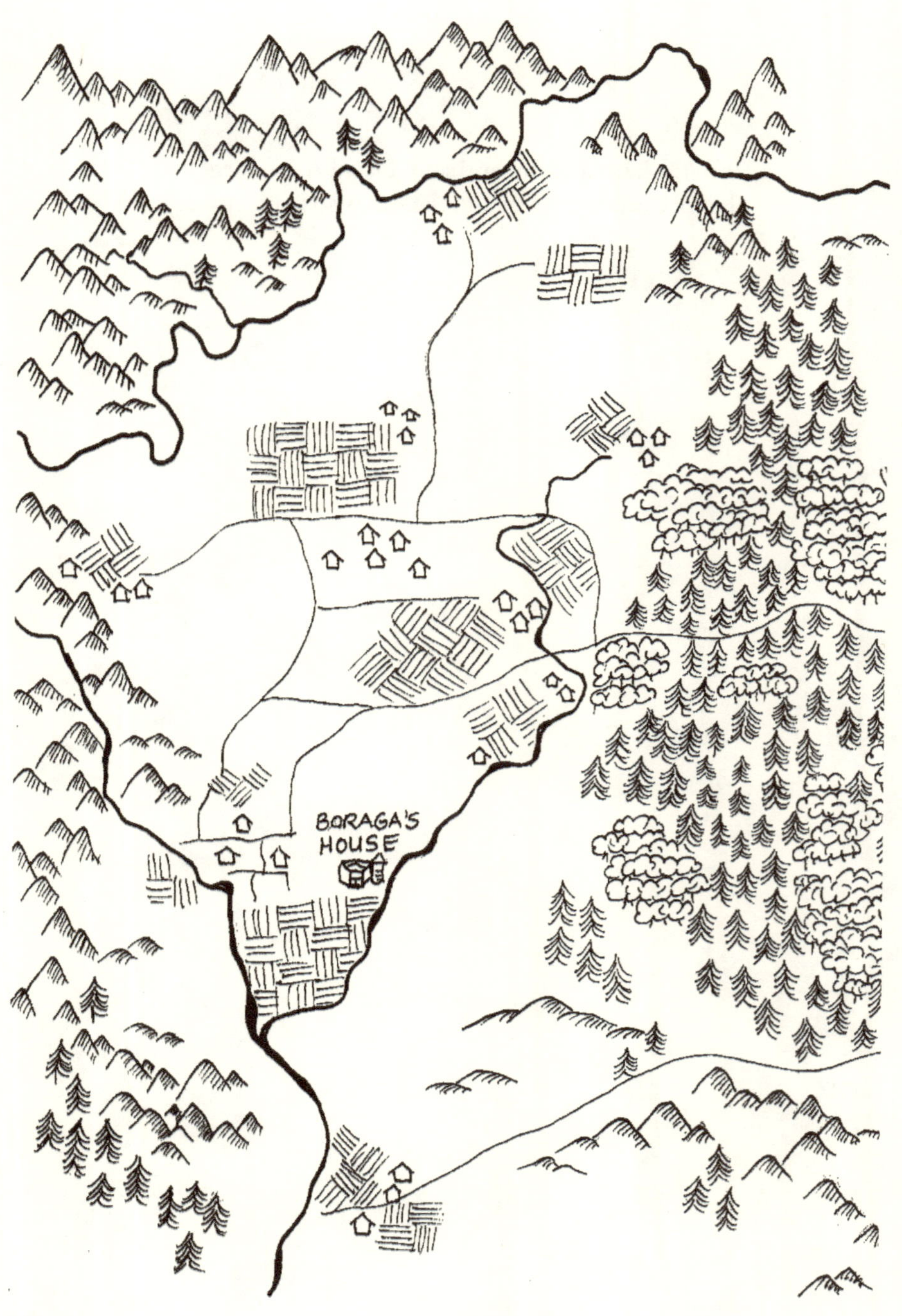

BORAGA'S
HOUSE

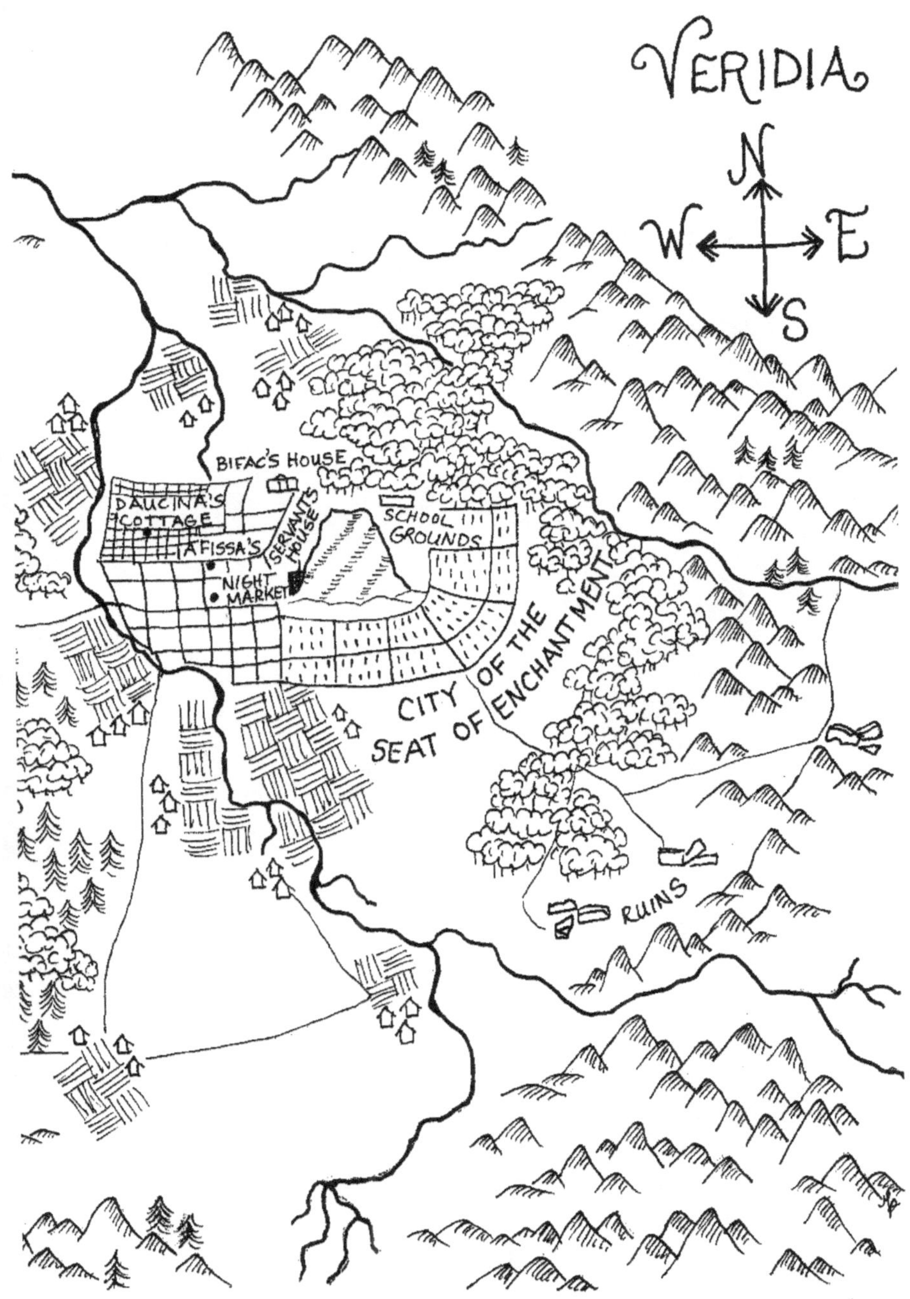

VERIDIA
N
W
E
S
BIFAC'S HOUSE
DAUCINA'S COTTAGE
AFISSA'S
SERVANTS' HOUSE
SCHOOL GROUNDS
NIGHT MARKET
CITY OF THE SEAT OF ENCHANTMENT
RUINS

Prologue

"WHAT DO YOU THINK the boys will blow up with their magic today?" Kassia bounced on her stool, her unusual pale hair fluttering.

Eight-year-old Fila mulled her cousin's question, the tip of her tongue sticking out of her mouth as she stitched to the rhythm of the gentle pattering of rain. "Another cooking crock, I hope. Father was grateful when I gave the pieces to him. He uses such things in the bottom of flower pots."

Someone in the circle of girls snickered.

Fila's head flew up, ripping out the hairs she had accidentally embroidered into her sampler. "Ouch!" she cried.

Astilbe's snickers turned into peals of laughter. Galium and Psoralea joined in, staring at Fila.

Heat climbed from Fila's chest up her neck to her face and ears. She rubbed the sore spot on her head with her knuckles, wondering what she had done this time to make the other girls laugh and wishing Teacher Parthena would return from her errand.

Kassia leapt up from her stool. Flower buds and skeins of yarn flew off her lap and landed in piles on the ancient oak floor. Knitting needles clattered to rest beside them; beads bounced and rolled across the room.

"How dare you?" Kassia shouted, hands on hips, glaring at the laughing girls until the last one dropped her gaze. "You know Teacher Parthena says we must not laugh at Fila because she's a Goodborn. She can't help being a toady."

Heat stung Fila's cheeks. She didn't know what a "toady" was, but it sounded warty and awful. She glanced toward the cloakroom. She longed to run inside, drop the bar on the door, and hide among the boots and long cloaks, imagining herself surrounded by the familiar, comforting smells of wool and herbs and oiled leather. Another girl might get away with it, but she was the daughter of the Servant of Enchantment. Everyone expected her to be brave.

She *was* brave. She had had lots of practice.

She stood, pulling at Kassia's sleeve. "Cousin, please don't scold them. They're just little girls."

"So are we, and we have good manners." Kassia put her arm around Fila. "When we grow up and I am the Servant, I will take care of you. No one will ever take advantage of you or make fun of you again."

Astilbe giggled.

Kassia scorched her with a scowl. "If someone does, I'll have them put to death."

The schoolroom fell into silence. Fila pulled away and knelt to collect her cousin's spilled things, starting with the soft bundles of colors right in front of their stools. Kassia was so certain she would be Servant one day. Did the Land already talk to her as it did to Mother? Fila had heard the grownups gossip; her cousin was a Talent, the greatest magical talent in two generations. That was why she was already doing advanced sewing while Fila still struggled with her sampler. And like Fila, she was a great-granddaughter of Granite, one of the few men ever chosen by the Land as Its Servant.

Fila reached up to deposit flowers and yarn balls on the chair seat and crawled toward some others. Good thing her amma had dressed her in a practical gray cotton dress with matching pantaloons; Kassia's mother would shriek if she came home from school with her pale pink silk dress filthy from crawling on the floor.

The door handle rattled, and the door flew open with such force that it hit the stone wall. Several older boys stomped in, smelling like wet dogs and snuffling like them too. Their wet boots squished. As they tromped by, drops of wetness splashed her face, and Fila scrambled to her feet.

Her brother, Urushi, five years older, shouted, "Look what we have!" The boys held up tiny balls of fur.

The girls jumped up from their stools and clustered in a half-circle around the boys.

Kassia pulled Fila's arm. "I want to see. Come on!"

The boys all stared at Kassia, as usual. It was not only her exotic paleness that drew their attention. She was the only girl whose laughter tinkled, the only girl whose cheeks flushed beautifully, not blotchily. She was the prettiest, too, and always wore beautiful clothes. Only Kassia's gangly brother, Celatu, did not stare at her, but instead studied the fuzzy creature in his hand.

Urushi stepped up to Kassia and opened his hands. "Which one do you want?" he shyly asked.

"Oooohhh!" Kassia bounced as she and Fila looked at the two baby rabbits. Both reached for the gray-brown one with fur as plush as a carpet and a twitching black nose.

"I want this one." Kassia grabbed it and held it to her chest, stroking it as it struggled to escape. Fila took the other one, a spotted bunny with only one ear.

"Thank you so much!" Kassia gushed. "It is so, so pretty." She looked up at Urushi. "You are wonderful to give it to me."

Urushi's chest swelled. He took a rabbit from another boy. The other girls crowded closer to the boys, pleading for rabbits of their own.

As Fila stroked her rabbit, amazed at its softness and warmth, her knees wobbled. Its eyes were glossier than a beetle's shell; its toenails delicate arcs of white laced with shell pink. When it stretched, yawned, and nestled into a ball in her hand, her heart sped up to match the beat of the rabbit's own. All animals trusted her, knowing by instinct she was Goodborn, but this time was different. She and this rabbit were meant to be together. It needed a name.

"Kassia, what do you think—"

But Kassia was guiding Urushi out of the crush of children and didn't hear her. She would have to choose a name by herself. Spotty? One-Ear? No, she should choose a name that highlighted one of its best features. "Bright Eyes! Do you like that name, bunny?"

"Watch out!" Kassia cried.

Fila ducked, then realized her brother was the one in danger. His feet skated and slid on beads that had spilled earlier from Kassia's lap … the beads that she had not yet picked up. Wincing, she bit her lip as he tipped this way and that, his magic building with his fear. Her nose and mouth filled with the odd moldy flavor of his magic; her skin tingled from her scalp to her toes. The bunny in her hands writhed. Then Urushi lost his balance and fell.

Just before his head would have smashed against the floor, he twisted. His elbow hit the floor with a crack. Urushi groaned, and a strange, wet noise that sickened Fila's stomach filled the room. Warm liquid splashed her face, its smell salty and metallic.

Outside, thunder exploded.

Fila wiped her eyes with a shaking arm. Her gray sleeve came away streaked with russet.

The other younglings, both boys and girls, looked as scared and confused as she felt. They huddled together, shoulders hunched.

"Ewww!" cried Astilbe. She pointed at Urushi; Fila followed the line of her finger. Her brother's tunic was soaked with blood.

Fila ran to him even though her needlework skills could not heal anything but the smallest scratch. "Let me see your elbow."

He didn't turn, didn't answer. Instead, he stared into his cupped, gore-filled hands.

Fila gasped. "Oh, Urushi! Your poor rabbit!"

Laughing nervously, most girls scurried away and clustered in a corner. The boys fidgeted with their rabbits, their hair, and the pouches hanging from their belts, looking everywhere but at Urushi. Fila was not immune to their fear and dread. She held Bright Eyes close to her chest and moved closer to Kassia.

Two boys whispered together and then broke into laughter.

Kassia's rabbit burst.

Shrieking, the girls scattered. Boys chased them, waving bunnies. A boy grabbed Astilbe's hair. He shoved a rabbit in front of her face and made it explode.

A tall, gawky boy blundered out of the classroom clutching a rabbit to his chest. Celatu had abandoned his sister.

Kassia's face was bone white, her mouth open but no sound coming out. She held her gory hands in front of her, clenching and opening them. Gouts of grey-brown fur and tissue spotted her beautiful clothes, and blood dripped down her face.

The classroom darkened as the rain outside became a torrent. Lightning split the sky, illuminating Urushi.

He sat on the floor staring at his hands, his face crumpled as if he were in pain.

I must help Kassia and Urushi. But which one first? It would be wrong to comfort one before the other. She stretched to touch her brother's shoulder, pressing her arm against Kassia's back at the same time. Urushi's body seemed carved from obsidian, so hard and cold it was.

He jerked at her touch. "I didn't hurt Kassia's rabbit," he muttered. "I did *not* hurt Kassia's rabbit. My rabbit was an accident."

Fila retched and clutched her stomach. It felt as if it would explode too. A wailing, icy gust swept in the unglazed windows as the Land reacted.

I must comfort him. Tenderhearted Urushi never went fishing with Father because he couldn't bear to pierce the worm with a hook. *He must feel even more sickened than I do.* Her Goodborn instincts roared at her to go to him, but disgust made her back away.

Someone shoved her from behind. Her heart beat like a crow's wings inside her chest. *Please, don't make Bright Eyes explode.*

The rabbit remained solid and whole in her hand. Her breath exploded in a whoosh of air. But the nasty boys still ran and shouted, out of control.

She had to find a place for her and Kassia to hide.

The cloakroom! She grabbed Kassia by the arm and pulled her to her feet. She seemed half-asleep. "Follow me," Fila told her. Kassia stared at nothing.

Fila hid the rabbit in the crook of her elbow, out of the boys' sight.

A gap opened in the fracas. She tightened her grip on Kassia and darted through. The stream of shouting, running younglings closed around them. Fila braced her feet to keep from being knocked over. She waited. Another gap, another quick dart. They were a few feet closer to the door. Again. And again. At last they were away from the herd of boys.

Pulling Kassia, she ran inside and shut the door. She wrestled the bar with her elbow until it clanged into place. Then she dropped below the door's window and tugged a still-stunned Kassia down.

Teacher Parthena's huge green cloak hung nearby. She longed to crawl under the hem and inside the heavy folds, where it would be dark and smell like lambs. But Kassia dripped with gore. Fila looked down at her own clothes; they were spattered too.

She sighed. She crawled toward the corner by the window, coaxing Kassia to follow with soft, gentle words.

Once in the corner, Fila placed Bright Eyes on her lap and hugged Kassia tightly. "You're safe now," Fila said. "The door's bolted. The boys can't get in."

Kassia flung her arms around Fila and sobbed. "My bunny! It was so pretty and then it was, was…." She sniffed back the snot drop threatening to fall from her nose. "I was scared the boys would hurt me too. You saved me, Fila."

"I hate boys," Fila said. "All they do is break things."

They held each other for hours, long after the noise in the classroom died down. The Toiler device implanted under the skin of Fila's arm vibrated.

She sagged with relief. "Spotted Turtle is looking for me. Our ammas will be here soon."

Kassia touched the quivering skin. "You're so lucky. Tell me the story again."

"A Toiler village flooded in heavy spring rains. The next week, a tornado came through and destroyed the rest of the village. Mother and Father spent weeks there using their magic to help them rebuild."

"Skip to the part about the eyebrows and the gifts. That's my favorite." Kassia rested her head against Fila's.

"Mother went to the Servant's library. She and Erudia the Melancholy studied maps and history books. They learned the village sat in a low place that had had many floods and tornadoes. Then Mother asked Father's Cousin Kriga to visit. She was a Talent like you."

"And her eyebrows were like caterpillars." Kassia giggled, though she kept strong hold of Fila.

"Fat and prickly like caterpillars. Mother and Cousin Kriga made a beautiful tapestry with strong magic for the village. It took a long time to make. Now it protects them from floods and tornadoes. The villagers were so happy, they created the tracking thing in my arm. Mother asked the Land whether she could accept the Toiler tech, and It said she could."

"When *I* am Servant, I will get lots of presents."

Fila nodded. "You will do many good things for Guardians and Toilers."

"That too. But mainly I will wear such beautiful clothes and have such elegant manners that everyone will want to give me presents."

Fila bit her lip. "I don't think that's how it works."

"Yes it is. Mother said so." Kassia squirmed. "Why aren't our ammas here yet? I want to go home!"

"Let's go meet them. I have not heard anyone in the classroom in a long time." Fila stood, but Kassia pulled her back down.

"No. The boys may be waiting to blow up our rabbit."

Something in Fila's chest tightened. *Kassia said* our *rabbit. I want him for myself.* Her Goodborn instinct flared purple and pleasurable in her mind, sparkling, glittering, reshaping her intentions, illuminating the right path, the good path, the path she should take.

"No," she whispered. "I don't want to."

"Hush, Fila! I hear something."

Fila squeezed her eyes shut and listened hard. Far away, Spotted Turtle bellowed her name. In the gaps, Two Sparrows' soft voice called for Kassia.

"Our ammas are almost here."

Kassia let go of her.

Blinking, Fila jerkily handed her rabbit to Kassia. "His name is Bright Eyes. He is yours now."

Bright Eyes looked up from Kassia's hand, his black button eyes wide with fear, and Fila's chest hurt. She stroked his tiny head one last time. Then she stood, brushed the dust off her clothes, and walked over to open the door. Kassia followed.

Just before Fila lifted the latch, Kassia whispered, "I won't forget today. We'll be best friends forever."

*   *   *

Celatu clutched the kit to his chest and let his long legs carry him through the school's network of hallways and arcades, around younglings and teachers whose mouths dropped open at the sight of his blood-spattered clothes, until he burst free of the school buildings into the pouring rain. He glanced back. No one had followed him into the storm. He slowed to a walk, his feet squishing as he climbed the grassy hill, heading for the forest path that led back to the cottontail nest.

I'm a halfwit. He never should have shown the nest to the other boys, certainly not in the very week Teacher Senecio taught them how to focus their male magic of destruction at a point inside an object to make it explode. He never should have gone along with Urushi's suggestion that they take the kits to school to show their sisters. Kassia would be furious he had left her behind with the magic-crazed boys. What a disaster!

At least I saved one kit from death. Celatu tossed his hair back from his rain-drenched face as he followed the path into the towering trees, the last stand of virgin forest in the Seat of the Servant or anywhere nearby. The cool air refreshed him like a drink of water fresh from a spring. He stomped the wetness out of his shoes. Little rain penetrated the dense woods of ancient beeches, tulip trees, sweet buckeyes, and sugar maples, so the path was hard and nearly dry.

He breathed in the perfume of leaf mold and decaying wood, glad to be out of the rain, glad to be in the forest where he belonged, instead of within walls. He patted the kit dry with his tunic as he walked, stirring the gray squirrels to chitter at him. Beneath their scolding, in the bushes to his left, something rustled. He stopped, waiting. A bobcat snarled as it bounded across the path.

The kit must have caught its scent; it struggled until he had to hold it with both hands. "You'll be back in your nest soon," he told it. The blazes he had cut into the tree trunks stood out in the dim light. He followed them over and around the hills until he reached one of the creeks. Jumping across, startling a map turtle off its log, he climbed the bank. His brightly colored books stood out from the forest's green and browns. An arrow of stones pointed to the nest.

Celatu stepped off the path and shuffled in the leaf litter. The mother cottontail jumped straight up, landed, and raced away in a blur of brown. Clasping the kit in one hand again, he brushed the other hand through weeds and wildflowers until he spotted the nest.

He removed the covering beard grass and leaves, slid the kit into the fur-lined depression, and covered it again. The fragile creature back where it belonged, he shoved his sleeves up and shouted all the curses he knew at the skies. "Tarnished silver! Corroded copper! Land take Urushi and all his friends!" They would not find the kit again; he would make sure of it.

He let his magic build inside him, enjoying the rush of pleasure as raw power thrummed in his limbs, feeding on his anger, flowing into his head, filling his torso, until his whole body was surging.

But something felt off. He wrinkled his nose. His power tasted strange, bad, like the smell of an egg abandoned by a hen.

For the first time ever, he didn't want to use his magic.

I don't have to. I have nothing to prove. His magic was already stronger than the other boys', and his skill exceeded theirs. He scattered the rocks with kicks.

Then he returned to his books and the drawing of a tree he had started on a piece of paper. He had never seen the species before, and the tree stood the only one of its kind among the thousands of trees in the forest. He had sketched its silhouette and started detailed drawings of two leaves. He would also need to draw its bark and a fruit. Then he should have enough information to identify the tree in his family's library, which had volumes dating back to the time of the first Servant.

Several hours later, he walked home in the dark. The rain had stopped. He pulled open the door and strode past the disapproving Guardian servant without taking off his boots. "Kassia? Are you home? Are you all right?" He headed for the stairs.

"Celatu! Attend me in the parlor," called a cold, imperious voice. Mother was angry with him. Again.

He squared his shoulders and walked down the hall past old paintings of scowling ancestors toward the sitting room. He smelled the magic and its results before he reached the archway. Father had made logs combust in the fireplace. Mother had altered a plant to emit light and had flavored the tea with an herb that was currently dormant. They must have an important guest.

He walked into the sitting room, his gaze flying to Kassia. She had washed and put on a clean dress, but her eyes stared wildly from her pale face.

"How are you?" he asked.

She opened her hands and held them out. One of the kits trembled on them, safe.

"She will be fine, no thanks to you," Father said. "Why haven't you greeted the Servant of Enchantment? Your manners are appalling."

He looked for the glint of copper. The Servant, his father's twin, sat on a cushioned bench in the corner.

"Good evening, Aunt Hyacinth."

She was the only person in the room who didn't look cross, and now she blessed him with a genuine smile he was happy to return. "You look cold," she said.

"You look colder, Aunt." He shrugged out of his tunic and draped it over the Servant's bare, blue-tinged feet.

Mother hissed at his action, but the Servant patted the cushion next to her. "Get yourself some tea and come sit next to me. I so rarely see my favorite nephew."

"No tea," Mother countermanded, "and no putting your dirty clothes on the furniture. You will go to the library and not come out for a week."

"But Mother!" He would die if he couldn't go to the forest for that long.

Father stood and glared at him. "You could be an important man in the Seat one day, but only if you learn how to behave in society. During your week in the library, think about what I've told you. You've got to go along to get along." Excuses bubbled up in his mouth, but he clamped his teeth together to prevent their escape. He bowed to his parents and the Servant and forced a smile for Kassia. Then he shifted the books under his arm and walked out.

"May I walk with you?" the Servant called after him.

"Of course." His palms slickened. He fidgeted as she walked toward him. She said nothing when she joined him, only laced her arm into his.

When they were out of earshot of the sitting room, she said, "Please tell me what happened in the schoolroom. Fila wouldn't tell me, and Kassia's story was incoherent."

Fila was the Servant's mousy daughter, his cousin, whom he rarely saw and could never remember afterward when he did see her. He hadn't noticed her today, either.

He started with the boys finishing their class assignment and looking for something else to do. When he finished, the Servant said, "you're leaving something out."

His ears burned. He nodded.

"For the same reason my daughter wouldn't tell me what happened." She said it with certainty, not with a question. "The Land is distressed. Tell me why. "

He stayed quiet. So many things had happened at once. His memory might be confused.

"Even if you're not certain, tell me. Your words may enlighten me even if they're wrong."

"I don't think Urushi meant to kill the kit when he fell. The other boys thought he did it to scare the girls. But he likes Kassia and wanted to impress her."

Hyacinth rubbed her forehead. Her eyes were scrunched as if she were in pain. "What do you think happened?"

"I saw Urushi fall. His magic, well, it just shot out of him like a fart. You should have seen his expression. Shocked. Bewildered. Ashamed."

Hyacinth gazed at a portrait of an ugly, frowning Guardian woman wearing an even uglier headdress. Several Toiler servants gathered around her. Their great height and broad shoulders made his ancestress look dinky and unimportant, while their smiles showed their embarrassment at their employer's foul mood and bad taste.

The Servant spoke softly as if talking to herself. Or to the woman in the portrait, who was probably a shared ancestress. "He may grow out of it. Some boys are slow to learn to control their magic."

He itched to go to the library now, to research Urushi's condition and to find out whether the treatment was Toiler tech or Guardian magic. "May I escort you back to the sitting room?"

Her head jerked as if she had forgotten he stood next to her. "That won't be necessary." She looked up into his face for a long while. Celatu studied the rug, wishing the inspection over. "You are different from the other boys."

"So Father tells me. Often." He winced. He had just insulted the Servant's twin.

"What frightens your father pleases me." She reached into one of the purses tied to her sash. She brought out a coin and pressed it into his hand. His fingers closed around it protectively; it felt comforting in his palm, as if cast to fit.

Celatu leaned down and kissed her on the cheek. "You haven't given me pennies for candy since I was little."

She laughed. "I know you're too old for candy. The … piece … is old, very old. All magic; no tech. No vendor would mistake it for money."

"What would you like me to do with it then?" The soothing power of the coin reached his chest. He took his first deep breath since things went wrong in the classroom.

"Keep it with you. Think of it as a good luck charm."

*　*　*

The rapid *clack clack clack* of her wooden knitting needles comforted Fila as much as the cool, welcoming dirt floor beneath her. Around her, in Mother's large workroom, looms and needlework frames of all sizes and shapes, overflowing baskets of yarns, large balls of scratchy hemp twine, and other tools of the Servant's duty surrounded and protected her.

Only moonlight lit the beloved space, glittering off Mother's needles neatly pinned in the felt hangings on the walls. The friendly dark hid her finished stitches, letting her savor the soft yarn and concentrate on the act and not the result. Next to her, her favorite doll, Green Bean, rested in a basket.

Lamplight warmed the room; someone padded into the room. "Fila? Are you in here?" Mother called.

Fila kept quiet, but her needles kept clacking.

Mother's feet approached. The lamp moved over the blue rectangle; the few metallic strands of Mother's copper hair woven in glinted.

Mother gracefully lowered herself to a cross-legged position on the floor. She sighed in bliss as she touched and joined with the Land. "What are you making?"

"A blanket for Green Bean to make her invisible to boys."

"You can do that?"

Fila hesitated. "Maybe."

"Why does Green Bean need to be invisible?"

"She doesn't. But if I get it right, I can make a blanket big enough to protect Kassia."

Mother stroked her hair. "I think Kassia will soon be good at handling boys on her own."

"She was so scared today." Fila pressed her lips together to keep from saying more.

"I heard about the rabbits."

"Boys are bad!" Fila burst out. "I hate them."

"To thrive, Veridia and its peoples need male magic of destruction as much as female magic of creation."

"I still hate them."

"You love Urushi, don't you?"

He killed a bunny. But he was sad about it. "I guess so."

"I would like you and Green Bean to come to my chamber now. Then before you go to bed, you can read a story to Urushi."

"Will he stop being sad if I do?"

"He will feel better."

"It's my duty then." She picked up Green Bean and wrapped her in her incomplete blanket, then followed Mother through the house and up the stairs to her chamber. As Mother looked through a cabinet, Fila sniffed Mother's dressing gown, a stack of handkerchiefs with crocheted edging, the lacy knitted shawl draped over the rocking chair. She could never get enough of Mother's scent.

"I'd like you to have this necklace." Mother held up a metal chain with a metal pendant, a hole in the middle. There was nothing soft or flowery about it.

"Is it Toiler tech? What does it do?"

Mother put it over Fila's head. Its warmth—and something more—radiated through her blouse.

Fila touched it with a fingertip, and her eyes wanted to jump from her face. "It's full of magic. Very old grown-up magic."

Mother nodded approvingly. "Good awareness! I was going to wait until you were older to give you this. But it feels appropriate for you to have it now."

Chapter 1

Ten years later...

To WEAVE THE WORLD was a woman's highest calling. So it was said, and so Fila believed. On an afternoon like this one, with the scent of honeysuckle and lavender wafting warm through the open windows of the needleroom, it was also a woman's highest joy. Fila stuck out the tip of her tongue as she and the other young women her age stitched under the watchful eyes of their teachers. In and out, in and out, her needle wove the twined threads through the needlepoint canvas. Green cotton thread, to make the newly planted fields fertile. Red wool, to make the ewes bear twins. Hair pulled from her own head as the sacrifice to set the magic.

She beamed, shutting out the mindless chatter of the other students. She delighted in this part of their training. Tonight, some students would grumble about the boredom of the needleroom; they always did. Others, such as her cousin Kassia, would stand with their looking glasses in the fading light by the windows, searching their scalps for bald spots.

But not Fila. For her, the ancient designs and techniques were a link to the original Guardians, who had joined forces with the living Land of Veridia, sealing its borders with magic and ushering in a thousand years of prosperity.

The rhythm of the needle lulled her into a blissful state in which the world compressed to a few sensations. The coos of mourning doves on the tower roof. The soft-prickly yarn against her calloused fingers. The distinctive scents of the turning year—fresh-turned earth during the sowing season, flowers and herbs during the growing season, sweet hay during the harvest season, and burning wood during the fallow season. And always, always, the earthy scent of the bare Land beneath their slippers.

She threaded her needle with a different yarn, blue this time, thinking of the unknown Toilers whose work in the cornfields today had been eased by her needle. Of course, she had worked hard too. She rubbed her neck, stiff from hours in the same position.

Next to her, Kassia whispered, "Are you bored too? At least our lesson today is easy."

Kassia was a Talent; all magic came easily to her.

Fila looked at the lumps and bumps in her stitches that would weaken the magic of her canvas and bit her lip. "It's not easy for me, Cousin." She threaded two extra hairs through her needle, glancing up to make certain none of the older Guardians had noticed. They would scold her and tell her to make her stitches more precise and even, like Kassia's; then she would not need extra magic to bolster their power.

She sighed. Her mind always foresaw success; her inept fingers instead often met with defeat. She had one consolation: When Mother was her age, she too had struggled to train her fingers. When Fila was home last, she and Mother had laughed together, comparing their first poor efforts at concentrating the essential oils in herbs and playfully arguing about whose early crochet knots were worse.

One day Fila too would conquer her clumsiness and be a good Guardian, one whose skill matched the strength of her magic, one who did her duty, one who healed the sick and helped the Land prosper.

A vibration tickled the back of her neck.

She ignored it. Odd sensations were common in this room, where so much magic had been woven over the centuries. But then, as if a curtain had been pulled across the sun, the room plunged into twilight.

"What's happening?" Kassia asked.

The tingle raced down Fila's spine, an agony of torturous pleasure.

Her back arched, her body rebelling against the growing pain. She gripped her frame with white knuckles, waiting. Powerful magic was building, magic like none she had ever experienced. From what cause? To what end? She didn't know and couldn't guess. She could but wait and grit her teeth.

Women's magic had taught her patience.

An unfamiliar magic raged through Fila—burning, biting, stinging, stabbing, throbbing.

She writhed, and a moan escaped her lips.

"What's wrong with you?" Cousin Kassia chided. "Everyone is staring." Then she spoke loudly, indignantly. "I cannot stitch in this light. You there, Toiler, do something!"

The Land erupted in rage. Thunder shook the tower; lightning ripped open the sky. Cold air blasted the room, knocking over chairs and frames.

The students snatched up their balls of yarn and held onto their frames. "Why is the Land doing this?" Kassia demanded.

The Toiler servants thudded quickly from window to window on their huge feet, slamming the shutters closed and bolting them against the unnatural storm.

Burning. Fila's scalp began to burn, starting at the base of her skull and rolling up and over her head.

Screaming, desperate to flee, Fila scraped her chair back across the dirt floor and leapt up. She staggered forward a few steps, but waves of pain forced her to her knees. The ground rippled when her knees touched it. Her hair burst free of its ribbon, clumps falling to the floor, and her silver pendant swung like a pendulum.

She reached her hands forward, beseeching.

The other students backed away, even Kassia; one fled the room, shrieking. *They blame me for angering the Land!* But she had done nothing, just as she could do nothing to stop the storms, neither the one outside nor the one racing through her.

Then massive, comforting arms enveloped Fila. She leaned against her old Toiler nursemaid. "Too much magic, Amma." Her limbs jerked. "It's tearing me apart. The Land...." Her fingers curled, the nails gouging her palms.

"Hold on," Spotted Turtle's deep voice crooned.

Fila's scalp stretched tight, and it felt as if it were being pricked with thousands of pins. She buried her face in her amma's shoulder and pressed her lips together to hold back her screams.

Slowly the pain eased, and Amma picked her up and placed her in her chair. Fila focused on stilling her shaking hands, refusing to think about what happened, refusing to look up at the other students, refusing to acknowledge the self she had been for eighteen summers had been gutted.

"Fetch a looking glass, please," Boraga, her teacher and owner of the manor, ordered a servant between claps of thunder. "Blankets and candles, too. Students, return to your work." She walked over to Fila and put a steadying hand on her shoulder. The Toiler returned with the looking glass, and Boraga held it out.

The silvered glass was confined in a ring of dull brass etched with glyphs of the Old Language. To grasp its handles was to take hold of a future she was not ready for, a future in which her choices would be as circumscribed as the looking glass. She shook her head.

Boraga placed the looking glass in Fila's trembling hands and closed her fingers around the handles. "My dear, you must look."

She closed her eyes.

"You can't avoid your destiny. Or your duty."

Duty. Fila opened her eyes and raised the looking glass slowly. At first she saw nothing but the pale oval of her face. As the Toilers lit the candles one by one, the image sharpened, and she sucked in her breath.

Her hair! Gone were the limp brown strings that never held a style. Her head was now wreathed in copper, glorious, gleaming curls of copper wire finer than baby hair and the color of a new coin, copper that graced only one head in the land.

Mother is dead.

Fila clenched her eyes against hot tears. Memories assaulted her. Mother twirling her around a field, the flowers around them a rainbow blur but her mother's face clear, her copper hair streaming and her head thrown back in laughter. Mother demonstrating the difference between a yarn-over after a knit stitch and after a purl stitch. Mother teaching her the ninety kinds of yarn and their names. Now an angry Land mourned her death and inexplicably chose her clumsy daughter as Its spokeswoman.

If only there were a magic for traveling long distances in an instant. She would go home to mourn with Father and poor Urushi. Her brother would take their mother's death hard. Keeping him alive and sane would now be Fila and Father's burden.

The storm outside echoed the whirlwind of memories. Blasts of wind wrenched wooden shutters from their hinges. Pulling free of Amma and Boraga, she strode to a window, letting hail scour her face. Mother was gone, leaving a deep, sucking hole inside Fila's chest that threatened to devour her.

Hands touched her shoulders and gently turned Fila to face the room.

The students and teachers knelt before her, all except Kassia, who stood hands on hip. The Toilers also stood, but with hands clasped in respect.

They are all my charges now.

Boraga came around to face her, looking at her with eyes grown suddenly old. She grasped her hands and said the time-honored words: "Welcome, new Servant. May you mediate between the Land and Its people for a hundred years."

Under the heavy weight of her responsibilities, Fila sagged and fell; Amma caught her. She must take up her duties right away. Judge disputes. Parcel out resources. Preside over festivals. Make new laws and amend the old. And a hundred other tasks, including keeping peace among the advisors on her council. But how could she, when inside her, grief and disbelief warred?

Boraga knelt and slid off Fila's slippers so her feet touched the cool, damp earthen floor of the classroom. Alien thoughts and emotions flooded her as she endured her first full communion with the Land of Veridia.

Overwhelmed, she rose onto her toe tips, straining upward to reduce her contact with the Land. A new feeling rose from her toes, an invitation sent with love.

Her fear fled. She set her feet firmly down, dug her toes into the dirt floor, and opened herself to the Land.

Its screams of anguish felt as if they were her own. Her mother's death was ripping the soul of Veridia apart. Or was something more wrong? She was too young, too inexperienced, to know. But she did know her duty. She lay down and pressed her body against the ground, desperate to comfort, to draw out the Land's distress.

Boraga gently shook her shoulder. "Fila, my dear, that is not the way. Get up, now; you must weave the world back together." Boraga turned to the cluster of wide-eyed students who huddled like sheep. "Wrap her in blankets and pick up your frames. Strong magic is afoot. We must fight it with all our might."

Hands tossed blankets around her shaking body. Amma placed a carved bone needlecase and yarns on Fila's lap and set her needlepoint frame before her. Boraga pulled several strands of copper hair from Fila's already smarting scalp, wound the fine metal threads around her fingers into a neat coil, and set it next to the yarns. "There's a breach in the magic like none I have ever known. None but the Servant can mend this gash."

"What must I do?" Fila's teeth chattered, and she clutched a blanket to stop her hands from shaking.

"Embroider over your needlepoint. Strengthen every pattern of harmony and growth and peace with yarn and copper."

Fila took a crewel needle from her needlecase.

Boraga placed her hand on her shoulder. "You must wield your needle as you never have before, quickly, precisely. Calm the Land or many Guardians and Toilers will die."

Fila sewed as icy rain soaked through her blankets. She sewed as her feet grew numb. She sewed as the ground under the manor convulsed and Spotted Turtle knelt with her shoulder against the frame to keep it from tumbling over. She sewed until bright copper gleamed from every symbol of harmony, growth, and peace. She sewed until her fingers bled and still she sewed. She sewed until the lightning stopped and the earth stilled and the clouds gave birth to the moon. Then she tumbled from her chair into the mud and sewed no more.

Chapter 2

Fila woke shrieking. Nightmares of a world gone mad, where rain froze into pellets and the earth rippled like a rug shaken at the start of sowing season, had pummeled her slumber. Massive arms engulfed her, gentle and comforting. She found herself in the rough-plastered room she shared with her amma, Spotted Turtle, a coverlet over her body and her feet wrapped in blankets as snug as a babe in the womb. Night had fallen; no light snuck through the shutters of the lone window.

All is well.

The bed groaned as Amma rocked her and stroked her hair. Fila leaned against the ancient Toiler, inhaling her beloved cinnamon scent, feeling her pebbled pale skin, safe in her powerfully muscled arms. "What a nightmare," she murmured, her scalp still burning from the dream.

Something cool and charged with magic brushed her cheek.

She lifted her hand to her face, and fine, bright wire curled around her fingers. The memory of the afternoon struck her like a slap.

She plucked a copper strand and stared at it. "Why me? Of all the Talents and Goodborns, why did the Land choose me?"

Amma squeezed her eyes shut, but it did not dam her tears. "Who can say? The Land does not think like either Guardians or Toilers. Your mother once told me—" Sobs strangled the rest of her sentence.

"Don't cry, Amma." She grasped the old Toiler's strong, knobby hand, so much bigger than her own. "Perhaps Mother isn't dead, but sick. Perhaps the Land had another duty for her to fulfill. Perhaps...." She could not think of another *perhaps* that would mean her world had not ended. "Mother cannot be gone. She is too young, too strong in her powers."

"It's natural to deny a grief at first." Spotted Turtle spoke with great tenderness, as if Fila were still a youngling. Her sturdy body slumped, for once showing its ninety-eight years. "If only her death were all that's amiss."

"Urushi." Her brother had seen twenty-three summers, yet his hair was not fully silver, and he often lost control of his magic of destruction. Mother always healed him after his accidents, time after time, no matter how much precious copper hair it cost her. Now he was her burden. "Do not worry. I'll take care of him."

"I know you will, my sweet child." Amma kissed her forehead. "But something new is wrong. I've never seen the Land so riled."

Too much to take in. Fila shifted her attention to the prickling in her scalp, the unaccustomed heavy weight of her hair, the fire spitting sparks in the fireplace, the rolling hills and valleys of the quilted coverlet.

Amma stroked her hand. "I was amma to your great-grandfather when he was little, before the Land chose him Servant of Enchantment and he took the name Granite. He was a Goodborn too. I was amma to your mother and then to you." The Toiler's deep voice shook. "I have been threefold blessed."

"Are you sure it's a blessing? I do not know enough about magic. I have years of study left."

"The Land made Its choice, and It has never before changed Its mind. Boraga has already sent messengers to your Uncle Bifac as head of the Servant's Council."

"Messengers? Why not ask Mourning Dove to contact Toilers at the Seat?"

"The investiture of a new Servant is ringed with rules and ceremonies." Amma tucked the blanket tighter around Fila's shivering form. "The announcement of a new Servant can't be sent by Toiler tech. Two Guardian messengers are required to carry the news." She put her finger on Fila's chin and turned her head so they were face-to-face. "Listen carefully, little one. You need to walk a lot to start toughening the bottoms of your feet. In just a few days, an honor delegation will come from the Seat of Enchantment to formally welcome you as Servant and escort you back. Are you listening?"

Fila nodded, her head spinning. Someone rapped at the door, and she ran gratefully to answer it. Her cousin stood smiling on the other side.

"Come in, Kassia, come in."

"You have so many procedures to learn. I thought I might help. I know a lot about the process, considering...."

Guilt burned through Fila's heart. "You always wanted to be Servant."

"And you never wanted more than to live in a Toiler village healing sick bison and strengthening the growing crops."

They looked at each other in silence and despair. Then they fell into each other's arms, Kassia weeping. "How did the Land get things so wrong?"

"I would let you be Servant if I knew how."

Spotted Turtle clapped her hands. "Fila has a lot to learn, but she has it in her to be among the greatest of the Servants," she said briskly, moving to a chair built to accommodate her wide proportions. "Both of you, come over here. We must prepare her the best we can."

Dazed, Fila nodded. Her curls grazed her cheeks, and she flinched from their raw power and frigid touch. She took her cousin's hand and sat on the edge of her bed. Kassia sprawled behind and around her, just as they had done as girls.

"Your first duty is to name your Consort," Amma said. "Have you anyone in mind?"

She shook her head, twisting her hands. Unlike Kassia, she had spurned parties, even family ones. All those cousins! Too noisy, too … draining. She preferred to help her parents with their duties or to wander the gardens by herself. She knew no young men other than Urushi.

Amma continued briskly, ignoring her distress. "You have many first- and second-cousins of the proper age to choose from."

Kassia propped her head up on her hand. "My father can make a list of men whose magic best balances yours, and then I'll tell you who kisses the best and gives the most expensive presents."

Kisses? Presents? She cared only that her future Consort be gentle, honest, and devoted to duty. "What happens after I choose someone?"

"There will be a grand ceremony to install you formally as the Servant of Enchantment and your husband as the Consort," Kassia said. "The Seat will be more crowded than you've ever seen it. You'll be invited to dozens of parties and will need many elegant new dresses. I'm so envious."

"Don't look so alarmed!" Amma said. "I've been through it twice and can guide you at every step."

"You're expected to go to every party," Kassia added. "But don't worry. I can go with you and tell you what to say."

Marriage to a stranger. Big ceremonies. Dozens of parties. Getting measured for new dresses. She had worried about the wrong aspects of being Servant. The worst came first, while she was deep in mourning and completely unprepared.

"Land take her!" Despite the evening's coolness, Kassia burned from her toes to the top of her head. She stomped about her room, moisture beading her forehead as her amma, Two Sparrows, chased after her with a hairbrush. "It isn't fair! Fila gets the best of everything. I always get the dregs."

"It's not our place to question the Land." Two Sparrows bent over and grabbed her side, panting with exertion. "It chooses Goodborns like Fila more often than Talents like you."

Kassia sniffed. "Talents make far better Servants than Goodborns, as you surely know. Talents can do what's needed, even if it's not good. Fila does not deserve to be Servant."

"You shouldn't speak so of your cousin," Two Sparrows scolded. "She's always been your good friend."

Kassia rounded on her amma and slapped her on the arm; the Toiler's third eyelids slid automatically over her eyes, annoying Kassia further. "I love Fila, as you well know. Who protected her from taunts and teases from the time we were little girls? Who guided her to choose less unflattering clothes? Who helped style her stringy hair?"

"You did."

"After all that, she *betrays* me! If she were my *good friend*, she would try to convince the Land to let me be Servant. But did she? No!" Kassia tapped her toe on the floor. "And I cannot wait all night for my hair to be brushed."

"Of course not, of course not." Two Sparrows rubbed her arm as if she wanted Kassia to feel guilty, her tone now more appropriate for a servant. "But it is the Land's gift we Toilers are conciliators. How can I help but urge peace between you and Fila? Here, sit, and I'll pour you a nice tisane to drink. The mountainmint and rose petals will relax you while I brush your pretty hair until it gleams like basswood honey in the sun."

Kassia ignored the chair and sat on the feather mattress. Two Sparrows eyed the indentation she made and frowned sadly.

Kassia felt a twinge of regret her amma would have to roll the lumps out of the mattress again, but only a twinge. After all, taking care of her was Amma's job.

Two Sparrows filled her favorite cup—made of the finest high-kaolin whiteware, Celatu had informed her when he gave it to her, and decorated with delicately painted red trilliums and pink lady's slippers—and applied the hairbrush to her hair. "You have been bored out here on Boraga's country estate," her amma said. "Time at the Seat of Enchantment is the tonic you need."

Kassia nodded; her hair snarled in the brush.

"Ouch! Have care!" She pinched Two Sparrows, who had the temerity to wince. "Yes, it will be good to be home. No more plodding about fields weaving tokens for the growth of strawberries and ducklings. No more sitting for hours in a windy classroom while the birds make too loud a racket to chat. I shall sleep under soft silk sheets and eat broiled quail with Mama, Papa, and Celatu."

Two Sparrows leaned close and whispered. "Aye, and you will see your young man."

"Him and Wiggle." Kassia pulled out the ring she wore on a gold chain hidden under her blouse. She studied it in the flickering firelight, turning it this way and that, admiring the way the opal flashed the colors of the rainbow. "We won't have to hide our love anymore. I can display all his gifts openly so everyone knows how much he cares for me. I'll be the envy of every woman."

"See? There's no reason to fret. You'll wear pretty shoes while Fila slogs barefoot through the mud. You'll have the husband of your choice, while Fila takes a Consort for his strength of magic. You can do as you please, and she will have duties upon duties. I feel sorry for Fila and Spotted Turtle."

Kassia considered Two Sparrows' words. The brush strokes had calmed her temper. But her ambition burned as fiercely as ever. She set her cup down carefully in its saucer. "When does the escort arrive?"

"In two or three days. Then we'll be on our way!"

Kassia dismissed the joyful comment with a nonchalant wave of her hand. "Oh, Amma, I neglected to tell you. You're not coming with me."

Two Sparrows' mouth gaped like that of her namesake bird, and her round, violet eyes shone with tears. Count on Amma to get in a twitter.

"I shall send an escort for you as soon as I can. I promise."

"Please don't make me stay here," Two Sparrows begged. "I dearly want to see the ceremonies, and you need someone to take care of you." She enveloped Kassia's hand in her own great one. "The Land has never mourned a lost Servant so violently. It is greatly out of balance."

"Yes, I shall be making a great sacrifice to leave you behind. But just between us, it's best this way. You'll be safer. Trust me." She smiled at Two Sparrows and patted her hand. Kassia longed to tell her the full truth and see the excitement and admiration in her amma's eyes. But that would have to wait. "I promise you'll not only see the ceremonies, but also have a seat of honor. You deserve no less."

She went to the shell-inlaid chest at the foot of her bed and took out a folded dress of white silk. She handed it to Two Sparrows. "See? I've already had a lovely dress made for you. It was very expensive, particularly all the pearls on the bodice. Now do you believe me?"

Two Sparrows clutched the dress to her chest, and a tear trickled down her face.

Chapter 3

C ELATU BENT LOWER over the ancient book on the desk in front of him and pulled the engraved brass lamp closer, but the faded glyphs on the parchment remained stubbornly the same. He had not misread the characters; he merely lacked the wit tonight to grasp their import. Staying up late arguing with Father always dulled his mind for the next day's studies.

He rubbed the spot between his eyebrows and wrote down his translation, with his gloss next to it: *Plural pronoun used for Servant; perhaps Consort was considered Servant as well?* He puzzled over the glyphs again and added another note: *Or distinction between soul and body? Or between pre-Servant self and Servant self?*

He blotted his quill, set it down, and reached for his lucky coin. Absent-mindedly fingering the ancient copper disk, he looked out the glazed casement windows. It was bad for the books for him to have placed his desk there, where sunlight streamed in, particularly when the fretwork shutters were open. But without good light, he had difficulty discerning the details in the tiny glyphs.

He had to credit the pleasure of it as well for his choice of location. His skin drank in the sun's warmth as he studied. After he had stared long at a book, it eased his sore eyes to look over the carefully manicured gardens and watch the water in the fountain splash and sparkle like stars. In the evenings, moonlight and shadows changed the garden into a festival of grotesques he never tired of watching.

Tonight, though, torrents of rain hid all from his view as he pondered the meaning of what he had read. The book dated from the time when magic had first appeared among the Guardians. Toilers had gained speech then, Guardians had discarded technology, and Servants had replaced kings and queens. Celatu hoped to puzzle out the reasons for these revolutionary changes; toward that end, he had spent years teaching himself to read the glyphs of the Old Language.

At the click of the library door, he turned, frowning. His parents knew better than to disturb his work.

Father padded toward him in his beaded velvet slippers and high-collared nightshirt, his face grim, his eyes red, his figure stooped. His gaze, as always, darted to the portraits of his ancestors and the hand-tinted map of Veridia hanging on the one stone wall not lined with tall oak bookcases. "I thought I would find you here, wasting your day as usual. Your mother complains and complains you never spend time with us." Father glared at the copper coin Celatu turned idly in his hand. "Put your toy aside. We must discuss the new Servant of Enchantment."

New Servant? *New* Servant? *No! It cannot be!* Last week when Aunt Hyacinth visited Father, she had glowed with vitality.

"Why do you look so surprised?" His father's expression changed from puzzled to enlightened—and angry. "You didn't even notice, did you? The storm? The earthquakes? The sudden cold? The Land mourned the Lady's passing, and you sat here as heedless as your quill." He shook his head in disgust. "You're lucky no books fell on your self-centered head."

Unlike Aunt Hyacinth, Father did not understand his gift of focus or his scholarly bent or his moral code. He considered them failings. He wanted Celatu out in society, jostling for prestige and power with other men his age, using his size and strong magic to advance the family's interests. *You must go along to get along* was Father's favorite saying.

But Celatu's hair had turned fully silver seven years ago. He passed his Test shortly afterward, doing so well Aunt Hyacinth treated him to lunch and presented him with the gold and diamond earring he still wore and asked after the ancient copper coin she had given him. Tarnished silver! She was too young to die. How could the Land allow such a tragedy?

He touched his earring, remembering her many kindnesses. She had been the only one who accepted his differences. Grief extinguished his irritation.

"Father, I'm so sorry about Aunt Hyacinth. I was proud to be her nephew. She was a good Servant. Some claimed her one of the finest successors to the good Dimidiata."

"Yes, she likely was. Stronger than our grandfather, certainly." Father stared at the floor, head bowed and shoulders slumped, a frail figure in his silk nightshirt. He looked so worn and tired, so … old.

Something clenched in Celatu's chest. One day his powerful father would grow old and feeble, and the sad figure he was tonight would be his constant state. Celatu would have to put aside his important research and take Father's place as an advisor to the Servant.

Father shuddered and raised his head. "We must think ahead. Trouble lies before us if the Land did not choose Kassia."

"Ignore her tantrums. She'll get over it. Buy her some new dresses or a silver necklace."

Father's eyes hardened. "Your sister deserves more respect from you. You don't understand what's going on."

"Oh, I understand the politics of the Seat. But in truth, it matters not a whit to me who holds more influence with the Servant or who aligns with whom this week." Celatu picked up his quill to resume writing. "Not a whit."

"Then make it matter." Father pulled a stool up to the desk and shoved Celatu's papers aside. "Urushi has more power than you imagine. You must decide whether you will back his ambitions. He requires it."

"My cousin knows I want nothing to do with politics. I'm neutral."

"Not to Urushi, not anymore. I have argued on your behalf. He will not accept your soaring high above the fray like an eagle." Father slammed his fist on the scarred oak desktop, making the inkwell jump. "So much book learning, so little wisdom! Maybe some books *should* fall on your head. They could knock some sense into you. For once, don't be Celatu the Coward." Father leaned in close, his eyes intense. "Do you know that's what everyone calls you?"

Celatu's jaw clenched.

Father leaned back, smug in his small triumph. "Choose a side and act, or hide in the library and wait for death."

"Death? Urushi knows I disavowed magic years ago. He wouldn't squander his limited magic killing me."

Father reached out toward Celatu's hand, but drew back without touching him. "Land knows we rarely see eye to eye."

"Father—"

"No matter what, you are still my son, my *only* son. Urushi needs my backing on the Servant's Council and so has tolerated my divided loyalties. But I can no longer protect you from him."

Celatu knuckled the spot between his eyebrows. "He taunts and teases, but he never goes further. I intimidate him too much. Do not fear for me, Father."

Father shook his head. "Your size can't protect you now. You must either support your cousin or flee the Seat of Enchantment." Father stood. "Sleep on it if you must. But I fear by morning you must decide, or it will be too late." Father padded toward the door. "Visit your mother. We won't live forever, you know."

As his father left the room, Celatu marked his place in the book, closed it, and placed it on top of his translation. His concentration was ruined; his father's words echoed in his mind.

He could not believe Urushi thought him a threat. His cousin had visited a few weeks earlier, wanting Celatu to back him on the Servant's Council so he could nudge his mother into irrelevancy. What foolishness! Servant Hyacinth would never cede her political power to anyone, let alone to a damaged son who could not pass his Test and whose hair held little silver. Celatu had refused and considered the matter closed.

But Father was not given to melodrama, nor did he scare easily. He was scared now, scared enough to taunt him as a coward. *He knows something he does not say.*

The true cowards were those who fawned over Urushi because he was Servant Hyacinth's son. They rushed to follow his whims and dictates for fear of his volatile temper and lack of control over his magic. It was not cowardly for Celatu to stay away, but common sense, something that should be obvious to someone as astute as Father.

He swallowed. Of course Father understood. *Father angered me on purpose to bend my will, to move me to action, because of Aunt Hyacinth's death.*

Servants lived much longer than other Guardians, sometimes almost as long as Toilers, according to his recent research. Aunt Hyacinth had seen only fifty summers; last week, she looked far younger than her twin.

Wide awake and restless now, despite the late hour, he rose from his chair. Pacing always helped him think, and the situation called for clear thinking.

Aunt Hyacinth should have outlived him. Father had not said how she died, and he never mentioned funeral plans. Instead, he talked with fear about Urushi's ambitions.

The individual facts were like glyphs he needed to decipher. He pulled out a clean sheet of paper and noted them, one per line, then studied them as he walked to the end of the room and back. As with glyphs, the separate meanings gradually merged into a coherent whole.

His spine turned to ice. Land protect them all! It was clear now: The Servant did not die naturally. He needed to heed Father's warnings.

Celatu rubbed his face with his hand. If only Father had shared what he knew earlier. If only he had paid more attention to gossip and politics. If only he had questioned Cousin Urushi more. His hands dropped to his sides, heavy as lead, and a lump in his throat threatened to choke him. Aunt Hyacinth could have been saved. *If only....*

Chapter 4

U RUSHI PACED his dark room at the Servant's House, tears streaming down his face in torrents to match the tempest outside. He pounded his fist into his palm over and over, letting the pain of swelling flesh overwhelm the agony in his mind and the roiling in his stomach.

He did not know how others stood him; he found himself sickening, a poor excuse for a Guardian. Better he had been born a Toiler than to be such a disgusting, defective wretch. Now he had killed the two people who loved him most with an accidental discharge of power. But who would believe it an accident? History would remember and revile him: Matricide. Patricide. The first person ever to kill a Servant.

Oh, Mother! She had healed his wounds time and again when his magic turned on him. She had spent long nights in the library searching for a cure for his lack of control.

He repaid her love and tears with death.

He couldn't call his magic back. Couldn't divert it. A boy of ten summers had better control. Did Mother die loving him? Even knowing his warped Power killed her and her Consort?

The Land had shown Its displeasure violently. Here at the House of the Servant, the Land still protested. Thunder rumbled, and lightning blazed from the sky into ground that rolled and shuddered in response. If life were fair and he were made to pay, the ground would open to devour him. Yes! Devour him whole. His loathsome carcass would feed beetles and flies, become feces to enrich the soil!

A candle flickered into life.

He halted his pacing and stared. The narrow column of smoke sparkled as it rose and twisted. Urushi wiped his wet eyes. "How could you allow this?" he howled at the smoke. "You promised me the power of a Servant. You said nothing about my parents dying!" He put his hands to his head, and then held them out imploringly, palms up. "The blood of my parents is on my hands! I shall never be clean!"

"Calm yourself," a voice whispered. The smoke drifted toward him and enwreathed him.

Urushi struggled to maintain his anger, but Shadow's caresses drew it out. She slurped it with a sigh. "They were a hindrance."

Urushi shook his head hard, like a muddy dog trying to fling off filth.

"Their demise brings you closer to power."

"I am ruined. Even if the Land chose Kassia as Servant, I'm ruined. Who will allow her to name me her Consort?"

"*I* will allow her. Take advantage of the unrest, my pet."

"How? By the Land, how?"

"Seize power. Now. While the Seat is without a Servant and everyone is paralyzed by shock and grief."

"My broken magic—"

"—does not matter while I help you. Profess this deed proudly; strike fear in all. Then cleanse the Seat of those who oppose you."

"You planned everything! You pushed my temper over the edge at just the wrong moment." Urushi balled his fists, loathing the sly creature as much as he loved her. *I bear the blame no matter what she did. If I weren't a disgusting, defective freak, Mother and Father would still be alive.*

The smoke swirled around his face, caressing his cheek with a touch he almost felt. "You cannot change what is done. But you can use the deaths to your advantage. You will have everything you want: Respect. Kassia. Flawless magic."

"You will heal me?"

"I will heal you, my love."

"My parents—"

"—made the ultimate sacrifice for you. Will you squander it?"

Shadow is right. I can't change what happened. But I can put it to good advantage, let their deaths have meaning.

"I will not squander the opportunity they gave me. I will reign as in the Old Times. As a king."

"You and I. Together," she whispered. The smoke unwound from his body, slithered through the air to the looking glass, and disappeared into its depths.

The candle flickered and went out. Urushi sagged in the dark, breathing heavily, feeling Shadow's departure as a physical rending.

He dried his damp face with his sleeve. He would mourn later. Now was his moment to act.

Chapter 5

Early the next morning, Boraga stopped at the top of the steps to the courtyard and snipped off a rose. Somehow it had escaped the depredations of last night's weather with little damage, only a pinhole in a petal surrounded by a now-darkening bruise. Its bedmates had not been so fortunate. Where yesterday hundreds of blossoms stood at attention, their velvet petals of red and pink and white complementing the glossy green foliage, today branches leaned at odd angles, naked and broken.

I will be stronger than they were. She drew the blossom's heavy tea-and-lemon scent deep into her lungs, but it did not revive her. The students waited for her below, but she wasn't ready to face them.

A heavy hand landed on her shoulder.

Boraga spun.

The Toiler leader, Mourning Dove, leaned on her cane, huffing from the climb from the Toiler village. "We need you desperately today. Our crops suffered as badly as your roses." She shook her ancient head. "Before yesterday, the harvest had promised to be abundant. The rains couldn't come at a worse time for our cecropia moths. They are getting drenched and battered as they emerge from their cocoons. There'll be fewer to breed this year, which will lower our silk production next year."

"Once the ceremony is over, I'll spend the rest of the day in the village. Do you need my husband's magic too?"

"Aye. The wind toppled old red oaks and shagbark hickories onto the sunflower field. If he could destroy the roots, we could haul the trees to the sawmill. Some of the flooded fields will take weeks to dry. We need him to clear some pastureland for planting."

Boraga shut her eyes for a moment. The situation was worse than she had guessed. "Can we avoid famine?"

"With wise management and magic, perhaps. Bartering for provisions won't be possible this time."

"I know." At least the village and her estate wouldn't lack for firewood; the downed trees were hundreds of years old. Boraga looked at the leaden sky. "The Land has not finished its grieving."

"Aye."

"At least It has paused for this morning's Burning of the Shoes."

The Toiler elder squinted down at the stone-paved courtyard, where students, teachers, and some Toiler villagers awaited Boraga. "That's Fila with the new copper curls, isn't it? Servant Hyacinth's daughter?"

Boraga nodded.

"Fila's a polite girl. Of course, the Goodborn always are." She scratched her wrinkled neck.

"Faint praise, my friend. You doubt she's ready to be Servant?"

"Don't you?"

"The Land knows things we don't." Boraga twisted her ring of intertwined iron and gold. Her students were not scheduled to start their study of the magical uses of metals until next year. Fila knew nothing about them, about the casting of spells with words, about so many areas of magic. She was only a middling student. Her raw power was enormous, but she lagged behind the other girls in technique, and like anyone her age, she lacked wisdom. "For both our people's sakes, I hope the Land has not made a mistake."

"You're so very young, too young remember other transfers."

Boraga smiled. All Guardians seemed young to Toilers. "I've passed the half-century mark. Servant Hyacinth and I were students together. She was Concinna then, before she chose her Servant name."

"I'll miss her." Mourning Dove continued to watch Fila. "Her grandfather Granite was one of the few men ever chosen by the Land to be Servant, the only one during my lifetime."

Boraga raised her eyebrows. "You're never this chatty, especially first thing in the morning."

The old Toiler licked her lips. "We don't interfere in Guardian affairs. Still, how well do you remember the last transfer?"

"Very little. I was in childbed with my first son."

"The Land mourned Servant Granite's passing with a gentle rain that brightened the grasses and sedges and hastened the crops' growth. So has It always mourned Its Servants, until now. I'm reminded of an old prophecy."

Boraga's arms goosepimpled. "Do I know it?"

The Toiler shook her head. "Unlikely. Not even I know the whole of it. But it starts with storms springing from the grieving Land after a Servant dies."

"Does it end well?" Boraga whispered.

"That part is lost. Let us hope it predicts an innocent such as Fila restores harmony."

Boraga looked down at the students. Orange-yellow sashes, the traditional marker for mourning a Servant, fluttered. Even at this distance, Fila looked lost, fingering her silver pendant. She wore a simple yellow cotton dress, its skirts blown tight against her legs by the breeze. The other students talked and gestured; no worry touched those innocent faces.

"Fila has little idea what awaits her." Boraga snapped the stem of the rose she held. "Concinna was still young. We thought we had so much time to train the Talents and Goodborn. Now that time is gone."

"Gone," Mourning Dove agreed. Leaning on her stick, she turned.

"Aren't you staying for the Burning of the Shoes?"

Mourning Dove shook her head. "Too much to be done." She limped away.

Boraga twisted her hands together. Her messengers would reach the Seat of Enchantment today, and the escort would set out soon after. She had little time to prepare Fila, even if she knew what to prepare her for.

"Concinna, my friend, forgive me," she whispered. She took another whiff of the rose cut down before its time, then tossed it aside.

"Mourning Dove!" She hastened after the village leader, who stopped at her call and waited. "Unusual times call for unusual measures, do they not?"

Mourning Dove narrowed her eyes. "So the good Dimidiata claimed. What do you have in mind?"

Boraga looked around to make sure no one could hear them, then whispered, "I need a great favor from you. Something prohibited." She waited for Mourning Dove to protest. When she didn't, Boraga spilled her request. "I wish to send a message to a Guardian friend at the Seat … by your communications tech."

As Boraga made a stately descent down the stairs of stone, the students, teachers, and manor staff arranged themselves in a respectful circle along the wall enclosing the courtyard. Fila stood in the middle, her hair bright despite the gloomy sky, her shoes and slippers piled at her feet. The girl's eyes were puffy and red-rimmed, but she seemed composed, if somewhat withdrawn.

Tiny tips of flame sparkled in the sugar kettle in front of her where Boraga had asked the house servants to improvise a fire pit.

Boraga knew what needed to be done, but not the proper words. She took a deep breath and hoped her improvisation would be as good as the Toilers' makeshift fire pit. "The Land has chosen a new Servant of Enchantment. Although the Servant has the most powerful magic in the kingdom, she is not the highest of the high, as in the long-ago days of kings and queens. Rather, she is the lowest of the low, a servant to the Land and Its two peoples, following the footsteps of the good Dimidiata.

"As token of her status of Servant to all, she will tread the earth unshod from this time forward, her feet always in communion with the Land that chose her." She nodded.

Fila knelt and gathered up all of her shoes.

"Save a pair. After you reach the Seat of Enchantment, you'll repeat The Burning of the Shoes."

Fila set aside a pair of beaded slippers. She strode toward the fire, then stopped. She set down a pair of work boots. Changing course, she carried the other shoes to Kassia, who stood with her arms crossed.

"Cousin, we've been through all our training together." She knelt and placed the shoes in front of Kassia. "I know how much you love these shoes. You chose the colors and trims. Please accept them as a token of my love."

The students murmured in excitement; the Toilers, with approval. Kassia nudged the shoes with her foot, her eyes and mouth hard. Envy and annoyance radiated from her like heat from a blazing stove, and no words of thanks passed her lips.

Fila as usual did not notice her cousin's bitterness.

Boraga suppressed a shudder. *Thank the Land Mourning Dove agreed to my request. I must contact Erudia the Melancholy, certainly. And my old classmate Elata. Without allies, Fila going to the Seat of Enchantment to assume control is like a downy duckling walking into the den of a wolf.*

Fila picked up the work boots and walked to the kettle. The moment seemed to overwhelm her; she opened her mouth to speak but nothing came out but a croak. She drew a deep breath and began again. "The Land has honored me by choosing me Its Servant. I accept the honor and from this moment forth shall go bareshod upon It, so I may always be attuned to Its wishes and always remember I am to serve, not to be served." Fila pulled several strands of copper hair from her head and tied them into a monkey's fist knot.

She heaved the boots and the knot of hair into the center of the fire. Flames shot up several times her height.

The students gasped and backed away, bumping into the other spectators. But Fila, her hair glowing fiery as the flames, her body a dark silhouette, gazed into the fire as if the knowledge and strength she would need for her duties could be seared into her.

* * *

Urushi stood in front of the open wardrobe, holding his besweatered terrier, Wiggle, and tapping his toe. He needed to dress to intimidate at the meeting of the Servant's Council tonight, but he could not choose a jacket with Hooting Owl standing so stiff, so cold, so formal next to him.

"Appa, I want you to know the truth."

"Suspecting what happened is painful enough. I don't want to know for certain." He refused to meet Urushi's gaze. "I think the blue jacket would suit the meeting tonight."

"Forget the jacket." He drew a deep breath. "Do you think I murdered my parents?"

Hooting Owl's gaze dropped to the floor. "What else am I to believe? They never would have attacked you, but that's what you told your uncle Bifac."

"That's what I'll tell the rest of the council tonight too. But you deserve to know the true story."

"No!" The Toiler took a step back, fear showing in his violet eyes. "I'd rather not hear the details."

"I lied, Appa." He sat down on the bed with Wiggle and patted the space next to him.

Hooting Owl paused, then sat in the indicated place.

Urushi grasped the Toiler's hand. "I told Uncle Bifac I killed them in self-defense so people would fear me, so they would believe my magic is strong. But it was an accident. I swear on the Land Itself and on my love for you I did not mean to harm them. Please believe me."

Appa's eyes were heavy with sympathy. "I think you should tell me what happened, Lad."

A Toiler, pitying me. What a goat I am. He clenched his jaw, set Wiggle on the floor, and fought to smother his shame before it escalated and sparked his magic. The dog trotted off to sniff in the corner. "Hirtu came to visit."

"Aye."

"He brought his new puppy to play with Wiggle. The dogs were having fun. Wiggle knew to be gentle with the puppy. Hirtu went to use the water closet. The dogs were just having fun...."

"And then?"

"Mother and Father came in. They had found out I was recruiting supporters on the Servant's Council to back me instead of Mother. Father said I deserved to be removed from the council."

Hooting Owl put one arm around Urushi and pulled him close. "Is that when you lost your temper?"

"No. I was upset, of course, and my magic was tingling, but I didn't lose control." That would have been a better time to do so. Their deaths would have not been so absurd, so meaningless. "It wasn't Father's decision. And you know Mother. She wouldn't have forced her son from her council." Urushi leaned against Hooting Owl, wishing he could be four summers old again and forever. "I thought I could hold my magic back long enough for the argument to end."

"What went wrong?"

"Hirtu's puppy ran to my parents and rolled on their feet. He was exuberant, elated to meet two new people who rubbed his belly and talked baby talk to him. The puppy couldn't control himself. He pissed on the carpet, the beautiful carpet I commissioned your sister's village to make for the anniversary of my parents' investiture."

Hooting Owl held him tight.

"He was only a puppy, doing what excited puppies do." *Did Shadow hiss then, or did I imagine it?* "I became angry, so angry, and magic swept through me. My parents didn't notice. They were watching the puppy." He panted as he fought to calm himself. *Deep breaths. Deep breaths.* "I woke up lying on the floor, Wiggle licking my nose. My lungs hurt, my tongue, my skin; I didn't remember any of those wounds."

His hands shook, and he watched Wiggle dig with intent purpose and great enthusiasm in the corner. He relaxed completely against the huge Toiler beside him. "Oh, Appa! Blood was everywhere. Soaking the carpet I was so worried about, the walls, the furniture, everywhere. Wiggle was wearing his protective sweater.

"Everyone else was dead."

The clock Appa's village had made him ticked on the wall. "When Hirtu returned, he cried over his puppy. I was too weak from my wounds to say anything, let alone give my condolences. He shouted I was a monster."

"You're no monster, Lad," Hooting Owl said firmly. "I would know it if you were."

"I'm not normal, though. You—"

Wiggle barked furiously in the corner, his body braced for a fight. Something hissed.

"He's cornered something."

Appa stared, then sprang from the bed and shoved his sleeves up. "Of all things! It's a mink. They're nasty creatures. I'll take care of it before it bites him."

The sleek, long body turned transparent.

Urushi blinked. The mink was solid and dark, as before. He held out his arm. "Wait! Take Wiggle away. I'll deal with the mink."

His appa shook his head.

"I order it. Go!"

He shut and locked the door behind Hooting Owl and Wiggle. He was alone with the mink. But when he turned, the animal had disappeared, and sparkling smoke wafted upward.

Urushi rubbed his half-numb hands and arms, trying to encourage his reluctant blood back into them. The ancient dungeons were cold, colder than they should be, and an impossible breeze gusted through untarnished bars made of an unfamiliar metal. The lamps gave off a sunlight-yellow glow that was not magic-based, but some kind of tech. Toiler tech or tech from the Old Times, he could not tell, but the lamps had been placed to make the cells much too bright or too dark for comfort. He heard scuttling all around him, but never saw the vermin. The stink unsettled his stomach.

"Hundreds of years have passed since anyone was here." Shadow wore the form of an alluring woman with mink-dark hair and too-sharp teeth. "Still the perfume of terrified people lingers. Do you find it as arousing as I do?"

Something clanked in the dark; he flinched. *Nasty* and *scary* were better descriptions. "I thought I'd been through all the caves and secret passages under the House of the Servant," he said diplomatically. "But I never knew we had dungeons."

"No one knows. So no one will interfere."

Relief rocked him. He strode toward her eagerly, the cold forgotten. "You'll merge with me at last!"

Her façade faded into insubstantiality before his fingers touched her. "Soon, soon," she whispered.

She kept putting him off, and he had to keep blustering and bluffing to keep people cowed. He wanted her powers now, not soon, *now*, before he had another accident of magic. "What are we here for then? I have a meeting. I can't stay."

"I know of your gathering. I know everything you do."

His skin crawled as if the scurrying creatures he heard were just underneath its surface.

"We're here to make children. Now, before your gathering." She materialized again, more tantalizing than before, dressed as a warrior woman of the time before the first Servant.

He gaped. She was smoke, vapor, gossamer, not flesh. "Children?" he choked out.

"Fear needs renewal. I'll birth you new weapons to menace the council members. They'll fall on the floor before you. Would such please you?"

"Yes!"

She smiled, her skin translucent and sparkling like the night sky. "Draw nigh. We shall show them ice and fire such as the Land has never known."

Chapter 6

H ANDS. *Hundreds of hands, dark Guardian and pale Toiler, reach toward her in supplication. Fila backs away, but there's nowhere to go. Hands surround her. The hands rise higher and higher until everywhere she looks she sees nothing but hands. Around her, mouths cry out for help, begging her to listen, to attend to them first.*

She turns in a circle, looking at one pair of hands after another. It's impossible to choose among them. The hands become more demanding. Some tighten around her arms, others around her legs, her torso, her neck. She looks down and screams. Her body is gone. All that remains is a shell of seething, writhing, grasping hands. It's hard to catch her breath; she stops screaming.

She struggles to break free. But there are too many hands; they weigh too much. Her own hands are trapped.

Slowly, gasping for air, she collapses under the weight, the weight of the hands. She is helpless. She will suffocate.

An animal hisses nearby. Sparkling haze drifts before her face. Soft in her ear, warm breath whispers, "I'll help you. Let me in, inside your soul."

Fila knows nothing of this creature. But the hands only want to take; the creature wants to give. She wants to live. She opens her mouth to speak—

She woke screaming. Heart pounding, she grabbed the coverlet and pulled it up over her nose.

Amma dropped a towering pile of newly washed clothes and rushed to her. "What's wrong?"

Fila could not answer. She could not draw breath, and her legs jerked with the need to run.

Amma pounded on her back until she coughed and gasped. Her lungs sucked in a deep breath, and the cramps in her limbs eased, to be replaced by shudders that wracked her body.

"I had a nightmare." She wrapped her arms about herself and told Spotted Turtle most of the dream.

Amma sighed. The deep sound rumbled inside Fila's ribcage. "Your mother sometimes had dreams like that. It's true everyone reaches to the Servant for help. It can be overwhelming when a flood strikes or disease smuts the rye, and hundreds need your help."

The weight of her duty to Veridia settled on Fila's shoulders like a wet wool blanket. She would bear this load for the rest of her life, but even the thought drained her.

"Fila?" Amma's eyes looked worried and weary.

"It's my duty. I will uphold it. Somehow." She looked down at her hands and thought about the part of the dream she hadn't told Amma, about the dream creature's offer and how she almost said yes.

After eating a quick lunch of corn bread and elk cheese curds in the kitchen with the Toiler servants, Celatu headed back toward the library with anticipation. He had reached a passage in the ancient book that sometimes referred to the good Dimidiata, the first Servant of Enchantment, as the Lady and sometimes as the Duality. Here was a clue to the book's earlier use of plural verbs to refer to the Servant. Perhaps this very afternoon, he would untangle the secrets.

"Celatu." Father stood in the door of his study, his face dotted with perspiration, looking even more haggard than he had last night. "Come in. We must talk."

Celatu's annoyance at the curt tone dissipated when he got closer. Father looked worse than distressed; he looked ill. He retreated into his study and shut the door firmly behind his son. Instead of sliding the bolt, he locked the Toiler-made lock, constructed from the hard metal the Toilers made and called *steel*, and then pulled the key from the lock and pocketed it.

His father sat behind the desk stacked with neat piles of papers, motioned for Celatu to take the chair in front, and pulled out an ivory silk handkerchief to wipe his forehead. His face was gaunt.

How had Celatu not noticed he had lost weight? Anxiety bubbled up from the pit of his stomach. He did not take the proffered chair. "I shall send for some refreshment."

"We have no time! Sit and listen." Father drummed his fingers on the desk. The sound echoed in the bur-oak-paneled room. "Last night the Servant's Council met. Urushi announced he has these … creatures. Icedragons and firehounds. They sense magic. He will send them to kill Guardians who have not pledged him their support. Icedragons for the men, firehounds for the women. You must throw in your lot with him. Now."

"He's bluffing. Remember how I loved the outdoors as a boy? I read every natural history book in our library. There are no such animals. Even if there were, Urushi knows I won't act against him."

Father looked pointedly at Celatu's hair, which had remained silver during his years of abstinence from magic. His eyes had kept their silver flecks as well. "If you did use magic, you'd be as powerful as you ever were." Father shook his head. "*More* powerful. Your magic has been building for a long time. Urushi's no fool. You're a threat."

"Father, people respect you. They know you had Servant Hyacinth's trust. Why don't you oppose Urushi? People would follow you. You could stop his threats and bullying once and for all."

"I cannot." Father dabbed his forehead again.

"What frightens you so?" Celatu leaned forward, his jaw tense.

"Urushi loves Kassia. He intends to marry her."

Celatu blinked. *No wonder Father does not oppose Urushi.* His cousin would be even more dangerous if he had an immense Talent like Kassia by his side.

Father's color heightened. "The family has to stick together, now more than ever before. Give him your support."

Celatu batted the idea away with his hand. "We're cousins, soon to be brothers-in-law. He would not harm me."

Father answered obliquely. "A cousin is a more distant relative than, say, a mother or father."

An ache began in the pit of Celatu's stomach, and he gripped the arms of the chair. "What are you saying?"

Despite the locked door, Father spoke softly. "There's an old fragment of prophecy. Only the beginning survives, but I think it may refer to our times: *A Servant dies by a loved one's hand; Dire storms spring from the grieving Land; the Servant can—*"

Dust motes swirled. Their breathing rang loud and harsh in the locked room, almost as loud as the sharp tick-tick-tick of the cherrywood clock. Father dabbed at the moisture gleaming on his forehead, apparently waiting for Celatu to deduce what he could not bear to say.

"You can't mean—" Celatu got out before his throat choked his words. He tried again. "Urushi murdered the Servant and the Consort?" Anger sparked his magic, and he yearned to rip or break or smash. Clenching his fists, he forced back the lust to destroy.

"I wish I knew," Father said. "Soon after they died, he told me it was an accident and begged my forgiveness. Later, and again last night at the council meeting, he bragged they had tried to kill him and he had acted in self-defense."

"Neither explanation makes sense." Celatu's voice shook a little. "How do *you* think they died?"

"I don't know. The bodies looked as if they had been—" Father's voice caught and, blinking, he turned his head away. "—exploded from within."

"Land preserve us!"

"I've watched Urushi's ambitions grow. We both know how volatile his temper is. I may not know what really happened, but I've drawn my own conclusions."

"Which are?"

"You should either flee immediately or tell your cousin your magic is at his command."

As he considered Father's words, Celatu gazed at the map of Veridia on the wall, larger than the one in the library but otherwise its twin. Male magic of destruction was too easily turned toward wicked purpose. He had discovered that ten years ago and had no illusions he could resist temptation better than other men. "I will not abandon my vow to abstain from magic, not for Urushi, not for anyone."

Father's face grew redder.

"I won't oppose him, either, Father. I'm not suicidal."

But flee? Leave his books and studies behind? It was what gave his life purpose and would be his contribution to Veridia's future, if he could unlock the secrets hidden in the old books.

Father snapped his fingers. "Well?"

"If Urushi threatens you or Mother or Kassia, I will protect you with my life. Otherwise, I will remain here." Celatu moved to leave.

"I told your mother you would act the donkey … again. It's a wonder you haven't grown furry, pointed ears." Father's voice sounded both exasperated and exhausted.

Celatu snapped back, "I'm a scholar. Not a donkey, not a lazybones, not a good-for-nothing, not any of the things you think me. A *scholar*."

"How would you know what I think? You're always in the library."

"I can see it in your eyes."

"If you're a mind reader now, read my mind and see the true danger you're in."

Celatu spoke slowly and deliberately. "I take your warning to heart. I will be on my guard."

"To live, you must flee." Father stood and balled his fists. "I was by Servant Hyacinth's side for many years. To keep her safe, I learned everyone's business.

I made certain the Servant always knew whose advice was made for the good of the Land and whose came from self-interest."

"Then why didn't you warn her about Urushi?" His shout echoed in the paneled room.

Father startled—Celatu had never raised his voice to him before—then he slumped into his chair, bowed his head, and rubbed his forehead.

"Land forgive me," Father whispered. "Urushi made promises for Kassia. I stayed quiet for her sake."

His words knocked Celatu's world atilt. *So Urushi does not bear all the blame.*

Father bowed his head and rubbed his temples. "I sent the grooms home, and I saddled a horse for you myself. It's large enough to carry you, and it's the fastest in the stable. If you need to leave quickly, it is ready. Go to your Toiler village and ask for help."

A lump filled Celatu's throat.

"You still remember how to ride, don't you? How to get to the village you've neglected for so long?" Father asked with a note of sarcasm. He followed Celatu to the door.

"I can ride." He had passed many a pleasant afternoon ambling about the grounds on a horse to think over problems in his research.

Father put his hand on Celatu's shoulder. He seemed about to say something, but instead returned to his desk, rummaged in a side drawer, and pulled out a knife sheath. "You are not so foolish to go about without a weapon as well as without magic, are you?"

He patted his hip. "I always carry the dagger you gave me when I passed my Test."

"Good. This is its mate. Both belonged to my mother," Father said gruffly. He held it out.

Celatu accepted it and pulled it from the sheath. It was as well cared for as his own. Perhaps better. A gift of great sentiment.

"I will prize it always. Thank you, Father." He strapped it onto his sash.

"Don't be afraid to use it." Father unlocked the door, looked out to check the corridor, and let him out.

A Servant dies by a loved one's hand; Dire storms spring from the grieving Land. Celatu rolled the two lines of prophecy through his head over and over as he walked to the library. He had read those words before, had come across them in his studies of ancient texts, even though he had not told Father. He remembered reading more, perhaps the entire prophecy. But in which book or manuscript? If he could only remember.

Chapter 7

ON A TYPICAL AFTERNOON, the lavender garden beside the tower smelled clean and fresh and buzzed with bees. Kassia went there when she wanted to remember the past or daydream about the future. Exotic lavender, which had been brought here from the lands beyond the mountains before the first Servant closed Veridia off, reminded her she would be Servant one day and have all the luxuries she wanted. She might even open a passage to the outside world so the Toilers could increase genetic diversity of their non-native plants and animals, and Veridia could again import gemstones, linen, exotic flowers, cheap silver and iron, and that most precious and rarest metal of all, copper.

She came this day, despite the heavy rain and the threat of the damaged tower falling on her, to get away from Fila. Her cousin needed her more than ever since becoming Servant, but oh, how it hurt to see her wearing the copper hair that belonged on her own head!

She stretched out her arms to feel the Land's tears, the sign that It already regretted Its choice. She had known since she was a tiny girl that her destiny was to be Servant; why else had It made her a Talent of extraordinary power? Fila had always sucked attention away from her, but one day people would look at Kassia and admire her.

To be sure, she got plenty of attention … for her beauty. Few men looked deeper or expected more from her than to be an ornament. Just as people looked at Urushi and saw only his damaged body and hair that wasn't silver.

I wish Urushi were here now. He would comfort her and remind her that she *would* be Servant and he her Consort, by her side always. It was hard to be so far away and to communicate only by letters snuck back and forth by a long chain of Toilers passing them hand to hand. She missed his kisses, his gifts, his compliments, his deep need of her, greater even than Fila's.

She pulled the gold chain over her head, sat on a bench, and caressed the ring Urushi had given her. She remembered the evening two years earlier so clearly. They had met secretly in the Servant's private garden courtyard in late summer, when lavender and other exotic plants from beyond Veridia were blooming. She arrived early, as usual, to admire its jewel-like beauty in the moonlight and to plan the changes she would make when she became Servant.

A thump alerted her that Urushi had come over the wall. She ran quietly in her silken slippers toward the sound, snuck up behind him, and put her hands over his eyes.

He must have jumped a foot! He shot an accidental spark of magic across the patio, breaking an old clay pot.

She broke into giggles that would not stop, and he grabbed her roughly, covering her mouth with his. "Shhh! We do not want Mother to discover us."

She pulled away and whispered, "Isn't that why you like to meet here? Because you find it exciting that she might?"

"*You* think it's exciting. I don't need any excitement but you."

Kassia stood on her tiptoes and kissed him hungrily. He answered her in kind, then took a step back. "I can't stay long. I have a meeting with Mother. She wants my advice. I am finally getting the respect I deserve."

"Then why did you ask me to meet you here?"

He led her by the hand to a stone bench set in a semicircle of flower bushes. "I want to give you something." He pulled a ring off his finger and gave it to her.

At first glance, she was disappointed with the white, waxy stone. Then she turned the ring, and the stone caught the light of the full moon.

Blue and green flared, and she gasped in awe. She turned it another direction and saw pink.

"It's even more brilliant in the sunlight. It flashes all the colors of a rainbow, and more," Urushi said.

"What is it?"

"An opal. Imported from outside Veridia before the days of the Servants."

It was very valuable then. He must really, really love her to give her something so precious. "I'll wear it always."

"Out of sight, of course."

She nodded. "Until the day your parents no longer think I'm *shallow* and *selfish*. Or until I'm old enough their objections don't matter."

"I … I chose this ring because it's like you. So many moods. Unique. Perfect. Precious."

She ducked her head so he couldn't see her sly smile. "Me? Perfect and precious?"

"Yes. You'll be the best Servant Veridia ever had." Urushi stroked her hair. "You're the only person who isn't afraid of me, the only person I don't have to fear being around."

"Why?"

"Because you're perfect. You never make me angry. You soothe me. You see past my faults. You believe in me, in my ability to rule Veridia by your side."

"I love taking care of you," she confessed. "I love that my magic is helping to heal you and turning some of your hair silver. When I am Servant, I will make you whole. You will be so handsome, the most handsome Consort ever, and everyone will be jealous of me."

"Every man is already jealous of *me*." He forgot his appointment then and kissed her for a long time.

A bolt of lightning brought Kassia back to the present. Frowning, she rubbed at the ring's stone, but the dark splotch remained. She held it to her eye. She was still perfect, but the opal was not. In its depths lurked a murky something, bleak and black.

Humming despite the downpour, Afissa walked up the stairs and through the main doors of the House of the Servant into the waiting area. Even with no Servant in residence, the house bustled with Toilers and Guardians carrying on the business of the Seat. The sight of so many yellow sashes silenced her and sombered her expression.

My life is so happy, yet here everyone is in deepest mourning. Her Goodborn instinct flared golden in her mind, insisting she forego her errand and knit charms of comfort instead. She fought the urge. Those who needed such could call on any of the Guardian women here for help.

A Toiler attendant, his hair in disarray, approached her, nodding in recognition. He kneeled to towel off her bare feet.

She spoke first. "My deepest condolences on your loss, Hoary Bat."

He looked up. His eyes, an unusually dark and expressive purple, glossed with tears. Not his first tears of the day; his eyes were bloodshot and red-rimmed.

"May I help you in some way?" golden instinct made her ask.

He shook his head. "Servant Hyacinth deserves to be mourned," Hoary Bat choked out. He stood and wiped his eyes on his embroidered silk tunic. "You're here to see your mother-in-law?"

"Yes. I brought her strawberries from my garden. Some for you as well." She slipped the smaller basket off her arm and handed it to him.

"They look delicious. Thank you. Go ahead to the library. I'll mark your visit in the guestbook."

By the time she had threaded her way through mourning functionaries and council members to the back of the north wing, she was near to crying herself in sympathy. She knocked at the library door; her hands could not manage the handle. Slow footsteps came toward her from inside, and the door swung inward. Dry air drifted out to caress her cheek.

"I brought you some strawberries from my garden, Mother Erudia." She let the heavy basket slip down her arm.

Erudia relieved her of the burden. "Land bless you, Afissa. Come in and chat, would you? Just no politics." She gestured toward the table where she most often worked.

"Gladly." Afissa entered and drew a deep breath. Paper. Ink. Glue. Age and wisdom. All those gladsome scents and more, overlaid with a slight metallic tang: Toiler tech. The Land had made an exception to Its rules and allowed tech in the library to preserve Guardian records and books by maintaining constant temperature and humidity.

They sat at Erudia's worktable, which was barely visible under the clutter of brushes, knives, pots of glue, rolls of dyed leather, balls of book-stitching thread, stacks of heavy paper held down by leather punches, and other repair tools she did not know the names of. Before they could say a word, a Toiler dressed like a farmer and carrying a portfolio entered the library and walked up to Erudia.

"It is urgent that I speak to you privately."

Mother Erudia raised her eyebrows, but led him away. Afissa occupied herself by smelling the glues, the papers, the rolls of leather, recognizing many of the individual notes that contributed to the library's perfume.

Erudia rejoined her, her face sadder than usual. She balanced a folded paper on a paper press and kneaded her eyes with her palms. "I have just had news from the countryside from my friend Boraga," she said softly.

"That Toiler was not a messenger," Afissa replied just as softly.

"Thank the Land you are a Goodborn. I have to share this with someone. We must talk politics after all." Erudia opened the document for Afissa and turned it so she could read it.

It was a letter, brief, to the point, and forbidden, by both custom and the Land. Ice grew beneath Afissa's breastbone as she read Boraga's news and plea for help, sent by Toiler tech from her village to one near the Seat.

"Do you know this girl Fila?" Afissa asked.

"She's Servant Hyacinth's daughter."

Afissa caught her breath. "Urushi's sister! So you know her well."

Erudia shook her head. "I of course saw her many times over the years, but she was a quiet child who faded into the background, not like her charming cousin Kassia. I probably haven't seen her in four years, since she went off to Boraga's for schooling."

"Do you still fear that you-know-who may be a danger to the new Servant?"

"More than ever."

"His own *sister*?" Afissa whispered.

"At the Servant's Council meeting last night, he claimed he murdered his parents." Erudia shook her head. "Whatever the truth is there, he has changed. Changed even since you and I last talked."

"How?"

"Here, in the privacy of the Servant's House, he seems sad, tormented even. When I can't sleep and take a walk, I see him wandering the halls, muttering to himself. But in the Servant's Council, he is brash and arrogant, giving orders he has no right to give. Even to Bifac."

Butterflies fluttered in Afissa's stomach, and her head spun as her Goodborn instincts staggered and stumbled, weighing her filial duty to her mother-in-law against her citizen's duty to the Servant. "I worry you aren't safe here. Please, come stay with us."

"No. I am a member of the Servant's Council. I must do what is right for Veridia. Once I figure out what that is."

"Will you help the new Servant as Boraga requests?"

Erudia picked up the letter and read it again, then sighed. "I do not know." She carried the paper outside, into the library's courtyard under an overhang, and set it on fire. She did not return until the letter dissolved into ash and floated away in the rainy gusts.

Over the next few hours, Celatu made little progress on his translation. His thoughts jumped about like rabbits, and the remaining lines of the prophecy tickled the edge of his mind like a half-remembered song.

He stood up and stretched. A flash of brightness outside caught his eye, and something scraped against the outer wall. He looked out the third-floor window.

Nothing.

Still, his father's warnings made him pull out his pocketknife. *Never give Father a reason to say, I told you so.*

He cranked opened the casement windows and leaned out into the rain. The storm made the afternoon so dark he could not see the courtyard or gardens below. Then lightning flashed, three bolts, one after another. Their light glinted off something large and curved to his right.

He jerked back.

A scimitar sliced the air where his head had been a second before.

"Land preserve us!" Celatu whipped his knife up. But it was dark again, rendering his assailant invisible. Meanwhile, with the bright light of the library behind him, his large silhouette made an easy target.

Keeping a tight hold on his knife, he quickly cranked one casement shut and reached for the other knob. Vicious, hissing curves of blue swung together through the open window.

What weapon has three blades?

The blades pulled back, scraping clumsily against the window edge, and Celatu darted forward. He lunged, striking blindly, trying to hit the hand or arm wielding the triple scimitar.

His blade hit, but did not enter flesh nor snag in clothes. Yet there was no screech of metal against metal, just a high-pitched scream and the sound of beating wings, as if a colony of bats flew in perfect unison. Before his opponent could attack again, he pulled the open casement shut with all the weight of his body.

He stumbled backward, his heartbeat pounding in his ears. He dropped his knife on his desk, leaned over with both hands on his knees, and sucked air like a bellows. When he could breathe again, he yanked the bell pull for a servant—Father must hear of this right away—and returned to the window, looking out cautiously from the side.

Something gleamed on the outside windowsill. Two scales lay on the damp sill. Not the tiny, leathery scales of a lizard or snake, but huge, iridescent plates the blue-white of a frozen lake, each larger than his thumbnail with a luster like mother of pearl.

His heart thudded again. These came from no known beast, living or extinct.

This attack could be no coincidence. Father had been right—about Urushi's intent to kill him, about the impossible but just-proven existence of magic creatures called icedragons.

Celatu swore and fought the urge to punch the stone wall. Urushi insulted his honor by not taking his word he would not meddle in politics or use magic.

He strode out of the library and met the servant coming toward him in answer to his call. He spoke quickly, his voice shaking, outlining for the Toiler female what to tell his parents and then the staff.

She leaned close and sniffed his breath.

"I'm not drunk, Green Frog. This house is in danger. Hurry to my father."

She blinked lavender eyes, assessing him, then turned and ran.

He returned to the study to pace and think. He picked up his knife from his desk, feeling safer with it in his hand, and listened. He heard only the storm.

The icedragon would be back to finish its mission. Meanwhile, the scales might tell him more about his enemy and how to injure it. He oiled the hinges of one window, then cranked it open, staying to the side. No claws reached in. He reached out, snatched the scales, and pulled back, all in an instant. *Success! But—*

He bit his lip to keep from screaming. The scales were colder than ice, colder than frosty metal in deepest winter, colder than any natural thing could be.

His fingertips turned blue. He shook his hand frantically, but the scales stuck fast to his skin. Cold fire burned into his hand and into his arm. Blue crept into his palm.

Groaning, he scraped his fingers against the nearest edge, the window frame. Too dull. The scales tugged at his skin but remained attached.

He still held his knife. *Quickly. Quickly.* His eyes opened wide. The point. Blunted and bent. On the animal's hide.

Burning raced faster up his arm. He turned his knife and used the blade as a lever to pry the scales off.

His skin came off with them. The scales clinked to the floor.

Blood welled from his wounds. He slumped against the wall and rubbed his arm and hand until they turned brown again, then wrapped his handkerchief tightly around his bleeding fingers.

Outside, something scraped against the wall.

Glass and wood glazing bars exploded inward. He fell backward, his arms rising to protect his face. A scaly snout pulled out of the window, lunged forward again.

He rolled backward to gain momentum, then launched his legs forward, driving his heels against the icedragon's nostrils. The creature thrashed back and forth, hissing. Celatu rolled to his feet. His eyes burned; his vision blurred. He ran for the stables.

He did not look behind him.

Chapter 8

FILA STOOD IN THE CENTER of a field newly planted with beans, corn, and squash while rain pelted her and pooled in the depressions her bare feet had made. Water spiraled down the coils of her hair and dripped onto her face. The Toilers must be fretting as they waited out the downpour in their rambling thatched cottages. This rain could wash away any seeds that survived yesterday's onslaught or bury them under so deep a layer of mud that their struggle to fulfill their destiny would be futile.

She must learn to be a Servant.

She had skipped class to come here, to this field that would be her test. If she calmed the storm and reversed its damage, the Toilers and Guardians of Boraga's estate would have food for the winter. If she failed, people would starve.

She swallowed, and her head buzzed. She had never tried magic of creation without needlework crafted for a specific purpose. There had been no point. Only a Servant could do such magic, and not every Servant at that. It was time to discover the extent of her powers.

She tipped her head back and stretched her arms toward the angry sky. She closed her eyes against the downpour and let the rain beat against her face. Toes squishing in the mud, she set her feet farther apart to brace herself. Tentatively, she sent a few strands of her consciousness down into the ground and up into the sky. She tensed when she touched the soul of the Land, but It barely noticed her, occupied as It was with Its grief. Boldly, she sent more of herself out, letting grief meet grief and emptiness meet emptiness.

The Land responded. Her copper hair rose, defying the Land's pull, and cast off sparks. A pulsing jolt of agony and rapture shot through her and out of her.

Now what? How had Mother talked to It? She had never asked. So she formed her request in her mind.

Please. Stop the storms and the earthquakes. You are hurting both Your peoples.

The ground beneath her shook. Emotions as wide as the sky, and as high, shoved themselves into her heart. The Land hurt too. It didn't want to forgive.

It withdrew. Its emotions and thoughts still entered through her bare feet, but they felt distant, impersonal. It wasn't ready to become acquainted yet.

Her arms fell, no longer suspended in the air by her magic. She crossed her arms over her chest and drew circles in the water with her big toe.

She would not go back to Boraga's yet. She would keep trying. She sent her consciousness out again, down into the Land, up into Its sky, her tongue sticking out as she concentrated.

She and the Land joined souls right away this time. But the Land had no interest in communicating with her, let alone cooperating.

She had magic of her own. Maybe she didn't need the Land's cooperation. She stretched her arms as high as she could and twisted her feet back and forth to bury them deeper in mud. No words this time, no pleading, and no worrying she could not do it. She would rely on instinct.

She took deep breaths and opened herself to all the urges inside her. Her stomach urged her to eat; she blocked its message. Her goosebumped skin urged her to go back to the manor; she shut it out. Another urge welled, one she did not recognize. She let it grow, let it take her over. Her body vibrated and prepared itself. It knew what to do.

Then she did too. *How simple.* She stretched her arms wider and spread her fingers, willing the storm to stop.

Lightning exploded from her fingertips and raced toward the clouds. Power! Raw and wild and wonderful. She gloried in her full abilities, always hidden before because her needlework skills lagged.

The rain lost its force and became a gentle, nourishing drizzle. Her arms still in the air, she danced about the field wildly, plowing the ground with her feet.

When she could no longer draw air into her heaving chest, she surveyed the field, and a slow smile grew. She was not done yet. She pulled out a few hairs, carelessly made a lark's head knot around a single hair, and tossed it.

Nothing.

Butterflies fluttered in her stomach, and she tugged at a curl. If Kassia were Servant and here in her place, she would find it funny that after a great magic, she could not get a simple charm to work. Fila had little sense of humor; she was not amused, but discouraged. Sighing, she walked to the charm, picked it up, and stared at it, her forehead wrinkling. She was almost certain the lark's head was the correct knot. She wiped away the water dripping from her hair into her eyes. Was the knot too small? Should it have more than one hair as the support? Did it need some yarn? Or a plant stem?

Back to basics. Color: Green was generally useful for encouraging plant growth. Every little girl learned that early. Texture: She could not remember whether it mattered. She bit her lip again, then stopped, not wanting a swollen lip Kassia and the other students would notice. Fiber: Fibers were particular to the woman, and plant fibers always worked better for her than animal hair or tissue. Thickness: She guessed that a thicker support would yield sturdier stems.

She rummaged through her needlework bag, chose a length of green cotton yarn, and folded it in half and then in half again. Hands shaking, she tied a lark's head knot about it, using more hair than before. She held her breath, tossed it into the bare field, and squeezed her eyes shut.

The ground quivered. She opened one eye.

A pair of leaves, then another, broke through the soil. She opened the other eye and watched with wonder as leaves popped up in a dense circle around the charm, a miracle that she, Fila, had worked. She laughed, her head tipped back, a final few raindrops splatting on her face. She skipped about, pulling hair and tying knots around green yarn and watching the bare field spring to life.

She was strong. Powerful. Formidable. She had soothed the storm and caused the seeds to germinate. She was truly the Servant, the conduit of the Land's power, the one who effected Its wishes.

The Land drew back Its power, and their bond returned to its usual calm communion without pain or ecstasy. She reeled and stumbled to her hands and knees in the furrow. She felt almost too tired to breathe.

"So this is what it means to be the Servant," she whispered to the mud. "This is what Mother experienced and I share with her still, what no one else alive understands."

She should head back to the manor before she was missed. She tried to stand; her exhausted body collapsed. She lay half-dazed in the mud, watching the lazy turning of windmill blades, until a large calloused hand slipped under her elbow.

"Lady, let me help." The young Toiler female lifted Fila from the mud, set her upright, and roughly wiped the mud from her face with a cloth. Several adult Toilers stood nearby, their violet eyes darting between her and the newly green field.

"Thank you for your kindness." Fila stood on her tiptoes and kissed the Toiler's cheek.

"We have been afraid since Servant Hyacinth died. But no more," said the oldest adult, Mourning Dove, whose ragged white hair hung below her waist.

"I knew Hyacinth and Granite and the Servant before your great-grandfather. You are more powerful. You lack only training and practice."

Despite her protests, the Toilers insisted on helping her back to Boraga's manor. She slipped through the kitchen entrance and went through the back halls so no one would see her so bedraggled.

At last, she reached her room. Shaking, she closed the door, fell back against it, and broke into laughter racked by weeping.

A Toiler pup opened the door to Boraga's chambers, and Fila peeked in before crossing the threshold onto the cold dirt floor. The door swung shut behind her. She was alone with her teacher in a sitting room as dark as her grief and as severe as Boraga's face silhouetted by the single candle.

"Sit, Fila." She pointed to a straight chair facing her own. "I cannot in a day or two teach you what you would have learned here over the next three years, but we can work on a few useful lessons."

Fila sat in the indicated chair. It was too tall for her, and her legs dangled like a child's. She smoothed her skirt and folded her hands in her lap. She repressed a yawn; her exertion of her powers had drained her of motivation and energy. And now she had lessons.

A band tightened around her forehead, and her stomach leaped about and gurgled, just as they sometimes had on test days when she was a child. *What I need now is time alone. Even just an hour or two. No more can fit in my brain, so full of grief it is, and struggling so hard to accept life's changes.*

As Boraga watched her, the backs of Fila's legs and her bottom began to itch. She let her hand drop to the thin cushion. Horsehair. She pressed her lips together to keep from squirming; the itch turned to pain as stiff hairs pierced her clothes and drilled into her skin like hungry mosquitoes.

Sighing, Boraga swept her raven curls back with a graceful hand, rose, and stood behind her chair. Her hands gripped the back. "First lesson: You no longer need to obey me or anyone else. Second lesson: Kassia will not always be around to stand up for you. You must make your own desires and needs known."

Childish giddiness rushed through her before her Goodborn nature chided her for selfishness. "Goodborns put others first. We cannot help it. Please, explain what I should have done differently today."

"Do you find your chair comfortable?"

She shook her head.

"Then for Land's sake, child, get up and request a different chair. Your job may be to serve others, but you should not tolerate any attempt to undermine your authority as leader of the two peoples of Veridia."

Fila jumped up and shook her skirt until nothing prickled or tickled her skin. "What else?"

"First, you could have declined my invitation to come here. Mourning Dove told me of your magicworking today. You are probably exhausted. Second, your every hour, minute, and second belong to the Land now. You should have asked why I called for you rather than wasting the Land's time waiting for me to say something. Third, it is no longer my place to give you orders. You should not have sat docilely, like a child, when I told you to."

She bowed her head. "Yes, Boraga."

Boraga's knuckles turned white on the chair back. "Think, child, think! You owe me no deference." She took a deep breath. "I confess, dealing with Goodborns is not easy for me. My apologies, Lady. But you must think before acting on your urges now you are Servant. You are only one person. Do the good that is most urgent, that helps the most people, that makes the biggest difference."

"Your words make good sense. But my Goodborn instinct responds to every person's need as if it's urgent. How can I learn to tell the difference?"

"I do not know. Perhaps your future Consort can help."

Someone rapped at the door.

Boraga sighed heavily and strode to answer it. Then she turned back to Fila. "You'll have to excuse me now. Several Toilers need healing."

Fila started obediently toward the door. *I'm acting like a submissive child again.* She twisted her cold hands together. "May I—; no, I would like—." *Bad starts. Try again.* "I will stay and help. I need to learn as much as I can." She took off her needlework bag, set it on the prickly chair, and opened it wide.

They worked quickly for the next hour and healed all four injuries—a cooking burn, a finger crushed in a grain-sorting machine, a hand cut by careless use of a band saw, and two toes broken after being stepped on by an elk—without leaving a single scar. Boraga explained in great detail as they worked what she would do, in what order, and why. Fila memorized some new healing charms and grasped some concepts that had eluded her when discussed in class, but now she had new questions.

"Katydid arrived first, but you did not treat her first. Why did you make her wait? Why did you ask her to help us with the others? Why did you assign her a task we did not need done?"

"Perhaps I can help you understand different levels of urgency after all. Do you remember when we discussed triage in class?"

"Yes, but I did not understand it. Every person should be healed right away."

"Usually that's not possible. For example, what if you were called, by yourself, to treat three Toilers and ten elk that were injured in a barn fire? Whom would you treat first?"

Fila closed her eyes and pictured the barn and the injured. Purple flooded her mind, but instinct proved useless. It urged her to help them all.

Boraga waited two long minutes, then said, "It would depend on the severity and type of their injuries. Those who will likely die or be seriously maimed if you don't treat them right away are class one. You treat all the class ones first.

"Those who will likely die or be seriously maimed no matter what you do are class fours. If you have time, provide class fours with a charm to ease the pain or help them sleep. But don't treat them until everyone else has been treated."

Fila gasped. *I cannot do that!* "That would be wrong, to not treat an injured person."

"As Servant, you will have to make hard choices. Every second you spend with a person you can't help is a second stolen from a person who could benefit from your magic. That would be a greater wrong. Do you understand?"

"Are you saying that instead of doing what is right, I should look at the harm each right action would cause and do what is least wrong?"

"You have a rather convoluted way of putting it, but yes. You may be Servant and able to draw on the Land's power, but you still have limits. You have only two hands, even when ten or twenty are needed. You still need sleep, even if a disaster requires days or weeks to fix. You should do the most good you can given your limits."

Fila's tired mind struggled with the new concepts until they abruptly made good sense. She sighed with relief. "I think I understand now. What are class two and class three?"

"Class two includes people who need treatment as soon as possible, but they aren't going to die right away if they have to wait. Class three is people whose injuries can wait for treatment. They might even eventually totally heal on their own if left alone. You can distract class threes from their pain and fear by asking them to help you with more urgent patients."

Fila rubbed her forehead with the base of her hand. Her head would rupture if she learned one more thing. Her brains would explode out and splat on the walls. *I would be a class four.* She giggled with fatigue and quickly covered her mouth with her hand. "Thank you for your time, Boraga. I have learned all I can for today. May I call on you tomorrow?"

Boraga bowed. "Of course, Lady. I aid the Servant in all things." She rose and smoothed her face of all expression, but not before Fila had seen there deep doubt and fear.

Chapter 9

KASSIA RAN HER HAND over her hair to smooth it, then knocked on Fila's door. She had not seen Fila or her amma, Spotted Turtle, since morning. She imagined them shut up in their room all day, wailing, weeping, and generally acting as if the world had ended. It was up to her to shake them out of their gloomy self-indulgence.

Fila answered the door herself.

Kassia rolled her eyes. Fila had never gotten the knack of delegating tasks to servants. Kassia tossed her hair. She had no such problems. Her amma knew her place and her duties.

"I've come to cheer you up." Kassia held out the bag she carried. "I've brought you your favorite honey drops to remind you of the sweetness of life."

Fila took the bag and rested her head against the doorjamb. She looked terrible. She wore an outfit so plain, it should belong to a Toiler who worked in the fields. Her usually warm face was bleached to parchment, dark hollows circled her eyes, and her hair—Kassia's eyes lingered on the brilliant copper that should be gracing her own head—stuck out at all angles. A curl hung annoyingly in front of Fila's eye, and Kassia resisted the urge to brush it back. She was right to come. Fila needed her.

"Thank you, dear cousin, but we're not really in the mood for company." Fila looked at the candy. "Not even honey drops could make this evening less bitter."

"I had the kitchen Toilers shape them to look like bare feet, just for you," Kassia wheedled.

Fila peeked in the bag, giggled, and slapped her hand over her mouth. "I hope Boraga doesn't find out and punish you." She hugged Kassia. "Thank you for your thoughtfulness." Her face drooped again, and she started to withdraw.

"It's my duty as your cousin to ease your grief. Please let me in." Kassia made her voice soft and sweet. "You wouldn't keep me from doing my duty, would you?"

Those were the right words. Fila immediately opened the door wider into her austere room. "I would never keep you from your duty. Please come in and sit down. Would you care for a tisane of mountainmint?"

"Yes, please."

Spotted Turtle set two undecorated earthenware mugs on an unattractively grained chestnut table.

Kassia wrinkled her nose. Fila cared as little about her surroundings as about her clothes. "I brought cards so we could play Rose and Briar."

"Cards? Thank you, but you know I do not care for frivolities."

"There's more to life than duty, you know. Besides, cards have a function. They're fun!"

Fila gave Kassia's hand a squeeze before wrapping her hands around her mug. "Good cousin, you always take care of me."

"As a cousin should." Kassia relished Fila's words, repeating them over in her head as she sipped her tea. "Do you want to go riding instead? We may not get another chance soon."

"It would be unkind to the horses to take them out in this weather. I'd rather sit and talk. That's something else we won't get much chance to do when we first get back to the Seat. Oh, I wanted to tell you first. I've chosen my Servant name!"

Kassia almost choked on her tea. "Who shall you be?"

"Violet. Violets have a beautiful smell and are useful for many purposes."

Trust Fila to choose a tiny, insipid flower. When Kassia became Servant, her name would be Cat's Claw. She sipped her tea slowly until she could speak calmly, without criticizing Fila. "I know something fun we can do that's also practical. Let's fix your hair! Just between us, it's a disaster."

"Yes! I can't figure out what to do with it." Fila pulled her hair on both sides then let go. Curls jumped out into a lopsided nimbus. "See? It sticks out every which way and gets in my eyes." She looked down and shook her head. "I'm being vain. Thank you for your offer, but what I look like doesn't matter. I'm *servant* to Veridia's peoples, not their mistress."

Kassia hid her shock. "On the contrary, your appearance matters very much. You're not an ordinary servant, you're *the* Servant, the most important person in Veridia. You should respect your peoples and look the part. Here, let me help. Spotted Turtle, watch what I do so you can do it later."

The Toiler didn't move until Fila nodded to her. Kassia seethed at the amma's impertinence.

Fila sat listlessly as Kassia bustled around her, tucking and twisting and braiding and even pulling jeweled pins from her own hair to jab into the unruly, springy curls. Once finished, she stood back and took a long, appraising look.

Fila's copper strands were a challenge, but Kassia had outdone herself. The top and sides were pulled back in flat plaits, and a loose tail draped down the neck. The style would be too plain for her, but it suited Fila. "There, that's better. The hairpins twinkle prettily in your hair. Like stars."

"Stars," Fila echoed. She touched her hair and turned to Spotted Turtle.

The Toiler nodded. "I think you'll be more comfortable now. Kassia did an excellent job." The Toiler stroked Fila's head. "It took your mother a while to get used to her Servant hair, too, and her hair was much . . . calmer."

Fila smiled. "Thank you, Kassia. I could never have done this on my own." They returned to the table and their now-cold tea. "It's like when we were schoolgirls. Remember? You always liked to style my hair."

"And then, somehow, you'd always get your knitting needle or your crochet hook caught in it and pull it apart." Kassia pursed her lips, remembering her annoyance.

"What I remember most was watching the boys playing outside," Fila said. "How we envied them! It never seemed fair we girls had to work so hard to develop our magic. Theirs flowed naturally, and they only needed to learn control."

"Hour after hour at the loom and embroidery frame for us, while they'd be having fun crushing pebbles and breaking tree limbs into firewood. Only at the end of the day did the teacher let us out of the classroom to heal their wounds."

Fila's hand trembled so hard that tea sloshed over the edge of her mug and pooled on the table. Her face was stricken, and her eyes, haunted.

Kassia's annoyance fled. They looked at each other in silence, then reached out and grasped hands.

"Did you ever watch the boys again after—after that day?" Fila asked.

Kassia shook her head.

"I know I have to have a Consort, but I don't want one. I feel sick every time I think about marrying someone whose magic only destroys. I do not want to spend my life with a man who enjoys killing baby animals."

"Boys mature, especially once they pass their Tests and their hair silvers. Surely you've noticed."

"No. I haven't had much contact with boys. When I was home during school breaks, I'd sometimes see Urushi during our family suppers. But otherwise, he often sat in on the Servant's Council, while I helped Mother or Father at Toiler villages."

"That sounds quite tedious."

Fila's eyebrows shot up. "Not at all! I loved going to the villages. What could be more thrilling than seeing a sick lamb stand up and run to play with the other lambs? Unlike you, I never had ambitions. I wanted only to be a good Guardian. Mother helped me learn the nonmagical skills we are not taught at school."

"Hair styling should have been part of those skills, don't you think?" Kassia joked.

Fila nodded solemnly, as always missing the humor. "Yes. Instead, we visited Toiler villages. Mother settled disputes and healed wounds, and Father helped the farmers prepare their fields and stripped the rust from their equipment."

Is that why the Land chose her Servant over me? Because she had helped a Servant and I had not? She let go of her cousin's hand and picked up her tea, hoping the mountainmint would drown the bitter taste in her mouth.

Fila hunched her shoulders. "It does not matter if the boys are different now. I still have to marry someone who *once* exploded rabbits."

"Not all the boys did that. I'm surprised you don't remember. My brother refused. The other boys made fun of him for years."

"Good for him. Your parents must have been proud."

Kassia snorted. "Mother made him eat and sleep in the library for a week. Father lectured him on how important it was for his future to *go along to get along.*"

Fila joined in on the last five words; they had both heard them often enough from Bifac when they were young.

"My brother was never the same afterward. He became a recluse; he talks to himself. Those boys still call him *Celatu the Coward.*"

"How sad. And how cruel. I never knew how he got that nickname. I dislike those boys even more now. They're nothing like my father."

Kassia leaned forward, needing to talk about some of the ethical questions she had been pondering alone. "Just between us, do you think Celatu should have gone along to get along? Should he have exploded his rabbit, as my father thinks?"

Fila grimaced. "I do not know much about being sociable or making friends. But I do think it's important each person follows her own heart and does what she believes is right."

"What she believes is right. Do you think it's better to do what's *good* or what's *right*?"

Fila's forehead wrinkled. "If you do what's good, shouldn't it also be right?"

Kassia rolled her eyes. Fila was no help, even if she was a Goodborn. She was so naïve she had never had the vagues, never had her soul sickened by doubt or confusion.

But Kassia knew how the world worked. Good for one person usually meant bad for another. Fila got to be Servant, and Kassia got stinky old shoes.

Unless she took steps to change her fate.

The next day, Fila was packing the last of her books when Amma flung open the door. Her large, pale hands fluttered like doves. "The honor guard is here! They want us to leave now!"

"At last!" Fila was tired of crying, tired of thinking she caught a glimpse of her mother from the corner of her eye, tired of hearing her mother's voice in every squeak of a hinge and rustle of a bush. She yearned to see her father and feel the comfort of his arms. She would need to lean heavily on his advice as former Consort in her new role as Servant, no matter who her own Consort was. She and Amma hurried to finish their packing.

A male Toiler pup appeared at the door. He stared down at Fila's hair, his mouth a round *O*.

Her face warmed. "I am ready to serve, if you will tell me who is in need."

"Boraga sent me to help with your bags, Lady."

She twisted her hands and looked at the floor, though of course it bore no instructions. She pointed to the box of books, and the Toiler tucked it under his arm. She and Amma hefted their own bags. The three headed down the wide stone hall to the manor's reception room, making slow progress. *This has been my home for years, and I will never see it again.* She peeked in every open door, sniffed every bundle of drying herbs and every vase of flowers, stroked every fabric. *Remember!*

"Starting the work of a servant already, I see," Kassia said, looking askance at the bags Fila carried. She herself was empty-handed and immaculately dressed in a nobby green silk riding jacket and split skirt. Instead of being sensibly braided, her hair was swept into an elaborate style held in place by one of her extravagances: wide gold hairpins decorated with polished milky-white spheres of fossil coral, cut so each appeared to contain a star.

"My goodness, you even look the part of a servant. Your clothes are rumpled from carrying those bags." Kassia ran her hand over the wrinkles in Fila's brown cotton blouse and split skirt and fussed with her hair. Then she dropped Fila's necklace inside her blouse. "Just in case we run into thieves."

Fila looked again at Kassia's hairpins, each worth more than her necklace except in sentimental value.

"No thief would dare attack the Servant's honor guard," Spotted Turtle protested.

Kassia adjusted the collar of Fila's blouse. "Now you're almost presentable."

"Where is Two Sparrows?" Fila asked.

"Amma is unwell. I told her to stay here until she feels better. Father can send someone for her later."

"That was kind of you. I know you rely on your amma as much as I do on mine."

They followed the hall to a set of carved double doors that opened onto a large room with windows swagged in leaf-green velvet. Fila became breathless, and her stomach fluttered. In seconds, she would be in Father's arms. Her gaze passed over the students gathered in one corner to the other side of the room, where Boraga spoke to the guards. They were crowned with the silver hair of Guardian men in their prime of magic and wore uniforms the color of indigo buntings.

She stood on her toes, straining to pick her father out of the crowd. The men all faced Boraga; no one watched the hall door or even glanced at it. She compared the men's physiques and stances, but none were familiar. *Why isn't he looking for me?*

Kassia clapped her hands. "What a magnificent honor guard! Sixteen men just for us. I can hardly tell them apart, they match so perfectly. We shall be the center of attention when we arrive."

Fila shuddered, and her feet stopped of their own accord. *I don't care what the protocol for the arrival is. I will have Father walk beside me.* "Does anyone see Father?"

"Not yet," Spotted Turtle said, her great brow wrinkled as she scanned the men.

Fila's stomach tightened with apprehension. She could wait no longer and called out, "Father? I can't see you. Where are you?"

The room silenced. The men turned, their gazes locking on her hair. One man stepped away from the others and came toward her, sinking to his knees in front of her. "Lady."

"Cousin Durio! How wonderful to see you." She took a breath and smiled, relieved he would be among the guards. Durio had worked as her father's secretary for many years. But it was odd that investiture protocol called for him, not her father, to greet her.

He rose and placed his hand on hers. The dark skin around his silver-flecked eyes looked sunken. "You have my deepest sympathies on the loss of your parents, Lady. Be assured, I shall help you in every way. May the Land flourish while you are Servant."

Parents.

Fila's mouth went dry, and the room spun around her, a blur of silver and green and blue. Her bags slipped from hands gone weak. Panic clawed through her insides and up her throat. Durio misspoke. He must have. "*Mother,* you mean."

"My sincerest sympathies, Lady. Both your parents have returned to the Land."

Not Father! Please, no, not him, too! "How did this happen? Did they catch a fever? Is Urushi in good health?"

"Your Uncle Bifac prefers to explain all when we arrive."

Fila wrapped her arms around her chest, gasping like a fish pulled from the water. *Father Father Father Father Father. Oh, Father, don't leave me!*

Next to her, Amma sobbed, her nictitating membranes covering her eyes as if the blow of the news were physical.

Boraga rushed over to Fila. "I am so sorry, my dear, for your double loss." She leaned over and whispered in her ear. "Lady, take great care. I fear whoever or whatever put the Land out of balance will try to stop you from fixing It."

Father, I need you so much now. "I'm joined with the Land now. Don't I have the most powerful magic in Veridia?" Fila whispered back.

"Your magic is incomplete until you have a Consort, my dear. Remember, even together, your parents couldn't stop what happened. Unlike you, your mother finished her training before she became Servant." Her eyes glistening, Boraga pulled something from her pocket and folded Fila's hand around it. "When you have no time to sew or knot a proper spell, this may help." She turned away quickly.

Fila's gaze followed Boraga as she rejoined the guards. An invisible wall separated their world from hers. She had borne every previous piece of bad news, even the ones she had thought *too much*; now her grief crumbled into dust, along with her dread and all her hopes. She was like one of the automaton toys the Toiler pups played with. She would talk and act as the Servant should, do all the right things, as if she were real. But inside she was empty. Hollow. As dead as her parents.

Kassia sidled up beside her. She no longer looked excited; her face showed puzzlement and confusion instead. "I am so sorry about your father," she said, taking Fila's hand. "He was always kind to me."

"May the Land preserve Uncle Bifac so that you never know this pain."

"Land hear your words!" she exclaimed. "You are so Goodborn, even in your grief. You didn't even look to see what Boraga gave you."

"Gave me?"

"In your hand, scatterbrain." She turned Fila's hand over and tapped the closed fingers. "See what it is. Maybe it will make you feel a little better."

Fila uncurled her fingers. A charm, its knots unfamiliar, tied with only the copper hair of a Servant—*Mother's?*—and the silver hair of a Guardian man.

"How lovely!" Kassia gasped, caressing it. "Very valuable—look at all the copper beads woven in. Powerful, too. Can you feel it? How lucky you are!"

Lucky only that I have so little left to lose. But Fila would not utter such a gloomy thought. "The best luck would be never to need the charm," she said instead, tucking it into her waistband where she could reach it quickly.

Chapter 10

KASSIA WATCHED from the terrace as Fila, stone-faced, limped across the courtyard, leaving a trail of blood from her swollen feet on the sharp rocks and sticks. The guards fussed over the new Servant and jostled to be near her. One guard brought her a horse garlanded with flowering herbs.

It felt strange not to be the center of men's attention, stranger yet to feel sorry for her cousin instead of jealous. But it was a strange day. Their lives had followed parallel courses. Now their paths diverged. They would no longer be *best friends forever*. Fila was an orphan; Kassia had two parents. That alone built a wall between them. They would never again sit next to each other in Boraga's tower room. Kassia would marry and be loved and given gifts.

But who could love Fila, especially now that her face had lost all expression and she walked like an old woman? Her future husband would marry her only for the prestige and political power conveyed by being the Consort.

Kassia touched the opal ring through her blouse and smiled. In minutes, she would be on her way to *him*, to happiness. He had promised she would be Servant. How lucky she was her father had sent only horses, even for the baggage and Toilers. She would reach the Seat much sooner if they weren't slowed down by wagons.

"I brought your father's horse for you," said the man Fila had called *Cousin Durio*.

"A Servant does not ride," Fila told him. "I will walk to the Seat of Enchantment as every new Servant before me has done."

Land take her! She knows a single tradition about the Servant, and it has to be the one that will slow my travel.

"Please, Lady, you must ride." Durio looked up at a gray sky that threatened rain. "You must reach the Seat and your uncle quickly. Trust me, as your father before you trusted me."

Impatient, Kassia joined them. "Fila, think. There will be no order in the Land until I'm invested at the Seat. If my father thinks our trip is dangerous and that you should ride, you should."

"What a wonderful idea," Fila said.

"What idea?"

"Your pretending to be me and going through the investiture in my place."

Coldness crept up Kassia's spine. Her slip of the tongue would have made Fila suspicious if she weren't so naïve. She grabbed the nearest guard. "Which horse is for me?" He led her to a small one. She had her foot in the stirrup and her other foot over the horse before his fingers clasped to form a step. She touched her hair and smiled sweetly in case she needed a favor later. "Please help Spotted Turtle with her horse. She hasn't ridden much."

While Spotted Turtle and most of the men mounted, she called back to Fila. "These aren't normal circumstances. The Land needs you in the Seat as soon as possible. It's your duty."

Fila looked at her dully, then mounted her horse.

Durio led the party away from the manor at a brisk walk. When the road left Boraga's open fields and gardens and entered the forest, the guards closed in around the women, forcing them into a tight cluster, and picked up the pace. Kassia sighed with relief.

But only twenty minutes later, at a fork in the road, Durio halted the group. He motioned to two men to ride ahead.

Kassia sighed and tapped her fingers on her skirt.

Next to her, Fila slipped off her horse. She pulled several copper strands from her head and hair from the horses' manes, took her crochet needle and a strand of pale blue yarn from the needlework bag that hung from her belt, and began a triple treble chain stitch.

Kassia curled her lip. It was an easy charm, but her cousin's tongue stuck out, as it always did when she was working or thinking hard.

The two scouts took so long, Kassia could have made charms for half the party. Fila finished only two. She gave one to Amma and one to Kassia before she climbed back on her horse. "Tie the charm in your horses' manes," she told them.

As if I didn't know that! "It will keep our horses surefooted and calm," Kassia told Spotted Turtle. Then she whispered to Fila, "dark blue would have been a better choice." To her disappointment, Fila didn't blush.

Under a darkening sky, the scent of storm in the air, Celatu gingerly touched the eye that was swollen shut, blinked the blurry eye, and swore. The huge, spirited, high-strung stallion Father had saddled for him would have been perfect … if the icedragon had not raked his eyes with its claws back in the library.

The horse had sensed his desperation to be far from the Seat and had obliged by keeping up a fast walk all night and through the morning with only short breaks. But now the creature—he would call him Spicebush Swallowtail for his beauty and his size—smelled the forest ahead and the storm on its way and broke into a canter. Celatu needed all his strength to hold him back. He, too, was eager to get under cover before the storm broke and before the icedragon found him. But even walking, Swallowtail went faster than Celatu could see. Any faster, and he could lose his head to a tree branch.

Celatu would have rather the icedragon found him than that. The Seat population ledgers would then read *killed by dragon* instead of *killed by twig*.

Though wood frogs occasionally quacked and house finches and several species of sparrows trilled in the trees along the road, they could not drown out other, more eerie sounds. The corn and barley fields on either side sighed and whispered. The trees themselves creaked, although his skin felt no wind.

He looked up at the sky. It seemed darker, but perhaps he had lost more vision since he last checked. His nose, though, confirmed the storm was nearer. The birds and frogs silenced.

Was that normal behavior before a storm? Some knowledge from his years wandering the primeval woods by the school remained as fresh as if he had learned it yesterday; some had vanished as if he'd never had it. He would need all of it when he entered the forest half-blind.

Swallowtail snorted, his ears flicking.

Celatu's taut muscles squeezed painfully. He looked around for the threat that disturbed the horse, but saw nothing. Of course, his good eye was producing so much mucus he probably wouldn't see a black bear strolling alongside, let alone a massasauga coiled to strike.

He closed his eyes to force himself to depend on his hearing and sense of smell. After several breaths, his senses opened to the world. Ahead sounded the whoosh of heavy rain, getting louder by the second. He leaned forward, and Swallowtail burst into a canter.

"Whoa! Whoa!" he shouted, opening his eye and pulling on the reins.

Something ahead moved quickly.

He yanked up his tunic and wiped the mucus out of his good eye to give himself a few seconds of decent vision.

The icedragon! It drifted high in the sky, body glittering as if covered in crystals, its shimmering frost-blue wings spread wide.

Celatu gaped at its brilliant beauty, almost impossible to bear but completely impossible to look away from.

The icedragon folded its wings back and dove right at him, scimitar claws forward.

Celatu's heart dropped into his stomach. Before he could prod Swallowtail with his heels, the horse leaped forward and galloped toward the woods.

The icedragon grew larger and larger as it hurtled toward them. Swallowtail screamed, and Celatu leaned low and clung to its neck.

As the icedragon passed close overhead, its painfully cold body burned his neck.

The horse devoured the road with its long stride. Celatu urged it faster, and he horse surprised him with a burst of speed. The forest expanded to fill his vision. Behind, the icedragon's wings whooshed as it turned to chase him.

Celatu's life depended on Swallowtail's instinct for self-preservation. He loosened the reins. The hammer of horseshoes against the packed dirt road did not blot out the increasingly loud sound of the icedragon's beating wings.

Ahead, thousands of passenger pigeons exploded from the forest, their wings roaring like a tornado.

Chilly wind blasted his hair from behind. The icedragon was closing fast. Pigeons plummeted around him, spraying blood, as the icedragon ripped through their ranks.

He had only seconds.

Cold. His tunic ripped. Fire rent his back.

A scream of rage.

Darkness.

Calm.

His eardrums rang from the icedragon's screams and the thunder of the passenger pigeons. His legs and back ached from galloping. Lines of excruciating pain scored his back.

All seemed good signs that he might not be dead.

Chapter 11

HIGH IN THE SADDLE, separated from the Land, Fila felt disoriented. Haze curtained everything she looked at. The clipclop of their horses' hooves and the singing of the forest birds sounded muffled. The bottoms of her feet burned and throbbed worse than before.

I have been Servant only a few days, and already the world feels wrong if I am not connected to the Land.

Against her waist, Boraga's charm still radiated its magic, reassuring in its constancy. She concentrated on the charm while she and her party moved through an an unchanging landscape of shadowed forest under a pewter sky.

Something jostled her from her trance. Her nose tingled, and scents of all kinds reached her. Male magic gathered and built. Not from her guards, but behind the travelers. *Something is very wrong.*

"Durio!" she called. As she turned, an ancient black oak crashed across the road behind them. The ground trembled as if giants danced upon it. *We are trapped. We can't return to Boraga's; we can only go forward.*

The Land shared her distress. The sky opened; rain poured.

In a flutter of loose robes, figures in billowing brown galloped from the forest on either side, swinging swords. Their magic smelled violent, merciless. Ice formed in Fila's guts and crawled up to freeze her chest.

Durio shouted orders. The guards formed two lines between her and the ambushers. Two attackers had bloodied arms from downing the tree—the price of exerting such titanic magic—and they wobbled on their horses.

Durio spurred his horse straight toward those two.

Fila leaned forward like Durio, her muscles taut in sympathy.

An attacker stood in his stirrups and turned with the grace of a dancer, sword in hand.

Fila shouted a warning.

Durio's horse impaled itself on the blade. It screamed and stumbled to its knees.

Durio rolled off and out of the way. But as he tried to stand, he slipped on the rain-slick leaves. His feet rammed his horse, and it collapsed sideways, crushing Durio's legs. His attacker slashed him with his sword and rode off.

Kassia's mouth opened in a silent scream. Fila leaned over and vomited, trembling like a candle flame on a breezy night. Amma reached over to pull Fila onto her own horse.

She shook her head and gripped her horse's mane to still her shaking hands. She had to help her men. *But how?* No war had troubled the Land since the first Servant had ousted the last king. Fila had not been trained for battle, and clearly, neither had her bodyguards' panicky, wild-eyed horses.

Two of her guards' horses bucked off their riders, and the attackers dispatched the men with quick sword thrusts.

The horses of the remaining guards danced, bumping into each other, biting, splashing mud, getting in the way of the guards' attempts to fight.

The disciplined horses of the attackers bared their teeth and pressed forward, squeezing the bodyguards' horses into a confused knot.

The attackers slew at will.

Meanwhile, ignoring shrieks of pain and shouts of triumph, the women's horses ambled calmly forward. "The charms are working," Fila whispered to Amma and Kassia. "Stay quiet and make ready to ride to freedom." She swatted their horses; they broke into a jolting trot that carried her cousin and her amma ahead of the fighting.

Trembling, Fila slipped off her horse and dropped into a crouch.

A jolt ran through her when her bare feet touched the ground, and power surged. The men were too busy fighting, or the rain poured too heavily; no one saw her. She crawled through the mud toward Durio. By the time she reached him, she had her needlework bag in one hand and a clump of copper hairs clutched in the other.

"Durio!" she whispered, gently poking his uninjured face. "Wake up!" He groaned; his eyes opened to slits.

"Run!" he groaned. "Don't let me die in vain."

Fila threaded a needle with a hair and jabbed it in and out around the slash wound, creating a complex design of hexagons, a pattern for knitting together. "I need you to magic the horse off you. I can't reach your other injuries."

He shook his head, moaning. "Too weak. I'll die from the effort."

"You will die if you don't. Please try."

Cedar-scented magic streamed from him into the limp horse and made Fila's skin tingle. The animal's skin dried and curled up like parchment. The exposed fat underneath melted. Organs appeared between the horse's ribs, only to dissolve into red pools. Durio's skin split open in several places, the price of his magic, and blood wept from his wounds.

The new surface wounds could wait. She reached through the horse bones to assess his life-threatening injuries.

His leg bones were crushed in three places; a ragged-edged bone with horsehair caught in the cracks protruded from his thigh.

She grabbed two needles from her needlework bag and knitted a thin rope of hair, letting the growing rope with its healing powers fall onto the protruding bone.

It started to retract into the leg, then stopped. She knitted faster. It didn't help.

Durio's injuries were no longer bleeding.

"Oh no, oh no," she breathed. Tears clouded her vision. She should have done more needlework, practiced more often in the evening, studied ahead on her own as Kassia had.

"There's the Servant! There, in the trees, by Durio!"

"I'll get her! Someone go after the other females!"

A brown-cloaked figure ran toward her, arms outstretched. Fila emptied her needlework bag onto a large leaf and grabbed embroidery scissors and a tapestry needle. She knelt, absorbing power from the Land through her shins and knees.

The man lunged; she thrust the scissors into his chest.

Grunting, the man grabbed her hand and tried to pull the scissors from his body.

She thrust the needle into his eye.

His huge bulk collapsed onto her, smashing her into the mud and trapping her beneath him.

Fila struggled, but she could not move the dead thief or slide out from under him. Pinned down, Fila had only one hand free, and her needlework kit lay out of reach.

The other men stalked toward her, bodies rigid with anger, their masks slicked flat against their faces with rain.

A large, hissing mink darted between the men's legs. As they stumbled, it slithered across her face. Its fur brushed her ear, and it nipped her before it ran off, leaving behind a tingle of magic, the taste of caramel in her mouth, and unfamiliar desires throbbing throughout her body.

She wanted—no, she needed!—to hit, to scratch, to bite, to humble all around her. Fila instinctively encouraged the urges to build until the edges of her vision blackened and she was on the verge of fainting. Then she sent her consciousness into the Land, slapped Boraga's copper and silver charm on a root, and exerted her will. *Grow!*

Veridia's power poured into her. It raced in cold lines to her arm, united, and ran down to the hand holding the charm. Under a burst of sparks, the root writhed and rose till her hand could barely reach it. Shoots exploded from the ground between her and the attackers, showering her with dirt and pebbles and flooding the air with the scent of fresh earth.

"Pus and blood!" a man cried as he tripped. She couldn't see the men behind the growing tangle of roots, but they shrieked in pain, and the ground vibrated with their falls.

She laughed. A small, sane part of her recoiled in shock and horror, but she laughed until she screamed at their suffering.

The sane part took control, and she sobered. Her magic had only bought her time. She was still trapped, and in a moment, the remaining attackers would squeeze between and around the roots.

Out of the forest stepped a glowering giant of a Guardian with a bloody, swollen face. He wiped one swollen eye with the corner of his tunic and leaned over her, putting his finger to his lips. He rolled the dead attacker off of her as if he weighed nothing. Then he dropped to his knees and crawled into the forest, motioning for her to follow.

Chapter 12

A S HER RESCUER PEERED about the small, dim clearing in the forest, Fila studied him. Knife slashes criss-crossed the upper half of his face. One eye was buried in swollen, bruised tissue; the other he dabbed with his tunic edge.

"This may be where I dismounted when I heard you scream," he said.

Fila shook like a willow in the wind, her sides heaving. Strange, she was more frightened now than during the attack. "Are you sure? Our tracks in the mud will be easy to follow. We need to get away before the attackers catch up."

"I think this is the spot."

"Where is your horse?"

"He should be right here." He turned in a circle, squinting with the eye that dripped mucus down his cheek.

"Can you see *anything*?"

"A bit."

"Corroded copper!" she cursed. "Do you remember what you tied it to?"

"Nothing."

"Nothing?" she screeched. "*Nothing?* You idiot. It could be anywhere." Fila imagined her fists pounding his face, feeling the tissue break down beneath her blows, seeing the tissue tear and bruises grow beside the ones he already had around his eyes, all accompanied by the scent of caramel.

She gasped and knotted her hands behind her back. *What is wrong with me?*

"No need to panic. I'm sure I'll find him in a moment."

Fila only stared at him as he bumbled about looking for his horse. His posture was proud; his face, alert and intelligent … perhaps even handsome when his eyes were not sliced, bruised, and burned.

I must heal his eyes and face as soon as we are safe. The normal thought and the purple of her Goodborn instinct suffusing her mind calmed her. *I had a brief moment of hysteria. I am fine now.*

She continued her study of his face. His silver hair was combed straight back, its fullness and waviness preventing it from looking severe. His black eyebrows did not curve, but instead slashed downward toward the center of his face, guiding her gaze away from his injured eyes to his perfect nose and lips.

She lowered her eyes, embarrassed, only to stare at his broad shoulders. *He is a man. Men enjoy destroying things.* Even Father, who scrupulously used his magic of destruction only for good purposes, enjoyed it.

Had enjoyed it.

Her attackers enjoyed it too. And they were looking for her this very moment. She fidgeted and lost patience with the slow pace of her rescuer's search. "I'll help you look; we need to get away. Those men want to kill me."

"I did not tie the horse becaue your screams sounded so desperate. I thought I should reach you as fast as I could. Good thing, too. If I'd taken time to secure the horse...." He let the sentence trail off.

Fila shuddered. "I apologize for my harsh words. Thank you for saving me." She glanced over her shoulder at the signs of their passage. No one yet followed, but she could not see far; they had crawled through a patch of dense, dark new-growth forest in the otherwise ancient wood. "That oak over there? It must be eight feet thick and a hundred feet tall. Use your magic to knock it down across our path. That will slow down our pursuers."

"I'd rather not."

He'd rather not? Unfamiliar violent urges swept through her again. She tightened her clasped hands and walked around the clearing's perimeter, gazing into the forest in hopes of seeing the horse. After completing one round, she stopped by their trail and glared at the wide swath of broken vegetation, churned mud, and water-filled kneeprints and handprints. The murderers would have no trouble following it.

"Why don't we follow your horse's tracks?"

"Of course!" He slapped his forehead. "I'm not thinking clearly. No sleep last night. Please, could you help me find the trail?" He pointed to his injured eyes, then knelt and felt among the wildflowers that carpeted the clearing.

Fila knelt beside him and placed her hands on the spongy ground, connecting to the Land. It resisted at first. She opened to It and scanned the clearing, letting the Land guide her attention.

The expanse of green with its clusters of color disappeared. She saw instead each individual plant, its stalk, its leaves, its flowers; the horse's actions were clearly inscribed in a language of water-filled depressions, crushed leaves, and chewed stalks.

She stood and retraced them. "*Here's* where you left your horse. It cropped off the flower heads in this patch of white avens. It wandered over here, gnawed on some wild hyacinth leaves, and then headed this way." The horse's trail took her into old-growth forest where the various canopy layers were so high she could walk upright. "I think I see it. Follow me."

Hope and fear sped her steps. She wound around trees old, older, and ancient, each step snapping a branch or cracking something in the mast underfoot.

Her rescuer padded behind her without speaking, his nearly silent steps taunting her for her noisiness.

Her mouth erupted with the sweet taste of caramel. She clenched her fists and kept up her pace until she saw a horse grazing. "Is your horse large and black?"

"Yes. Do you see it?"

"It's right there." Fila pointed.

Her rescuer squinted in the opposite direction. She took him by the elbow and turned him.

"There you are!" The man strode toward the horse. It swung its head, nostrils flared and pupils ringed in white. He kept walking, despite its aggressive posturing. The horse escalated its warnings, swishing its tail.

She ran forward and grabbed his arm. "Stop!"

"What's wrong?"

"This cannot be your horse. It doesn't recognize you."

"How many huge black stallions can there be wandering in this forest? This has to be my horse."

"Then why does it want to bite you?"

"I never rode him before today. Last night, rather. He's high-strung. Aren't you, Swallowtail?" The horse stretched its head and neck out toward him.

Fila tightened her grip and pulled him away from the aggressive animal. "You're a thief! Or a madman. Or both. Get away from that horse, you fool, before you get bitten. What is wrong with you?" She was shouting by the time she took a breath.

He turned toward her.

The horse nipped his rear, and he jumped forward, straight into a white oak sapling. He raised his palms. "I'm quite sane, actually. And I'm no thief. The horse belongs to my father, but he did give me permission to ride it."

"Oh," she said, glad he could not see the embarrassed heat flooding her shoulders and face.

"Perhaps we should start over again. Hello, I'm … I'm Tul, your rescuer today. For our get-away, I present to you this fine stallion. He's fast, strong, and brave, and he'll get us well away from your pursuers. If we can catch him."

His joke made her giggle. She clapped her hand over her mouth.

"My eye injuries may seem less amusing when you learn that because I can barely see Swallowtail, you'll have to be the one to catch him."

"My deepest apologies. Never in my life have I spoken to anyone as rudely as I have today to you. I do not know what is wrong with me." The strange, violent urges rose in her again; this time she tamped them down firmly.

His mouth twisted. "Murder attempts do tend to make one cranky."

"I had not considered that." *I hope he is right. I hate these strange new feelings. I hate that I can now feel hate.* "Do not worry. I can catch your horse. I'm a Goodborn."

His eyebrows shot up, and he chuckled. "Right. And I'm the Servant."

He does not believe me. And no wonder. I have behaved in impossible ways.

She turned toward the horse. Swallowtail was chewing on some newly sprouted trees. She walked slowly toward it, giving it a chance to smell and sense she was a Goodborn. Its eyes remained unfocused, and it continued to eat. She took hold of its mane and reins and swung into the saddle.

"Now let's get far from here and your attackers."

"My amma and cousin escaped during the attack. We must find them."

"Absolutely not," he said, walking toward her. "It's too dangerous."

"It is our duty."

"My rescue, my rules."

She stared at him in disbelief at his callousness. "Please, have mercy on my amma and my cousin. What if those evil men find them?"

"Something worse than those men wants to kill *me*."

The horse shifted under her. *I disturb it with my anger.* "Once we find Amma, she will help you fight your enemy. Let us—" The horse stepped quickly toward a break in the forest.

"Whoa! Whoa!" She tugged on the reins; the horse snapped its head, pulled them from her hands, and broke into a rack gait.

She called back to her rescuer, "Follow our trail!"

He shouted, "Don't forget: Swallowtail is high-spirited."

Fila clung tightly to the mane and let the horse have its head while it got used to her. It sped into a reckless canter through the wood that soon had her ducking branches as they whizzed through a cluster of chestnut trees. It raced between two vine-covered oaks, snarling itself for only a second before bursting through. Wet vines slapped her; some tore away from the trees and clung to her clothing and face. Poisonous white snakeroot. Poison ivy.

"Whoa, boy, whoa!" she ordered sternly.

The horse did not even flick an ear. She reached for the reins, but the horse tossed its head, and she missed. Her breath rasped. *I'll be lucky to live long enough to break out in a rash.*

Then she saw the massive toppled oak and the abyss left where it had ripped out of the ground. "Whoa!"

The horse responded instead to the death grip of her legs around its abdomen. It galloped.

Her trembling hands dug deeper into the mane. The horse's massive muscles tightened; it took flight. As they soared, rootlets brushed her, flinging dirt into her face. Eyes. Mouth. Nostrils. Gritty. Stinging.

Tears blurred her vision; coughs racked her body; the percussive landing surprised her. Her feet flew from the stirrups. She lost her balance.

She fell. She could not stop it. She did not try.

She closed her eyes, focusing on keeping firm hold of the mane, letting her legs slip, preparing herself for the pain when her feet hit the ground and the horse dragged her.

Still, she screamed when branches and fallen nuts tore the skin from her feet.

She let her eyes open but did not let go. She raked her toes through the leaf litter and touched the ground. She heard foot bones crack. She moaned but held fast.

A jolt from the Land shook her, racing from her toes to the horse. Every hair of its body sparked, lighting the forest briefly, brilliantly green. The horse stopped dead.

The Land pushed strength into her. She clung to the shaking horse, stroking its neck and murmuring sweet words instead of the angry ones she was thinking, as the agony spread from her swelling feet until all her joints ached in sympathy. She needed to heal her feet now, before pain blotted out her ability to think.

But she dare not let go of the horse.

Beneath her, the Land tickled her feet.

Stop! Please!

The Land ignored her plea. Her agony increased until every nerve fiber flamed. Her skin burned, bubbled, and melted, the liquid skin dripping off her feet.

She pulled herself onto the horse, wincing, expecting the pressure of the stirrups against her raw skin to be unbearable.

Instead, the pain vanished. Yet she still had sensation; the stirrups felt cool, comforting. *I felt the blisters rise and the molten skin flow.* She forced herself to look down at the ruined stubs of her feet.

She sucked in her breath. Her feet were still there, skin intact. She wiggled her toes and flexed her feet; the bones were no longer broken.

She put a hand to her head, dizzy with amazement and awe. She had underestimated the Land because It communicated so poorly. But Its powers were immense. *I know too little about the Land to be a good Servant. I do not even know whether I serve It or whether It serves me.*

The horse stepped forward, and she grabbed the reins. Then it half-scrambled, half-slid down a zigzagging animal path into a rocky gorge.

With his injured eyes, Tul will never be able to track our wild path.

She rubbed the back of her neck as the horse picked its way around large branches and stones beside the stream at the gorge's bottom. The road from Boraga's to the Seat ran roughly east-west, so they had been heading east when attacked. She was on the north side of the road when Tul rescued her and led her to the clearing. If she could figure out what direction the horse headed now, it should be a simple matter to find the road and follow it back to the attack site to look for Amma and Kassia and then to find Tul to return his horse.

The sun provided no help; the sky hid behind four layers of forest canopy and forbidding black and pewter clouds.

The Land must know where the Seat was. But she feared getting off the horse; she could not hold it back if it wanted to run away. Besides, It seemed disinclined to communicate anything but anguish.

The horse stopped to drink.

Think! Surely the surroundings gave some hints. She looked around. The direction of the stream's flow might tell her—if she knew more about geology. She put a hand on her churning stomach. She could be lost among the trees for days. Weeks, even, if Swallowtail got away from her.

Woodsy mnium grew plentifully here, on the rock tops that broke the surface of the rippling water, on the toppled trees and half-rotted logs that had fallen into the gorge, and on the gully's rocky wall. Though abundant, the woodsy mnium and other, unfamiliar mosses did not carpet the surfaces evenly.

She straightened. The mosses grew thicker on one side of the gorge than on the other. They favored only some parts of rocks and logs. Even the mnium's orange spore capsules were denser in one direction. *What direction?*

At Boraga's, she and Kassia had studied wildflowers and their uses. The complex life cycle of mosses, though, made them magic-safe only for women with great talent and many years of study beyond the norm. She half-remembered the basics taught to every child: how to identify and find the most useful mosses, the ones collected for soft mattress stuffings and velvety ground covers.

Kassia and I planted mosses in wet, shady spots. She looked up. The canopy opened to the sky above the gorge; sunlight shone here. Her heart pounded. Most mosses preferred damp conditions. Did woodsy mnium? If so, then it preferred the north side. So she was facing … east. The road lay south, to her right.

When the horse had its fill of water, she nudged it into a walk, studying the gorge walls for an easy place to climb back out. They came to a low natural stone bridge; a waterfall splashed beyond and around slabs of shale tilted at crazy angles.

The horse balked.

Fila looked for another animal path. *There!* She nudged the horse to turn until it saw the path too, and she gripped both mane and reins as they climbed up. She coaxed it to head south, toward the road and, she hoped, toward Tul, keeping on track by watching for the mnium's bright-orange spore capsules.

She settled back into the saddle and licked her lips. They were either going exactly the right way or exactly the opposite.

Her survival depended entirely on the growth habits of woodsy mnium.

Chapter 13

WHEN HER HOSTESS LEFT to answer the pounding on the kitchen door, Afissa sprang up to investigate the odd little wooden cottage. She had never been to this run-down section of the Seat before—known for poetry readings that ended in fistfights, private clubs in which artists gathered to smoke dried tobacco leaves in pipes, and a yearly contest for the fruit and the vegetable that most resembled sexual organs—let alone to the cottage of Daucina, first-cousin-once-removed of her husband, Gramin. If her home was any indication, the woman was delightfully eccentric.

Wards wrought in dozens of shades and hues of hair-fine blue threads had been tucked into the frames of the mismatched, unglazed windows to keep out the cold and wind. Afissa cocked her head as she studied the fifteen shades of violet painted on the walls and woodwork. She leaned over to inhale the perfume of the ancient books piled on most flat surfaces and caressed the balls and skeins of yarn and threads everywhere else with her eyes, cheek, and back of her webbed hand.

What Guardian woman could resist the sensual delights of this room and the magical possibilities of its contents! Textures from prickly-scratchy to velvety smooth. Weights from cording to spidersilk-light. So many colors, dozens of which could not be produced with modern dyes, many of which she'd never seen. No wonder Daucina's bookcases held old chemistry and botany texts.

Above her, something burbled, and a soft gray form winged past her face and flew through the window despite the wards.

She tilted her head back. The room had no ceiling; the sitting room opened to the rafters. *No wonder it's so cold in here, despite the lovely fire.* Another mourning dove, perched on a rafter next to a nest, returned her look of curiosity in equal measure.

Afissa laughed, then slapped her hand to her mouth to smother the sound. *Here I am, goggling at the furnishings while waiting for some of the most important women of the Seat. What an idler they'll think me.*

Afissa settled herself again on the low, wildly striped hassock, dug into her large needlework bag with her feet, and pulled out the knitting needles that held a half-finished sock.

Her current project was to knit warm socks and decorate them with embroidery for all of the Toilers in the village she was Guardian of. Toiler tech allowed them to whip out dozens of socks in the time it took her to knit one pair, but machine-made socks were utilitarian and plain. Her Toilers deserved beautiful socks. She balanced her feet on the floor and picked up knitting where she left off.

Daucina returned to the sitting room leading the newest arrival, an older woman with bushy eyebrows, who tossed back her hood and said, "Fortunate for us the rain continues. Half the city is wearing hooded capes or cloaks. No one gave me a second glance." As her gaze assessed the room, her eyebrows rose ever higher, but she made no comment on the house or décor. "I'm Kriga. Cousin of the late Consort."

Afissa rose, needles still clicking between her toes. She was proud of her hard-won grace and balance. Smiling warmly, she said, "You have my deepest sympathies, Kriga. I'm Afissa, Erudia's daughter-in-law."

"Afissa is my cousin by marriage," their hostess added. "She has two adorable daughters nearly ready to go to Boraga's for the next stage of their training."

Kriga nodded gravely; her gaze flickered down to the knitting needles between Afissa's toes and back up, pausing to take in her fused hands. "My cousin could have fixed you."

Afissa refused to drop her gaze, refused to let her smile wilt. "The Consort tried to 'fix' me. Many times. The webs grew back."

Kriga looked away first.

Afissa sat back down. *I hope the meeting will be small.* It grew tiresome explaining her fused fingers to each person she met. She socialized little, preferring to be home with her family and gardens. But Mother Erudia had begged her to come. The women would need a Goodborn.

Someone rapped on the kitchen door.

Daucina went to answer it and then ushered in Mother Erudia—*Land be praised!*—and a woman she introduced as Elata. After that, Afissa lost track of the names. Soon, the other conspirators numbered twelve, all women about Mother Erudia's age. As they settled in and took out their handwork, Daucina and her Toiler helper, Ladybug, served mugs of fragrant violet tea.

Erudia called the meeting to order over the pops and clicks of women's needles mending the world. "I hope you were all able to keep the meeting a secret from all Guardians."

A chorus of yesses replied, but Afissa remained quiet. As she had told her amma about the meeting, something crashed in the hall outside. She rushed out; the hall was empty, but a vase of flowers lay broken in front of its nook.

"How much Servant hair were you able to bring to strengthen our magic?" Mother Erudia asked.

The rustle and clinking of needlework bags opening sent the remaining mourning dove shooting out the window. Afissa pulled from her bag an envelope of hair from Servant Granite, a wedding present from her mother-in-law she had saved for eighteen years for a project that needed the strongest magic possible. As the women unwrapped packets of bright copper hair, reflections multiplied the light of the fire until the room seemed aflame.

"Sneaking around, keeping secrets, gathering hair—do you have us playing a children's game?" Kriga raised her bushy brows.

Erudia sat, frown lines criss-crossing her face like irrigation canals on a map. "Since Servant Hyacinth died, Urushi has been acting more like a king than a Servant's son. At the most recent Servant's Council, he announced he has created creatures of magic to kill his opponents."

"Surely a bluff," Elata objected.

"Even a woman Talent can't create living beings. How could a man do so, much less a defective one?" Daucina asked.

"And yet." Erudia sighed again and bowed her head. "And yet my uncle spoke out against Urushi's usurpation of powers in the Servant's Council. Now he and his son are missing."

Land watch over them! Like most Guardians, Afissa spent more time with her Toiler family than with her blood family. Even so, she knew both of the missing men and respected their integrity. People did not just go missing in Veridia, not with the double guard of mountains and magic wards serving to keep people in as well as intruders out.

The fire crackled and popped as other women considered Mother Erudia's words.

"Evidence?" Kriga barked.

"A pool of blood and a pile of broken timbers where something large crashed through the roof."

The room closed in, thick and fuzzy. Afissa bent over and took gasps of air.

Erudia continued. "Boraga sent messages to Elata and me. Our new Servant is Servant Hyacinth's daughter, Fila, who has not yet finished her training. She's a Goodborn, not a Talent."

"What a time to have a Goodborn Servant," Kriga grumbled.

"We Goodborn are not feebleminded," Afissa said gently.

"No, dearest, but neither are you well equipped to understand men like Urushi, who put their own desires above the needs and even lives of others," her mother-in-law said. "Boraga begged me to do what I can to ensure Fila is invested as Servant. She did not, of course, know what Urushi does here, but the Land's violent reaction made her suspect the new Servant might be in danger."

"I still find it hard to believe a brother would harm his sister," Afissa interjected.

Some women chuckled.

She compressed her lips. *I'm here to make ethical judgements about their proposals, not to share thoughts of my own.* Still, their laughter stung. She knitted faster.

"I have a plan," Erudia said. "You come secretly to my quarters at the Servant's House. I invite Urushi to tea to discuss an urgent library matter. I put a strong sleeping charm on him while he is distracted. Together, we pool our magic and Servant hair and heal him. Afissa, is the plan acceptable?"

She closed her eyes and summoned the golden glow. "Your plan is ethical. Even though you don't get his consent, you are doing something that benefits him and that he should be grateful for."

The other women spoke, one on top of another. "If Servant Hyacinth couldn't fix his defective magic, how can we?"

"You assume his destructive bursts of magic are the problem. What about his craving for power?"

"Fixing his magic will make him *more* dangerous if we cannot fix his damaged spirit."

Erudia sighed. "Does anyone have a better idea?"

Elata set her mug down daintily and folded her hands in her lap. "When you invite Urushi to tea, why not simply poison him? When he is dead, Fila and Veridia—not to mention the rest of us—will be safe."

"Excellent. Solves everything." Kriga set her knitting aside and stood. "Are we agreed?"

"No!" Afissa leapt up. "If you choose murder, I must warn Urushi."

Kriga glared. "He's a threat to Veridia. You can't understand evil. You're Goodborn." She did not sit.

Neither did Afissa. *Your eyebrows do not intimidate me.* "I recognize evil better than anyone else here. If you fight wickedness with wickedness, you become your enemy."

Women whispered to each other, then Elata spoke for the group. "Erudia, ethics does not belong in this discussion. We must do what is necessary."

"We must do what is necessary *and right*. That is why I invited Afissa. That is why she will stay."

The room hissed with grumbled whispers.

Erudia heaved a long, lingering sigh. "Daughter, Kriga, please sit."

Kriga glowered, her eyebrows bunched together. Then she harrumphed and sat.

Afissa looked around the room at the unsympathetic faces, then sank onto the footstool, the golden light in her mind brightening to illuminate the branching paths of actions and consequences, some good and some not-good. *No one is* for *the new Goodborn Servant. Everyone here is* against *Urushi. I must protect the Servant … if I can.*

"Back to our business," Erudia said. "Urushi dotes on that little terrier of his. What if we kidnap it?"

A woman asked, "Which does he care about more, the dog or his power?"

The room fell silent.

A wave of cold rolled over Afissa. Shivering, she said, "He wouldn't believe you'd harm his pet until you did so. Which of you will be the one to hurt an innocent dog?"

Silence again.

"What if we lured him to his Toiler village and kept him from leaving?"

"Keep him from leaving? Our magic can't do that."

"Guardian men with strong magic and weapons could."

"Excellent idea," Elata said, tidying a stray curl.

Afissa shook her head. *I can't believe what I'm hearing.* "Weapons in a Toiler village? Magic of destruction? It would break the agreement between Guardians and Toilers."

Silence leaden as the skies outside fell over the room, broken occasionally by a sudden intake of breath and then a sigh—the blossoming of an idea and its death.

Then Daucina said, "What if we lure him to his Toiler village and while he is on his way we dose him with spores of various fungi?"

Erudia leaned forward. "Go on."

"Our magic could invigorate the fungi, make them grow and spread, make the rashes itch worse than poison ivy. He'll be trapped in the village, disabled by the itch and the pain. After Fila is invested, we reverse the magic. He recovers without any lasting harm."

"Your creativity is remarkable," Elata said, "but you must admit your plan is rather elaborate and relies on everything working perfectly."

"I've been to Urushi's Toiler village," Afissa said. "Its tech specialty is biochemistry. It produces many remedies for both Toiler and Guardian disorders. Its remedies may cure any infection you give him."

"But otherwise the plan is moral?" Erudia asked.

Afissa attended to the gold shimmer, then shook her head. "Whatever is biologically different about him could change his response to disease. A fungus that's a nuisance for others might be deadly for him. Or it could strengthen his faulty magic." The skin on the back of her neck crawled; some of the women were staring at her hands, she was sure of it. *They think Urushi and I are alike. Freaks. Cursed by the Land. Yet Servant Hyacinth said the Land doesn't curse people, that It may have given me webbed hands as a blessing.*

"The dog's sweater!" Erudia exclaimed.

"What?" said several women at once.

"I do hope dogs wearing sweaters is not a new trend," Elata said.

"Urushi's dog wears a sweater with a hood and legs," Erudia explained. "It contains magic to protect the dog when Urushi loses control of his magic." She clapped her hands. "Oh, I have a beautifully simple plan for a trap. We weave a net to do the opposite of the dog's sweater: We toss it over Urushi, and his magic can't escape. It will be trapped inside, unable to hurt anyone."

"Except Urushi," Afissa objected. "That's not right."

Elata said, "We can fix that simply enough. The net could absorb and destroy his magic. Or convert it to light or heat or sound that passes through harmlessly."

"Yes!" Kriga exclaimed. "Let's do it."

Erudia said, "Afissa?"

"It would be wrong to trap him forever. But you would have to: If he's a danger now, he'll be a danger when he's released."

Some women murmured agreement.

"We must hope after the Servant and her Consort have been invested, they'll be strong enough to either heal him or control him," Erudia said wearily. "The Land chose Fila for a reason, however unsuited she seems to us. I say we make the net and trap Urushi now and worry about how to release him later."

Afissa's abdomen and chest buzzed, then her extremities shook. *The vagues! Not now, not again.* She closed her eyes and breathed deeply, waiting for her body and mind to accept that Mother Erudia's suggestion was not clearly right or wrong.

Not every Goodborn fell sick when a situation was morally ambiguous, but Afissa did. This time the sense that the world had turned inside out and been wrung out like a washcloth just got worse. Every muscle and nerve demanded she escape. She dropped her knitting and ran for the kitchen.

She slammed the door behind her and leaned back against it.

Ladybug set down her tea with a clatter.

Sweat poured down Afissa's face, and she slid down to the floor. Limbs twitching and jerking, her back arching farther than it was designed to, she mewed.

The Toiler placed a wet cloth against her forehead, and delicious cool drops ran down Afissa's face. "Do you want a towel to bite on?"

Afissa couldn't answer; her head jittered too hard. She signaled "no" with waves of her hand.

Ladybug sat on the floor beside her, pulled her onto her lap, and held her tightly to stop her flailing. Then she rocked her and sang a children's bedtime song:

> *Who takes care of Guardians?*
> *Toilers do. Toilers do.*
> *Who takes care of Toilerkind?*
> *The Guardians, of course!*
>
> *Who takes care of both these folk?*
> *It that made them. It that made them.*
> *Who serves Land and people both?*
> *Servant of them all.*

The deep voice calmed Afissa's spasms. Her muscles relaxed, fiber by fiber, until she no longer needed to flee. When she felt strong enough to sit upright, she laughed with joy. "Thank you," she told Ladybug. She reluctantly climbed out of the Toiler's lap and stood and stretched.

"Come back to the kitchen, Young One, if their questions give you the vagues again. Better yet, stay in here and help me drink the rest of the violet tea. There's no ambiguity about the goodness of tea."

Afissa chuckled. "I am tempted to. But the women need my help." She took a good look at Ladybug's feet, memorizing their size and shape. Then she walked down the hall to the sitting room, humming "Who Takes Care" and mentally designing a pair of socks with embroidered violets for Ladybug.

She opened the door and stopped short. Each woman had already knitted or crocheted or macraméd a substantial portion of net. Goosebumps erupted on her arms: These women were not merely Mother Erudia's friends. Each had an unusual skill.

Her skin tingled as she watched them work, her gaze moving hungrily from one to another, trying to memorize the technique of each. *I'm not worthy to work among them.* Then: *I am the only woman who does needlework with her feet. I'm as skilled at my ability as they are at theirs.* "What should I do?"

Erudia looked up. "You can put the finished squares together, starting with the ones I've laid out on the floor. Link them with white yarn."

Afissa returned to the striped hassock and rummaged through her bag for white yarns and a crochet hook. Once she stopped examining each square for clues to the purpose of each unusual design or color combination, her toes flew through their task. The repetitive rhythm lulled her into rapture. The web burgeoned, and its magic with it.

I should be the triumphant spider in the middle, but instead I feel like the fly. The web's growing magic exuded an aura, sticky and ominously alluring. Caught, her needles dragged and her toes slowed. The magic was trapping her in a haze of euphoria.

A heavy hand stroked her head.

She tried to shake it off, to return to the half-dream world of the web.

"Afissa? Afissa!"

The seductive voice pulled her back to awareness.

Mother Erudia's voice, sharp and high, said, "What are you doing here, Gramin?"

My husband, here? Afissa kicked the net off. "I didn't see you come in."

"I noticed, love." He bent to kiss her lips. "I stopped by to see you and Mother. I thought afterward I could walk you home."

Mother Erudia's face shriveled like a dried-up apple. She bolted to a window. "Did anyone follow you here? You didn't tell anyone about our … sewing circle?"

"Actually, yes."

Afissa's stomach flopped like a beached fish. *The broken vase. He had overheard her plans.* "Gramin, you didn't!"

"What's wrong? Bifac invited me to the Servant's House to discuss a commission, and Urushi was there. Urushi asked how Mother was, and I said I hadn't stopped by your suite because I knew you were meeting with several friends to sew."

Erudia wheeled from the window. "Oh, Gramin. What have you done?" Breathing heavily, she put her hand on her head. "Friends, gather your work! We must flee now. Daucina, you and your Toiler as well."

Afissa's face burned, but she stayed where she was, trusting Gramin. As the other women jammed items into bags and totes, she pulled the partially finished net onto her lap.

Her husband's brows knitted as he watched the flurry of activity. "I assured Urushi strongly your group was sewing, not plotting. He asked me to tell you about his new edict. Starting tomorrow, no more than four Guardians can gather at once."

Deep howls shook the front wall of the house, knocking charms from the window frames.

"Out the kitchen door!" Erudia cried, leading the way down the hall. Terrified women ran after her, all trying to squeeze into the hallway at once.

Gramin went to the window and peered in both directions.

"Do you see anything?" Afissa hugged the net to her chest.

He stuck his head fully out. "Flaming dogs!"

"What are you cursing about? What do you see?"

"Flaming dogs the size of ponies are running this way."

Urushi's creatures of magic! "The firehounds must not see, hear, or smell us!"

Gramin slammed the shutters on both windows and bolted the door. He slipped his hands under the base of a tall china hutch and dragged it toward the door. Yarn balls and skeins fell off and rolled every which way.

He'll slip or trip! With her feet, she swept the yarn from his path.

Something outside slammed against the door, and the heavy oak vibrated.

The hutch must be very heavy; Gramin still had two foot-lengths to drag it before it would block the door. "Hurry, Gramin!" Afissa pled, shaking like laundry on a clothesline on a windy day.

Screeching, the door hinges ripped from the wall. Two slavering, blazing monsters pushed inside, knocking Gramin over. The hutch crashed to the floor.

The dogs bounded toward the women clotting the hall. Baying, each seized a woman by the neck. Growls and screams filled the room.

The firehounds shook their victims like chew toys and then tore out their throats.

Afissa scrambled around the hutch and helped Gramin stand. He kissed her hard, then pulled out his pocketknife. He threw himself on the dogs, stabbing and slashing.

Afissa shivered at the familiar, beloved tart-sweet persimmon scent of Gramin's magic.

Unheeding, the firehounds climbed on the dead women to reach for other potential victims. Gramin's shirt caught fire; several women's skirts were smoking.

In the hall, Ladybug's face appeared. She threw a woman over each shoulder and ran back to the kitchen.

Thank the Land for Toilers!

Two more dogs squeezed through the door, heads raised and nostrils sniffing. One swung its massive head toward Afissa.

She cowered. Her heartbeat pounded in her ears. She had no pocketknife, of course. She was helpless against the firehound.

Except for the unfinished net.

She flung it over the dogs.

Crazed, they howled, scratched themselves, and nipped each other, entangling their legs and snouts in the net. Their struggles twisted them into a rolling ball of fire. Yarn ate the sparks and spit them back out tenfold.

Sobbing, Afissa skirted around them to grab first her needlework bag and then Gramin's elbow. "Let's get out while we can."

"But the women!"

"Toiler Ladybug is rescuing them from the hall."

The firehounds snapped and growled. The remaining women pushed each other, frantic with fear. One woman's hair caught fire.

I can't bear to watch anymore. She pulled Gramin toward the nearest window.

He swore. Flames danced between them and escape. "Stand on the back of the hutch," he told her.

She did.

He stretched out his hands, palms down, and widened his arms, eyes ecstatic, leaning forward as if pulled by the call of music. As his magic crushed the air from everything it passed over, flaming balls of yarn crumpled and shrank into charred spots on the floor. His wild and reddened eyes stared from skin gray with ash.

"Come away, Gramin!"

Groaning from the cost of his magic, he stumbled toward her.

"Just a few feet more," she urged.

Howling in triumph, a hound slipped out from under the net, its glowing red eyes fixed on Afissa.

As the dog leapt, she threw herself against a window. The shutters held firm against her weight.

"No!" Gramin howled, shoving himself in-between the dog and Afissa.

She popped the latch free, pulled the shutters open, and vaulted over the sill. She fell and scrambled out of reach. The monster hit Gramin with a thud of its bricklike head.

He crumpled. The dog trained its gaze on her and lunged.

"Gramin!" The old stone buildings across the street echoed her wail: *Gramin!* The dog's thick chest lodged in the window frame.

She cowered as it growled, snapped, and writhed to free itself, its fangs long and sharp and bloody.

The scent of persimmon perfumed the ashy air, and the firehound shrieked as it was jerked backward into the house. Afissa scrambled to her feet and took a step toward the window. "Gramin?" she whispered, her voice gone after her despairing scream. Blackened fabric and crispy white ash floated out and stuck to her face and lips.

The tangled net of fighting dogs ripped; dogs tumbled out. They reared, heads back, snuffling the air.

Gramin's charred arm rose into view; its hand gracefully carved the air.

The flaming firehounds ignited and burned for real, their howls of agony tearing Afissa's heart.

Through the thick smoke, what was left of Gramin struggled toward the sill and locked eyes with her. "Run, my love," he murmured, his voice hollow, resigned.

"No!"

Two firehounds, bone glistening through the burnt skin of their faces, staggered toward her.

Gramin's hand danced. Furniture, rafters, floor: All became fire.

I must save him. Gasping for breath, she swung a leg inside.

He looked at her with longing and made one last gesture. His clothes exploded into flames.

She threw her arm over her eyes. She turned from the cottage and stumbled blindly down the street. *My fault. All my fault.*

Chapter 14

S Fila guided Swallowtail through the forest toward the road, noting the evidence of the mnium, she listened for voices or clashing metal ahead. She did not want to at last find the road, only to find the attackers as well.

But the forest remained innocent of violence. A scarlet tanager swooped in front of her; blue jays squawked and clicked nearby. Ahead, on a mature black oak, gray squirrels chased each other. A preternaturally beautiful mink ran right in front of her, stopped, and hissed.

She stopped the horse and admired the glossy animal, whose shape seemed misty in the odd forest light. The mink ran off. When Fila looked up, she spied daylight.

She clicked her tongue against her teeth, heedless now of making noise. They left the forest, and there was the road, its damp mud churned and pocked. The horseshoe marks all told the same story: The killers were heading east toward the Seat of Enchantment.

She rode west, toward the site of the ambush, scanning the road and roadside for signs of Amma and Kassia.

They crested a hill; her lungs squeezed painfully. A crumpled figure lay ahead, clad in a brown cotton riding skirt made from the same material as her own.

"Amma!" she cried, sliding off the horse. She ran, pulling the horse. When Swallowtail balked, she dropped the reins.

She fell to her knees by Spotted Turtle and cradled her face in her hands. *So cold. So very cold.* Amma's body lay twisted, torn, and bent, like a discarded toy, and glossy pink tumors had torn through the skin of her arms and legs and face. The nictitating membranes over her open eyes were neatly sliced. No weapons had done this. Magic had.

Fila rocked side to side, pressing Amma's stiff, mutilated hand to her cheek. Mother. Father. Amma. All dead. Possibly Kassia as well. She longed to lie down next to Amma and never get up. But someone had to take care of her damaged brother now her parents were gone. Poor Urushi, whose hair had never silvered and whose magic flared when he was upset. Mother was always healing wounds and treating scars caused by explosions of his uncontrolled magic.

At least Kassia did not lie here beside Amma, thank the Land.

Amma would no longer need the Toiler tech device that let her locate Fila. *I could give it to my future Consort.* Amma had carried the device in a small pink felt envelope that Fila had made when she was little. Amma had strapped the envelope to her wrist or put it in her apron pocket or hung it from her sash when she wore one.

Fila searched those places, then everywhere else she could think of.

The tracking device was missing.

Sweat broke out on her upper lip. If the ambushers had taken it, they could find her and kill her too.

She shook her head. Surely the envelope had fallen during the trot to safety. Or Amma had tossed it to the side of the road to prevent the ambushers from getting it. Who would give a second look at a not-quite-square pink envelope sewn together with uneven orange stitches? Even if an ambusher had found it, he would not know what the device did.

Unless they tortured Amma to find out.

A crow cawed above, and she flinched and dropped into a crouch. Her heart beat faster than she had known it could.

She raised her head and looked in every direction. The road was still empty. She scooted over to the hoof prints in the mud going east. On second examination, she still believed they belonged to the ambushers: they were fresh, the party was large, and the prints were made by Guardian horses, not the massive, big-footed Toiler work horses.

She squished back to the site of the ambush, crossing the road back and forth. She found neither the tracking mechanism nor any sign of her cousin, not even a dropped gold hairpin. Her needlework bag still lay where she had dropped it, and she tied it on her sash.

Someone whimpered.

She froze, her gaze darting about. Two bandits remained, one impaled, and the other, glassy-eyed, trapped within a strangling prison of roots. She doubled over and vomited for the second time that day.

The impaled man whimpered again. Blood bubbled from his lips. Instinct and pity propelled her feet; a whiff of caramel and a whisper in her ear made her falter: *He sought to slay you. He deserves death.*

She shook her head to clear it of the dishonorable, unwanted thought. *It is my duty to help him. I am Servant to all the Land's inhabitants, with no exception for evildoers.*

She did what she could. It was both good and right.

It was also too little. Shaking, she pulled back from the limp body. She had protected herself by making the roots grow, and her Goodborn instinct had not objected. Yet her action killed two men.

She moaned. *How will I ever forgive myself?* Beneath her self-revulsion, other emotions pulsed. Her feet burned to dance and prance with joy; her hands rubbed together in satisfaction.

Fila pounded her fists on her thighs, then jumped up. She did not have time to commune with the Land, to pry from It how It felt about the deaths or the pleasure she took in them. She had to find Kassia and Tul; bury Amma; and get to the Seat to comfort Urushi and claim her position.

By the Land, I hope Kassia lives; I have had my fill of death for today.

She trod the muddy road east, her gaze sweeping the road and the woods on either side, dark places that could hide a hundred Kassias. She shouted her cousin's name until her throat burned. Eventually, unsuccessfully, she went back to Amma's body. Mud caked her feet like custom boots. Stomping free, she pressed her lips together. She had no tools to dig a grave.

Footsteps squelched nearby.

She grabbed Boraga's charm and swung around, standing protectively in front of the corpse.

Tul. He *had* managed to follow the tracks of their wild trek after all. The diamond in his earring gleaming, he frowned down at her. "Why did you take such a roundabout route?"

"We became lost."

"Lost? In a forest? Why didn't you look at the moss to get your bearings?"

She crossed her arms protectively over her abdomen. "Be silent. Just—be silent."

"Your temper has gotten no better during our separation. Where is Swallowtail?"

She swallowed guiltily. She had not tied up the horse. "Hush! My amma lies here dead. Murdered." She stepped aside so he could see.

He drew in his breath sharply and wiped his eye with the edge of his ripped tunic. As he gazed at Spotted Turtle, his nostrils flared, and his face mottled with righteous fury. Two long steps took him to her side. He dropped to his knees and felt for a pulse.

"She is already gone," Fila whispered.

He ran his large hands over her the tumors on Amma's arm. "It's easy to kill quickly and painlessly," he growled. "These men were monsters, to torture an old Toiler." He looked around, his visible eye wild. His gaze settled on a gnarled white oak whose many thick branches dominated the sky and hung over the road.

Magic tingled in the air, and Fila threw her arm over her eyes.

No flames, no quake, no flying debris. No smell of magic. Only thuds and grunts.

She uncovered one eye, then let her arm drop slowly. Her hand pressed against her chest. Neck muscles bulging, Tul pummeled the tree with bare fists, smearing the bark with blood. She winced as each powerful blow struck.

The ripped back of his tunic flapped, revealing more knife wounds, more swelling, more bruises.

She gasped. She had to stop him from hurting himself any further. She ran to him. "Stop! If anyone deserves pain, it's the killers. Let me tend to your knuckles. And your eyes and your back."

He dropped his arms and panted. His tunic stuck to the wetness on his broad chest, revealing the dark curls of hair underneath. He leaned against the tree's rough trunk.

"You didn't use magic to vent your anger," Fila said. "You didn't use it earlier against the men attacking me."

"Where is my horse?"

"Why did you not use magic?"

"I don't."

"Don't what?"

"I don't use magic."

Her breath stopped; her lips parted. Was he teasing her? Shakily, breathily, she said, "I have never heard of a man who did not use magic."

"You have now."

"Why?"

His face closed against her. "You are covered in mud. Even your hair."

Fila made a token swipe with the back of her palm at her cheek. "Let me heal your wounds. Then you can help me—" She stopped to swallow the lump in her throat. "—help me bury my amma."

His face softened. "Now *I* am the one who must apologize for my rudeness. This day has not been pleasant for either of us. Please accept my condolences on the loss of your amma, Little One. Certainly I'll help you bury her."

Her face burned from the endearment. "My name is Violet," she said eagerly, happy for a chance to tell someone her new Servant name.

"One of my favorite flowers." He sat cross-legged in front of her.

She pulled the pins from her hair and ran her fingers through the curls that fell. Others stayed glued to her head by mud. *He has so many injuries that I'll need a lot of hair.* Wincing, she yanked some out and scoured the remaining dried mud off with a clean corner of her blouse. She knotted two hairs in a triple half-hitch around a plant stalk and laid it in turn on each of his knuckles.

His skin knitted together and the redness disappeared.

"Now for your eyes and back."

"One eye. I'm in a hurry," he reminded her.

She rose and searched the roadside for useful plants. The more powerful the plant, the less her weak skills mattered.

Softly, he said, "You didn't think to tie Swallowtail when you saw your amma lying in the road, did you?"

She winced at the contrast between her earlier harsh words and his kind ones. She knelt to pull up a wild ginger plant and broke off part of its root. "You are more than kind, considering how badly I treated you."

"Perhaps I shall shout at you later. Right now, I'm saving my energy for digging and healing."

She didn't find the other plants she needed. She concentrated, sending her thoughts like roots into the Land, feeling It acknowledge her.

It didn't tell her where to find the plants, nor where Kassia was. It sent her nothing but rolling waves of grief.

Sighing, she pulled her spirit back and plucked bee balm. She folded and rolled the leaves between her hands, crushing them as she returned to Tul, releasing the astonishing, resinous enchantment of its scent. She was grateful Tul remained quiet, even when she took his chin and turned his face so she could examine his eyes from different angles. "What happened to your face and back?"

He shrugged. "This and that."

She emptied her sewing bag and chose soft materials that would be gentle against his skin. A blue ribbon to cool the burn. Purple and green ribbons to draw the bruise out of his skin. Yarn of golden cat fur to give substance and to put the light of life back in his eyes. Several hairs from her head to strengthen and set the magic.

She tied the ends together, took up her crochet hook, and with the speed of years of practice worked a simple bag in a mesh stitch. She sliced the ginger root and put it and the crushed bee balm inside the bag. She mashed the charm between her hands until the ribbons were damp with juice from the plants.

Fila placed the charm on his eye as gently as she could. His face showed none of the pain she knew he felt.

After several minutes he sighed and the tightness in his face eased. As the lines softened, she realized he was not as old as she had assumed.

Above, clouds rolled away. The sun appeared, and its light lit the road, highlighting how badly injured his other eye was.

She moved the charm to it.

Tul grasped her wrist. "I can see well enough to dig a grave, Little Violet." He looked up at the sky as if searching for something, and his shoulders loosened when he didn't find it. His gaze dropped and wandered over her face and hair.

He sucked in his breath sharply, and his hand tightened on her arm. His other hand rose, trembling, and touched her hair. "It's copper. I can't believe it," he breathed.

He released her and knelt. "Forgive me, Lady. I could not see before you were the Servant. This changes everything."

"Why? I do not understand."

"We can't take time to look for your cousin. The Seat is in turmoil. Lady, you must go there right away to take your place as the Servant."

Chapter 15

CELATU'S FATIGUE SLIPPED OFF like a heavy cloak. "I have to find Swallowtail. He'll get you to the Seat faster than than if you walk. Where do you think you left him?"

She nodded toward the east, and he jogged in that direction, whistling and calling for him.

A horse whinnied ahead. He glanced at the sky for the icedragon and then ran toward the sound. Swallowtail stood at the forest edge, tail swishing indignantly, his reins tangled in a sycamore sapling and his headstall caught on a limb.

He stroked the horse's neck. "You're in a predicament, aren't you? Hold still and I'll have you free soon. Then you'll be on your way home with the Servant on your back."

Meeting the Servant changed everything. As he babbled to the horse, his racing mind created and discarded plans. The crucial question was whether he should accompany the Servant to the Seat. He could protect her if her attackers waited ahead—but his presence would attract the icedragon. Would it attack her too? According to Father, icedragons targeted Guardian *men* … but Urushi might have misled the Servant's Council.

When Swallowtail calmed, Celatu worked at the knots in the bridle, finally losing patience and pulling out his knife to cut the branch that snagged the horsestall. The horse shook his head. Celatu grabbed his bridle and forced him around the sapling.

"There you go!" He searched the saddlebags for oats and offered Swallowtail a handful. Flexible, fleshy lips tickled his palm until it was empty.

Then he investigated the cloth he'd glimpsed in a saddlebag. Spare clothes! *Thank you, Father.* He pulled off his shredded, mud-covered tunic and put on a clean one.

"Now let's get you properly introduced to the Servant," he said to Swallowtail. They crested the hill; he could see the road and the sky above it and some of the forest for a long ways. No icedragon defaced the sky, thank the Land, but a Toiler wagon approached from the distance.

He changed course, nudging Swallowtail into the shadows under the trees. They sidled along the woods' edge and stopped when Celatu could clearly see the Servant.

Violet startled at the sound of the wagon. Instead of slipping into the forest as a sensible person would do, she brushed off her split skirt and walked into the middle of the road, waving her arm to hail the wagon.

Celatu slapped his head. *Why did I think she would be sensible?* He pulled his knife and readied himself.

The wagon rumbled closer. No Guardian rode in it, only a male Toiler who dozed with his head back and mouth open.

Celatu maintained his guard; Toilers were neutral in Seat politics and Guardian disputes, but their fierce loyalty to the Guardians associated with their villages meant that the Toiler could still be a danger.

Violet ran to meet the wagon. "Excuse me!" She shook the Toiler by the arm.

"Eh? What? Am I home yet?" The male opened his eyes and looked around, then looked down at her.

His mouth dropped open. "Whoa!" he shouted to the horses, pulling on the reins. He stared at her hair in wonder, then leapt off the wagon, grabbed her hands, and kissed them.

"I am Growling Dog, Lady, and am honored you sought me out," he rumbled as he knelt. "How may I help you or the Land?"

Celatu had to smile at the new Servant's shy awkwardness as she reached up to lay her hand on his head. "I am most pleased to make your acquaintance, Growling Dog. I am Violet. I have a great favor to ask. I was attacked on the road. My amma was killed, and my cousin abducted."

The Toiler's face became stormy as he rose. "Someone dared attack the Servant?"

She nodded. "I beg your leave to bury my amma in your graveyard, and I would like to talk to your neighbors to see whether any may have seen my cousin or her kidnappers."

"All that you shall have, and more. You must be hungry and weary. My mate, Bluebird, will care for you."

"My deepest thanks."

"First, let's put your poor amma in the back of the wagon."

"I will do that." Celatu was out of the shadows leading Swallowtail toward them before he realized what he was doing. He handed the reins to the Servant and went to her murdered amma. He lifted her carefully and carried her to the empty wagon, where he laid her down and arranged her limbs. *Now she looks at peace.*

Violet said, "You are almost as strong as a Toiler!"

He returned to the stained place in the road and collected the fingers. Those he placed on the amma's lap. Tears burned his eye wounds like fire. "Lady, who could hate you this much?"

The Toiler interrupted before she could answer. "That's a discussion for tomorrow. Be at ease; Servant Violet will be safe in our village tonight."

For all Celatu knew, this village owed its allegiance to Urushi. "Who is your Guardian?"

"Tul, you're being rude," Violet scolded.

"I know what's happening at the Seat, and you do not. Lady, do not trust anyone unless I say you can. I ask again, Growling Dog, who is your Guardian?"

"Celatu the Coward." Growling Dog spit.

Head spinning, Celatu grabbed the side of the wagon to stay upright. "I have heard of him," he said carefully. "A scholar who rarely goes out in society, is he not?"

"I know nothing of that, but he never shows his face here. We have to do all the work ourselves."

Celatu broke out in goosebumps from the cool breeze that hit his skin, making him feel even more naked and exposed. *I worry needlessly. No one in my village knows what I look like.*

"He is a sorry excuse for a Guardian," Violet said hotly.

Celatu broke in before she or Growling dog maligned his character further. "I'll let you go to his village. This Celatu is renowned for his disinterest in politics."

Violet put a hand on her hip and tipped her head far back so she could look down her nose at him. "I do not need your permission or approval." The most bad-tempered Servant ever shoved Swallowtail's reins toward him.

Growling Dog held up his palms. "Please, you're both exhausted and in need of baths. Tul, join us tonight. We'll take care of both of you."

"Land bless you," he blurted out with such enthusiasm the Toiler chuckled.

"I'll take that as a *yes.*" Growling Dog climbed back into the wagon and patted the bench next to him. "Good. We need some Guardian help. Tie your horse to the back of the wagon and sit here, Tul. We'll be to my village soon."

Violet walked alongside as the Toiler told her about his village, his plots, his mate, their five pups, and their seven dogs.

Celatu fidgeted. By *Guardian help*, Growling Dog meant the village needed magic. He had no intention of breaking his oath; he should get off the wagon before taking advantage of their hospitality. But oh, for hot water and clean skin and a bed! He would fight an army right now for such little comforts.

Fila nearly clapped when the lights of the Toiler village at last shone through the trees. Growling Dog recruited the first several Toilers they encountered and sent them and Tul to dig a grave. He then took Fila, Amma, and Swallowtail to his cottage, made introductions, and explained to Bluebird what had happened. She agreed immediately to his suggestions.

"You have the thanks of the Servant, Bluebird, for—"

Bluebird stopped Fila with a wave. "My dear Violet, no formalities. To a hot bath with you." She led her through the kitchen to a huge room for cleaning. She pointed to a handbasin hollowed from a boulder by Guardian magic, then to a rack with unfamiliar Toiler tech. "After you rinse out your clothes—there's soap on the lip of the basin—hang them on the rack and pull down this lever. They'll be dry before you finish your bath." Bluebird bustled out.

Fila shut the door, privacy during bathing being the custom among Guardians, and groaned with pleasure as the heated floor warmed her chilled, wet feet. The room was full of luxuries provided by Toiler tech. An artificial pool set in the floor and lined with smooth, rounded stones. A device that lowered one into the pool. Polished flint knobs to control the flow of water and its temperature. Glass bottles of perfectly uniform sizes and shapes and of many unusual colors, holding cleaners and softeners for the body and hair.

She chose a small, elegantly shaped bottle, pulled out a stopper, and sniffed. The thick garnet liquid inside smelled like strawberries, not like turpentine. She dripped a little into her palm. It didn't sting when it touched her scrapes and cuts, and it felt smooth, not sticky. How lucky the Toilers were to have such a luxury!

Sighing, she stripped, rubbed and rinsed most of the dirt from her clothes, and hung them up as instructed. When she pulled the lever, the rack turned her clothes in a circle, and warm air blew onto them.

She got into pool and turned the handles for warm water to rain from above. She pulled another handle, and soap squirted onto her. Lather, rinse, done.

She dried under the warm air and put her still-damp clothes on. *I should go into the kitchen, but....* She looked around, then slunk over to the pool and slipped the small bottle of garnet liquid into her pouch. *The Servant deserves a little treat now and then.*

Her step had a bounce as she moved toward the door. As she reached for the latch, she froze. Goodborn did not steal. Or envy others. Or justify bad decisions. Goodborn couldn't; their instinct stopped them.

What is wrong with me?

Am I breaking, like Urushi?

She put the bottle back where it belonged and sat on the edge of the pool, trembling. She rubbed her forehead; her hand came away damp. *I cannot believe what I did. Everyone will see guilt on my face and know I committed wrong.*

I cannot let that happen.

She slid the bottle over slightly so no one could tell she had picked it up, then went to the mirror and studied her reflection. Color stained her cheeks. From guilt or her warm dousing? Her chin quivered. Guilt or exhaustion? She took deep breaths to slow the pounding of her heart.

My magic is not breaking. The circumstances are trying, that's all. I became Servant unexpectedly. My mother, father, and amma died. Robbers tried to kill me too. My cousin was kidnapped. I have many new and frightening responsibilities. I had to spend most of the day with that annoying Tul. I am badly in need of sleep. There are many possible reasons for my uncharacteristic behavior today.

She stopped shaking. She would get a good night's sleep, and tomorrow she would again be herself.

When Fila went into the kitchen, Amma's body lay on the kitchen table, already washed. Bluebird was working the dust, leaves, and knots out of Amma's gray-streaked hair with a wide-toothed tortoiseshell comb.

Fila climbed up on a chair on the other side of the table. She stood on it and began untangling Amma's hair with her fingers, avoiding looking at the rest of her savaged body.

"My amma's name was Spotted Turtle. She saw ninety-eight summers. She had ten pups from three litters. When I was little, every night at bedtime she told me stories of their pranks and escapades."

"You should not have to see your amma like this."

"Spotted Turtle did so much for me. I want to do this one last thing for her."

"Tell me more about her."

The tightness in Fila's chest eased as she told stories of Spotted Turtle. How she comforted Fila when she came home crying from school because she'd been teased for being a Goodborn. How she taught Fila to grow herbs and flowers in the corners of her own plot. How she taught her the folktales and customs of the Toilers so she could be a better Guardian. "She was proud the Land chose me as Its Servant. Yet she will never see my investiture or wear the embroidered white dress of a Servant's aide."

When Fila finished telling Bluebird about Spotted Turtle, they worked in companionable silence. Fila's thoughts returned to the ambush. *When I sent Amma and Kassia ahead, away from the attackers, I was trying to save them. What did I do wrong? What should I have done instead?* Every scenario played out the same, with her guards and Amma dead. Becoming Servant had strengthened her magic, but her training and knowledge remained the same: inadequate. *Mother would have saved them all.*

When Amma's hair was detangled, Bluebird braided it, then arranged and pinned the braids to hide some of the wounds and tumors. But Amma's face remained disfigured, a final indignity she did not deserve.

Although it was wasteful to use magic on the dead, Fila crocheted a hexagonal charm and fixed the visible injuries on Amma's face. "Spotted Turtle will go to her grave looking like herself."

"As is right. She can have one of my dresses. Her own clothes are in tatters."

"Did you happen to find in her clothes a pink felt envelope containing a small Toiler device?"

Bluebird shook her head. "Nothing like that. Only some pretty stones and a bird feather."

Fila's stomach flipped. *Where is the tracking device?*

"Would you like her clothes back?"

"No, thank you." Mindful of the village's relative poverty, she added, "Are you sure she cannot be buried in her own clothes? I cannot accept your kind offer of a dress."

"Lady, it's not your decision. You're not the one needing a burial outfit." Bluebird left the kitchen and came back with a simple dress of unbleached cotton decorated with embroidered acorns from several species of oaks. "Go sit by the fire. I'll dress her."

"No. I owe it to her to see what she suffered on my behalf." Fila looked at each wound, memorizing it. The strange and unpleasant emotions that started during the attack returned. She hated the robbers and longed to torture them as they had tortured Amma.

I will not give in to evil feelings again, not now, not here. She thought about how much she loved Amma, how much she missed her; love and grief expanded to fill her, driving out rage and hate, bloodlust and savagery.

Soon after they dressed Amma, the gravediggers returned, sweaty and tired, carrying a plain wooden coffin that smelled of freshly planed wood. Pups carrying vegetables followed. The males placed Amma gently inside, and the pups scattered the vegetables around her body. Adults carried her coffin to a horse-drawn wagon, where other villagers waited. Fila joined them.

The wagon rumbled over the dirt road out of the village and past the fields. Fila, Tul, and the Toilers followed on foot. Each stone that cut or bruised her feet reminded Fila of Amma's sacrifice.

The wagon stopped outside the cemetery. Even though the village lacked a functioning Guardian, the graveyard was well cared for and offered a lovely setting for Amma's rest. Spiderwort carpeted the square in soft, spiky green. Clumps of bee balm softened the graveyard's edges and perfumed the air with a dark, citrusy aroma.

The Toilers held no service, but instead honored Amma with stillness as the lingering solstice sun dropped behind ancient trees. Then they lit their lanterns. Fila took one last look at Amma's broad face, pebbled skin, and heavy brow ridges. She closed her eyes tightly.

She heard the hammers as the villagers nailed the lid on. The grunts as they lowered the coffin into the ground. The staccato thuds of dirt shoveled into the grave. The Land sent a few waves of comfort into her, but not enough. It could never be enough.

She breathed; her heart beat. Such simple acts, yet they separated the quick from the dead. A fine line, and she was on the wrong side from almost everyone she loved.

She couldn't give in to grief. She had duties. She must not think about her lost loved ones or she would fall into a dark hole, never to emerge.

A light hand touched her hair and pulled at a curl. She raised her head and looked into the somber violet eyes of a female Toiler pup who held Tul's hand. He nudged the little one, and she held out her arm. The flickering lantern light revealed a long cut, swollen, red, and oozing white and yellow fluid that ran down her forearm.

Class four.

"When my appa died, distraction temporarily lessened my grief." Tul's gruff voice sounded embarrassed. "So I found some people who need your help."

"Thank you." She reached out and squeezed Tul's hand tightly.

He squatted down and looked at her. His dark eyes radiated concern and compassion.

She let out a huge breath and with it, her sense of isolation. *Someone understands a little of what I feel.* Despite the wounds he had not let her heal yet, she could tell he had a kind face, one that made her feel safe and tempted to let down her guard even though he was a man. Perhaps because his kindness revealed itself in his refusal to use male magic of destruction.

The harsh light of lanterns and moon cast shadows where he one day would have lines. He would have two vertical lines above his brow from pursing his face in thought. Two curved lines would bracket his mouth from smiling. His cynicism and distrust had not yet left their mark. *What a shame if such a handsome face became crabbed and closed in!*

She dropped her eyes and let go of his hand. Her thoughts about this man she might never see again were far too intimate. "Thank you for your kindness tonight, Tul. It means more than you can guess."

She held out her hand to the pup. "Come here, little one. I will make you feel much better."

Chapter 16

Urushi wrapped his brown scarf high around his face and drew his hood up to shade his forehead and eyes. He studied his image in the looking glass by the door and nodded. All of his scars from magic gone wrong were hidden. "Tonight, Appa, I will again be Jugland, a collector and seller of antique coins."

"Jugland. I'll remember."

"Let us head toward the night market and see what we can learn. Be alert for any mention of giant red dogs." He opened the door and shuffled out, head down and hands in his pockets.

Appa joined him, his slouch and sneer masking him as well as any physical disguise. They eased into the foot traffic without catching anyone's notice.

Although the rain had stopped, the crushed-aggregate street gleamed darkly, and damp seeped like long, cold fingers beneath his cloak. Around them, Guardians and Toilers alike discussed the foul weather, with the new Servant rare as a conversation topic. He picked up a pebble from the street and, with great care and concentration, sent his magic inside to agitate its molecules.

The pebble warmed without exploding and without pieces of his magic heading off elsewhere to cause havoc. *Yes! I did it!* He rolled the pebble between his hands until they reached the half-empty night market, where he headed for the stand of Curious Raccoon, his favorite roasted meat vendor. The flames from the braziers at the back caressed his face with warmth.

"Four sticks of venison, please," Hooting Owl said. "Well done, with a cup of herb sauce."

Grinning, the Toiler handed them sticks of already cooked meat and laughed at Appa's surprised expression. "I saw you coming. I hope your business fares well today, Jugland."

"Well enough, well enough," Urushi said, pulling a sweet, crisp bit of venison from its stick without dipping it in the herb sauce Appa loved so much. "Why is the market so empty? On such a chilly night, I expected you to have a long line."

"A fire broke out in one of the arts districts. You know how it is. People get careless with their fires when it's cold and wet; I've been warning my customers for days to be careful. Anyway, most Toilers and a few Guardians went there to rescue people."

A thrill tickled Urushi's spine from his tailbone to his neck. Perhaps Curious Raccoon was right, that simple carelessness was to blame. But two of the firehounds he had sent for Erudia and her co-conspirators had returned, gory-jawed. If they had caused a fire, Guardian women would be afraid and support him. "Has anyone returned from the fire with news?"

"Returned, yes. With something I'd call news, no. Rumors. Women with flippers for hands. The howls of hundreds of dogs. Red monsters with flaming eyes. Bah!" Curious Raccoon looked in both directions and then leaned toward them. "Some blame the Pretender."

"Pretender?" Urushi asked, keeping a wary eye on the other people in the street. The small, random clusters of passersby were coalescing, like raindrops flowing to a low spot to make a puddle.

Appa threw his remaining stick of venison to the ground, grabbed Urushi by the shoulders, and pushed him away from the crowd.

Urushi shoved one of the massive hands from his shoulder, dug in his heels, and looked straight into Curious Raccoon's lavender eyes. "What pretender?"

"Urushi, of course. The late Servant's son." As the Toiler looked from Urushi to Appa and back, his smile twitched at one corner and then faded.

Under his wraps, Urushi sweltered. Sweat dripped into his eyes, and his muscles twitched as magic ran through them. *How dare he? I'm Servant Hyacinth's son. I have as much right to rule Veridia as Fila does.* His hands flexed and released, and his nose filled with the sour scent of his magic. He shrugged off Appa's grip on his shoulder and raised his hand.

"Your meat was wonderful, as usual," Hooting Owl told Curious Raccoon, throwing Urushi over his shoulder.

Overhead, thunder rumbled.

"Put me down! I order it." Magic sparked from Urushi's body as he struggled against Appa's tightening arms.

Curious Raccoon hid behind his braziers; parents picked up their pups and young and ran. Appa strode toward home, paying no more attention to Urushi's kicks and stinging sparks of magic than he would to a fly.

"Put me down!" Urushi roared. Magic shot from him.

He screamed as skin tore and internal organs split. The colorful canvas covers of vendors' booths burst into flames.

Toilers ran from every direction and tried to beat out the fire. Still, the magic poured out of him, flinging him about like a doll. His hood fell back; his scarf unfurled from his face.

"It's Urushi!" someone shouted.

"The Pretender!"

"He set the market on fire!"

"Someone stop him!"

The clots of Guardians he had watched earlier now stalked toward him.

Hooting Owl broke into a jolting, wound-opening run.

Like packs of wolves, the groups of Guardians loped after them.

"Look at him, the coward!"

"He's running from us!"

Appa ran faster. A woman laughed contemptuously; he pinpointed the sound.

Gritting his teeth against the agony to come, he sent a burst of magic toward her and those around her. Lightning cracked the sky.

The mocking laughter abruptly silenced.

He woke in the infirmary, blessedly burdened with only his usual pain. His hazy vision made out three of his nurses bustling around him. "How am I?" Urushi asked the room at large.

"One of your kidneys ripped open," a nurse answered. "It's healed now. But you should rest for the next few days."

"Hooting Owl?"

"I'm here." Appa walked over to him and grasped his hand.

Urushi felt his face, hairline to chin, ear to ear.

"No new scars," Appa reassured him.

Urushi let his head drop back onto the cot. He clenched his fists; he wasted precious time. Again. He had so many ideas for freeing Guardians from the shackles of the Land's rules and for giving Toiler tech to everyone.

But here he lay, instructed to rest. He was a half-man with a half-life: Other people had sixteen hours a day to work, to plan, to play, to strive after goals; it was a good day when he managed four productive hours. What houses in Veridia had an infirmary with women Talents on permanent staff? None but this one. All for him. *Once Shadow and I merge, I will be a full man. Once I'm not a monster anymore, once I free us from the Land's tyranny, people will respect me, even love me.*

"Urushi needs his rest. I'd like everyone to leave, please," Hooting Owl said. Urushi lifted their joined hands to his cheek.

When the room was empty, Appa sat on the cot. "I worry about you. Once, you harmed others only by accident and were sad for days afterward. Now you send out magic creatures with no purpose but to kill. Worse, tonight you killed directly, on purpose, yet I see no regret on your face."

His conscience did sting for ordering Fila's death, but he could not yet bring himself to confess that deed to his appa. "I hate being the Land's joke. I hate all the resting, hate spending hours in this room while nurses heal my injuries. I hate my life more than you can possibly imagine."

Hooting Owl's forehead crinkled, and his massive brow ridges drew together until they looked like one of the forests' craggy gullies. "You don't want to live?"

"I *do* want to live. But not like this, cursed by the Land, waking each morning to a burden of pain and despair that keeps getting heavier, having to talk myself into getting up and enduring another day of being pitied, mocked, and hated."

Appa shook his great head so hard the cot shook. "I love you more fiercely than any bear mother ever loved her cubs. Kassia loves you. Fila. Wiggle. Aren't we enough? How much more love do you need?"

Even Appa can't understand how I long for what others take for granted. He rolled away, pulling his hand from Appa's. "How much love do I need? Enough to feel like an ordinary person instead of a freak!"

Appa sang a lullaby and stroked his head. "I would do anything to take away your pain," he said when he finished.

"I know."

"There's a Toiler philosopher who studies gratitude and its cultivation. I'll invite him to visit you."

"I do not want to be grateful for a life that crushes me. I want a different life."

Appa's shoulders sank. "How can I help you?"

"You can't. No human can."

"Your despair grieves me. Sleep now, lad." Appa kissed him and left.

When the door shut, something hissed by Urushi's ear. He rolled onto his back, and a mink, sparkling like the stars in the night sky in the countryside, shimmered into being on his chest. "Shadow, I am so tired of waiting, so tired of being trapped in this body. Why can't we merge now?"

"Soon, soon we will be one," she crooned, "and every day you will wake overflowing with thankfulness."

"Every day?"

"*Every* day. Have faith."

"I do trust you," Urushi said. Warm tears rolled from his eyes, stinging recent wounds and soothing his heart.

Chapter 17

GROWLING DOG AND BLUEBIRD had offered Tul and Fila the use of their bedroom.

"We do not want to be any inconvenience," Fila said. "We will be happy in the barn with some blankets." Now she was up in one corner of the hayloft, hollowing out a nest in the hay and attempting to make a comfortable bed with the thin blankets. The village was not prosperous, which was not a surprise, given the poor Guardianship. The villagers worked hard. Their cottages were in good repair, and their fields were clear of weeds. But she knew to credit hard Toiler labor, not Guardian magic.

She had healed several cuts and a broken leg before Bluebird shooed away the Toilers still in line. She would tend to them tomorrow, as well as go to the many flooded fields to encourage more seeds to germinate. She rubbed her aching forehead. She had to choose between helping the villagers and looking for Kassia; both were right and good. But one must go undone. Which one?

She rolled to her left side, but the straw poked her face. She yanked a blanket higher, but then her feet were uncovered. She rolled to her right side, and straw poked her rear. She flopped on her black and blew out her breath in frustration.

"Can't sleep either?" Tul called.

"No. And I was so exhausted."

"I as well. Why don't you come over here? Conversation might distract us from our misfortunes."

She grabbed one of her blankets and waded across the hayloft with only thin slats of moon glow to light her way. Tul had not dug out a nest, but merely thrown his blankets over a lumpy mound of hay.

"No wonder you cannot sleep. This hardly counts as a bed."

"Personal comfort is not high on my list of priorities. When I was a boy, I enjoyed hiking and sleeping in the woods, even in winter, even when it rained."

"Yet here you are, unable to sleep in a hayloft."

"Despite a wonderful long, hot bath." He looked at her face and grimaced. "So many bruises! What a day you had, Violet. But at least you are clean now, and your hair is no longer caked with mud."

He glanced at her hair, a look of longing, or possibly sorrow, flickering through his eyes. He truly was a handsome man, despite the injuries to his face. Fila conjured an image of what he might look like fully healed. Her heart stuttered. She let her gaze linger on his face just a little too long.

"I should heal your other eye now."

"No! I mean, you need sleep, and I won't be using that eye tonight."

She knelt, spreading the straw of his bed into a depression, stopping to sneeze every so often from the dust she stirred up. She measured the depression with her eye, compared it with his size, and then spread one of his blankets inside it. "Have you never slept in a barn before?"

"No."

"Where do you sleep when you visit your Toilers?"

Tul smoothed the already smooth blanket in his new bed and picked off a piece of straw. "Not in the barn," he said gruffly. "Besides, Toilers aren't helpless younglings. We need *them* far more than they need *us*."

"We're symbiotic species. We need each other equally."

"Are we Guardians the elks or the organisms in their guts?"

Fila drew her brows together. "Is that supposed to be a joke? Just look around. Tools need cleaning. Land needs clearing. Rotted stumps need removing. This village is proof Toilers need Guardians."

"Guardians who don't use magic?"

She sat down and draped her blanket around herself. She had to admit—to herself, not him—that without magic, a Guardian would be of no more use here than a child. "If you don't help your village, what do you do all day? That is, when you're not conducting rescues?"

"I eat, of course. I read. I study ancient texts. When my eyes get tired, sometimes I watch the fish in the fishpond."

"How monotonous. I would think you'd be glad to visit the villages and do something, even if you don't use magic. There is always a different problem to solve."

He perked up and leaned toward her, his voice taking on new animation. "There are many problems of our *history* to solve too. For example, why did magic suddenly appear in the world? Why do Guardians have magic but Toilers do not? Why did the Guardians renounce technology, and why did Toilers embrace it?"

"That happened long ago. The answers cannot matter."

"But they do! We need to know as much as possible about those early times."

She yawned. "Why do you think so?"

"We may need the knowledge one day. What if magic disappeared as quickly as it appeared? What if a dangerous new magical being appeared in the world? The old texts may hold clues to solving these problems." His shirt rustled as he shrugged. "Besides, the world holds so much pain and suffering. I'd rather be in the library."

"You're a Guardian. You could relieve some of that suffering. Helping me rescue my cousin from her kidnappers would be a good start."

"Lady Violet, you're naïve in the ways of men. If your attackers didn't hesitate to kill a *Toiler*, an act the Land considers an abomination, they wouldn't hesitate to kill a Guardian."

Fila gasped, her stomach tying itself in a knot.

"You're Servant now. Veridia has no leader until you get to the Seat of Enchantment and take your proper place. Your public duties come before your personal ones."

Fila wrapped the blanket around her tightly. Her Goodborn instincts recoiled; she could not abandon her cousin. She felt it throughout her body and deep into her toes: It would be utterly, unforgivably wrong. *What am I to do?*

"I've seen more of the world than you, Violet. One person, even the Servant, can't make much of a difference for good in the world."

"You are wrong. I healed painful injuries and maladies tonight. I made a difference."

"If your cousin is still alive, and if we search for her, we'd be two against many. Your attackers have men's magic and weapons. We're more likely to be captured and killed than to save anyone."

"They tortured Amma for the fun of it! Who knows what they'll do to my cousin? She's alone and scared, at the mercy of evil men. Like … like … a helpless little rabbit in the hands of cruel boys."

Tul gasped. He grasped her hand and held it too tightly.

"Tul? What's wrong?"

"Nothing. Forgive me. It's nothing." He let go of her hand and stood. "I must walk and think."

He paced the length of the loft and back so many times Fila lost count. Then he returned to his bed and sat cross-legged in front of her.

"Lady, I truly wish we could help your cousin. But we must leave tomorrow early and make fast progress to the Seat of Enchantment."

"You still have not explained: What is so urgent about getting to the Seat that I should abandon my cousin?" Her skin tingled against her will at his nearness. In the chilly night, his body radiated warmth and comfort.

His words, though, were precise and cold. "Are you certain you want to know, Trusting One? You will find the truth hard to believe and harder to bear."

Fila took a deep breath and nodded. "I suppose it is my duty as Servant to know more about the ugly side of life."

"The men who attacked you? They weren't thieves. They were assassins. That's why we can't look for your cousin. *You* are the killers' target."

Fila's heart sped up, but she shook her head. "Only someone as cynical as you could suspect such a thing. No one has ever assassinated a Servant. No one has ever tried."

Rain pelted the roof, thundering like the drums Toilers used to pace their labor.

"There's more." Tul continued without mercy. "Servant Hyacinth and her Consort did not die naturally. I suspect they were murdered. In cold blood. I fear for you, Violet."

Grief upon grief upon grief. The tattoo of the rain quickened. She buried her face in the blankets and rocked.

Rocking, rocking.

Faster, faster.

Tul's heavy arm around her shoulders stilled her. "I'm sorry," he said. "In my anger at the traitors, I spoke carelessly. Becoming Servant at so young an age must be hard."

"I never expected to be Servant, or that my parents would … would...." She swallowed hard. "I always thought it would be my cousin when the time came."

"Your cousin. The one you are looking for?"

Fila nodded. "She's probably so frightened. Kassia was never one for the woods. She likes dressing up and shopping and...."

"Kassia?" Tul's arm fell from her shoulders. "Your cousin is named Kassia? Does she have pale hair?"

"Yes. Do you know her? You must. She goes to all the parties."

A crack of lightning revealed Tul's look of confusion. "The only cousin she has … I mean, the only cousin she's mentioned.… Who were you, Violet? Before you were Servant?"

Her scalp prickled beneath the copper curls. Tul's eyes were wide, his manner intense, as if her previous identity were important. He seemed … almost frightened.

"I was no one," she said. "Fila. Daughter of the Servant and her Consort."

He shook his head. "No. You can't be. The Servant's daughter is Good-born."

"I *am* Goodborn. I told you that already."

He gripped her wrists tightly. His voice shook. "You're not Fila. You're joking."

"I do not know how to joke." She dropped her face. "But I can understand why you were confused. My behavior today was deplorable."

"But, but, how could a Goodborn behave so?"

She batted the question away with her hand as if it were frivolous. "I had a difficult day." *I truly hope that is the explanation.* "Anyway, I am Fila no longer. I'm Violet now. Or will be after the investiture."

He rose and paced the hay loft again, faster, swearing under his breath. Outside, the weather worsened. Cold air whooshed in through the slats.

She shivered and cast a glance across the barn at her waiting nest and blankets. "Can you not think without walking?"

"No."

"What are you thinking about this time?"

"Kassia."

In the tense silence that followed, Fila twisted her hands together. "I know she is sometimes thoughtless and selfish, but she did not deserve to be kid-napped by evil men."

"No one deserves such."

"Yet you would leave her to the mercies of men you believe are assassins," she said with contempt.

"Don't judge me," he snapped. "I haven't finished telling you what you need to know."

She crossed her arms. "Get on with it then. I'm sleepy."

He returned to that end of the barn and sat next to her. He spoke in a strained voice. "Your brother.... "

She tingled with fear. *Is Urushi hurt? Sick? Murdered?* "Please, I must know." Her voice came out an octave too high.

Tul took one of her hands, gently, as if she were a fragile vase. "I wish I didn't have to tell you. I'm very sorry, but Urushi's the one who killed your parents."

Like a fragile vase, she broke.

Fila ran screaming into the night. Rain-laden gusts drenched her before she had gone the length of her noontime shadow, but she did not care. She dug her feet deep into the mud. *Tell me the truth*, she begged the Land. *Please. Please.*

She waited for It to let her know Tul spoke falsely.

Instead, ambiguous as always, It sent her Its own grief mixed with gentle waves of comfort.

What use are You? She stamped and grabbed her hair with both hands. *What use are You?*

"Violet! Fila!" Tul shouted from the door of the barn. "Come back inside."

She shook her head. "Now *I* am thinking."

He strode out to join her. "What's wrong?"

"My poor brother! How can he live with the pain of accidentally killing Mother and Father? I wish I were there with him."

His eyes broke contact, and he pulled at the neck of his tunic as if it were suddenly too small.

"What are you not telling me?" she asked. Her forehead pulsed with sudden pain. "Wait—you said—" He had said so much, it all mixed together in her mind. "Did you say that my parents were, were...."

"Murdered. I believe so."

"By Urushi?"

"Yes."

She shook her head. "No. It doesn't make sense. He depended on Mother's strong magic to heal his wounds. It had to be an accident." Her head kept shaking in denial for long moments after she stopped speaking. Rain flew from her swinging curls and hit Tul's face.

He did not flinch. He put his hands on her shoulders. "It may not make sense, but people say he admitted killing them."

"No." Her hands flew to her mouth, and she wrenched away from him. She turned in circles, muttering "no" over and over. *If only I could unwind the past week.*

He stopped her with his hand. She rounded on him. "Could you not tell me in a gentler way? You were cruel."

"Drag it out? Make you wait for the bad news you knew I had?" He shook his head. "That would be crueler. I may be many things you don't approve of, but I am never cruel." His eyes winced as if he understood or shared her hurt.

He did not, of course. She suffered alone. "You hurt me anyway," she threw at him.

"I'm sorry. But you needed to know the truth about Urushi. That he killed your parents. That he sent assassins to kill you."

She put her badly shaking hand to her mouth. "Urushi sent the attackers? No. You're wrong. You have to be wrong."

"I'm sorry, Violet."

She pounded on his chest with her fists. "Don't say you're sorry. Fix it. Fix it!"

"I can't change the past."

"Then you're no good either." She whirled away.

"I can protect you. I won't let him hurt you."

She ran without thought to where she would go, changing course on the slightest whim. The Land sent more feelings of comfort. She blocked them, pummeled them with her will, shoved them away, back into the ground.

The Land hid the truth from me. Me! Its voice and companion for decades to come. She stopped and stomped on the ground, howling her rage. She opened her defenses a crack and blasted the Land with one thought: *I will never forgive You this betrayal. Ever.*

Her headache worsened, and her head threatened to explode from the devastating knowledge it carried. She ran and ran.

Eventually a faint scent of honey broke through the taint of ozone in the air.

The graveyard.

She ran with purpose now, looking for the fresh mound over Amma's grave. The rain had carved the mound's smooth top into a series of bowls, each of which overflowed, their brown tears running down the side. She flung herself on the grave, digging her fists and feet into the mud as if to embrace Amma again.

The Land tried again to soothe her, but she was beyond soothing, beyond wanting soothing. *I hate You,* she told It.

It would not leave her alone. It sent tendrils of Itself into the tender muscles in her thighs and arms and the bruises and scratches she had sustained during the day.

She jumped up and ran to the nearest tree. Her feet slipping and scraping on its rough bark, she climbed high, as far from the ground and the Land as she could get.

The Land could not have her pain. She wanted it, needed it, craved it. Her body should mirror the state of her soul, as the weather did. She sat in the tree and rocked as the moon traced its path across the starless sky, alternately hiding behind the storm clouds and peeking out.

I am the sister of a murderer.

Today, I killed too.

And I behaved as no Goodborn should—or could.

The Land had made a serious mistake when it chose her. She did not deserve to be Servant. She did not even want to be Servant, tied to an unknowable, alien intellect that let her wander lost in the woods for hours and lied to her through Its sadistic silence.

Higher in the tree, claws scrabbled on bark.

Whatever creature lurked in the dark could not be more daunting than the day she had lived or the choices she faced. "Come, friend," she whispered, looking up into the branches. "I will dry your fur and keep you warm this miserable night."

Something dark and slinky dropped into her lap. A mink. The beaded water on its coat caught a glint of moonlight and sparkled like stars. It bared its sharp teeth and hissed, then curled up on her lap like a housecat.

She brushed the water from its fur. Then she squeezed water from her skirt and bunched it around the animal. It yawned and sneezed, then burrowed into the fabric.

Stroking the animal soothed her and allowed her to think. Three duties, each urgent, each necessary: To find Kassia; to help this needy village; to go to the Seat and restore harmony to the Land. The mink wiggled in her lap, warming in the nest of her skirt.

Boraga was wrong. Triage was no help; the duties could not be slotted into four simple boxes.

Her Goodborn instinct was useless too. Its purple glow urged her to attend to all three duties. At once. Right now.

The Land *should* help her as It helped Mother. Why would It not? She detested It! It was fickle; It was distant; It gave her no information or guidance.

Three duties, each urgent, each necessary. She was lost.

Chapter 18

Fila's shoulders dropped as tension flowed out of her. She set the mink on a branch, climbed down from the tree, and trudged back through the sheets of rain to the shelter of Growling Dog and Bluebird's barn, her mood darker than the night.

She pulled herself up the ladder, her exhausted body somehow double its usual weight.

"Lady, where have you been?" Tul shook her shoulders. "How can I protect you when you run off?"

"I'm sorry."

He let out a whoosh of breath. "Now you're Servant, you must be careful to stay healthy. The people of Veridia depend on you for so much."

His words made it clear his concern was for Veridia and the Servant, not for the woman who inhabited the role. Her hair, even heavier filled with rain, dripped freezing drops that ran down her neck and back. She shivered, despite Tul's warm hands on her shoulders and his body heat.

"The rain cleared my head. My way is clear now."

"Land be praised! You seemed lost and confused earlier."

"Thanks to you."

"I apologize. I know from my research that too much information at once can be hard to take in."

"But you were right: I needed to know it all. Others kept their suspicions secret, as if I were a child."

"I will accompany you and make sure you reach the Seat safely. I can be ready at dawn if you wish it."

"You did not ask what my decision was."

His body stiffened. "Why would I need to?" he asked, his careful tone indicating it was more than a rhetorical question.

She tipped back her head and looked up at him, making her expression as serious and determined as possible. "I will not be going to the Seat of Enchantment. I am giving up my role as Servant."

He took his arms from her shoulders and stared into the corner of the barn, where nothing was visible in the dark. He paced to the wall and back several times.

He is thinking again. Always thinking. She interrupted the silence. "You don't need to protect me anymore. You can go back to what you were doing before you rescued me from the thieves."

He snorted and brought his gaze back to her. "You're soaked."

He picked up a blanket and wrapped it tightly about her. He patted her awkwardly on the back. "You had a terrible day. I had a terrible day. Probably the worst day of both of our lives."

She nodded.

"And then you made a decision while it was dark and gloomy and wet. Get some sleep. We'll discuss this with Bluebird and Growling Dog in the daylight. They're sensible people."

"You think I am not being sensible? That I let my mood dictate my decision? I assure you, I thought everything through quite thoroughly."

"Shhh. Shhh. We'll discuss it in the morning."

"*We*? It is my decision."

"One that affects the whole world."

"Tul, that is why I cannot be Servant. My unfinished training; my mediocre skills. I will lead Veridia into disaster."

"The Servant doesn't act alone. You'll have the Land's help."

"I wish you were right. So far, the Land has given me nothing. I am on my own."

He whistled. "I have never read of the Land choosing a Servant and then abandoning her."

Fila choked on a sob. "So you understand?"

"If you are not Servant, what will you do?"

"I'm staying in this village."

He said sharply, "You would abandon your cousin?"

She lowered her head. "I was hoping you would look for her. I doubt she still lives, but if she does, I would be a liability in the rescue. You said it yourself: I'm naïve."

"I spoke hastily. Why, for Land's sake, did you believe me? Especially after naming me an idiot?"

"Idiot or not, you were right. Here, in this village, I can help, not harm. The T-t-toilers need a Guardian who will t-t-take care of them."

"Your teeth are chattering. Sit."

She obeyed, too weary and worn to refuse.

His fingers felt like a brand against her chilled flesh. He put one arm around her and drew her close; he used his other arm to chafe some warmth back into her arms and legs. She stiffened at the intimacy, then leaned against him. He radiated heat like a Toiler's furnace, and she was so, so cold.

Feeling returned to her fingers in dozens of wasp stings, hundreds of pinpricks. Her teeth stopped chattering. She melted further into his embrace, sighing and closing her eyes. For the moment, she could pretend everything was all right.

"I mentioned someone was trying to kill me, but not why." Tul's deep voice vibrated within her ribs, a strange feeling, but soothing, like a cat's purr. "Urushi intends to rule Veridia. While the Seat is leaderless, he consolidates support. Those who don't back Urushi die. His first attempt to kill me failed. I didn't wait for a second. I got on Swallowtail and left the city."

A chill blossomed deep inside her chest, ice that Tul's heat could never melt. She did not know her brother at all. "The few men who were Servants all had powerful magic and strong Consorts. Urushi is … flawed." She paused. "Or has his hair turned at last?"

"No. He still can't control his magic or his temper. But it may not matter. He wants to be king, not Servant."

Fila gasped. The long-past days of kings and queens were violent and unhappy times. "King? I wonder why anyone backs him."

"People fear his anger. When someone opposes him and Urushi falls into a rage, his magic breaks free and strikes where it may."

She had helped Mother heal his magic wounds and comforted him when he released his frustration in shouts or tears. But never had she tried to imagine what it was like to be him, to live with painful scars, to be the object of pity, to spend each day in fear of hurting his loved ones or himself. Had his loneliness made him a power-hungry murderer?

"Before I fled," Tul said, "my father told me Urushi had magical beasts at his disposal, creatures designed to kill Guardians."

"It cannot be true. No one has such power."

"I thought so too. But one of these beasts, an icedragon, tried to kill me. It found me again after I fled the city, but I reached the forest just in time. I assume it still seeks me."

Acid scoured the back of her throat. "Is that—is that how Mother died?" she asked, not certain she wanted to know the answer. "Killed by an ice-dragon?"

"No; icedragons kill Guardian *men*. Urushi has *firehounds* to kill Guardian women." She jerked, and he put his other arm around her. "Forgive me; I'm being pedantic. To answer your question—I don't know."

Thunder crashed outside, and they both jumped. The storm worsened. She pressed herself against him, not caring he was a stranger and sometimes an idiot, only that he was big and strong and warm and, most important, next to her. She drew strength from his powerful body almost as she drew it from the Land.

Unlike the Land, he had saved her from assassins and warned her of danger.

"Lady, you still tremble, and your skin is icy. Take off your clothes."

"You overstep yourself!" She pulled away.

"No, no. You misunderstand. I'll give you my dry clothes. There's no need for embarassment; this barn's as dark as the inside of a sheep."

Heat rose to her face. She dropped the blanket, scooted away from him, and stripped. She wrung the water from her clothes and draped them over the rail of the hayloft to dry.

His clothes rustled. "Here. Take this." She reached out blindly; cloth brushed her skin. She grabbed it—it was his tunic, still warm from his body and smelling enough like him she felt another blush rising. She put it on. It fell below her knees.

"Here," he said again. This time he handed her his pants. She grabbed them and yanked them on, stumbling a little as her foot caught in the unfamiliar garment. *Ah!* What bliss to have on something dry and still warm from his body heat. She shivered, from pleasure this time.

"Better?"

"Yes, thank you. But what about you? You must be cold now. Without your clothes, that is." Her voice hitched.

"Don't worry; I've got a blanket wrapped around me. We can share the rest, and we'll both be warm." He drew her to the nest she had made in the straw for him. They sank down together awkwardly and tugged the blankets around themselves.

She marveled at the experience of being in his arms. Although Amma had held her so many times, this was different. His touch reminded her of the Land's, comforting and protective—and alien.

Her foot accidentally brushed his leg; the spark made her jump. For a moment, the briefest moment, his mind touched hers. *Impossible. That only happens in Toilers' tales.* She waited for him to make a joke, but he merely shifted away. *I must have imagined it.*

Something was bothering her. "Why did you stop to save me when an icedragon was after you?"

He waited so long to answer she thought he had fallen asleep. Then he said, "I cannot bear to see others suffer."

* * *

Celatu held the Servant—*my cousin*—as she slept. The most powerful person in the Land was as frail and vulnerable as any of the Land's other creatures. She thrashed about as if nightmares plagued her, but calmed when he stroked her arm. *My cousin.* She needed a Consort, soon, and according to tradition, his qualifications were perfect.

He could do worse than to become her Consort. After only a day with her, he knew she wasn't one of the frilly, frothy women his parents invited to dinner, ostensibly for a boring evening of conversation about politics, parties, and infrastructure repairs, but in reality for consideration as his wife.

The potential brides always thought him too eccentric, too solitary. Violet probably did too. But his quirks were a minor problem compared with his lies and half-truths. She would be furious when she learned he wasn't Tul, but Celatu. Celatu the Coward.

He sighed and closed his eyes, but sleep didn't come. He was too aware of his nakedness and her closeness, too aware of her woodsy, earthy scent and the wiry tresses that tickled his nose, too aware he wanted to protect her, not only because she was an innocent creature at the mercy of someone evil and not only because she was the Servant and he owed her his protection. He wanted to take care of her because she was the Once-Fila-and-Future-Violet, an infuriating, endearing mix of power, naïveté, and dogged devotion to duty.

The hammer of rain grew louder, thunder boomed, and Fila stirred.

"You're safe," Celatu said. She rested in his arms without saying a word. Winds lashed the barn, and its old boards creaked. Below, the elk cows, heavy with calves, were restive, stomping and grunting. Pigs squealed in fear. Swallowtail nickered. The cracks of lightning quickened.

Violet sighed. "I am weary to my bones, but the storm keeps me awake. I worry the Toilers' fields will flood again and the vanes of their windmills will break."

He dared to stroke her cheek. "Put it on your worry list for tomorrow."

"I do not have a worry list."

"Then give me your worry so you can sleep."

She giggled and nestled more snugly in his arms, and he smiled for no reason. He would ask her soon to unite. He would present his argument to be her Consort in practical, logical terms, building it on facts she could not deny. His powerful male magic, even if he never used it, would greatly strengthen her female magic if they joined. His knowledge of the world and his physical strength would protect her against any who sought to harm her. He would promise to always treat her with kindness and respect and to give her many children strong in body and magic.

How could she turn down such an offer?

Chapter 19

WHEN CELATU WOKE, the Servant was gone. He went to look for her to tell her of his plans to look for Kassia.

Violet may have given up on Kassia, but he believed his sister was still alive; she could charm the skin from a snake.

Father had said Urushi wanted to marry Kassia, that Urushi hoped she would be Servant and he her Consort. For all Celatu knew, the assassins were Kassia's honor guard, not kidnappers.

But he had enough distrust of humanity in general and criminals in particular not to believe his sister inviolate even if she were under Urushi's protection. She loved to talk and tended to fuss. What if a kidnapper tired of her babbling or of having his collar adjusted?

Had Kassia any idea of the plots entangling her?

He was impatient to go after her and get her out of the clutches of bad-intentioned men. But first, he had to find Violet.

He found her walking from house to house, surveying the villagers about their needs and problems. Her little bone tablet was already covered in neat graphite notes. She had tied a cloth over her hair, but many copper strands had escaped.

He rubbed the spot between his eyebrows in frustration when she ignored him. "Lady, I'll look for your cousin as you requested, but I cannot leave you here alone. The assassins are probably looking for you. Firehounds too. You should come with me."

"I'm staying here." She angled her tablet toward him. "Look how much I need to do." Her voice held no emotion, no vitality. Her face had aged overnight.

"Then I'll stay here to protect you, at least until you're not Servant anymore. Rescuing Kassia is less important than protecting you."

"Go. I won't be Servant much longer. The Land must accept my decision. I'm Servant by mistake."

In all his research, he had never come across any Servant who had not been Servant until death. But he played along; in time, she would learn the truth in her own way. "Until you're no longer Servant, you're in danger."

"I don't care. Please, Tul, find Kassia. If she is still alive, rescue her and take her safely to the Seat."

He opened his mouth to protest, but she cut him off with words more desperate than rational. "She is not married. She would be so grateful that she might choose you as her husband."

"I'd rather be yours." *Oops.*

She drew herself upright, flushing as bright as her hair. "Do not make fun of me. Just because I am Goodborn does not mean I fall for sarcasm or false flattery."

"I meant what I said. Not every man wants a well-dressed, sophisticated beauty."

For some reason, his comment did not go over well. Her eyes flew wide open, and she pursed her lips.

He braced for an upbraiding.

"So I would make a good wife because I prefer practical clothing and would not draw other men's attention? In other words, I'm unattractive and cheap to maintain? Faint praise, that."

He tried to soften his offense with a joke. "Maybe I've grown to like your bad temper. High spirits, I'll tell people."

Her hands and jaw clenched. "I have not been myself. You do not understand what I am going through."

"Then help me understand."

She shook her head, turned away, and walked toward the next Toiler house.

He followed. "Wait! Please. Give me another chance to say what I mean without making an idiot of myself."

She stopped; she turned. "Is that even possible?"

Ouch. "What happened to Sweet Violet from last night? I grow tired of spending so much time with Mean Violet."

She flushed, and her eyes glistened. "I must apologize. Again. Say what you want to say, and I'll do my best to be polite."

I must remember to treat her gently. Her losses have taken a heavy toll. "There are good reasons for you to take me as your Consort. Based on my research in old documents, the Toiler legends are true: When the Land created Guardians, It molded us genetically to serve the Servant and keep her safe. Just as It gave Toilers an irresistible, overwhelming desire to take care of Guardians. Violet, I vow to protect you any way I can. I want to marry you so I can protect you always. My magic is very strong. If we bonded, it would boost your power greatly."

"Only until I am no longer Servant, which will be soon. Then you are stuck with me, the real me you have not met, not the Servant who triggers your inborn protective instincts now." Violet wrapped her arms around herself even though the morning was warm. Lines radiated from her eyes, and under her bruises the skin of her face looked dull. "Please, Tul? Look for Kassia. She is my best friend."

He had to do something to relieve her suffering. "You win. I won't go far, but I will look. Growling Dog mentioned three other villages lie nearby. I'll visit them today and hurry back to you."

"You won't help with today's work?" Growling Dog, holding some kind of farm tool with sharp prongs, scowled down at Celatu. He felt ten summers old. "What kind of Guardian are you? Last night, several families asked whether they could have your help today. There's a wasp's nest outside a pup's window and a rotted tree limb high above the reach of our ladders. If the Servant can't heal Hummingbird's foot, we'll need you to amputate it cleanly. Not to mention the fields need weeding."

Celatu shifted under Growling Dog's disapproving gaze. The villagers under his Guardianship needed a magic-wielding Guardian more than he had realized. "Servant Violet begged me to search for her kidnapped cousin. Land willing, I'll find her still alive."

Growling Dog harrumphed and headed toward the fields. Guilt twisted Celatu's insides, even though he knew it unwarranted. Without magic, he could do nothing for the villagers they couldn't do themselves.

Celatu headed toward the barn to get Swallowtail. Violet sat in the barn's shadow on a borrowed stool as a line of villagers waited to talk to her. "I hope to bring Kassia back to you when I return," he murmured.

Her face transformed. The fatigue dropped away, and she favored him with a smile so brilliant that his toes curled.

"Thank you. You will have my gratitude for ever."

The memory of her smile kept his spirits soaring as he rode the back roads, visiting widely scattered Toiler villages and isolated homes. Unfortunately, no one had seen a group of Guardian men, with or without a pale-haired woman in tow. He took heart no one had found her body, either.

He checked the sky often for the icedragon. Once something flashed overhead, and his heart lurched. But whether real or mirage, it appeared no more. Still, he kept under the trees and on the narrower paths that would be less visible from above.

He was on the way back to Growling Dog's village when he came upon a ramshackle cottage with a broken-down cart outside. He stopped, tied Swallowtail tightly to a tree, and studied the cottage. No dogs slept on the stoop, and no geese wandered about. He doubted anyone lived there, but to be thorough in his search he knocked at the door.

Someone screeched, "Just a moment!" Odd bumping and clanking noises issued from the house. When the door at last opened, he had to look down instead of up to see the Toiler female. Scrunched-faced and squint-eyed, she sat in a chair whose legs ended in mismatched wheels.

Her gaze took in his Guardian features, and her eyes lit up. "Mud's clogging my gutter." Her voice was hard to understand; he guessed some teeth were missing. "Take care of that first."

"I fear you mistake my intentions. I'm not here to work. I am looking for some people. Several Guardians, possibly dressed in brown robes, and a woman they may have kidnapped. You would have noted her if you saw her. Exotic light skin and hair."

She shrugged, but Celatu caught the flicker of interest in her eyes.

"Intentions or not, you'll work or Granny Earwig won't tell you anything." She rolled back so he could enter her house. He followed her in.

"What possessed your mother to name you Earwig?" The inside of the cottage was neat and in better condition than the outside or the wagon.

"I named myself, I did. People have more sympathy for 'poor old Granny Earwig the rag collector' than they ever did for Lily the weaver."

"I take it you've seen the people I seek? Where? When? Is the woman unharmed?"

Granny Earwig cupped her hand around her ear. "It's hard to hear when my gutters are dirty."

Celatu looked at the greasy hair hanging in strings about her ears. He did not know what a gutter was, but if dirty ones impaired her hearing, he did not think cleaning them was a chore he wanted to take on. "Did I mention there's a reward for good information?"

He looked about the room, and his gaze alighted on a small workbench with a variety of tools and wheels neatly arranged in cubbyholes. He looked again at her wheeled chair. "I could change the wheels so they're all the same diameter. You'd have a smoother ride."

She frowned, rose from the chair, and walked with a steady gait toward the large table. She picked up a pipe, lit it, and tapped the side of her head with a bony finger. "Think, man, think! Would the villagers feel as sorry for me if I made my rounds in a chair that rolled evenly instead of lurching along with an annoying clack-clack-clack?"

"You're a fraud!" Celatu recoiled, then broke into hearty laughter.

Granny Earwig clicked her tongue against the roof her mouth. "What a nasty word, fraud. All I'm doing is making the most of my poor assets to make a living since that idiot Celatu the Coward took away my trade."

His stomach dropped even though she was lying. "He did nothing to you. I happen to know he hasn't visited his village in four years."

She nodded so hard that ash bounced out of her pipe. "That's the problem. When Nightingale accused me of stealing wool, the village council deadlocked and appealed to Celatu for help. He 'declined to come.'" She perfectly imitated an upper-class Seat accent. "Meanwhile, Nightingale made dove eyes at all the males on the council until one fell for it. When the council voted again, I was declared 'guilty' by one vote and banished. Every village was notified of my 'crime.'

"Lily had to disappear. 'Granny Earwig' couldn't afford a new loom, so she became a rag collector."

The world tilted, and the room spun fast around his head. Celatu braced himself with a hand against the wall. He didn't want to believe her story. But it was true the few times the Toiler council had asked for his opinion on a trial, he had declined to go. *Granny Earwig's predicament is my fault.*

"I can see you are moved by poor Granny Earwig's plight. If you ever meet up with that poor excuse for a Guardian, give him a kick in the behind for me." Her articulation had improved remarkably. She pulled off a wig and tossed it onto a table.

He leaned against the wall for support and squinted at her. Her clean hair was neatly pulled back into a knot, and as she unscrunched her face the lines disappeared. "Did you steal the wool?"

She snorted. "Not that it matters now, but no. I was as honest as a person could be. I don't have that luxury now."

"I am truly sorry for your misfortune." He emptied most of his coin purse onto her table. She looked at his earring. He took it out and set it next to the coins. "Lily, can you tell me about the people you saw?"

She gathered up his guilt offerings, took them to the window, and counted the coins. She turned the earring, examining the diamond. She nodded. "This morning, a group of Guardians stopped me. One was a woman with pale hair. They asked whether I'd seen the Servant on my rounds. The Servant, of all people! I said no, and they rode on. They didn't toss me a single silver piece for my trouble!"

Celatu's heart sped up. "How was the woman? Was she injured?"

"I didn't notice. Kidnapped, you say? She didn't ask for my help."

In her Granny Earwig getup, she didn't look as if she could give any. "Did they mention where they would look next for the Servant?"

She shook her head. "They were on the main road heading in the direction the Seat, if that's any help."

Chapter 20

A FISSA SAT on the hard terrazzo floor of the entry hall of her house and lifted her feet to tie her daughters' gray mourning sashes, then tugged them into perfect bows. "When Grandmother Erudia arrives, please set aside your own grief to comfort her. She wrongly believes she is to blame for your father's death."

"Yes, Mama," Nandina and Typha said in unison. Neither was Goodborn, but like all young ones, they had copied her behavior and grown into kind, well-behaved near-adults.

Not all young ones. Urushi did not copy his parents—or did a poor job of it.

What of our new Servant, Fila? The firehounds made me her strong supporter, yet I know little of her.

"Mama? You're daydreaming again." Nandina put her hand on Afissa's cheek.

Afissa started, stood, and brushed off the back of her skirt. *I hope I thought of everything.*

Daucina and Ladybug came down the corridor lined with representatives of every family in Gramin's Toiler village and joined them in the entry hall. They had stayed with her since Daucina's cottage burned. Gray and drawn, her late husband's cousin had aged at least ten years. Still, Daucina smiled at the girls and grasped both of Afissa's hands. "You've done a wonderful job of planning this memorial, given … the circumstances and the ban on gatherings. I will sit across the street so you can have two other adult Guardians here."

"No, I won't hear of it. I don't want you falling ill from the heat."

"Ladybug talked to your neighbors in the green wooden house. We can sit in their garden in the shade and the fresh breeze."

Ladybug added, "They are too frightened to come over to comfort you, so they are happy they can show their support in this way without risk."

I wonder how many other friends won't come today because they're frightened Urushi will consider any mourners as traitors. They had prepared enough food for a large crowd but chosen dishes that would keep while the Toilers took them back to their village if no one came. "Thank you, Ladybug. I don't know what I would have done without your help."

Ladybug stroked her hair. "Toilers and Guardians exist to serve each other. If I hadn't helped you, I would not have met Gramin's valet. Buckeye and I plan to marry." She grinned, and her bumpy, huge Toiler face looked beautiful, despite the silvery scars of healed burns.

"Buckeye caught himself a hero for a bride. He must be bragging to all of his friends about you." Afissa stood high on her tiptoes to kiss her cheek. "Please, take cider and food for both you and Daucina. If Daucina tires, bring her back here, even if you have to carry her. If we can have only one Guardian guest at once, that's what we'll do."

"I'll take good care of her. And you." Ladybug hugged Afissa and then headed for the courtyard, where tables of food and drink awaited guests.

Afissa stepped out the front door and checked the sundial's pale shadow. Guests should be arriving soon. She adjusted her own sash again. The overcast sky dulled and muted everything, even the flowers. She gazed up and down the street, looking for gray sashes, but spotted none. *I hope someone is brave enough to come to honor Gramin.* She rejoined her daughters in the entry hall; Daucina and Ladybug left.

"You girls remember your duties, right?"

Both nodded. Nandina said, "No more than four adult Guardians, including you and Grandmother Erudia, in the house at once."

"Make sure of it. We don't want to give Urushi a reason to arrest our friends." She fussed with her sash, then went out to survey the street again. This time she saw Mother Erudia walking slowly with a cane toward the house.

Is no one else coming? She wiped damp palms on her skirt and walked down the street to meet her mother-in-law, who had aged as much as Daucina. "Mother, I would be honored if you would stand with Typha to greet the guests."

"But don't you need me to—"

"No." *I've never interrupted her before.* They arrived at the house. Erudia kissed the girls, gripping her cane with visibly shaking hands.

"Nandina, come with me." Afissa had dreaded this moment. She led Nandina between the rows of Toilers to the end of the hall, where Gramin's masterpiece stood. It had taken two Toilers to carry in the high chest, made from old-growth black walnut and carved on every surface, even the back, with the leaves, flowers, nuts, and fruits of all the trees of Veridia.

"Mama, what is the chest doing here?"

Afissa sucked in a deep breath. "The mourners must have a memento of your papa."

"And they can't clip his hair, as usual. But why is the chest here?"

Afissa's throat constricted; she could not answer.

Nandina's brows drew together, then, as meaning dawned, the color fled her face. "Not the chest. Please, Mama, not the chest!"

Afissa hugged her daughter. She had run the backs of her hands and her lips over the carvings often over the past day, trying to memorize the size, shape, and feel of the grain of each lovingly researched and carved rendering. The bottom "drawers" were a false front; it tipped out into a desk surface for when Gramin needed one. He had decorated even those hidden surfaces. His Toiler village had hand-forged the hinges at his request.

Losing the chest piece by piece will be like losing Gramin all over again.

"Your grandmother will send each mourner down the hall. You will invite each person to take a carving to remember your papa by. With a knife, with magic, however each person desires. Did you sharpen your pocketknife as I told you to?"

Sobbing, Nandina nodded.

Afissa said, "Help the older people and younglings if they can't remove the carving themselves. Then send or guide them into the courtyard. I'll stand with you for the first guest or two."

Minutes passed. At last, someone arrived, a neighbor couple. They spoke to Erudia, then came down the hall between the Toilers. The wife put her hand on Nandina's shoulder and whispered, "We must be brave now."

Nandina nodded.

"Your loss is our loss." The husband said the traditional words.

Afissa nudged her daughter's shoe with her foot.

Nandina bowed. "You honor our dead with your visit. Please take home a part of, a part of my father, Gramin."

The neighbors looked at the chest, then at Afissa.

She nodded. "This chest is as much Gramin as his body ever was. He spent months researching and making drawings for the carvings and schematics for the chest. It took him years to find wood of the right quality and age, have it milled to his specifications, season it, carve the boards, cut the pins and tails of the dovetails, and put it together."

The husband asked, "Is there a sycamore fruit?"

She resisted the urge to stand in front of the chest and protect it. "The finials are sycamore fruits. Please choose your favorite."

The husband reached up to touch each. When Afissa smelled the cherry scent of his magic, she shut her eyes. A soft crack; it was over. "Beautiful workmanship," he murmured. When she heard the finial slide into a pouch, she opened her eyes. She did not look at the chest.

"Please come with me," she said loudly to cover the sound of Nandina's snuffling. She led them into the courtyard.

"Your loss is our loss."

"You honor our dead with your visit. Please eat in memory of my husband, Gramin." She bit her lip, feeling awkward. Ordinarily, the bereaved merely said the ritual greetings over and over, and the guests passed by and talked among themselves. Now, silence screamed. The neighbors picked up plates and stood looking at the food. "Please, eat," Afissa urged.

Each took a few strawberries and a small square of cheese. They gulped them down and hurried to the sacrifice table. Here, Afissa had been able to keep tradition.

The couple visibly relaxed at the familiar setup. "Your loss is our loss."

"You honor our dead with your sacrifice."

She and Gramin had not known these neighbors. She expected small tokens—a coin, a button, a few strands of hair, a flower from their garden. Instead, the husband cut off a chunk of hair as wide has his thumb and dropped it on the platter. Before Afissa recovered from his gesture, the wife sliced her palm over the copper chalice. The first drop of blood struck with a ping.

Afissa drew a sharp breath. In silence and stillness, blood trickled into the copper chalice until it stopped on its own.

The neighbor woman whispered, "Your bravery inspires us. We will not support Urushi."

"More is needed," Afissa said. "We must also support the new Servant."

The woman blinked at her firm words, exchanged a glance with her husband, and nodded. "It is not enough to be against something, you mean. We must choose something to be for."

The vagues wavered at the edge of Afissa's awareness; she could not answer except with a nod. *Is it wrong if my actions or words inspire rebellion in others? What if they are hurt or killed?*

A Toiler ushered the neighbors out. The gong sounded; footsteps entered the house.

Mourners came and went, far more than she had expected. Many left immoderate tokens or made lavish sacrifices. Mild vagues clung to her, but she hid her discomfort until the last mourner left.

Dizzy, she held on to the table as she drank mug after mug of cider to moisten a throat dry from hours of repeating the ritual words. Her mother-in-law and Daucina joined her in the courtyard.

"Mother Erudia, I'm surprised Gramin's murder inspired so many to put themselves in danger." Afissa's arms jerked with the vagues, and she sunk into the sedge to keep from falling.

Erudia snorted. "They are fools. *I* was a fool. Urushi killed my boy. Now I see clearly our efforts were not worth the cost."

"*I* see more clearly too," Daucina said, her eyes red and swollen. "I see how unsuitable Urushi is to be king or Consort, how truly dangerous he has become."

"I have known Fila since she was a little girl. She's too weak to win her Seat against Urushi," Erudia retorted.

"Mother! Am I weak because I am Goodborn? We must support our Servant."

"I agree," Daucina said.

Erudia shook her head. "All I want to do is go back to my rooms at the Servant's House and mourn my son and my friends."

"What about other women's sons, other people's friends?" Daucina asked. Erudia shrugged.

"Mother, listen to me." Afissa enclosed Erudia's hands in her own. "Urushi is more of a threat than we thought, and we have less to lose. Don't let grief keep you from doing the right thing."

"I do not care what is right. I care only that my son is dead."

"See through what you started," Afissa urged. "Help the new Servant restore harmony to Veridia."

"Why? She cannot bring back Gramin. The world has ended." Erudia sighed and shrank into herself.

"Not for your granddaughters. Do you want them to live in a Veridia under Urushi?"

At last Erudia raised her head. "We don't know Fila would be a better leader. She's his sister. Her magic or character may be tainted too."

"She's also Servant Hyacinth's daughter. The Land chose her and bonded with her! Trust the Land. Fila deserves a chance to show what kind of Servant she can be."

Erudia pursed her lips. "I agree she deserves a chance ... to prove she is worthy to be Servant. I will agree to test her."

Chapter 21

BLUEBIRD HAD GIVEN FILA her place at the head of the supper table, despite her protests. Now Fila sat contentedly on a stack of books as she and the family ate their dinner of vegetable soup, bread, and blackberries. For all the times she had helped out at a Toiler village, Fila had never eaten with a Toiler family before. They joked and laughed and the pups kicked each other under the table, just as in her family.

Just as her family had once done on the occasions they were all together. *Who knew those times would be so few and thus so precious?*

She put down her spoon; the previously delicious soup no longer appealed. The day of helping the village had let her stuff her sorrow into a far corner of her awareness. Now it burst free, buffeting and clawing her with grief raw and agonizing.

After supper, the family cleared plates and gathered near the fire in the sitting room.

Someone banged on the door.

Bluebird got up to open it, and Tul came in.

Fila jumped up from her chair. "Did you find Kassia? Is she safe?"

"Please, sit down, Tul. I'll bring you some food." Bluebird took a chair from a hook on the kitchen wall, took it into the sitting room, and set the chair next to Fila's. Tul slumped into it as Bluebird got him a plate.

"Did you find her?" Fila asked.

"No, but I did find a Toiler who saw her with the assassins. She's alive."

"Land be thanked!" She sat back down, taking deep breaths as one worry melted away.

Tul looked up to say something, then stared at her face.

"What's wrong?" She self-consciously smoothed her hair and tucked in an errant strand.

"You're smiling. I never saw your smile before. It's beautiful." Flushing, he looked at his plate and started on his meal.

Her ears burned. Bluebird had placed his chair too close to her, so close she could count the exact number of black whiskers growing out on his cheek and jaw, so close she could hear his stomach gurgle and see a tiny freckle by his ear, so close his warmth and the scent of Swallowtail reached her. He did not need books to sit on, and despite the Toiler-wide chairs, his right shoulder almost touched her cheek.

She scooted her chair away a little and remained silent. She had never been as social as Kassia, but she knew how to carry on a conversation. Now, that knowledge fled, and her tongue lay heavy and wooden in her mouth.

The Toilers and Tul kept up a lively conversation on their own, Tul firing questions at them about Toiler legends, village crimes, the network of Toiler roads and paths, the treatment of criminals, mythical beasts, something called a "steam engine," and other random things. His curiosity knew no bounds; no wonder he loved his library. She had to admit Tul had profited from his book reading. Whatever topic came up, he knew something about it, and often she did not.

Then Growling Dog asked Tul to do some Guardian chores.

"I appreciate all you've done for us, but I can't help in the village tonight," Tul said. "I must talk with the Servant."

"I can wait." Fila wanted to check a field of lettuces again before it got too dark.

"That won't be necessary, Lady."

"Yes, it will be." Growling Dog's voice had dropped an octave.

Tul put down his flatware. "If the Toilers want reimbursement for their hospitality, I can send money later."

Growling Dog stood and scowled. "That's not how things are done. Guardian guests repay with magic."

Tul's fists opened and closed. He kicked back his chair and stomped out.

Fila stood too. Tul obviously did not want to tell them his secret, that he did not use magic. But now the two of them looked like boors and freeloaders. "I apologize for Tul's manners. I will do enough work here for two people, I promise."

"You already have, Lady." Bluebird tugged on her husband's sleeve until he sat. "That doesn't lessen *his* obligation."

"I will talk to him."

Fila found Tul in the barn pouring oats from an oversized barrel into a trough. Swallowtail, still saddled, dug in as enthusiastically as Tul had earlier.

The dust made her sneeze. The barn smelled of caramel. "You did not feed your horse before you came in for dinner?" Her voice rose in pitch and volume, as Kassia's did when she was in a state, and she could not stop her anger. "Or remove its tack?" She kicked the side of the barn: "Mean Violet" had returned.

Tul's large muscles bulged as he righted the barrel and set it down. He fiddled with a clasp on a saddle bag. "I thought you'd want to hear the news about Kassia right away. Then Bluebird put a plate in my hand, and I was starved." He smiled at her. "So horses first, Guardians second? I'll keep that in mind."

His smile was affectionate, as if they were friends, as if she had agreed to his courtship; his asumptions fed her anger. "You shamed me. I worked hard all day, but now I feel like a freeloader." She undid the buckles under the horse's belly. "Go apologize to Growling Dog and Bluebird and ask how you can do your duty."

He stiffened and shook his head. "No. You asked me to find your cousin. She takes precedence over chores, over everything, except your safety, of course."

She yanked on the saddle.

It flew off, sending her tumbling backwards. She landed with a hard, loud thump.

Tul offered her a hand up.

She paused, then took it and pulled herself back on her feet. "Thank you." The words came out automatically, sounding silly in the middle of an argument. She hoisted the saddle and slung it over a stand.

"You're welcome, Lady."

"Why couldn't you have displayed those manners in the cottage? You acted as if you were too good to do manual labor. Why not just explain you do not use magic?"

His gaze flicked away, and he pulled a copper coin from his pocket and turned it expertly and rapidly between his fingers. "It's not something I talk about."

Her rising curiosity and the calming effect of watching the coin spin gave "Sweet Violet" a chance to re-emerge. "Why? Is it a secret?"

"No. I just do not want to hurt anyone's feelings."

"My feelings were not hurt."

"You are not a man who enjoys destroying things with his magic. If you were, you might interpret my choice not to use magic as a moral judgment on your choice."

Fila nodded with understanding. "Many people think that because I am Goodborn, I am constantly judging them and finding them lacking. It makes it hard to make friends."

"I understand. Although I am no Goodborn, I try to consider how my actions might affect others. Sometimes that angers or annoys people who act without thinking."

"You are always thinking. Your legs must be very strong from all that pacing." She covered her mouth with her hand.

Tul chuckled. "You made a little joke! You have a sense of humor after all."

She let her hands fall to her lap. "Apparently I do."

"I wasn't making an excuse when I said we had things to discuss," Tul said. "How long do you plan to wait for the Land to choose someone else as Servant?"

"As long as it takes."

He shook his head. "No. You have to set a deadline, and it has to be soon. I won't let you wait longer."

"Or you will do what? Do not threaten me."

"Violet, *you're* the threat. While you wait for the Land to make someone else Servant, icedragons and firehounds are hunting down and killing Guardians. While you delay, Kassia may say something to annoy the assassins and they may hurt her. We need to set a deadline for the Land to decide."

Her eyebrows and eyes drooped. "For the most part, the Land ignores me. It does not talk to me as It should. Giving It a deadline is pointless." She turned away, took the curry brush from the wall, and brushed Swallowtail's mane.

"Then you must set a deadline for yourself. How long are you willing to leave your cousin and everyone else in Veridia in danger?"

She brushed harder, removing even the tiniest knots from the horse's mane. Then she worked through the forelock until it too was sleek and shiny.

"Did you know you stick your tongue out when you concentrate? It looks adorably silly." *Land take me, I've said something idiotic again.* "I mean, you look natural and free, not sophisticated, with all your personality grounded like a Toiler's." *That is not quite right either.* "Anyway, we should get back to the topic, which is setting a deadline."

Violet stopped brushing and leaned against Swallowtail. She spoke slowly, with gaps. "What if I set a deadline, and when it passes, I am still Servant?"

"Then we head as fast as we can toward the Seat on the main road, hoping to rescue Kassia from the assassins on the way."

"I am not making myself clear. If the deadline passes and I am still Servant, I will have no more knowledge or training than I do now. The Land may still ignore me. How can I help Kassia or Veridia without the Land's aid? Tul, I am so afraid of making things worse."

"Worse than Urushi sending animals to kill people in the streets of the Seat?"

"Yes, worse than that. Urushi sits on the Servant's Council. He knows something of governing; I know nothing."

Celatu walked back and forth beside Swallowtail, his hand stroking the coarse-silky coat. Meanwhile, Violet brushed the other side of Swallowtail, slowly this time.

"Lady, I cannot think of a reason the Land has abandoned you. Such a thing is unprecedented. But I suggest It chose you Servant because It knows you can develop into an excellent one."

"It sounds vain, but I believe I could be a good Servant in ten or fifteen years … if I continue my training and choose a good council. But as you keep pointing out, the present emergencies require a good Servant now." She walked over to the ladder and gripped an upright tight in both hands, looking him straight in the eyes. "Help me sort out what to do, what is right," she whispered.

"I do not know what's right any more than you do."

"You have read all those books. Do you not have any ideas?"

"People have been saying 'The Land doesn't make mistakes' for hundreds of years. Perhaps in your case, It did make a mistake. But you can't make good decisions if you believe that. You have to trust in the Land and in yourself."

"Without evidence."

"I'll quote another saying, this one from the thirteenth or fourteenth Servant: 'Pretending works just as well as being.' Can you pretend to be a competent Servant?"

"That would be lying!"

"Let's call it instead, say, *inspiring those who depend on you and scaring those who oppose you.*"

"Misleading in the service of good, in other words. That would work?"

"Better than allowing your fears and doubts to show. Even the gentlest dog growls at a person who's afraid of it."

"I suppose I could pretend I was my mother."

He smacked his fist against his palm. "Yes! Perfect! Servant Hyacinth was one of the greatest of the Servants. Do what you think your mother would have done, and you can be an acceptable Servant now, even without the Land. It's not lying; it's good leadership."

She heaved a long, relieved sigh. "I can do that. If the Land does not change Its mind by dawn, I will accept Its decision. We will leave for the Seat and look for Kassia as we travel, as you suggested."

Celatu woke before the dawn deadline, his heart pounding from a dream in which a spider of huge size and row after row of sharp teeth held Kassia in its web while he read a book. Not so far from the truth. He'd been prepared to leave the Servant's cousin to her fate until he found out who she was, just as he'd left the Toilers under his care to theirs.

He shuddered at his callousness. Violet's comparison of the captured Kassia to a helpless rabbit in the hands of cruel boys brought back vivid memories. When the boys started killing the rabbit kits, he had run away, taking his kit back to its nest and safety.

The boys had called him "the Coward" after that because he had not killed his rabbit.

He thought the epithet fit, but for a different reason: He had not stopped the other boys.

Yet now, despite all his thinking and all his efforts not to hurt anyone or anything, he had harmed both his sister and his Toiler village.

Things would be different here on out. He would make things up to his village. He would *not* let Urushi turn Kassia and the Servant into his next victims.

At least the Servant was safe right now. He had moved his blankets to the top of the ladder before he went to sleep. Any firehound or assassin would have to crawl over him to reach the Servant.

He listened for her breathing, the sound of her shifting on the hay. He heard only Swallowtail snort.

Berating himself under his breath, he crawled across the loft, stopping to listen every so often. He reached the pile of hay she had shaped into a nest and felt inside for her.

Empty.

His breath left him. *Father says I'm a heavy sleeper, but I didn't believe it. I should have slept next to her.*

His hands kept searching. He found her blankets, neatly folded. He tried to imagine bloodthirsty assassins folding blankets and failed.

She had left on her own. But where had she gone in the night?

He put a blanket under his arm and climbed down the rickety ladder. He greeted Swallowtail and walked out into the chill, clean-smelling air. A tinge of pink in the east was the only hint of the coming day. No light shone from any cottage, and the night was quiet except for the hoot of owls. Violet was nowhere in sight.

She had talked with great excitement the previous day about helping the Toilers harvest their broccoli crop. He smiled to himself. He found each little quirk and eccentricity she revealed enchanting.

Celatu turned his steps toward the fields. When the trees opened up, he scanned the sky for the ice-blue glow of an icedragon.

He saw nothing. Still, he felt uneasy and kept looking up at the sky. The dark was intense and eerie, and clouds hid part of the moon. *I'm being foolish.* He pulled out his lucky coin for comfort, but his worry increased.

A Toiler village was about the safest place in Veridia. But Servant Violet was somewhere in the dark fields, well away from the village, vulnerable. Assassins or wild animals could creep up on her unnoticed, and the sleeping villagers would not see or hear her trouble.

Sweating, he broke into a run. He didn't call out. If his worst fears were true, his calls and her answers would tell the assassins where she was.

He did not know where the broccoli was planted. He ran up and down the lanes edging the alternating rows of field and fallow, imagining in each bush and tree a danger to Violet.

When he came upon her, he almost didn't see her, a black silhouette against a black background, a place empty of stars. He sensed rather than saw her hands moving.

Thank the Land. Thank the Land. He stood and looked at her for a long minute, unable to speak, trying to take in that she was safe. "I wish you had wakened me. I would have come with you."

Her knitting needles never stopped clicking. "I did try to wake you. I didn't want you to worry. You just snored all the louder."

"I don't snore," he said.

"How would you know? You are asleep when you do it."

Father was right about my snoring too. "I am so relieved nothing happened to you. When I couldn't find you, I imagined firehounds carrying you away to who-knows-where."

"Perhaps if I were 'Mean Violet,' they would quickly bring me back."

"To be safe, let's sleep close together on the road. I need to protect you better."

The even rhythm of her needles faltered for a moment. "It's not dawn yet."

"You're right." He hopped up on the wall next to her and listened to the night. They were still close to the village but there was so much more to hear: the forlorn songs of coyotes, the rustling of rodents among the plants, the angry howl of a bobcat, the buzzing wings of a matutinal bee searching for nectar.

Over the next hour, those sounds faded, to be replaced by an occasional trill of bird song and the bang of a door in the village. The sky grew pinker, and Fila's hair glowed. Behind her, thick crops grew where yesterday stood only stubble. Fila had worked hard. Unaccountable pride welled up in him.

In the growing light, he watched her light up, admiring the tilt of her head and the strength of her delicate fingers, smiling at the tongue tip peeking from the corner of her mouth as she concentrated on her work as if nothing existed but this wall, this project. *If only this moment could last forever, if time could freeze and dawn never come. I could gaze at her for the rest of time.*

The curve of the sun broke the horizon. He willed it to slow its ascent, but it rose quickly. Half up. Three-quarters up. Almost fully above the horizon. Dawn.

Violet's hair flamed like a quick-burning fire. He lifted his hand to shield his still-sensitive eye against its brightness.

She lifted her hand, too, lifted it slowly toward her head. The hand hovered like a hummingbird around a flower, dipped into the red curls, and darted away.

She drew a deep breath, held it, and sighed it out slowly. Her eyes spoke her grief and despair, cutting him like a blade. "All I ever wanted, since I was a little girl, was what I had here in this village. The chance to spend each day quietly working magic and helping Toilers with their work."

"I know this isn't the way you wanted things to turn out—"

"I will do my duty," she interrupted. "I will give up my dreams." She slid off the wall and slowly put items into her needlework bag.

His chest tightened. *I would rather die than give up my life of study. She is doing the equivalent to do her duty to Veridia.* He felt diminished, even though his research was valuable.

"I have been hiding something from you, Tul. Something I should have told you earlier. Before you accompany me to the Seat, you need to know."

The hair stood up on the back of his neck. "I'm listening."

She looked up at him, her lower lip trembling. "I think I am going mad."

Chapter 22

CELATU COULD DO NOTHING but stare at Servant Violet, his mouth hanging wide open as if inviting small birds to take up residence.

"I will understand if you do not want to accompany me now," Violet said, her voice shaking.

He sat back down on the wall, closed his mouth, and remembered some of her brother's rages. He swallowed the lump in his throat. Veridia was in serious trouble if both of Servant Hyacinth's children went insane.

"What makes you think you are going mad?" he asked, proud of the calm tone with which he asked the question.

"I am behaving like a different person, a person I do not like," she said. "You yourself did not believe I was Goodborn at first. Within a short time of meeting you, I cursed, I was rude, and I was overcome by rage several times. Do you remember?"

His mouth wanted to tug into a smile. "Yes, I think so."

"I did worse things you did not see," she whispered. "Right before you rescued me, I watched men die and laughed out loud at their suffering. I almost stole a bottle of strawberry-scented something from Bluebird and Growling Dog's bathing pool."

His head reeled. The Land's chosen Servant, a Goodborn, could control her behavior no better than a child. Never in his books had he read about such a thing.

She looked at him from under her eyelashes, apprehension apparent in the hands she twisted together and in her tight, hunched posture. "Am I going mad?"

"Are you sure you were a Goodborn? Did the Toilers come and do genetic testing on you?"

"Yes and yes."

"How old were you when your … problem started?"

"It started only a few days ago. When the assassins attacked my traveling party."

What was different about that day? he almost asked, but he knew. Everything in her life changed for the worse. "Did the assassins force anything into your mouth or nose? Did they rub anything on your skin?"

"Not that I remember. But much about that day is already foggy in my memory. What are you thinking?"

"A wild guess. I thought perhaps Urushi's goal was not to kill you after all, but to poison you and then take over your duties slowly as you got sicker and sicker." *Or fell deeper and deeper into madness. What am I going to do about Servant Violet? Is she fit to rule?*

"Poison. Hmmm. Something odd *did* happen. Right before you rescued me, a mink ran by and bit me! On the ear. Is it possible for an animal to transmit disease?"

"Not nowadays, or so the Toilers say. But long, long ago there used to be a disease of mammals called rabies." He clasped his hands together so that Violet would not see them shaking. "It was transmitted by bites. The infected mammal often behaved oddly and became aggressive."

"Do you think I have this rabies disease?"

"I hope not!" he blurted out. "It does not seem possible."

"Is there a treatment I should take?"

"No one made it anymore after rabies was wiped out." The back of his tunic was soaked with sweat. *If only he had rescued her a minute or two earlier, before the mink bit her and possibly doomed her to a painful, dreadful end.*

"How long until I am my normal self again?"

He kneaded the spot between his eyebrows with a knuckle. His first thought was not to tell her. But she had been outraged that everyone except him hid from her the truth of what happened to her parents. He would not, could not, treat her as a child.

"If it's rabies—and again I point out that it seems impossible that it could be—it was wiped out long ago—also, your symptoms started too soon after the mink bite—but if it is rabies, then, then…." His voice stopped working for several moments. "Then you will not get better. Most victims die. But not all of them!" He would not tell her yet how rarely victims survived or how horribly they died.

Her face turned the color of old parchment. "What other ideas do you have for what is wrong with me?"

"Whatever … happened to Urushi could be starting in you."

It did not seem possible, but she paled even more.

"What else? There must be something else." She grabbed his arm and held onto it.

"Perhaps this is to be expected after having your life turned upside down. Only the strongest, or the stupidest, person could act normally after becoming

Servant, abruptly leaving school, losing their parents and amma, having a friend abducted, not getting enough sleep, eating an unaccustomed diet—"

She interrupted. "I understand." Her hand slid down his arm and clutched his hand. They sat like that, not speaking, for a long time. Toilers passed them on their way to the fields, giving them curious looks, but no one disturbed their thoughts. At last Violet reached up and touched her hair. "Copper. The Land does not care that Its Servant may be mad or have an ancient fatal disease."

"What will you do?"

She spoke softly. "Go to the Seat; defeat Urushi; take my position. Nothing has changed, in truth. I know I may fall out of the hayloft onto my head or be trampled by panicked bison later today, but that is no reason not to follow my plans until then."

"How sensible. You're picking up some of my good qualities."

She rolled her eyes at him.

"For once, I cannot be the logical one," he said. "All I can think of is all the terrible things that might happen to you and to Veridia. They go round and round in my head. I compare them in various dimensions, weighing them against each other to rank them from best to worst. I change the weights of the variables and go through the whole exercise again. I think about each terrible result and how I will help you bear it. I worry how I will bear any of them. I see your sad eyes and can't think of any way to make you feel better. I feel stuck, unable to see a reason to continue while your future is uncertain. I want to stay right here on this wall until we know what will happen."

"Sometimes you think too much."

Celatu stared at her in speechless, horrified disbelief.

"I am leaving today. Will you sit on the wall and wait for the icedragon, or will you come with me to restore harmony to Veridia?"

"I'll boost you up." Celatu had saddled Swallowtail and double-checked that all the buckles were tight.

"A Servant walks."

"Usually, yes. But we're in a hurry."

"Today, then. No promises for tomorrow."

He picked Violet up and set her on Swallowtail and climbed up behind her. "I promise to give you time to connect with the Land and gather power."

"Good. We will need my magic at its strongest."

They traveled in silence in the direction of the Seat, taking the road that "Granny Earwig" had seen Kassia on yesterday. Several times they passed Toilers in their wagons, traveling from village to village with goods to trade or sell.

Violet spoke to everyone, asking whether she could do anything for them. Usually they wanted only to touch her hair and tell her their names; some asked her to heal blisters or rashes or to pluck out splinters. Celatu asked each about the assassins and Kassia, but no one had seen either.

Celatu scanned the sky often for the icedragon. It didn't appear, but his frequent checks made the progress of the sun across the sky obvious, and he increasingly fumed at how little distance they covered.

Midafternoon he heard the clip-clop of a single horse and a male Guardian voice singing a bawdy song.

"We didn't learn *that* song at Boraga's manor," Violet said.

He laughed, but she held her hand up and cocked her head.

"What is it?"

She cocked her head. "I feel … something."

"Something?"

"Yes," she sighed. She looked at him flirtatiously over her shoulder, her eyes unfocused and her eyelashes batting. "The song makes me feel so nice."

He furrowed his brow. Was this a new sign of her possible madness?

Violet sighed again, and the song trickled through him, making it hard to think. But a thought tickled at the edge of his mind, trying to make itself known, getting lost in the captivating song.

Magic.

Danger.

Celatu dismounted and lifted Violet from Swallowtail. "Into the woods, Lady, quickly." He grabbed her hand and pulled her toward the forest. "Hurry!"

She tried to pull free of his hold. "I want to listen."

He held her tighter. The singing grew louder, unbearably beautiful, irresistably enticing. "We must get as far from the singer as possible."

"I don't want to." She twisted and squirmed. "Let go of me!"

"No!" His spinning head tilted the road and his grip on her loosened.

She pulled free and stumbled, steadying herself on his arm and giggling. She teetered drunkenly toward the road.

He could not stop her. That tingling memory burned. A sound like wind or rain or the rushing tide swept through his head, then cleared it.

Tone magic.

He pinched himself, forced his mind to focus. "Violet, stop! The song has magic."

She stumbled, her steps forced and grotesquely mechanical. "I cannot stop." Her hand stretched toward him, shaking and jerky. "Tul! Help me!"

Her cry freed him from the song's allure. He lunged for her, grabbed her about the waist, and pulled her toward the horse. Her feet kept moving, her toenails scrabbling to get purchase in the dirt.

"I can't fight it." She grabbed fistfuls of his clothes in a death grip.

"I'll keep you safe." He carried her to Swallowtail and threw her over the saddle. He jumped up behind her and urged Swallowtail deep into the woods. He stopped in the shadows under a huge oak. The trees and leaves distorted the song; his compulsion to go back to the road weakened. Violet, though, still fought to get free.

He held her tight against him. She put her fingers in her ears; he listened to the progress of the tone musician. The plod of hooves deadened; the horse trod on the soft forest floor.

"Lady, listen. We must go quietly. A tone magician is after us," he murmured. Sweat broke out on his face and torso. Celatu knew no way to counter his singing.

He rode Swallowtail deeper into the forest. They came to a towering rock outcropping, and he slowed the horse to climb the narrow trail that led around and up the rock to the top.

The space was flat and larger than he would have guessed. He saw only the tips of trees, their limbs hiding the forest floor. He dismounted and strained to hear the tone magician.

They waited for many minutes, Celatu constantly scanning the forest. The birds remained silent except for an occasional tweet. Were they safe or not? Celatu pulled at his sweat-soaked tunic.

"What have we here?"

Celatu spun. The tone musician was a silver-haired man of middle years with a cudgel and a face crisscrossed with scars, a sign of an outcast or outlaw.

"Tell me what treasures you have, and I'll tell you whether they're enough to buy your life."

"I have nothing you'd want."

"You've a horse and a woman. One can never have too many of either."

"You do not want these. The horse is skittish and wild, and the woman is mad."

The thief frowned. "Just the horse, then."

Celatu turned to help the Servant down and grinned despite their predicament. She had found a spare sash and wrapped it around her head, hiding her telltale copper hair.

"Now you two, walk away slowly and I'll let you live."

"Why should I trust the word of a thief?" Celatu fruitlessly scanned the ledge for potential weapons. His chest tightened. How would he protect the Servant?

There! A deep, shadowed crack ran across the ledge. If he could maneuver the thief to its other side....

"You win. The horse is yours." He dropped the reins just out of the thief's reach, pulling the Servant away.

The thief stepped over the crack and bent to pick up the reins.

Celatu sent out a spurt of magic and split the crack open.

The thief staggered and flailed. Just as the rock sheared away, he gained his balance and jumped across the rift. His scars purpling with anger, he started another song, one even more dangerous: It called to Celatu and Violet to jump off the ledge.

Celatu sent his power out, seeking every rootlet that broke the rock's surface, every grain line and crystal, every flaw.

The rock bellowed like a dying buffalo, and he groaned with it, his skin ripping. The rock vibrated beneath his feet. Gasping, he pushed his magic to its greatest extent—and then beyond.

The magician's song cut off abruptly as the rock's surface cracked. The rock crumbled into sand that streamed outward in every direction.

The thief and Swallowtail fell, screaming.

When Celatu woke, the light had changed, and birds sang loudly. Fila was gone, but a trail of bare footprints wound its way down the mound of debris.

Gashes slit him from breastbone to navel. He pressed his tunic against his injuries. His arms and legs were torn as well, and his skull burned. He pushed unsteadily to his feet and staggered after Violet's footprints to the forest floor.

She knelt next to the body of the thief, whose descent had been stopped by an oak's trunk. She knotted a charm, her fingers a blur of motion.

He grabbed her arm. "What are you doing? That man would have stolen our horse and possibly killed us. Heal Swallowtail."

She glared and pulled free. "*Heal people before animals.* Kassia and I learned that rule the first day of our first class in healing charms."

"Hurry then. Have you seen him? Spicebush Swallowtail?" He whistled and called, but the horse that whinnied did not sound like Swallowtail. "Lady? Have you seen him?"

Violet said nothing. The thief's injuries absorbed her totally; her eyes were closed, and her lips mumbled something as she knotted.

He limped around the disintegrated rock, using the larger pieces as props to push off from. The thief's horse whinnied agan when it saw him, but he ignored it, continuing his circuit. A large rock gave under his touch, and he backed up to look at it more carefully.

Swallowtail.

He was twisted and covered in sand and stones and clots of soil, but it was him. Or rather, his body. He had suffered.

Celatu closed his eyes to avoid seeing the broken form.

He and Fila were safe, thanks to his magic, but at the high price of both his principles and Swallowtail. He shuddered with disgust at himself; he had thrilled with pleasure while causing all this destruction.

He undid the saddle, but could not lift the huge horse to pull the saddle completely off. Instead, he unpacked everything he could reach. It took him three trips to lug clothes, blankets, and food to the thief's horse. It was a sorry creature, bony and missing an eye, but it stood placidly as Celatu examined it and its tack. The thief's saddlebags contained a cloth bag of dried beans, a cookpot, a travel-sized Court and Villages game set, and, of all things, a shiny copper skillet. He repacked both sets of equipment in the thief's saddlebags.

Fila still sat next to the thief, slumped. "He's dead."

"Better him than us. The tone magician lived to rob and kill."

"You called him that before. What's a tone musician?"

"Something I learned about in my research. In the years of the early Servants, magic was not cleanly divided into female magic of creation and male magic of destruction. There were other kinds of magic. Breath magic, the ability to slow time by holding one's breath. Clay magic, the ability to create beings of clay so lifelike that a word from their creator gave them breath and heartbeat. Tone magic, the ability to control the will of others by singing."

She shuddered. "So that is why I wanted so badly to go toward the music. And later, to jump off the rock."

"Yes."

He knelt and searched the thief's clothes, pocketing everything of interest except the man's knife.

"Robbing the dead? That's disgusting."

"We can't return these things to their owners; we don't know whom he stole them from. The thief no longer has any use for them."

"*Disgusting* is too good a word for you. Better are *vile* and *repulsive*."

His face grew hot, first with humiliation and then with anger. He kept his gaze low as he emptied the thief's purse and removed his belt, his own blood mingling with the corpse's. Then he sat and caught his breath.

"Practical."

"Excuse me?" she said, looking at him instead of the thief for the first time. Her eyes widened at his blood-soaked clothes.

"I'm practical. I'll do what it takes to get you to the Seat safely so you can stop Urushi and set things aright. And by the way, Mean Violet, you're welcome."

"For what? Oh, of course! Today's events still have me flustered. Thank you for rescuing me from the tone musician. I would have been lost on my own." She looked at his blood-soaked tunic and then up into his eyes. Softly, she said, "I know what a steep price you paid to save me."

Gruffly, he answered, "I promised to keep you safe."

"You did. Now take off your tunic so I can heal your wounds."

He complied. With businesslike efficiency, she examined the gashes on his arms and chest. She picked up several charms of pink and blue yarn and pressed one against his largest chest wound.

Her touch was gentle, but even so the pain made him gasp. Agony gave way to soothing warmth moving into the wound and spreading in all directions. Then came the part he hated, the terrible itching and the sensation of hundreds of insects crawling on his skin as the wound knit itself.

Fila examined the ridge of pink healed flesh with a critical eye, nodded with apparent satisfaction, and moved the charm to his next chest wound. He closed his eyes and focused on naming all the Servants in order, over and over. It seemed hours later when she announced, "Your chest is done," but when he opened his eyes, the sun had barely moved.

He started to put his tunic on, but she shook her head. "Arms next."

"They're scratches," Celatu protested.

"Yes, if scratches were the length of a hand and the width of a finger. You worked powerful magic."

"It was worth the pain to save you."

She blushed. "You need to be whole and strong in case we encounter the assassins. Give me your arm."

"You have to admit now not everyone on the road is a friend."

"And you have to admit not everyone is an enemy. The Toilers gave us information and fed us even though we were strangers."

"I'm too exhausted to argue. What if we agree we both are right and you take the thief's knife? You need to be able to protect yourself with more than magic."

She hesitated. "I'm no better than you are," she muttered as she took the knife from his hand and slid it between the folds of her needlework kit.

She could never be as bad as I am. She was a woman and could not be tempted by the heady power of destruction. Even at the height of his pain, he had gloried in his ability to reduce the huge rock outcropping to sand and send the man who had threatened the Servant flying.

It was the ultimate in sensation. He still tingled with delight even as he loathed himself. It had been better than anything he'd known, even books.

Fila dug around in her needlework bag and pulled out her flint and its striker.

Tul looked astonished. "Women can make fire on their own?"

She shrugged. "Of course. Sometimes a wound needs to be cauterized, and there's not always a man around when you need one. Do you have an idea how we can carry water and cook those beans?"

She clapped with delight when he took the cookpot out of the thief's saddlebags.

He fetched the water; she started the fire and hunted for herbs to add to the pot; the completed meal was tasty and filling, although she yearned for bread or some roasted corn. Anything to offset the monotony of a meal of nothing but beans.

Tul said nothing. He brooded as he ate, scooping beans into his mouth, chewing, and swallowing in a steady rhythm.

"Is something wrong?"

He spoke to the ground. "I broke my vow."

"To save me. It was my fault. Are you angry with me?"

He continued as if he had not heard her. "I've always despised men who took delight in hurting and killing with their magic. Now I am one."

"No! How can you class yourself with them? You did not enjoy—"

"I loved it, every moment, even as my skin ripped. I'm disgusted. You must be too."

Shock rang through her like a peal of bells. She twisted the point of her knife in the dirt. Since the attack in the forest, good and evil had become difficult to tell apart.

She had been both astonished and horrified by Celatu's power and what he did with it. The Land had broken its silence and reached into her, soothed her, told her he did what was right. She did not understand how.

"Good isn't what I always thought it was," she said. "All my life, I thought men were evil because they destroyed things. But if the Land gave men the magic of destruction, It must have meant for you to use it."

"I could have stopped him without magic if he hadn't been a tone magician. I should have at least tried."

"And your Servant might have died." Fila ran her hands through her hair, most of which had fallen free of its braids. "Since becoming Servant, so many things I thought right and true are proving to have wavy edges. That day you came to my rescue, I made roots grow to stop the assassins. I thought it was right to protect myself. But in doing so, I hurt some men. I caused them to die.

"Perhaps that's why the Land rarely helps me. Perhaps that is why I am going mad."

"We don't know that you are going mad."

"We do not yet know that I am not."

He returned to his brooding.

For the first time, Fila understood what an ordeal it was to be a man. Men could not bring forth babies, and they could not make plants grow or wounds heal. They could only impair, maim, break, wreck, rend, erode, spoil, ravage, destroy.

And in doing so, they impaired, maimed, and destroyed their own bodies and sometimes their souls.

Tul's soul suffered. It showed in the squint of his eyes, his hunched shoulders, his slumped back, and the motion of the copper coin he turned over and over between his fingers.

She pulled out the elaborate charm Boraga had given her and studied it. She did not understand most of its patterns, but she did recognize some meant for healing. *Perhaps it will help him.* She reached over and placed the charm over Tul's heart. Power moved along her arm and out through her palm and fingers.

He raised his head, his expression curious, then he put his hand over hers. It was large, warm, and uncalloused except for the end joint of the middle finger. She shivered at his touch and scooted closer. As the charm drew her magic into him, the signs of his sadness gradually faded.

When Tul looked his usual jaunty self again, she sat back with a deep, satisfied sigh of fulfillment. She tucked Boraga's charm carefully away.

"Thank you, Lady. I did not know that healing a wounded soul was even possible."

"Neither did I. But it was my duty to try."

"Praise the Land for your dedication to duty." He got up and took a box out of one of the thief's saddlebags. "Care for a game of Courts and Villages?"

She shook her head. "I have never enjoyed games. I will heal your other eye now."

"My eye can wait. Why don't you like games?"

"They are frivolous and without purpose. I would rather do something useful." *Such as heal his eye. Why does he keep putting me off?*

"There's more to life than duty. Joy is essential to a life worth living."

"Doing my duty makes me happy."

"Then you'll be happy to know playing Courts and Villages will help you do your duty better."

She crossed her arms. "I truly doubt that."

"Please, Lady, play a game with me. I need a distraction." Tul brushed away the leaves, twigs, and stones from the space between them and emptied the pieces from the box onto the smooth space. The box folded outward to make a playing surface. He separated the tokens into groups. "This copper disk is the Servant, and the silver disk is the Consort. You can be Servant this time around, and I'll be Consort." He put the Servant and Consort disks in the centermost oval on Fila's side of the board.

"Courts and Villages is about loyalty, alliances, betrayal, proper and improper use of one's allies, and the duties and responsibilities of Guardians and Toilers." He made the first move, sliding a brass counselor token into the green box of jealousy. "If you can't win at Courts and Villages, how will you ever understand and control your unruly counselors? How will you fairly judge the problems and grievances the Guardians and Toilers bring to your court?"

The problems Mother had dealt with were delicate, complicated, and multifaceted. Sometimes they took months to resolve. Courts and Villages, with its simple moves and simple tokens, was no reflection of the Servant's life.

But Tul had saved her life. If she could help him by distracting him, it was her duty to do so.

She made a move. The game was on.

She lost miserably. Her most trusted ally turned out to be the leader of the coalition against her, and she rebuffed the help of her most powerful councilor, who was loyal. They played a few more rounds, with the same result. Tul played the way he lived, trusting no one. His strategy was the stronger.

She bit her lip. She had wanted to impress him in Courts and Villages. Instead, she had made a fool of herself with her naïve moves and misplaced trust.

"Do you see now why you need me as your Consort?" he crowed.

"Being Goodborn is not a genetic defect. If you consider it so, why do want to marry me?" she replied tartly. "Do you so crave the power of a Consort?"

He recoiled. "Not at all. I care naught for politics and will be ecstatic to return to my books once you have restored order and balance. But I do not want to spend the rest of my life hiding from icedragons. I'd become Consort and help you defeat Urushi for that reason alone."

Her mouth dropped open. "If you were Consort, you would neglect your duties? That's shameful."

"The Consort's main duties require him to use magic. Breaking my vow yesterday makes me even more determined to keep it in the future. I'll never use magic again."

"I admire your principles, but they rule you out as a potential Consort."

"Rule me out? You would not consider me under any circumstances?"

"When Toilers fight, that's when I'll marry you."

Fila stands in a forest at twilight. She knows for a certainty she is not alone, but each time she turns, she sees no one. Fear creeps through her, turning her limbs to lead.

"Where are you? Come out where I can see you."

The air shimmers, sparkling with speckles of light so bright they dazzle her eyes and speckles of dark so ebon they swallow the light near them. Light and dark coalesce into an ill-defined figure whose edges blur against the tenebrous forest. The slim, dark figure wears the sleeveless shift and dozens of long beaded braids fashionable among women a millennium ago, in the days of the first Servant. It moves like a mink—sinuous, slinky, slithery, and utterly inhuman except for her eyes.

Fila can hardly bear to look at those eyes. They hold the sorrows of ages.

It coils around the trunk of a large oak tree with a double knothole, its head weaving. As it drifts, the switchgrass and dead leaves beneath its feet smoke and wither.

"Who are you?" Fila asks.

"Shadow." It drifts closer. Its features sharpen and become vaguely familiar. It wraps itself around Fila as it had around the tree. "Don't you want to know whose shadow?" it whispers. Its breath chills her skin.

"No," she whispers back.

"I'm the Servant's shadow," it hisses. It doesn't move, yet it now stands a few steps away. Its face mirrors Fila's own. "Your shadow." The face lengthens and the nose narrows. "Your mother's shadow." The jaw thickens, and a moustache sprouts. "Your great-grandfather's shadow." The face changes faster and faster

until the features dissolve into a flicker. "The shadow of every Servant since the first, a thousand years ago."

"What do you want?" Her heartbeat is as loud as her voice.

"The question is, what do you want? I've been helping your brother. But I like you more." Its tongue flicks out. "So much more. I want to merge with you." The creature weaves itself around Fila again.

She tries to run, tries to push it away, but her limbs are mired in molasses.

"Remember how good you felt when you tripped and entangled those men who wanted to kill you? That was my doing, you know."

"No! It was Boraga's charm."

"My doing," the creature says. "I can give you so much more. Everything you lack. Ambition and the power to fulfill that ambition. The ruthlessness to do what needs to be done. The Servant can become the Mistress and rule the Land and Its two peoples. Anything you want, you can have. I would complement you well, you see."

"The Servant already has a complement. The Consort."

"You won't need a Consort. There will be no more female magic or male magic. You will have the powers and pleasures of both—without the price of either."

"Why change the way things work now?"

Shadow solidifies more. She is almost human. "Imagine all the good you could do." Her voice, oh, her voice! Soft, soothing, seductive. Sweet as honey— and as sticky.

Fila leans toward her. Shadow holds out her hand; images dance on the palm. Toilers play games in the shade as fields plow themselves. A woman gives birth with screams of laughter instead of pain. Machines cook food and heat homes. "You are already powerful. Join with me, and your power shall grow beyond any ever known. Your dreams"—she nods at the images in her palm—"will become real."

Possibilities flood Fila's mind. She could turn the Land into a paradise. Everyone would be happy. She would be the greatest Servant ever. She would be remembered as the greatest Servant ever.

She blinks her eyes. How quickly her thoughts turn from selfless to selfish. Wary now, she says nothing.

Shadow shrinks into a mink, glossy and sleek and sparkling with dew. She circles Fila once more. "I'll return. Mayhap once you see what I do for Urushi, you'll accept my offer."

Fila woke with a start, drenched in sweat.

Tul jumped and knocked the mug of tea warming on a rock into the fire. The splattering tea made a mink-like hiss, and Fila cried out.

"It's all right. You were dreaming."

"It was so real." She sat up and looked around the clearing. The moon was full, and the campfire added its own light. Then she saw it—the oak with the double knothole. "There! We were right there, by that oak."

"'We'?"

She told him about her dream. He listened with a frown of concentration. "I never left the clearing after you fell asleep. You slept soundly until now."

"I've never had a dream so real."

His frown deepened. "I wonder whether Urushi has more creatures of magic at his command than just icedragons and firehounds."

She pushed the blanket off and got up. "I must look at that tree."

"I'll come with you. Perhaps I dozed off without realizing it." He found a thick branch and lit it in the fire. They walked together, slowly, toward the oak.

It was identical to the one in her dream. She stood staring at the double knothole as Tul wandered among the trees nearby, kicking the undergrowth and looking up into their canopies with his torch held high.

"No one here but us. I see no mink or any other creature. Lady, I think perhaps you noticed this tree earlier, and your nightmare incorporated it."

"I hope so. Thank you for looking for the creature." She took a few steps toward their campfire.

"Lady—" His voice came out strangled.

She whipped around.

He pointed to the ground by the oak where she had been standing.

"Oh my." Her voice trembled as she looked at the spot. Where Shadow had stood in her dream, the plants were seared to brown crisps.

Chapter 24

SWEAT RAN DOWN Celatu's back. Here was magic he did not recognize, dangerous magic. "Lady, I need to think. Come with me. I don't want to leave you alone."

She put up no argument, though her eyes were half-shut with drowsiness. *The dream really frightened her too. How can I protect her from monsters in her dreams?* He walked quickly, as fast as the torch glow allowed, reviewing everything he had learned over the years about Servants, Consorts, magic, and pre-Servant times.

After an hour of walking in large circles around the camp, he could no longer bring new facts to mind, so he made one final circuit to search his mind for every song, poem, popular saying, legend, and literary work that featured a mink or a shadow. There weren't many. None seemed relevant to the Servant's dream, except perhaps one phrase:

> *… can the shadow withstand …*

Shadow had tempted Fila, offering her some of the flaws the Goodborn lacked. If the phrase were actually *can the Shadow withstand,* it might provide a clue to Violet's dream.

He played with the line; if he reconstructed it properly, he would know it, he was sure.

> *Guardians can the Shadow withstand …*
> *Goodborn can the Shadow withstand …*
> *The Violet can the Shadow withstand …*
> *The Servant can the Shadow withstand …*

Yes! That's it! The *Servant* can the Shadow withstand.

Like gears in a Toiler machine, various facts meshed and separated in his mind, only to mesh with other facts in new combinations. An idea glimmered and shimmered, tantalizing in its wholeness and cohesion. Of course, ideas sometimes made sense in the mind, only to fall apart when analyzed on paper. But he had no paper.

Violet yawned widely and mumbled, "I am so glad I can get some sleep now."

He couldn't let her sleep, not until they had talked out his idea. "Did you study any ancient history during your training? Any myths or legends?"

Yawning again, she encased herself in a blanket and sank to the ground, leaning on her elbow. "Not yet. That's part of the training I lack. We spent our time on becoming skilled in the practical techniques of magic—embroidery, knitting, needlepoint, crochet, knotting, beading, weaving. We learned to spin wool into yarn and to make dyes. We tromped around every kind of ecosystem to learn to recognize different plants in different seasons and to help us remember where they grew. Most of our books were on botany or patterns and colors and their meanings."

"So you know nothing about the first Servant?"

"Mother told me the good Dimidiata abolished the old system of royalty and reordered society so Guardians and Toilers had complementary roles. What does she have to do with my dream?"

"The good Dimidiata and her siblings were the first people with magic. It just appeared in them, the way sometimes a white ewe bears black lambs, and Dimidiata had wits enough to work out its rules and limitations. She and her brother, her future Consort, unseated the last king through violence and intrigue and magic. People called her the Berserker."

Violet's eyes widened, sparkling with interest. "The good Dimidiata was called the *Berserker*?"

He nodded. "Once she had secured the kingdom for her own, everyone expected her to declare herself queen and to execute those who had supported the former king. She astounded them all by setting up a just system of government, naming herself Servant, and devoting her life to acts of generosity and self-sacrifice. She wasn't born a Goodborn, but she apparently became one."

Violet pushed herself up and sat cross-legged. Her eyes were wide awake now. "I have changed similarly, but in the opposite direction. How did the war-loving Berserker become the good Dimidiata?"

"The old books in our library have many theories. But listen to this: One scholar claimed she made a pact with the Land to give up some of her personality, the part that sought power, felt envy, and killed without mercy. I always thought this theory the stupidest of the explanations for the metamorphosis. But now you are offered some of these traits. What if the creature you met in your dream is real? What if she is the collection of flaws Dimidiata cast off?"

"The good Dimidiata made a fine bargain with the Land. She gave up only flaws."

Celatu snorted. The Servant really needed him as her Consort, whether she realized it or not. "The Berserker gave up the traits that made her strong, those that let her make hard choices and do what was necessary despite the cost. We may have discovered what makes the Goodborn good."

"What do you mean? Are you going to argue again that we are defective?"

"The Goodborn aren't defective. They're divided. *Divided!*"

He laughed and danced around the fire, twirling, reaching for the Servant's hand each time he passed her.

She refused to join his dance. "You need sleep. You are out of your wits with fatigue."

He knelt next to her, trembling with the excitement of discovery. "Before I fled the Seat, I had come across a puzzle in my research: Why do the manuscripts in the century after the first Servant refer to her sometimes in the plural? Now I can guess: She existed in two parts, Dimidiata and Shadow! She sacrificed half of herself and of every other Servant to become what we now call *Goodborn.*"

"So?"

"Don't you see? Shadow is *your* other half, too. That's why the Servant needs a Consort—for balance. To make up for what is lacking."

She shook her head so hard a pin flew from her hair. "I am not a puzzle to be solved. Neither am I a sport of nature, like a … two-headed frog."

"That's exactly what you are. Tell me, Lady: Before the assassin attack, when did you last do an unkind act? When did you last put your desires before your duties? When were you last angry?"

"Never!" she snapped without even thinking.

"If I'm right, you didn't even have the ability to do such things! Now you do. What happened during the attack to change you?"

Her forehead wrinkled, and she stared at the ground for a long time before shaking her head. "I do not know. So much happened so fast."

"You told me she said *I can give you so much more.* Not *so much,* but *so much more,* as if she had already given you something."

He watched her face as she thought through his words. He stayed quiet, wanting her to come to her own conclusions, hoping that they confirmed his own.

Her mouth formed an *O* of surprise, and she leapt up. "Do you not remember? The mink bit me. I am not mad; Shadow gave me part of herself then. Now she wants me to take back all of her evil! No wonder the Land hates me."

Before he realized her intentions, she dashed into the forest and out of sight.

<h1 style="text-align:center">Chapter 25</h1>

Tul's footsteps followed her into the forest, but Fila could not stop, not yet. Her body wanted escape; her mind no longer had a say in what it did. *If I run fast enough and long enough, I can put it all behind me: Tul's logic, Shadow, the mink. Surely what I feel inside me counts for something. Doesn't it? Doesn't it?* Her skin confined her like a too-tight bodice and she wanted to tear it off. She clawed at her skin; she dodged the soft layers of dead leaves and chose the stoniest ways instead, letting the rocks rip the skin from her feet.

Tul shouted for her to slow down, to let him catch up.

She shook her head and ran faster, not caring that she careered into trees. She had to get away and be alone.

A stream burbled nearby; she turned toward the sound. Its voice promised so much: Solitude. Forgetfulness. Release. *Lovely water, keeping singing! I am following your voice.* Closer, closer, closer, and then she was at the bank and she kept running and she flew over the stream and glided down like a great egret.

The water hit her like a wall of stone.

Coldness stunned her, tearing away all fear and every thought, stripping her of all but an animal's sense of existing. She bent her knees and sank to the bottom, a murky place where earth and water were not opposites but combined into mud, which hid her from everything and hid everything from her. She squished mud between her fingers, rejoicing in the act's lack of meaning and lack of consequences.

She scooped mud up and plastered it on her copper hair. For a moment, she could be just Fila again, bouncing on the bottom of the stream and letting the undercurrents roil and rush by without her.

Strong arms embraced her and thrust her up into the air. "Pus and blood! Lady, are you all right?"

She threw her head back and gulped air she had forgotten she needed.

"Look at you! So muddy, my poor Lady." He lowered her and held her with one arm above the stream and scooped water over her head over and over. "Are you all right?" he asked tenderly.

"Yes. I am fine now. I just needed a brief escape from my dreadful life."

He carried her to the bank and set her down. "You truly scared me. I thought, I thought...."

"Can we go back to camp? I need to sit by the fire."

"Of course." He picked her up again and ran a straight route back, leaping over logs, not complaining that she dripped cold water on him. He set her down by the fire.

She leaned close to the flames and rubbed her arms, speaking before he could. "Your reasoning made so much sense I believed it. But I am sensible now. I know I'm not a half-person. I am as complete as anyone."

He was silent for a long time. Then: "Are you certain? Rejecting my hypothesis also means rejecting Shadow as the cause of your behavior."

"Yes, I'm certain." She tried to forestall his next argument. "Even though I'm Goodborn, I *choose* to do the right thing, *choose* to put others first, *choose* to do my duty, as my parents taught me." *I do choose, do I not?* The Land beneath her, as usual, offered no answers.

Tul pressed his lips together and shook his head but did not argue. "Why did you run off?"

"You were cruel to tell me your theory so baldly. You dropped it on me all at once, like a passenger pigeon overhead opening its bowels."

"There's nothing upsetting in my hypothesis."

She stumbled as she tried to put her thoughts into words. "If I do not choose my own actions, if I am ... broken ... defective, like Urushi ... if I choose good only because I can do naught else, my choices are meaningless."

"I don't follow."

"I would be no better than one of the machines the Toilers build, a mechanical device that does only what it was designed to do."

"Please forgive me. I was so excited to have a possible solution to such an important historical puzzle I didn't consider you might find it dismaying."

"Not dismaying. Life crushing. If I were an automaton, I could only do the *good* thing, not the *right* thing. I could not kill Urushi. It would be evil, doubly so because he is my brother. But what if it is the *right* action to take to restore harmony to the Land?"

"Your Consort could—"

"Please let me finish. If I were half a person, and Shadow were my missing half, what would we be together? Not Fila or Violet. We'd be someone new, someone capable of enough evil to merit the name Berserker. No, I will not believe you. I would rather be mad."

* * *

Celatu watched the Servant sleep, bemused, fighting the urge to peel back the blanket and stroke her head. Her resilience was remarkable. Life had served her one bad surprise after another in the past few days. Though the burdens she bore grew heavier and heavier, she kept fighting to stay upright. Could he have done as well?

No, he had to admit. Though she was young, she had a mature woman's strength of personality. And an adult woman's body, he thought, admiring the drape of the blanket over the curve of her hip.

He should sleep too. He put the Servant's nearness out of his mind, but something else niggled at him, something important, something that would not show its face but had been tickling his mind since the Servant told him her dream.

Too tired to take a walk to think, he poked the fire with a stick and released his mind to drift as he watched the sparks leap about. It was a technique he had used in his research, letting his mind play with words and concepts as he watched. He was a spectator to his own thoughts. After a time, like grouped with like and cause with effect. Wholes grew from random parts.

The Shadow had sparkled, so he meditated on things that jumped and swirled and popped like sparks, then moved on to things that were the colors of sparks. Violet's hair. Her blushing cheeks. Blood. His wounded eye. Fall leaves. Bricks. Male house finches. Male orchard orioles. Male cardinals. Male summer tanagers. Red foxes. Red trillium and many other flowers. Many fruits too. Common serviceberries. The fruits of smooth sumac. Persimmons. Red raspberries. Red mulberries. Strawberries.

Strawberries!

He had received a rare invitation to a party from Urushi. Two years ago? Three? He remembered the attraction, though: fresh strawberries out of season. One of Urushi's friends had a talented gardener, and through a combination of Guardian magic and Toiler mechanical ingenuity, they had made a field of strawberry plants flower and set fruit despite the snow.

When he reached the Servant's House, Urushi and his friends were lounging on cushions around rock-crystal bowls piled high with plump strawberries the color of garnets.

His mouth watered at the sight. Urushi, his lips stained red, moved over to make room for him and gestured at the bowl.

Celatu took a strawberry, popped it in his mouth, and knew why no one spoke: The berries balanced tart and sweet, firmness and yielding, scarlet flesh and black seeds, in perfect harmony.

Only after the men had devoured every berry did conversation begin. The stranger sitting next to Celatu turned to him. "What do you think of the new statue of Servant Hyacinth in the Garden of Stone? Myself, I think the nose is too big."

Celatu had to admit he had not seen it.

Another stranger broke in. "Celatu the Coward doesn't get out much. He spends all day hiding in his family library doing nothing."

The words stung. "I don't laze about. I study. I know the history of all of your families, the stories of the greatest Servants, and the tales and legends the ammas and appas tell younglings." He should have stopped there, but he had to brag. "I am the only man in this room who knows how the first Servant, the good Dimidiata, defeated the great king."

Urushi twisted toward him, his unflecked eyes intent. "I've always wondered how such a gentle woman defeated a great army and a ruthless king."

"She wasn't gentle before she was Servant. In fact, her nickname was the Berserker." He had the attention of every man in the room. Celatu regaled them with old legends and various scholars' theories about why and how Dimidiata changed, including the one about Dimidiata's bargain with the Land to give up her dark half.

"Legends often have a kernel of fact," Urushi mused. "I wonder, if the good Dimidiata did throw away half of herself, what happened to it?"

It seemed an innocuous question. But now, staring at the fire, Celatu suspected Urushi had set out to find the answer. The library in the House of the Servant was the best in the Land and doubled as the official library of the government. If more information on Shadow existed, Urushi had access to it.

What if Urushi had found that information and summoned Shadow to ask for her help? This whole horror might be Celatu's fault: the deaths of Hyacinth and her Consort, the deaths of those who refused to side with Urushi, the death of Violet's amma. All his fault. He, the man who was so embarrassingly sensitive he could not bear to see any innocent, helpless thing suffer.

He stared at the fire again until mesmerized by bright flames against dark night, with smoke the buffer zone between. Shadow had told the Servant she was helping Urushi, but Urushi would not be the first choice of a liminal being in this liminal time. Urushi's soul tilted in the wrong direction: too much shadow and too little light.

Shadow's true complement would be her opposite, someone who was only good.

Violet.

Perhaps Violet *should* consider merging with Shadow. In one stroke she could weaken Urushi and strengthen herself.

He looked at the Servant's cocooned form and frowned. Violet was terrified of regaining her lost half. But what if she did merge with Shadow, if all that evil poured into her? The darkness might overwhelm her light. She could lose her empathy, her ability to see the best in others, her captivating combination of arrogance and unpretentiousness. She would be a stranger.

Worse, as Servant, she would be the worst thing ever to happen to the Land.

Perhaps Shadow would accept a union with him instead if he were Consort. He too was shadow, smoke, liminal, a being in-between: a Guardian who didn't use magic, a Guardian who didn't take care of his Toilers. He would have a better chance of keeping her under control than Fila, who had only a few day's experience of suppressing hate, envy, and a lust for destruction.

He rubbed the spot between his eyebrows. Whom was he kidding? Shadow might be mist and vapor now. But she had been the fiery spirit of a frenzied warrior and could be again, once ensconced in a human body. Neither he nor the Servant could control her. Rather, they needed to keep her away from Urushi.

By the Land, what a predicament they were in. He longed to be back in the library again, savoring the smell of leather, paper, and ink, no worries in the world.

When he sided with the new Servant, he had assumed she could restore order to Veridia and he could go home to his books again. Then the Land abandoned the Servant, and Shadow emerged from the depths of legend to help Urushi and tempt Violet. The odds tilted greatly in Urushi's favor.

Four days ago, presented with this situation, he would have given up this fool's quest and hidden out in a distant Toiler village to ride out the storm in safety. Urushi would eventually forget about him, and he could slip back home.

He looked at Violet's sleeping form, and waves of emotion rolled through him. Affection. A sense of duty. An overwhelming desire to protect her. Logic said it was time to leave, but he could never abandon her. She meant too much to him.

Chapter 26

MORNING SUNLIGHT streamed into the bedroom in the Servant's House, warming Urushi and relaxing some of his tight, injured muscles. He kept his eyes closed, the better to think. Events were not going as planned, and the improved weather was ambiguous. He hoped it meant the Land had forgiven him.

Toenails scratched against the wooden floor, then Wiggle landed on the bed. The dog planted sloppy kisses on his nose and forehead and snuffled in his ear. Despite his pain, he laughed to see Wiggle's delight when he opened his eyes. Quivering, the little retriever rolled on his back and kicked his freckled feet. He tickled the dog's belly. The tightly crocheted hooded sweater that protected Wiggle from Urushi's rogue magic surely must dull the pleasure, but he couldn't tell it from the dog's kicks and moans of ecstasy.

He scooped the dog up with one hand and limped over to the looking glass. He turned his head this way and that, searching for new silver hairs, slumping when he found none. His extra practice sessions in magic were not having any effect, and that witch Shadow had not yet merged with him, despite his pleas and her whispered promises.

She had vowed to give him control over his magic and everything and everyone else, but each time he asked when, she would say only, "Be patient."

He tired of patience. He tired of seeing fear in people's eyes instead of respect. He tired of using his temper, instead of reason or logic, to persuade people to do what he wanted.

The heavy rosewood door creaked opened, and Hooting Owl came in. "You look in better spirits today, child. May I bring you your breakfast and set out your clothes?"

"Yes, thank you, Appa." He only called Hooting Owl "Appa" in private. Officially, Hooting Owl was now his valet. When Appa volunteered to stay on even though Urushi was grown, he had jumped at his offer. The fewer people who knew about the magic-distorted body Urushi kept hidden beneath his loose clothes, the better.

Hooting Owl scratched Wiggle's head, and the dog flailed about in delight. "My sister has sent you a gift." The Toiler hesitated. "I'm not sure you will approve."

Urushi raised his eyebrows. He usually received presents only from Guardians who wanted either to appease him or to win his influence. Hooting Owl's sister lived in one of the villages under Urushi's guardianship. If she wanted something, all she had to do was ask. "What is it?" he asked, his curiosity piqued.

Hooting Owl pulled a blue-glazed ceramic crock sealed with red wax from his pocket. "It's a cream to put on your hair. Several females in the village have been working on it for months. It can turn a Toiler's hair silver. They send it with their best wishes it can do the same for a Guardian." Hooting Owl set the jar on the walnut shelf under the looking glass. He went to the bed and began rolling the lumps from the mattress.

Urushi stared at the jar with a mixture of longing and loathing. If it worked, his hair would no longer trumpet his defect.

Anger and resentment boiled red before his eyes, and he set Wiggle down. How dare the Toilers pity him? As magic built, he clenched his fists and fought it. *They are being kind. Kind. They are being kind.* More than kind: There had been no drop in the village's productivity. The women must have worked on the cream on their own time. *They are being kind. Kind.* As the pressure in his skull lessened and his magic retreated, he relaxed.

Wiggle whined, and Urushi leaned over and scratched his belly. "Please give your sister and her friends my thanks."

"As you wish." Hooting Owl went to the wardrobe, pulled some clothes off the hooks, and draped them over the now-flat bed. "I'll bring your breakfast now."

Hooting Owl stayed away for a long time. When he came back, he carried no breakfast but Wiggle's, which he set on the dog's embroidered mat of burgundy satin. "A Guardian has arrived. He refuses to give his name and insists on seeing you."

"Put him in the drawing room—no, have him await me in my garden." No sense taking chances with the furniture if the news was bad. "Tell him I'll join him shortly."

Urushi dressed as quickly as his limited range of motion allowed. He pulled a long scarf embroidered with healing symbols from a hook on the wall. Nearly all the magic had drained out; he had used the scarf to cover his shame too many times to count. He wrapped it around his face until only his eyes showed.

He peered closer in the looking glass; the tendrils of white scars in the blue irises had grown in the past week, he was sure of it. Blindness would follow, his head nurse had warned, if he did not learn to control his magic.

He gave Wiggle a final pat as the dog wolfed down his stewed rabbit, and he hurried down the stairs to his garden, which he had designed himself. It lay far from the house, and the beds were planted with soft-leaved, soft-stemmed plants. Instead of benches, there were chair-height mounds planted heavily with gaura. He could bring Wiggle here with no fear of his coming to harm from flying debris.

In the garden, Nelumbo, one of the assassins he had hired, stood awkwardly, twisting his hood between his hands as he gulped air. He must have ridden all night.

"What news?" Urushi asked.

The assassin swallowed visibly. "In most ways, your highness, the raid went well. We killed Fila's guards quickly. Sixteen fewer Guardians now oppose you. We have your Cousin Kassia, and she is safe and well."

"Excellent! Did the Land choose Kassia as the new Servant once my sister … once the deed was done?"

The man scuffed the toe of his boot in the dirt. "Your sister escaped."

So the sunny weather did not mean the Land celebrated Kassia as Servant. His world went red, and he bit his lip so hard blood flowed. He swung his fist blindly and connected with bone. It cracked; the man fell. "You killed sixteen armed Guardians, but you couldn't catch one small barefooted woman? What kind of fools are you?"

"Her magic … very strong," the man mumbled as he struggled to his feet.

"Of course her magic is strong. She's the Servant!"

"Unheard-of strong." Nelumbo touched his reddened jaw and winced. "She did things Servant Hyacinth never could have, and then she disappeared." The man was shaking now.

I will be calm. I will be calm. "Treat her Toiler amma with care. She's a lure to catch Fila."

"The old Toiler is dead."

Urushi's skin tingled as the pressure of his magic grew. "You killed Spotted Turtle? She was a hundred years old and harmless." Urushi shuddered as magic shot unbidden from his left arm.

Nelumbo spun as if to run. It was too late. Magic streamed from Urushi from every orifice and pore, crackling, spitting sparks, and stinking the air with sourness. His skin blistered and split open in dozens of places, and inside, deep in his chest, he felt tissue tear. His breathing roughened and shortened as he struggled to draw air in and push it back out again.

Urushi closed his eyes and collapsed.

When Urushi regained consciousness, Hooting Owl hovered over him. Urushi looked around. He lay in the gaura in the courtyard, with only four of his nurses nearby making charms. Not so bad, then, if the rest weren't here.

He gingerly lifted his head. Dozens of crocheted charms lay on his shirt and pants—he did not allow even the healers to see his bare skin—and only a few external wounds remained to be treated. The nausea and fatigue would take longer to go away, he knew from long experience, and the wounds inside would heal slower than those outside, if they healed at all. He'd have new scars and bumps and be even more bent and grotesque.

He was too angry to care. Fila was alive.

Pus and blood! He had cried for two hours before he ordered her death the first time. Now he had to do it again.

I must be a stone. Fila has to die for my destiny to be fulfilled.

"Did the messenger survive?" he asked Hooting Owl.

"Aye, and he'll recover."

"Bring him."

"The women aren't done treating his injuries. He has several broken bones and possibly internal bleeding."

He raised an eyebrow. "So?"

Hooting Owl frowned but said nothing. He nodded and left.

Urushi sent his nurses away next. The charms would do their work with or without their presence, and he preferred without. He lay on the mound, the warmth and an irritating tingling coursing through his body as the charms knitted together tissue and bone.

Several minutes passed before Hooting Owl returned, cradling Nelumbo in his arms like a baby. The Toiler laid the oddly bent man near Urushi.

"You realize you botched this mission?"

The assassin nodded. No fear showed in his unfocused, silver-laced eyes, only resignation.

"Would you like a chance to redeem yourself, perhaps earn yourself a place on my council?"

The man blinked; his gaze focused. "Yes, your highness. What shall I do?"

"Ride back to the others and tell them to stop searching for Fila. I want them and Kassia here as soon as possible."

"It shall be done."

"You are to take two firehounds and find Fila."

"Me?" The man paled. "I know nothing about dogs, let alone magic ones."

"I'll tell them their target. You need only follow on horseback, watch the firehounds do their job, and bring back proof she's dead."

Chapter 27

CELATU ROSE before the Servant and searched the forest for food. As a boy, he had often spent long days and even nights in the forest alone and had never suffered from hunger. He smiled, remembering his discovery of a patch of peat densely packed with grubs. They had tasted like a cross between pine nuts and elk bone marrow, so delicious he saved six, wrapped in his handkerchief, to take home for his parents and sister. He gave them to Cook and asked her to serve them at dinner on pretty plates.

Kassia screamed; Father looked disappointed and resigned; Mother pursed her lips and ordered him to the library until the next morning. The only person happy was Cook, who got to eat the grubs.

I miss those days in the woods dreadfully, but I didn't realize it until now. He would rather be in his library than on the run from an icedragon, of course. But he was enjoying his morning wander, the smell of the mast as it crushed under his feet; the tapping and rapping of woodpeckers and sapsuckers also searching for breakfast; the final rhythmic, cheerful calls of whip-poor-wills before they slept; the fresh, mossy scent when he neared the stream.

He had trouble remembering which insects and plants were edible, and he now had two adults to feed, one very large. He surprised himself and the Servant by bringing the cooking pot back to camp full of flowers, herbs, early fruits, still-flopping minnows, and a hunk of rotting wood with a partial colony of sleeping carpenter ants and larvae.

His buoyant mood did not last long. As they broke their fast, the Servant picked at her food and maintained a pensive silence. Only when they started packing up did she speak. "What happens when we catch up to the assassins? Do you have a plan for rescuing Kassia?"

"Let's make it up as we go. That worked quite well when I saved you."

"Quite well? That will go down in history as the worst rescue ever," the Servant exclaimed, indignation in her voice and her gesturing hands. "I cannot believe—" She cut off in midsentence when she realized he was joking. She wrinkled her nose at him. "You think you're funny, but you are not."

"You don't have much of a sense of humor. Shadow must have gotten that part."

She looked down her nose at him.

"Seriously, Violet, we have no idea where the assassins are or how many are left. We don't know whether they've stashed Kassia somewhere or whether she's still with them. We don't know how many horses they have or how injured they are from the magic they worked. We don't need *a* plan, we need twenty or thirty plans."

Violet chewed on her thumbnail.

"What are you thinking?"

"We do not have to confront them and fight. If we find them, we can wait until they camp for the night. I know a charm for helping injured people rest. It puts them into a long, deep slumber. We could put a charm on each man, free Kassia, and slip away."

Celatu fingered his lucky coin as he considered her idea. "Quick. Safe. Easy. I like it. But we need to make sure the assassins can't follow us when they wake up."

"We can untie their horses and scatter them. Horses tend to wander off if not tied, as *everyone* knows." Violet laughed, a startling, bell-like sound all the sweeter for being so unexpected.

"You should laugh more often. You have a lovely laugh."

Her face immediately sobered. "I shouldn't laugh at all, with so many people to mourn."

Soon after, they set off down the road at a brisk pace, Celatu holding the reins of the thief's bony horse. The assassins' horses had left plenty of dung on the road; he wished he knew how to tell its age. It did not look like the fresh deposits of either Swallowtail or the thief's horse, so they likely were not on the verge of stumbling upon the assassins unexpectedly, thank the Land.

Despite her shorter legs, the Servant kept up, her hands busy twisting and weaving colored threads and copper hairs together into the sleeping charms. She hummed happily as she lost herself in her work; he stole glances of her more often than he scanned the sky.

"Something sparkling. There." She pointed.

His gaze followed the line of her finger to a spot several feet in front of them.

He went to it. There were two things, one on top of the other. On top, a thingamabob of gold and white stones. He rubbed his sweating hands on his pants. His sister had many sparkling ornaments, but he wouldn't recognize even the ones he had given her, let alone the others.

On the bottom was a small, square Toiler device.

He looked around, noting a pile of duck bones by the roadside and a line of dung that started about ten feet away. The horses had been tied there for a while, perhaps while the assassins had a meal yesterday.

He showed Violet the hair thing first.

"It's Kassia's. She was wearing several hairpins like this the day we left. I remember thinking they were inappropriate for our trip."

"What about this thing? I can't imagine why Kassia would have it, but it was under the hairpin."

As the sky clouded over, so did the Servant's face. She took the Toiler tech from him. "This was Amma's. It was missing when I found her body."

A breeze picked up, unexpectedly cold, and the Servant shivered. "Do you think Kassia dropped them on purpose? For us?"

"As a message, you mean? Perhaps. You know her well. Can you guess what she means?" He wandered toward the side of the road as Violet answered, hoping he could estimate the number of horses and thus the number of assassins.

"It could mean all sorts of things. She may be letting us know she's still alive. That she's still with the assassins. She may be marking a trail to find her. She may be protecting … Do you hear a strange noise?"

He fumbled to open the pouch on his belt so he could store the hairpin there. "Protecting whom? What strange noise?"

"It sounds like wind blowing through trees in a storm, only deeper."

A gust blew Celatu's pouch to the side. The hairpin missed the pouch and landed on the ground. He bent over to pick it up.

An icy wind brushed his skin and his back instantly numbed. An icedragon swooped up, screaming its frustration.

"Run for the trees! It can't get between them!" he shouted. He leapt from his crouch and raced for the forest, not stopping until he was ten feet in. He spun, waving both arms, to ensure the Servant saw where he hid.

She had not followed him to safety. Instead, she struggled by the side of the road, tugging on the horse's bridle with one hand, a bunch of charms clasped awkwardly in her other hand, her needlework kit held under her armpit.

A large, sparkling blue form plummeted from the sky.

"Leave the horse and run!"

Ignoring Tul's shout, Fila tried to coax the thief's horse into motion. It dug in its hooves all the harder, so terrified that the white showed all around its one eye. By the moment, the icedragon's shadow grew bigger.

It was too late to pull out all of the long silver strands of the thief's and Tul's hair caught in the horse's saddle and coat, shining brightly. Pulling harder on the reins, keeping her eyes almost closed, she glanced up. The icedragon's target was clear: It was coming straight toward the horse.

She swiped a sleeping charm held in her cramping fingers across its forehead. If the Land were with her, the horse would relax enough to let her lead it.

Instead, the horse collapsed to the ground, asleep.

Fila jumped to stand over its belly. She braced her legs and held every sleeping charm she had above her head.

The dragon's descent slowed and leveled out, angled slightly downward. Its claws were like swords; its scales glared, making her eyes burn and run with tears.

Her arms trembled. Then her legs. Would the dragon rip her apart to get to the silver hairs on the horse? Blackness tinged the edges of her vision and grew.

I am about to faint.

Something long, sleek, and dark ran across the road, hissing.

Anger roared through her. The blackness swallowing her vision receded. Strength returned to her limbs. She giggled that she had worried about her own safety. Nothing mattered but hurting the icedragon.

Its belly smashed against her fingers and forced her arms down.

She thrust her hands back up, into its belly, mashing the charms against it.

A screech of agony struck her like a whip, ringing painfully in her ears even after the icedragon shied away and tumbled to the ground. The icedragon glared at her balefully, its belly plates split in many places with hair-thin lacerations that began healing within moments.

The charms she had shoved against its belly now lay on the ground, as rigid as if they'd been in a frozen lake all winter. Smoke rose from them. The creature dragged itself away, whimpering.

Fila swallowed several times. *How many people can there be who still support me if such monsters chase them?*

Her Goodborn instinct insinuated a tiny thread of purple into her thoughts, urging her to comfort the icedragon and fix its wounds.

She automatically took a step toward it, then stopped. *This is war. I still do not understand triage or the difference between good and right. But I know I must protect Veridia's children and eliminate Urushi's unnatural creatures of death and destruction.*

She turned to check on the horse. The beast still slumbered. As she leaned over to wake it, a man's arm grabbed her roughly around the waist, capturing one of her arms as well.

Goosebumps puckered her arms. Terror froze her, mind and body. But the fury still raging within conquered it.

"Run! Assassin!" she shouted, hoping Tul would hear her and get away. As she stomped on the assassin's foot, she fumbled in her needlework pouch. Her fingers locked on a knitting needle.

She pulled the needle out and viciously jabbed her assailant's arm.

Chapter 28

A T THE CROWN OF THE CALDERA at the center of the Seat of the Servant, Urushi stood in the Servant's private lookout, surveying the city. He had come alone, without even Wiggle or Hooting Owl for company. Below, dots of flame showed where his firehounds had been at work. He had sent out just as many icedragons; an occasional flash in the sky revealed one hunting.

Yet below, in front of the Servant's House, Guardians gathered illegally, protesting. A few Toilers stood among them. He had not quenched his opposition; somehow, he had encouraged it.

Slow, deliberate footsteps echoed in the stairway behind him, footsteps as weary as his soul. No anger rose in him; perhaps he needed company after all.

"May I join you?" Uncle Bifac asked.

"Please do."

Bifac leaned his elbows on the stone railing, taking deep breaths of the cool air as Wiggle liked to do.

"How did you find me?"

"Your mother came up here when she needed to think. So did our grandfather. Rulers always need a quiet place to consider their actions, and where better than overlooking their city and their citizens?"

"Uncle, I'm not winning the people over. I thought killing a few would cow the rest into supporting me. Instead, more people plot against me, even on my very doorstep. How many more do I need to kill before I can settle down to the business of ruling?"

"You're changing the way things have been done in Veridia for a millennium. Some people will never *approve*. Eventually, they'll *accept*."

"How? I'm tired of killing."

"Then stop. Call back your firehounds and icedragons. They're what I came up here to talk to you about. As you said, they are not working."

I don't know how to call them back. Shadow tells me so little. He leaned on his elbows, mirroring Bifac's position. He did not trust his uncle—or anyone—enough to tell him about Shadow. But Uncle had been Mother's closest councilor, for good reason. "What do you suggest, Uncle?"

"When punishment doesn't work, try reward."

Urushi slammed the stone with his fist. "That's ridiculous!"

"Plan a huge party for your crowning. Spread out your business among as many merchants and entertainers in as many different neighborhoods as possible. Plan events for the little ones and pups. Play up Kassia; having the most beautiful, best-dressed, greatest Talent in Veridia as your wife can only work in your favor. Show Veridia what it gains by having you as king."

"Hmmm." Bifac's idea could well stop the rebellion, but it stuck in his craw to let those who hated him or pitied him to continue doing so. "I want respect. Respect! Not toleration because I entertain younglings and marry well."

Bifac turned to face him. He looked even more unwell than when Urushi saw him last. "Ahh. Respect is hard to earn and easily lost."

"A saying of one of the Servants?"

"Personal experience." He clapped Urushi on the shoulder and headed down the stairs, his tread heavy.

The air sparkled a few feet out from where he stood. Shadow half materialized before him, floating high above the city. "Once you merge with me, you will no longer want that pale imitation of a woman."

He crossed his arms and frowned. "I've loved Kassia since I was a boy. She accepts me as I am. She listens to my ideas. She wants me to be happy: She gave me Wiggle to keep me company while she was at school. What have *you* done for me?"

Hissing, Shadow took the shape of a mink and settled on the ledge. "Our children kill your enemies."

"The result is that the number of my enemies grows."

"We will merge. I will make you a whole man and powerful beyond belief."

"We will merge. We will merge." He imitated her sultry voice. "So you keep promising. But when? Kassia promised to marry me and sealed her promise with the gift of her body, trusting me not to hurt her. But you—you promise and promise and then back away."

Shadow slid off the ledge and became womanlike again, shaping herself much like Kassia. She leaned against him, although she was too insubstantial for him to feel her. "I will give you more than she ever can. You will forget her."

Urushi smiled. "You're jealous! Despite your great powers, you're jealous."

One sparkling shoulder shrugged. "You prefer a weak mortal woman to me."

"Do not worry. I love Kassia and always will, but I need *you* to make my dreams come true. Please, I beg you, merge with me. Now. No more waiting. Together, we will control all you see below, and beyond."

"Soon, my love, soon." Her sparkles fizzled out, leaving him once again frustrated and alone.

"Land take you, Lady! Stop stabbing me!" Ignoring the injured icedragon, Celatu threw the Servant over his shoulder and ran back into the woods. When he set her down, he took two steps back, out of knitting needle range. Veins pulsed in his forehead; he pounded his clenched fists against his head to keep from shaking her. *I could have lost her. Forever.*

"Tul? *You* grabbed me? I thought an assassin had caught me." She beamed at him. "For once, *I* saved *you.*"

Her innocent joy did little to quench the boiling anger that kept him from speaking. In the road, the icedragon staggered to its feet and took off. It would come for him again when it had healed.

Her smile faded. "What is wrong?"

"What madness overtook you to put yourself in such danger?"

Her forehead wrinkled. "Danger? You yourself told me icedragons go after Guardian men."

"That was hearsay! My father passing on part of something Urushi said." His voice choked; his eyes blurred. *Corroded copper! I'm about to cry. In front of her.* He turned and pummeled a tree, pretending he was still furious. By the time he turned back to her, he had himself under control.

Now she was the one distressed. Her dark-honey skin had paled and was beaded with glowing drops of water. Breathing oddly, she held one hand to her forehead and one to her stomach.

Her knees gave way; he caught her and propped her against a tree. He fanned his hand to cool her face.

"It could have killed me. I thought as a woman I was safe." Her breath evened out. "In some ways I am glad I did not know. That gave me the bravery to injure it and keep it from going after you."

"Very sweet sentiments. But Violet, the icedragon can't fly into the forest; not enough space for its wings."

"So I did not save you? Only the horse? Pus and blood!"

The Shadow is acting through her again. He looked toward the road. The thief's horse stood at its edge, nibbling weeds. "We should check the horse for injuries. How did you know the icedragon would attack it?"

Wobbling, she got to her feet and headed toward the road. "I did not know for certain. But your hair was on it; your scent was on it."

"So it hunts, at least in part, by sight or scent. Useful. How did you drive it away?"

"The underside is heavily armored, like the rest of it. But the sleeping charms injured it. Hairline cracks split the scales. They started healing on their own."

"Those charms?"

She nodded.

He checked the sky, then approached the smoking charms slowly. He knelt by a cluster. The copper hairs woven into the charms had oxidized into broken lines of verdigris. On either side, the thread and yarn had blackened. Pus-yellow icedragon ichor had burned holes in the charms and made hollows in the ground below, where the thick fluid bubbled and smoked. Only this close could he smell its rancidness.

"The sleeping charms didn't injure the dragon. Your hair did."

She grabbed a handful of hair and wrenched it from her head. After making three small bundles, she tied one with a ribbon of orange-red the color of fire, one with a ribbon of blue the color of the icedragon, and one with a ribbon of white. "Here. These may protect you."

"Thank you, Lady." He tucked each bundle into a separate place. Then he got a copper trowel from the horse's saddlebags and dug a deep hole along the side of the road. He scooped up the charms with the trowel and dropped them in the hole. He also scooped up the ichor and the dirt around it and dropped it in the hole, then covered everything with dirt and leaves.

He walked back to the Servant and held up the trowel, now oxidized in places and riddled with holes. "The icedragon's blood did this."

Her eyes went wide. "To your eyes and back too, before I met you?"

He nodded. "Are you feeling up to going on? Now the icedragon has found me again, we'll have to travel through the woods."

"I'm going to walk in the road."

"It's not safe. We must stick together."

"It is bad enough I must start anew on the charms. I do not want to have to watch out for roots, gullies, and low branches at the same time."

He reached out, plucked a long silver hair from her shoulder, and held it up.

Her hand flew to her mouth. "Oh my goodness!"

"You will walk with me in the woods."

She sighed. "Yes. It will be safer." Then her eyes twinkled. "But I would be safer yet if you stopped shedding on me!"

By twilight, when crickets courted and owls hooted, Celatu's head hurt from hard concentration. Rarely had he found an established path they could follow east for more than a few minutes before it veered. They stayed close to the forest edge, within sight of the road to the Seat, and the extra light meant heavier underbrush. He constantly searched for the easiest route and often had to cut a way through with his knife when the bushes and saplings were thick or the branches low. The thief's horse was more interested in fresh green shoots than in covering ground.

It had been a long, hard day. They had one consolation: The horse droppings on the road were now nearly fresh.

He glanced back again at the Servant. Barefoot, she had had an even harder time. She looked weary; she had spent hours making charms while watching her step. Her dangling sewing case bulged; they were prepared.

As the night deepened, he could no longer see his way. "We should walk on the road now. The woods are too dark."

"My feet will be pleased. But are you not worried about the icedragon?"

"Reptiles are day creatures."

"What about icedragons?"

He stumbled and swore. "We would have to find a dead one and examine it to be sure." *All this time I've expected it to act like a reptile and a poikilotherm. Stupid, stupid, stupid. Magic creatures don't have to follow the design plans of real animals.*

"Have you seen it only during the day?"

He thought back over his encounters. "The first time it attacked me, it was technically day, but the sky was black and I couldn't see far through the heavy rain. Later, it chased me at a fast speed for a long distance." His stomach sank. No cold-blooded creature would have the energy reserves for a long chase.

"Homeotherm," they said in unison.

"We can't make any assumptions about the traits or abilities Urushi put into these creatures he created," Celatu said.

"If Shadow exists—*if*—she may be helping him make the icedragons and firehounds."

"You still don't believe she is real?"

She frowned. "I do not know what to believe," she said uncertainly. "I feel like a whole, complete person. But if Shadow is not real, how can we explain these magical creatures or my doing things Goodborn cannot do?"

"Maybe the changes in you happened because the Land needs a different type of Servant to fight the icedragons and firehounds and their maker. Maybe It altered you, not Shadow or the mink." He said it only to comfort her; he still believed his hypothesis about Shadow was the most likely explanation.

"Thank you! I knew you would come up with a better reason for my change. I feel braver now."

Her sweet, innocent smile touched his heart He wanted to stroke her face. Instead, he said, "It's dark enough that I suspect the assassins have stopped to camp. Let's leave the horse. I'll go barefoot too. Then we can get close to the assassins without their hearing us."

They tethered the horse in a grassy spot by a stream, in case they didn't return until daytime, and gathered brush and stones to scatter by the side of the road to mark the spot. Then they continued down the road in the dark night, with only the moon to light their way.

He caught a whiff of smoke and gestured her to a halt. "Smell that?"

"Yes," she whispered back. "Light ahead, to the left."

Energy surged through him, and by the way the Servant stood straighter and walked faster, he knew she shared his excitement.

He rubbed the back of his neck as they walked down the road toward the light. He still longed to return to his books and his studies, but such a life now seemed incomplete. If Violet continued to reject him, he would have a serious talk with Father when he got home. He would tell Father exactly what he wanted in a wife; it would not be one of the fluffy women who were invited to dinner.

But it's Violet I want, not just a wife.

I think.

They entered the woods near the camp, feeling with their hands to find gaps in the foliage, probing with bare feet to find soft mats of sodden leaves to cushion their footsteps. They made so little sound that their nervous breathing seemed a clamor.

When they could clearly hear the assassins laughing and talking, they settled with their backs against an old oak to wait for the men to go to sleep. The leaves under them were damp, and the evening breeze grew cooler.

Celatu sat stoically, too prideful to admit he was cold.

Violet had no such concern. She rubbed her arms, shifted position, and finally scooted so close they sat hip to hip and arm to arm.

He turned his head so she could not hear how his breathing quickened at her nearness.

"Perhaps we should have brought the horse for warmth," she whispered.

Her warm breath tickled his neck, and his goosebumps spread.

"Lady, if you are cold, it is my duty as a loyal citizen to warm you." He put his arm around her.

She trembled in his embrace. "I'm shivering only because I'm cold."

"As you say, Lady." He wrapped his other arm around her and held her close until she stopped shaking. He was warm now, too. Several coils of her hair danced against his neck, and a tingle of magic brushed him each time the breeze jiggled her curls. She felt good against him, and she had stayed "Sweet Violet" for hours. He rested his head on hers, not minding the prickling of her hair but rather enjoying its tickly sparks of magic. He could sit like this forever.

Too soon, the assassins' voices dropped to a murmur and then silenced altogether. Snores began soon after. They waited another half an hour.

"They must all be asleep now," he whispered. Neither of them moved.

"I am sorry I have been so rude to you so often."

"Shadow changed you."

She shook her head. "My behavior is always my responsibility."

"If so, Lady, I forgive you everything."

"That is gracious." She flexed her fingers and wiggled her shoulders. "I am stiff from sitting like this for so long."

"It's time to go."

"Wait a moment. I want to thank you for agreeing to look for my cousin." She twisted to face him and stretched up to kiss him lightly on the lips. The power of the Land pulsed in her lips and worked its way through him, warming his body as it spread from his mouth to the tips of his toes and fingers. "Blessings of the Land," she whispered.

It felt like finding a lost part of himself he had not known was missing. He pulled her roughly toward him and kissed her deeply, strayed to pepper her nose and forehead with kisses, breathing in her scent, then headed back to her welcoming lips. He thrust his hand into her hair and kissed her until he could not think straight. Soft, lingering kisses. Intense, passionate kisses. Panting, he stroked her soft face from brow to chin. Smooth, sweet, intoxicating, she was like no woman he had ever been with. He was drunk on her, and they had done nothing yet but kiss.

She pulled away; he growled "no," but she didn't leave his arms. She slid down and relaxed into his chest, caressing his bristly face, purring with contentment. Her silver pendant with the hole in the middle burned against his skin like a tiny sun.

He shut his eyes and closed his hand around hers, savoring her calloused skin, her warmth, the Land's silent approval pulsing between them like a warm current of water.

The Land's approval! After so many ambiguous messages, this one was clear: the Land wanted them to bond. He wasn't even the Servant, and he could understand Its desire for them to be together forever.

Violet gasped, "No!" She pulled away and crawled toward the campsite.

Yet her touch still warmed his skin, as if they still embraced. Emotions and sensations that weren't his—excitement mixed with confusion, damp leaves under knees, and the brush of a branch against a cheek—mingled with his own thoughts as he sat by the tree.

"Come back," he whispered. Her curvy bottom disappeared among the dark tree trunks and shadows.

He shook his head to clear it, but his lips still tingled and his mind still focused on their kisses.

He found her several yards from the edge of the camp, surveying it from behind a bush. Everyone lay still, and fires were banked for the night. The horses were tied to trees at the edge of the glade with no guard. They flicked their ears in Celatu and Violet's direction, then continued grazing calmly.

Violet handed him half of the charms. "Place one on each man's forehead and press it down. Do not let any of them touch your face," she instructed. "They will not take effect for a minute, so when you finish, stay still. I will search for Kassia."

The words entered his mind as she thought them; her spoken words were an unnecessary echo. "Violet, I hear you in my head. It is—you are—amazing."

She dropped her eyes and put a finger to her lips. She walked silently into the circle of sleeping killers.

Celatu followed. He placed one charm and then a second. As he moved toward a third sleeper, a woman called out, "Wake up! It's Fila!"

Celatu turned toward the familiar voice. The woman's silhouette, outlined by the fire, was familiar too, but his mind could not bring a name to mind.

His vision jerked and jolted into another perspective as if he saw through his own eyes and through those of another.

Violet. He was still somehow connected to her.

Violet recognized the woman's voice—and knew her name. Then Celatu did too.

His hand flew to his heart and clutched his tunic as he retreated back into the undergrowth.

Violet addressed the woman. "I'm no longer Fila. I'm Violet. I'm here to rescue you from the assassins, Kassia."

Chapter 29

FILA'S STOMACH TIGHTENED as she stepped closer to get a better look at Kassia. *Thank the Land, she does not look hurt.*

Relief swept through her like a wind before a storm, then ended abruptly. Kassia's smile. It was the smile she had worn when they were little when she had beaten Fila in a race or drawn a prettier picture. The smile she still wore when she wheedled an extra tart from one of the cooks or when her class project was the best.

Kassia smiled in triumph.

The assassins threw off their blankets and jumped up, even the ones with relaxation charms on their foreheads, fully dressed and knives in hand. Two kicked kindling onto the fires, sending the flames blazing high above her head. Another grabbed her and put his knife to her throat.

Kassia's smile grew wider.

She is in league with the assassins! Fila needed a plan of escape, but her mind, reeling from betrayal, had but a single thought: *I thought she was my best friend.*

The man holding Fila howled like a wounded wolf and dropped his knife. He and it hit the ground together.

Fila grabbed his knife and backed away.

Tears ran down the assassin's face as he screamed and screamed. His legs were bent in several places no human leg should bend.

Bent by magic. One of the assassins had helped her.

Why? It makes even less sense than Kassia helping the assassins. Jabbing the knife in various directions, she looked around the circle of assassins for some sign of who her savior was. Whoever it was had incredible pain tolerance; no one looked as if he had just performed painful magic.

Kassia sniffed the air. "Cinnamon. Do you smell it, Fila?"

Tul! He broke his vow against using magic again! But where was he? She caught a glint of silver in the woods. Tul was doubled over.

She returned her gaze to Kassia. "I smell only cloves. Have you injured your nose?" she asked in mock concern, aping "Mean Violet." *I will die before I let her see me afraid.*

Kassia shoved her hard.

Fila spun; an assassin seized her and slapped her. She dropped the knife she had just acquired, and he hooked his elbow around her throat.

"Careful, Hirtu," Kassia said, wagging her finger. "Don't hurt her."

Hirtu. One of Urushi's friends. She had not recognized him; he had grown at least a foot taller, and his jaw had widened.

"Our orders are to kill her!" Hirtu protested.

Murderous rage filled Tul's belly. How she felt it, she did not know, but emotions sparked between them just as when they had kissed. His anger tamped out her terror, leaving her recklessly bold. "Let go of me, Hirtu. My orders take precedence over those of my brother's."

Kassia placed her hands on her hips. "Don't be stupid, Hirtu. You either, Fila. Urushi did not order a murder. *I* am in charge here, and *my* orders are to keep her alive and unharmed."

Fila felt Tul's anger rise and overpower his sense. His muscles tensed. He burst from the forest, running straight toward her.

Two smaller men grabbed him; he shrugged them off with ease. "Kassia, what do you think you're doing?"

Kassia gasped, and her pale face turned even whiter. "Get her out of here, Hirtu."

Fila struggled. The elbow tightened around her throat, and she clawed and kicked with all her might. She was no match for Hirtu in strength. He dragged her, half-conscious, to the edge of the camp and pinned her between himself and a tree, and the effort did not even make him breathe faster.

She gasped when he released his hold on her throat. Her lungs burned for air; her confused mind thought she was drowning in sand. She clawed the air, trying to dig herself free.

The link with Tul saved her. Her mind followed it back to sanity.

She opened her eyes. Tul and Kassia stood an arm's length apart in the center of the clearing, glaring at each other. The assassins stood nearby, some restlessly playing with their knives, others juggling stones.

"Answer me! Why are you siding with assassins?" Tul shouted.

"As you surely know, there's a big difference between *honor guard* and *assassins*. I am going to Urushi to be his wife. I love him and want to help him rule."

"He's using you. If he were here, I would kill him for it."

"You lie," Kassia said. "He loves me and is going to marry me. We'll rule jointly as king and Servant."

"We don't need royalty, and we already have a Servant."

"Fila?" Kassia trilled a laugh. "Really? *Fila*? Hardly a suitable Servant."

"Better than you."

Kassia gasped and slapped him.

Tul smiled grimly, as if the blow had been a caress.

Kassia's face turned scarlet, and she gestured at the assassins.

Several tackled Tul, knocking him to the ground and sitting on his back and legs.

Fila felt his frantic panic through her link with Tul as the men squashed the air from his lungs. He stopped struggling to send a stream of magic fire at Hirtu.

Tul was too slow. Her captor dodged it easily and pressed Fila tighter against the tree.

Kassia looked down at Tul. "You bow to me now against your will. But when I am Servant, Brother, you will bow to me willingly." She looked at the assassins. "Take him to the road and send him on his way." The men slid off and hauled him upright.

"Stop! Wait!" Fila twisted sideways so she could draw a deeper breath. "Why did you call him *Brother*?"

Kassia's eyebrows flew up. "Fila, have you lost your senses? You know Celatu is my brother."

"Celatu *the Coward*," Hirtu corrected.

Fila's knees gave way; she would have fallen if Hirtu had not caught her and jerked her back to standing.

"No!" she breathed. Tul could not possibly be her scrawny, awkward, pimpled cousin. He looked nothing like the boy she remembered. Her gaze flicked between Tul and Kassia, trying to discern who was lying to her.

Tul refused to meet her gaze.

Her breath caught. He had not let her treat his worst face injuries, no matter how many times she asked; now she knew why. He thought she might recognize him.

A copper cord linked them and blazed and pulsed with their emotions: her horror, anger, and humiliation; his shame and guilt. His feelings were like a blow to her chest.

"You deceived me from the beginning. How could you? *How could you*?" Her voice broke.

He looked at the ground and did not answer.

"And you, Kassia. We were always best friends."

"We still are. Once I am Servant, everything will go back to normal. You'll see."

Never. Fila pulled her anger inside and boxed it up. She forced her face into a neutral expression that gave away nothing and hid everything. *Kassia betrayed me. Tul—Celatu—betrayed me. My own brother betrayed me. I cannot trust anyone.*

The fires popped and hissed like the anger waiting inside her.

Kassia turned back to the assassins. "Well? Didn't I tell you to take him to road?"

"But he'll come after us again. We should kill him and be done with it."

"He doesn't use magic, and you know he runs away when there's trouble. He's as harmless as Fila."

"He shot magic fire at my feet," Hirtu said. "We should kill him or keep him prisoner."

"He did *not* shoot fire at your feet," Kassia said in the same peevish lecturing tone she often used with Fila. "As I already told you, my brother does not use magic."

Heart pounding, Fila lied. "I saw no magic fire."

"Goodborn tell only the truth," Kassia admonished Hirtu.

He stiffened; Fila thought he would argue. But he merely shrugged. "Well, running away *is* what your brother does best."

The other assassins laughed. The several men holding Celatu dragged him toward the road.

Celatu did not struggle, did not try to get away, did not even groan or joke or complain when pulled him over fallen logs or through a stream.

Tears sprang to Fila's eyes. *Now that I know he is Celatu the Coward, he no longer pretends to be someone he is not. Such as my rescuer. My protector. My entertainer. My suitor. Those were Tul, who exists no longer.*

When the men pushed Celatu into the road, he at last turned his head to look at her. His face by torchlight was planes and angles; she could not see his expression. Was he sorry for deceiving her? Or was he laughing at her for believing his lies?

One of the assassins shouted, "You better run, and run far. If we catch you again, I'll make sure you meet with an 'accident.'"

Celatu nodded and backed away.

"Leave him alone and come back to the fire," Kassia ordered. "He's not worth your time."

The pain of Celatu's leaving her was almost physical, like having a tooth pulled. The pain of his betrayal was more like having a limb torn off. His eyes still looked at her.

"You're a liar and a coward," she said quietly.

He hung his head.

After a pause, she added, "But I forgive you." She tried to send her forgiveness through the copper cord. It faded.

Celatu limped west, away from the Seat.

Away from her.

Fila kept her face calm as Kassia stood in front of her, fists on her hips. Although her heart pounded like a hammer against an anvil, Fila refused to let her cousin know her fear. She was still the Servant.

"Take her needlework bag," Kassia ordered, her bravado blunted by the tremor in her voice. "Get boots for her feet, boots with the thickest soles you can find, and bind her wrists."

She pulled Fila toward the fire and looked her up and down. "I can't believe you've let yourself go like this. Your blouse and skirt are torn and stained, you know. And your hair! I don't have the words to describe it!"

"Unfortunately, Amma was unable to dress it once she was dead."

"I guess that's some excuse. But you surely know you can't go around looking like this. It's disrespectful and dishonors the office of Servant I will soon be holding. I'll have to lend you one of my dresses."

Shocked speechless, Fila stared at her cousin, whose primping and extravagant clothes and jewelry always struck her as self-indulgent, a way of showing off. "Do you not care about the people who died because of you and Urushi? Not even Spotted Turtle, who made you your first doll? Do not talk to me of respect until you show me the respect I deserve as Servant."

Kassia would not meet Fila's eyes. She circled Fila, pulling at her hair with a comb and tut-tutting. "Not caring for your appearance is disrespectful because you force others to look at an unpleasant sight. Now sit on this stump and hold still." Assassins bound Fila's hands and shoved stiff boots onto her feet while Kassia styled her hair.

Kassia pays no attention to anything I say. Urushi has filled her with dreams and delusions. Fila tried to think as Tul would—or rather, Celatu the Coward, Land swallow him for abandoning her to cutthroats without a fight. He had tried to teach her to be wary of whom she trusted; he had finally succeeded.

"You knew about the ambush. That is why Two Sparrows didn't come with us."

Kassia looked shocked. "I would not risk my amma's life. I'll need her once I am Servant."

Fila assumed an air of indifference. It was not hard to do so. So many emotions battled within her—grief, anger, confusion, fear, astonishment, sadness, betrayal—that none could claim dominance and rise to the surface above the others. Her mind floated above her body, cold and clear as a stream in the ancient forests, with the eddies below not visible from the surface.

"Servant? Poor Kassia. My brother has tricked you." Drawing on "Mean Violet" again, Fila filled her voice with pity and scorn. "You can't be Servant. I am."

Kassia jerked the comb in Fila's hair. "You think you know so much, but you do not know anything. Anything!"

"I am trying to help you. Just as you and I have always helped each other. Just as you are helping me with my hair now."

Her words did not soften Kassia. Stone-faced, her cousin finished dressing her hair, pulled a healing charm from her bag, and held it against a bruise on her face.

Fila flinched before she could stop herself.

"What happened to your face?"

"Urushi's assassins tried to kill me. I barely escaped."

"Don't assign yourself so much importance. It's unbecoming. Urushi's men are my escort."

Kassia had always been eager to be the center of attention. Now she was in some world of her own, one in which Urushi's men had not tried to kill Fila, a make-believe world in which Kassia could become Servant without harming anyone else.

"Why was Celatu with you? He doesn't like to be apart from his books."

"Urushi tried to have Celatu killed. He had to flee the Seat."

"Liar!" Blotches of angry red dotted Kassia's cheeks. "Urushi would never do that to my brother!"

"Cousin, when have I ever lied to you, to anybody? I am Goodborn."

Kassia looked away, pressing her lips together tightly.

Fila continued. "Maybe you do not know my brother as well as you think you do. Here's something else you should know about him." Fila paused for effect and to gather strength to say the words. "He killed our parents."

"Liar again!" Kassia ground the charm hard into the tender bruises on Fila's face.

She cried out and jerked her face away.

"Sit still. We need your face healed." Kassia applied the charm again with a softer touch. "We don't want anyone getting the wrong idea about why you're giving up your position as Servant."

"I have already tried to give it up. The Land refused."

"Try harder. Try again." She grabbed Fila's hand and squeezed it too hard. "Please, Fila. Do it for me. You know this has been my dream always."

Fila returned the hand squeeze and spoke calmly. "You know I never wanted to be Servant. I begged the Land to release me. It didn't."

"I *will* be Servant."

Fila's throat tightened. "I cannot believe you would kill me. We've been best friends a long time, since we were tiny and our ammas gave us bits of yarn to play with."

"Best friends, yes, but enemies sometimes as well, and you never noticed."

"How can you say—"

Kassia continued as if Fila hadn't spoken. "Don't worry; I'll make sure you live. I want you to see *me* be the center of attention. I deserve it more than you ever did just for being a Goodborn. Now it is my turn. I'll be Servant. You'll be the one wearing cast-off shoes."

Fila's head spun, and she feared she would throw up. She had misread everyone, even her best friend. Who would betray her next?

Who was left to betray her?

Her self-pity evaporated. The secrets were out; she knew where she stood. As she planned her escape, she could rely only on one person: herself.

Chapter 30

CELATU PACED THE ROAD in the moonlight, rubbing the spot between his eyebrows. The horse turned its head nervously back and forth to keep its good eye on him.

The Servant's expression when she had learned his true identity, and then again when he managed to escape, haunted him and interrupted his attempts to create a plan to rescue her. He had hoped she would get to know him well enough to look beyond his nickname and reputation, to see that he was cautious, not cowardly.

Whom was he kidding? He hadn't merited the nickname "Coward" when he received it, but he earned it later. He stood aside while Urushi terrorized the people of the Seat; he fled rather than face the icedragon; he was not willing to risk danger to rescue the Servant's cousin until he learned it was Kassia.

With his rescues of Violet and his efforts to protect her, he had only begun to redeem himself. He had to do much more to become the man he wanted to be, to become the man Violet deserved.

He started now. Without Violet nearby, colors lost their brilliance, and every act, even breathing, seemed a struggle. He missed her dark-fringed eyes, her blazing hair, and her soft body seeking warmth from his. He missed the way she challenged him to think in new ways and question old assumptions.

He rested his forehead on his palms and tears burned his eyes. He was no hero from an ancient legend, with magic and wisdom beyond all others. He had determination and great strength, but they were too little to defeat Urushi and Shadow united and to elevate Fila to her proper place. No Guardian could stand alone against firehounds and icedragons and an ancient evil spirit.

I do not have to stand alone. He wiped his tears away. He and Violet should face her enemies together. Her supporters would unite behind them once she arrived at the Seat.

And after being in the assassins' camp, he knew exactly whom he was up against there. He knew he could free Violet easily.

There was one more element he needed to pull in before forming a plan: the prophecy. He had the first two lines; it was now crucial to remember the rest.

A Servant dies by a loved one's hand;
Dire storms spring from the grieving Land;

He had a good memory for such things and had developed techniques for bringing lines learned long ago back to to the front of his mind.

He let himself daydream while he beat the rhythms of the first two lines on his knee: da TA da TA da da TA da TA; da TA da TA da TA da TA. Sometimes he hummed along and sometimes he was silent; sometimes he made up silly fragments of lines that matched the rhythm and rhyme schemes.

It was a common rhythm; his head soon filled with lines from songs that could not possibly be related to the prophecy. He chuckled at these and kept going.

The Servant can the Shadow withstand....

He remembered pulling up that line recently. It was the only reference he could find to Shadow in his memory, lacking any of the rest of the song or poem.

Celatu blinked. Could it be part of the prophecy? He recited the first two lines out loud and added the line about Shadow right after. It fit. It felt right. All three lines made sense together for the first time in history.

The remaining line stubbornly refused to appear, although he felt at the very edge of his memory, just out of reach, teasing him.

After many dozen of repetitions, his knee was bruised and swollen and he was no closer to the crucial line.

Sleep on it, Father always advised him when he couldn't make a decision or remember something important. It was one of the few pieces of Father's advice that had been useful for his research.

He piled dry leaves together into a bed. He sought the copper cord and sent feelings of comfort to Violet.

He received no response. He turned over and lulled himself to sleep humming the rhythm of the prophecy and running through all the words he knew that ended in *–and*.

His first thought the next morning was his self-pitying thought of the night before: No Guardian can stand against firehounds and icedragons.

No Guardian.

What about the Toilers?

He beat the rhythm against his other knee, this time trying out "Toilers" every place the rhythm called for TA da.

The prophecy popped fully into his mind.

A Servant dies by a loved one's hand;
Dire storms spring from the grieving Land;
The Servant can the Shadow withstand;
If Toilers fight, and a coward makes a stand.

What if the fourth line instead were:

If Toilers fight, and a "Coward" makes a stand.

He jumped up and shouted "yes!"
He knew the prophecy, and he knew its meaning.
He had the key to defeating Urushi and Shadow.

As he scratched Wiggle's head, Urushi watched a bead of sweat trickle down Uncle Bifac's face, and he smiled inwardly. His uncle knew to be summoned to the courtyard for morning tea was a sign Urushi feared he would lose control.

He had no intention of harming his uncle. Bifac was useful, and, more importantly, he was Kassia's father, and Urushi wanted to do nothing to upset his beloved. But his uncle was not wholeheartedly committed; he needed to cement his loyalty.

"Hooting Owl, please take Wiggle inside." Urushi handed Appa the dog.

Bifac's face paled, but he maintained his dignified pose. "Please bring me a cup of tea when you return.

Urushi ignored his uncle's attempt to assert rank and turned to face him straight on. "I'm disappointed in you, Uncle. The honor guard you chose for Fila was too good. She escaped."

"It would have been risky to send anyone but Guardians aligned with Fila's family. Boraga would have made alternative arrangements to get Fila to the Seat."

Urushi thumped his fist on the gaura-covered bench. "Forget excuses. I know you warned the honor guard. My men found them well armed and ready to fight. If their horses had been more seasoned, Fila's guard might have prevailed."

"The Consort trained his men well."

"Look which way the wind is blowing, Uncle. Be my man with your whole heart, and you will have an honored position as father of the Servant and father-in-law of the king. If you put your loyalty to your sister and niece first, you are only a liability to me."

Bifac's face smoothed into blandness; he often wore that expression in the council chambers. "I always note the winds, Urushi. Remember that."

A threat? Urushi wondered but said nothing. He would break this man to his will. The silence grew long as neither man spoke.

Hooting Owl returned with a tray holding a porcelain teapot and matching teacups and saucers. He poured the tea and stood to the side.

Bifac took a cup, cleared his throat, and spoke. "My loyalties are, as you note, divided, and you play games with me. You sent an icedragon after my only son, for Land's sake! My only son! Where is your loyalty to me?"

"I understand many people have claims on you," Urushi said carefully, gently, picking up his own teacup. "I understand you have loyalties that conflict. You are an important man of an ancient family." Urushi hardened his tone. "But if you do not choose me, you *are* making a choice. Against me."

Urushi sipped his tea, watching Bifac over the edge of the teacup. Calculation played across his uncle's face. Pressure was building.

Bifac looked straight into Urushi's eyes. "When we talked right after your parents' death, you told me you planned only to kidnap Fila. Now it seems you wanted her killed. Again you did not trust me."

"It's only prudent, Uncle. Your pesky divided loyalties."

Bifac leaned forward, his face intense. "I will ask the question I shied from before. If Fila is alive, how do you intend to make my daughter the Servant?"

Urushi picked a sprig of creeping thyme and inhaled the piney scent. "I will ask my sister to step down. Perhaps the Land will accept her decision."

Bifac frowned. "As far as anyone knows, a Servant is Servant until death."

"Some of the books in my library may have instructions for changing a Servant back into an ordinary Guardian woman. Or I may need to take matters into my own hands. Again."

Bifac stood so abruptly his cup chittered against its saucer. He set them on the tray and paced the courtyard. Urushi poured himself more tea. He now knew what Bifac's decision would be.

When he was young, many times his uncle had admonished the cousins to *go along to get along*. Bifac would stay true to his principles, such as they were. The only question was how he would justify his decision.

He came and stood in front of Urushi in his usual assertive pose. His face showed no regret or hesitation. "You have my full support...." Bifac let the sentence trail off and did not relax his stance or his gaze.

"You have a condition?" Urushi asked coldly.

"Yes. Two, in fact. First, I will not personally kill Fila or witness her death. I want no blood guilt on me."

"Agreed. And the second?"

Here his composure broke. "Spare my son. Please."

Urushi choked on his tea.

Bifac continued. "Celatu has left the Seat. If he knows what's best, he'll stay away." Bifac spread his hands in exasperation. "If he returns, I'll lock him in the library."

Celatu is alive? Urushi's fists tightened. His cousin was the first man to have eluded an icedragon. "What if he becomes a danger?"

Bifac pshawed and put a friendly hand on Urushi's shoulder as if Urushi had agreed to his second condition. "He's Celatu the Coward, remember?"

Urushi stood. "Uncle, you've chosen the right side, and you'll profit for it. I'm glad we've come to an amicable arrangement." He showed his uncle out personally, then stood at the door and watched him walk away.

For all his political genius, Uncle Bifac had a serious blind spot. *Bifac does not see Celatu's refusal to follow the crowd is a form of courage.* But Urushi saw it. Like a narrow vein of gold in a vast mountain, that thread of courage was thin but pure.

Urushi's eyes narrowed, and then he smiled. *This time, I'll send an entire pod of icedragons.*

Chapter 31

IT TOOK CELATU half the morning to backtrack to Growling Dog's village. He urged the horse into a canter as he neared the village limits, ready to explode with nervousness and eager to enlist the villagers in his plan immediately.

But only the hum of insects and the songs of birds broke the stillness of the near-empty village. He rode through without seeing a single soul other than a female pup carding wool and a ginger cat washing its face in the sun.

When he reached the far side of the village, he saw why. Two adults were high in the air, painting the water tower. In the pastures beyond, young pups and dogs kept watch over the grazing buffalo and antelope. In the fields and orchards, males, females, and older pups planted, hoed, weeded, pruned, and did other tasks he did not recognize.

He jiggled his lucky coin impatiently. No wonder the village was empty. The Toilers were toiling. That's what Toilers did, their half of the mutual obligations binding Guardians and Toilers.

He scanned the workers and located Growling Dog and Bluebird. He tied the thief's horse under a shady tree and ran over. They stood at his approach, Growling Dog rubbing his back.

The Toiler wrinkled his massive brow. "I did not expect to see you again so soon. Is Servant Violet settled into the Seat, then?"

"No. That's why I'm here. I've come to beg for your help."

Growling Dog and Bluebird exchanged glances. Growling Dog frowned. "You need Toiler help with Guardian business?"

"Urgently. Servant Violet has been kidnapped. Urushi intends to kill her."

Bluebird gasped. "Land protect her! I wish it were possible for us to help her."

"It is possible!" Celatu walked back and forth, waving his hands in agitation as he talked. "I have a plan to unseat Urushi."

"No more, Tul!" Bluebird said brusquely, holding up her hand. "What type of people do you take us for? This village follows the rules the Land set down for us. We do not meddle in Guardian business."

"Except as peacebuilders," Growling Dog said. "Go to your own kind if you plan war."

Celatu rubbed his chin in frustration. If only they would listen to him, they would understand that they needed to make an exception for Servant Violet.

He ran to the water barrel in the road and vaulted onto the lid. "Listen to me! Servant Violet needs your help!"

"Get out of our village!" Growling Dog bellowed back.

"Violet needs your help now, and I have the right to ask you for that help. My name is not really Tul. I am Celatu, your Guardian."

"Celatu? Celatu the Coward? Land take you, then!" Growling Dog whacked his hoe against a pile of stones, sending them flying. "You have much to account for!"

"I know I've been a terrible Guardian. But as your Guardian I call on you to listen to me. Not to help me, but to help the Servant and all of Veridia."

Growling Dog interrupted again. "You took advantage of my hospitality. You lied to me, Bluebird, and every other Toiler in this village. Now you ask us to break the most sacred rule governing interactions between Guardians and Toilers." He took a deep breath and bellowed, "Celatu the Coward, you're a scoundrel!"

Scoundrel. Celatu looked at his feet, hating himself for neglecting his village, wishing he could do that part of his life over. *Scoundrel.* The word would ring in his head for a long time.

Rubbing his lucky coin, Celatu forced his head up. "It *is* your business this time. It's the business of every person in Veridia, Guardian and Toiler alike. If you would just let me explain—"

"No." Growling Dog scowled fiercely, his arms crossed over his chest.

"Don't punish Violet for my shortcomings. Please, listen to me."

Growling Dog turned and walked away.

Celatu leapt from the barrel. He took two giant steps, grabbed the Toiler by the arm, and swung him around. "I won't let you ignore me," he shouted. "No matter what I've done, I'm still your Guardian."

"Prove your worth as a Guardian."

His head felt on the verge of bursting like a rotted wineskin. He ran his hands through his hair. He was sorely tempted to leave, to try another Toiler village. But would strangers listen to his plea to break the rules of Veridia? No. He needed to convince his own Toiler friends first. They would convince the other villages.

"Fine," he said through gritted teeth. "I'll prove my worth as your Guardian. I'll help paint the water tower."

"Toilers can paint water towers. You are going to use your magic to help Mosquito here clear his first plot." He gestured to a sturdy young male.

Celatu smiled a greeting, but Mosquito jerked his head and walked off.

Celatu followed. *Again I'm breaking my vow to help the Servant. I must be either the most patriotic person in Veridia or in love.* His face burned as they walked. Villagers stopped their work to watch him as he passed, their expressions ranging from disapproval to anger.

Mosquito paused at a fence, and Celatu walked up beside him. Now he understood why the Toiler struggled here despite advanced tech. Thick-stemmed bushes and hundreds of rocks jutted from the unturned soil. The young Toiler wiped his forehead with his sleeve and looked down at Celatu with challenge in his eyes. "I applied to you weeks ago for help clearing my plot. What kind of Guardian are you?"

"A bad one," Celatu admitted.

"That's the truth." Mosquito swept his hand in a gesture that encompassed his plot. "The roots go deep, and even a steel plow cannot get through until these rocks are gone." He loomed over Celatu. "What are you going to do about it?"

He echoed Fila's words. "My duty. I'll do my duty."

He chose a corner to start in and scanned the field. *Weeds first.* Concentrating on the sun's heat on his hair and the web of roots under the surface of the soil, he held out his hand. His magic roared up, eager to do what it was created for.

The ground closest to him sank as the root mass shriveled and disintegrated under the heat channeled by his magic. He pushed his hand outward, and the ground rippled away toward the forest. Already the weeds nearest him were collapsing in waves to lie pale and lifeless. He sent his magic out another time, and every plant disintegrated onto now-bare soil. Wisps of smoke rose from the ground.

He dropped his hand and turned his awareness inward to check for wounds. His palms were slightly burnt, but that was the extent of his injuries. The magic hadn't drained him, either; he had more energy than when he started.

Realization dawned: Male magic used as the Land intended, to help the Toilers, harmed a man less than magic worked for other purposes.

He called to Mosquito. "What about the rocks? Do you need them intact?"

"I just want them out of there."

Celatu pulverized a rock near his feet into gravel and grinned in spite of himself. It was still as fun as when he had three summers and had crushed his first hard-boiled egg. He focused on a pointed boulder a few feet from the fence. Because it was so close, he imploded it. One moment it was there; the next it had collapsed in on itself into a pile of sand.

Mosquito nodded with reluctant approval.

Celatu forgot everything except the field as he reveled in the joy of destroying rock after rock, trying to do each in a different way. His minor injuries did not lessen his glee. How amusing Violet would find this, Tul doing his duty as a Guardian and enjoying every moment.

"Seek shelter!" a deep Toiler voice called. Celatu and Mosquito looked up. The blackening sky spit out a bolt of lightning. He ran with the villagers as cold rain pelted them. He was soaked by the time he reached Growling Dog and Bluebird's house; the door was already closed.

He pounded on it, and Growling Dog opened it.

The Toiler frowned. "No refuge here for the likes of you." He slammed the door in Celatu's face.

Chapter 32

THE POUNDING at the front door rattled the wooden legs of Afissa's knitting caddy and startled her into missing a stitch.

She put down a half-finished mitten, went to the shuddering door, and pulled the leather thong to open it. "Why are you—" She had no need to finish her question; the Toiler kicking the door held a tower of cages so high that it obscured his face.

"Delivery. Two fence lizards, two five-lined skinks, two broad-headed skinks, two box turtles, two black rat snakes, four mastiffs. Where should I put them?"

Four huge dogs stood behind him, drool dripping in strings from droopy black gums.

She drew back, shuddering. "I am afraid there's been some mistake."

"I was told the pink stucco house on Street of Beavers. This is the only one I found. Are you Daucina?"

Her house guest had gone out very early this morning. Now Afissa knew why. "No, but she's staying here. Please follow me." She led him the shortest way to the courtyard. "Set all the cages here in the shade, and tie the dogs here too."

She let him out and returned to her mitten. Soon, another Toiler arrived with a delivery for Daucina. He was barely out of puphood and skittered off as soon as she took it, a child's needlework basket.

She inhaled the memory-laden scent of freshly woven reeds and grasses. She had started school with a beginner basket just like this; so had Nandina and Typha; so did every little girl. She ached for Daucina, who had lost everything, even the most basic of supplies. *I should have shown her my workroom and invited her to use whatever she wanted.*

She smiled for the first time since Gramin's memorial service. As a girl, she had struggled with manipulating the little pair of snips with her toes and had accidentally ruined the hems of two skirts. *Mother was so angry.* Afissa had to wear black skirts, increasingly patched, for the rest of that year. And the adorable cushioned wristband bristling with copper pins. This one had green fabric. Her own had a lovely blue print. How frustrated the teacher became when she wouldn't remove any pins because she didn't want to hurt her "porcupine."

Her gaze caressed the other supplies. A large quilted needlebook folded into a flower petal. *How proud I was to be entrusted with all those sharp needles!* Spools of thread and skeins of yarns in basic colors. Two leather thimbles. Three crochet hooks ranging from medium to large. Squares of unbleached muslin. *I felt sorry for the boys because they didn't get anything so wondrous to start their magic training.*

She carried the basket to the guest wing and placed it by the door to Daucina and Ladybug's suite. *I hope it brings back good memories for her instead of reminding her of her ruined cottage.*

Someone knocked on the front door again. "For Land's sake!" She lifted her skirts and ran to open it to find yet another Toiler with a delivery.

"Yarn for Daucina."

"Yes, I see." On the Toiler's arms and over her shoulders hung perhaps a dozen net bags stuffed with red, green, blue, yellow, and white yarn.

"Bring it in." Afissa motioned her into the sitting room, where the Toiler emptied her bags onto the floor. Light from the many windows there revealed not five colors of yarn, but at least five *dozen.*

Fascinated, Afissa sorted the yarns first into the five hues, then within each hue by purity, then separated the resulting groups into shades and tints. When she finished, she stood, stepped back, and looked at the array of colors. A thrill ran up her spine, and her feet ached to start knitting.

The front door opened, and Daucina's voice rang out. "Afissa? Are you here?

"In the sitting room with your yarn," she called back. "The animals are in the courtyard."

Daucina and Ladybug entered, laden with packages. "I had hoped to arrive before the animals. I hope they don't upset you."

"Not as long as I don't have to feed them."

Ladybug lined her packages up neatly along the wall. Daucina, looking frazzled, dropped hers where she stood and surveyed the yarn-filled sitting room. Her ear-high shoulders dropped into their proper place. "At last I feel a little at home."

"The colors are amazing. What will you do with all this yarn?"

"I have a project I could use your help with this afternoon. Your daughters too, when they come home from school."

"Why don't we have lunch now so we can get started sooner?"

Several mugs of tisane and a bowl of corn and pepper soup revived Daucina from her shopping. After Afissa served bowls of custard with dried cherries, Daucina delivered a whirlwind oration on her experiments with color.

"Red is red is red. At least, that's the way we've traditionally viewed color when we do magic. Yes, most women make distinctions between the pink produced by sumac berries, the brown-red produced by sumac bark, and the orange-red produced by bloodroot juice. But for the most part, we view the various shades and tones of a color as substitutes for each other.

"They are not! Alas, my old books are ashes now. But women's magic used to be more complex … and more effective."

Afissa leaned forward. "Because of making distinctions between slight differences in color?"

"Yes, and much more. Women have lost much knowledge over the centuries! I've focused my experiments on color almost exclusively, though."

"What are we doing with the new yarn?"

"I have an idea for controlling the magic of firehounds and icedragons."

Afissa's heart sped up. "Excuse me for a moment." She ran to her workroom, pulled out the net from its hiding place, and carried it to the dining room. "The net held in the magic of the firehounds, so perhaps we can use its patterns for inspiration."

"Excellent!" Daucina dropped her spoon in her half-finished custard, grabbed the net, and headed toward the sitting room.

Ladybug's violet gaze followed her, an affectionate smile on her face. She continued eating her custard, so Afissa did too. Then they joined Daucina.

"Ladybug, could you bring in some lizards and the turtles, please?" Daucina asked.

Afissa sat cross-legged on the floor, close to bouncing with excitement, full of questions. "Why do you assume reptiles and dogs will be good models for icedragons and firehounds? If Urushi'a creatures are made of magic, neutralizing their magic may be more like neutralizing a charm."

"I *don't* know. But we have to start somewhere."

"Why start with reptiles?"

"If war comes to the Seat, the combatants will be primarily men and their weapon of choice their magic of destruction. Urushi has icedragons; we does not. Our success rides on neutralizing Urushi's advantage."

Afissa nodded. "As we work, would you explain your reasoning? I want to learn to use colors too."

Daucina beamed. Ladybug brought in two cages and asked, "Are you sure you want the animals in the sitting room?"

Even for a good cause, Afissa didn't want her parquet wood floor or her upholstered furniture ruined. "Let's work on the terrazzo in the hall." They moved into the hall, Daucina's arms piled with yellow yarns.

"I'm starting with yellows because icedragons are bluish, and yellow is an opposite color according to some theories. To start, we'll work on creating a cord that will subdue reptiles. We women can help the men by getting close to the icedragons and leashing or hobbling them."

"You assume icedragons attack only Guardian men."

Daucina nodded approvingly. "You're good at seeing assumptions. Keep pointing them out, in case I've made some bad ones. Ladybug?"

"I've collected stories about icedragon and firehound attacks from every witness I could find. Toilers are never attacked. Icedragons go after only Guardian men and firehounds after Guardian women, unless someone gets in the way," Ladybug said.

"That's how Gramin died. He stood between me and the firehounds," Afissa murmured.

The Toiler wrapped her arms around her, and Afissa leaned her head against Ladybug's broad shoulder for several moments.

"Now we must try to prevent more deaths," Daucina said quietly. "What quick and easy crochet or knitting pattern do you prefer for making cords?"

Afissa swallowed a lump of grief. "I often knit *Bud and Stem* when I need a strand, but it's neither fast nor easy. It's strong, though, which could be useful in a leash." She thought some more. "Knitting bias binding is very fast and very easy."

Daucina shoved over half the balls of yellow yarn. "Knit arm-long pieces of bias binding in these yarns. I'll knit strands of *Bird's Eye*, and then we'll trade yarns."

As they worked, Ladybug repeated the stories of attacks she had collected. When the Toiler finished telling all she knew, Daucina asked Afissa, "What conclusions have you drawn?"

"We were luckier than we knew." Afissa swallowed the sour bile rising in her throat. "Few people have escaped either magical creature. The icedragon's scales are so tough and thick that knives often don't pierce them, and touching them causes frostbite. Water does not douse the flames of firehounds. Both icedragons and firehounds heal fast."

"Any traits we can exploit?"

"The preference for one sex or the other. Also, the creatures usually target a particular person."

Daucina nodded. "It makes sense for Urushi to single out his most dangerous enemies."

"Then women may be able to rescue other women and men rescue other men."

"Sometimes, when Guardians were close together, the creatures attacked indiscriminately," Ladybug pointed out. "At our cottage, the firehounds acted so."

Afissa knitted in silence, thinking. "Will the Land allow our magic to work on a battlefield?"

Daucina's mouth set in a grim line; Ladybug stroked her hair. "We may not know until we try."

"When I rescued your friends, I did not realize I was interfering in Guardian affairs," Ladybug said. "The Land did not stop me or punish me."

"What are you suggesting?" Daucina asked.

"Once you have charms that work, we Toilers could apply them to the beasts during battles."

"No!" Afissa exclaimed. "That breaks every rule of Toiler-Guardian relationships."

Daucina nodded. "It goes against your instincts as well. You might aid an injured enemy as easily as you help your own side."

"I long for simpler days," the Toiler said. She left and returned with a wooden flute. The Toiler played gracefully and expressively as Afissa and Daucina knitted until they had two ropes of each of the many yellow yarns.

"That went fast!" Afissa said.

"You know the old saying: *Music is Toiler magic*," Daucina replied. "Let's try the turtles first. We'll tie each rope around their necks to discover what effect it has on their desires and ability to move."

Heedful of scaring the turtles, Afissa took each out of the cage slowly, with one hand secure under its tickly claws and feet, and set it down in a space Daucina cleared of yarn.

Ladybug retrieved a bowl from behind her back and dropped vegetable scraps in the circle. Once the turtles caught sight of the food, they raced toward it, bumping shells and treading on each other's feet. Afissa was laughing hard by the time one extended its red-eyed head to an astounding length and seized a root.

"What's so funny?" Typha asked as she skipped in the front door, swinging her basket. Nandina followed at a more dignified pace.

"Running turtles are funny. Put away your schoolwork and come back with crochet hooks and knitting needles. We need your help."

"Hooray!" shouted Typha as she ran off. Nandina sat down and pulled out what she needed.

The adults each chose a turtle, tied a rope of yarn around its neck, and held it until Ladybug moved the food. They released the turtles; both raced toward the vegetables at the same speed as before.

"Failure," Daucina pronounced. "Next color."

Typha returned.

"You girls take charge of the turtles," Daucina said. "Repeat what we did with each cord of yarn and let me know their effects."

Afissa removed the five-lined skinks from their cage. They needed no food to motivate them; both were eager to escape. Within an hour, they had tested all the yellow yarns on the skinks and turtles without success.

"What next?" Typha asked.

"We started with yellow yarn because by some definitions yellow is the opposite of blue," Daucina explained. "However, fire and ice can be opposites, so perhaps in this case red is the opposite of blue. Girls, would you please return the yellow yarn to the sitting room and bring us the red yarn? Careful— keep the red yarn in correct order."

As the girls laid out the yarns, Daucina suggested the adults make red strands and the girls test them on the turtles.

Yawning, Afissa returned the skinks to their cages. She stretched and bent her feet and toes until she worked out all the kinks, then picked up her knitting needles again and began working. Time blurred with the rapid clicking of needles.

Nandina said, "Look at this!" She set down the turtle in her hands. It looked around for the food and plodded determinedly toward it. Nandina put a loop of dark red yarn over its head.

The turtle slowed and glanced around, food forgotten.

Nandina removed the loop, and it resumed its quest. "We've tried only five reds so far, but all affected the turtles."

"Excellent work!" Afissa noted how respectfully they handled the turtles, and her heart swelled with pride.

"Now work together, trying the same cord on both turtles. Then separate the cords into three piles according to how strongly they affect both turtles."

Boredom gone, Afissa's toes flew, churning out strands of crimson, cardinal, vinaceous, vermeil, russet, rufous, vermilion, maroon, orange red, cherry red, strawberry red, brick red, blood red, and reds she had no names for. She finished her ropes before Daucina and fetched a skink from its cage. She tested good, better, and best red ropes on it.

"The ropes work the same way on this lizard," Afissa said. "Look how docile it becomes when this rope from the 'best' pile is around its neck. It lets me pet it, even touch its ears."

Daucina asked Ladybug to bring the other reptiles. The women soon narrowed down the most effective colors to the darker reds and the most effective pattern to the simple bias edging.

Daucina said, "Now I think we should try simple crochet—"

Erudia burst in the door without knocking and slammed it behind her. "Quick!" she panted, red-faced, mud coating her clothes from neck to feet. "Block the door!"

"Mother Erudia! What's wrong?" Afissa jumped up and ran to her.

"Urushi, Land swallow him, sent a firehound for me. Me! I've been the librarian in the Servant's House for 50 years. I am going to strangle that boy if someone else doesn't do it first."

Afissa's hand flew to her throat. "Are you sure it was for you?"

"Of course I am! I looked out the window of the library into my private garden, and the beast was sniffing my shawl, my favorite bench, my hat, picking up my scent. If it had gotten inside, it would have destroyed unique documents! I left the library immediately, of course." She prowled as she talked, picking up lamp tables and other light furniture and piling them in front of the front door.

Shaking, Afissa stroked Erudia's back. "Mother, please sit. There are other doors and many windows, and firehounds are strong enough to jump through any of them. You're only tiring yourself out."

Erudia let out a sigh. "You're right." She rubbed her face and slumped into a chair. "I spent two hours getting here. I backtracked and circled blocks and public buildings. I went in the front doors of friends' houses and out the back doors. I even crawled through a drainage tunnel too small for a firehound to fit in. But eventually the firehound will pick up my scent and track me here." She took several deep breaths, and her color improved. "By the Land, I've put you all in danger. But I could think of nowhere else to go."

Afissa put her arm around her. "Daucina has a good surprise for you."

Glumly, Erudia looked at her friend.

Daucina beamed back. "We have been experimenting for hours. A dark red cord knitted in a simple pattern and placed around the neck of these reptiles makes them lose their desires and motivations. We may have found a way to keep icedragons from killing any more Guardians!"

"You will be a heroine in future books in the Servant's library!" Erudia sighed. "I only wish—selfishly, I know—that you had worked on fighting firehounds instead."

"If a simple dark red cord works on reptiles, let's see what the effects are of pale blue cords in complicated patterns on dogs."

Afissa took the girls to a neighbors' house in case the firehound attacked. When she returned, Erudia and Daucina already had lapfuls of cords of various tones of light blue. The panting dogs lounged by a window in the sitting room, pools of their drool spreading on her parquet floors. *I don't care about the damage if we can save Erudia.*

Afissa joined the other women and decided to make cords in three patterns for each color in hopes of speeding up discovery; she would crochet cords in *Scallop Stripe* and *Long Waves* and knit cords in *Ice Storm.*

They worked without talking or taking a break to eat. Ladybug played fast dance music, helping them keep up an even, rapid pace. After a long time, Ladybug was sweating, and her fingers trembled. She put down her flute. "I'll bring water."

"Bring back some elk bones too," Daucina called after her. She set down her crochet hook and started tying a running bowline in each finished cord.

Ladybug returned with bones with marrow still in them.

Daucina took a pile of leashes into the sitting room and let the dogs smell the bone she held. They jumped up and nearly knocked her over with their wildly wagging tails. She slipped a leash around each dog's neck and tossed the bone into the entry hall.

It landed in front of Afissa. She covered her eyes with her arm, expecting the huge dogs to skid across the floor and slam into her.

Nothing happened. She uncovered her eyes. One dog crawled on its belly toward the bone; the other nudged Daucina while she scratched its broad skull. "We're close!"

After further testing, Daucina declared the cerulean *Ice Storm* cord the most effective. It wasn't as strong as some of the other cords, so Afissa raced to make several more, working in lots of her hair and knotting in charms to prevent them from burning. When she finished, she leaned against the cool plaster wall and drank two mugs of water as Daucina braided the cords together and secured each end with a single copper hair. Servant hair was precious now that their caches had burned in the fire.

"We're ready if the firehound finds you," Daucina said.

"I'm not waiting for an *if*." Erudia moved enough furniture away to open the front door. "Bring my chair. I'm going to sit in the street until it picks up my scent and comes for me."

"Mother, no! I can't lose you too!" With a sinking stomach, Afissa waited for the vagues to attack. Instead, her Goodborn instincts told her this was the right thing to do. Her limbs filled with lead, and it took all her strength to stand.

"My stomach is in knots, waiting for the hound," Erudia said. "We have to test the leash on firehounds sooner or later. Let's get it over with." She marched outside boldly.

Afissa, Daucina, and Ladybug looked at each other, then followed her, carrying the chair, her cane, and the leash. Erudia planted herself in the chair and crossed her arms, determination on her face.

"I can't interfere in Urushi's business with Erudia, but I will pull the other two of you out of harm's way if necessary." Ladybug looked down at them with a fierce face, daring them to deny her intent.

Instead, the Guardian women nodded. "*Strange times call for strange tactics.* So said the good Dimidiata," Erudia said.

They spoke no more as the evening sky changed from a blue the color of the leash to the pinks and purples of spring flowers to star-spangled black. The wind picked up, raw and chafing in its chill. One by one, oil lamps and candles were extinguished in the houses on the street, leaving black holes like gaping mouths.

"I hear it," Erudia said with preternatural calm.

"It is only the wind," Afissa answered. But as the howling grew louder, she knew it was not. She chafed her cold arms, wiggled her stiff toes, and stepped in place, in preparation for what she might be needed to do.

"One of us must grip the end of the leash while the other puts the loop over the firehound's head," Daucina said to her.

"Erudia is my mother-in-law. I'll leash the beast."

The howling grew louder, and orange tinted the sky, as if a house burned. Afissa listened and watched until she figured out the firehound's probable path. Then she took the loop and placed herself about ten feet from Erudia, between her and the firehound.

The flaming creature bounded around a corner and headed straight for her.

Afissa gasped and froze, less prepared than she had thought for the fearsome sight. She recovered in a few seconds and hurriedly loosened the loop to make it much bigger.

Although the firehound was bright against the dark night, it seemed less than solid: The flickering flames altered its outline from moment to moment.

I must look at the head. It's a big target. How can I miss? Look at the head.

As the firehound ran faster, time slowed. Afissa lifted her arms, pulled the loop open, and waited.. The heat of the approaching firehound licked her skin, and the carrion-and-ash smell of its breath assaulted her nose. Confidence filled her, and she tossed the loop over the firehound's head with as little worry as if she played a game with the children.

Time sped up. To normal and then faster. She whipped around. "Pull tight!" she shouted. The firehound ran past. Her skin singed. The beast slowed. Crouched. Leapt.

And fell short as Daucina pulled the leash and the cord of magic tightened around the firehound's neck. The hound tipped and then, looking embarrassed, sat with legs splayed.

"Erudia, walk away from the firehound," Daucina said. "I'm going to loosen the loop a little. Afissa, stay beside the creature. Pull the leash hard if it tries to attack."

Afissa's neck tightened, sending sharp pains radiating through her shoulders, back, and jaw. She moved into position. "Ready."

"Now."

As the loop loosened, the firehound's ears perked up. It stood, sniffed the air, and drilled Erudia with its pitiless gaze. It stalked her slowly moving figure. Afissa swallowed the lump in her throat and walked alongside, keeping her hand near the leash, as close to the flames as she could tolerate.

Daucina pulled the leash snug; the firehound lost interest and wandered over to a tree to piss.

She loosened the leash; it swung its head toward Erudia and broke into a trot, Afissa running beside it, her lungs heaving as her hand blistered from the flames.

Daucina pulled hard.

The firehound sat.

"We've done it. We can control the firehounds." Daucina's voice held no triumph.

I don't feel triumphant either, just drained. Relieved. "Now we've caught a firehound, what are we going to do with it?"

"I said before I wanted to test Fila to see whether she's a suitable Servant," Erudia said. "Now we have the means to do so, as well as the means to find her."

* * *

Urushi lit a candle and took the rough stone stairs down eight flights to the lowest cellar. Magical light and torchlight danced in the looking glasses on the wall of the cellar. His shoes slapped against the stone floor. A bat squeaked, swooping down from the ceiling and then up the stairwell, its beating wings rustling Urushi's hair.

An icedragon roused at his approach, rolling first one iridescent ice-blue shoulder and then the other before rising. It strolled majestically to the bars of its cage and looked at Urushi with its head tipped.

"I have no treat for you now, but perhaps soon," he told it, rubbing his hands together to warm them in the icy den. Shadow had not told him whether the icedragons were intelligent—nor much else about the creatures they had birthed together. Never had an icedragon or firehound spoken, but their eyes looked at him as if they understood his words. They followed his orders. They killed the people he told them to kill.

They never came back. Shadow wouldn't tell him why.

He went to the looking glass and looked for a movement, a shape, a darkness that should not be there. "Shadow?" he called. As his voice echoed in the chamber, the mist from his words drifted into the frigid air. He watched it rise until it dissipated into the darkness of the ceiling.

His stomach fluttered. She should be here. Was she teasing him to heighten his anticipation, or had she changed her mind?

One moment the looking glass showed nothing unusual, and in the next moment a tenebrous figure lounged on the back of the icedragon's reflection, her head resting on the spikes of the creature's scruff.

"Fila is alive. You should have told me. I had to hear it from a messenger."

Shadow shrugged. "She is on her way here. We can deal with her then." Shadow rolled up into a seated position.

"I do not want to wait." Urushi frowned and rubbed his goosepimpled arms.

"I thought you longed for me as much as I for you. Instead you have no smile for me, only anger and harsh words. You wouldn't want me to leave you, would you?"

A frisson of fear ran up his back. She had to stay with him, merge with him. Without her ancient magic, his Gift would remain incomplete and uncontrolled. He needed her, desperately, and not only to gain control of the realm. If Kassia could not heal him once she was Servant, Shadow was his only hope of completeness.

Shadow needs me as well to become human again. The thought gave Urushi the confidence to reach out his hands toward her and say, "It's time for us to merge. We have no reason to wait."

"The time is coming, my love," she assured him. "But you have other, more urgent concerns. Celatu seeks to raise an army."

He inhaled slowly and nodded. "At last he comes to his senses."

"His army is to support Fila against you." She cocked her head; the position was one no human could have held, and he stepped back in revulsion.

"You did send an icedragon for him, my love. I have more news. Some Guardian women have left the Seat to find and protect the new Servant."

"Two reasons for us to merge now. I need your magic and strength."

"You need more icedragons and firehounds to put down the insurrections before they grow." Shadow slid off the icedragon like a sheet of water. "Come." She beckoned him closer. "Let us make *you* an army."

Urushi's blood ran cold. He knew the cost, now, of creating the magical beasts. But he would have to bear it. What was one more agony in a lifetime of them? He limped toward the looking glass; she slunk toward him. They pressed together.

He did not feel her body, her flesh, only cold, but their joining was unmistakable. Her Power shot through him like a lightning bolt, and his feet lifted briefly from the cave floor. Her magic, dark and sweet like molasses, flowed through his veins. He could feel the wounds from yesterday closing, his muscles regaining their strength, the pain leaching from his joints. He knew with absolute conviction he would be the most powerful ruler of Veridia since the time of the old kingdom once they merged.

The pleasure twisted as Shadow reached for his Power and grasped it. It was as if every bone in his body was yanked out at once, except the agony went on and on. Their minds joined into one, and a blue spark appeared, followed by a red one. Soon, their mind was full of sparks that grew and took animal form. As each sprouted legs and head and tail, it plummeted, burning through Shadow toward her womb. The animal-sparks there grew, and he knew the pressure and the pain as if they were his own.

Just when it seemed they would explode, they screamed in unison. Shadow birthed the caniculae and the dracoculi in a stream of coruscating red and blue. The little ones staggered as they hit the stone floor and scattered to make room for their dog sisters and dragon brothers.

Inside the reflection, the hungry creatures drank Urushi's energy and grew. Wings popped forth from the backs of the icedragons, and fangs from the mouths of the firehounds. Still they grew, draining Urushi until his legs wobbled and his knees bent. Weak as an infant, Urushi remained upright only because of his link with Shadow.

At last, Shadow broke their connection with a moan. Urushi collapsed to the floor, his limbs as limp as a fruit jelly. Still the icedragons and firehounds drank from him until Shadow passed her hand over them.

"Go forth, my dragon younglings, and kill the men who mean your father harm. Go forth, my hound younglings, and kill the Servant and women who mean your father harm."

The glass rippled like the surface of a pond in a light breeze, and the creatures slid through the looking glass in twos and threes and plopped onto the floor. Some stopped to rub their snouts against Urushi, but the others sniffed and ran knowingly up the stairs toward fresh air and their prey.

"Shadow—" Urushi whispered.

"My sweetness...." She was already fading, now merely a few wisps of smoke delineating the shape of a woman. "Need rest," she murmured and dissolved completely.

Urushi closed his eyes, exhausted and drained. But he could not rest here; he would freeze to death. Already his toes and fingers were numb. He forced himself onto stiff limbs and crawled to the cage of the icedragon. It pawed at the ground as if eager to join its brothers. Urushi opened its cage, and it sprang over him, its wings tightly folded against its body in the tunnel. Urushi longed to see it take flight, but it raced after its new siblings on foot.

Chapter 33

CELATU PACED in Growling Dog and Bluebird's barn as the storm continued. He should have read more broadly all those years he spent in the library instead of focusing on history and legends. It would be quite useful right now to know what Judex's *On Manners and Behaviors* had to say about making apologies and requesting favors.

There was no point waiting for the storm to let up. He was soaked to the skin already. He rolled open the barn door, half-ran, half-slid across the wet paving stones to the house, and pounded on the oversized door.

"I want to apologize!" Celatu shouted.

The door opened, but his triumph was brief.

"You left the barn door open." Growling Dog again slammed the door shut.

Celatu rubbed the spot between his eyebrows as his hopes sank like a stone tossed into a deep well. Grumbling, he splashed back to the barn. He took hold of the door's edge and shoved. Just before it closed, a squealing piglet raced through the crack and out into the rain.

He lunged for the sleek pink body and wrapped his hands around it. The mud was slippery, though, and he lost his footing. He struggled frantically to keep the squirming piglet above his head as he landed hard onto his stomach. Muddy water splashed into his eyes.

When he could see again, the piglet was gone.

He looked about but the only motion he saw was the falling rain. Splashing and thunder drowned out the piglet's squeaking, if indeed it still squeaked. He took a second look and saw a spot of pink in a muddy puddle. When the spot moved, he knew he'd found the piglet.

He trudged over to the puddle, picked up the piglet, and put it under his arm, wedging it against him with his elbow. Coated in mud, it was even more slippery than before. It slid out and plopped into the same puddle, giving an indignant squeal. It looked at him, then bolted.

Celatu had no choice but to give chase.

Under the benches, around the pot of rosemary, and around the well the piglet ran. Celatu caught up to it several times, but it could turn quicker than he, and it evaded him every time. He cornered it at last when it ran into a wheelbarrow lying on its side.

He blocked it in with his body. "Nice pig," he said soothingly as he pulled off his tunic. "Good pig," he said as he tossed his tunic over the pig and then grabbed it. "Aha!" he shouted in triumph, feeling ridiculously proud of himself. The cotton of the tunic was rougher than the pig's slick flesh. The piglet squirmed and kicked, but to no avail. He carried it back to the barn and prepared to kick open the door and shove in the creature.

The piglet's heart beat rapidly against Celatu's chest, and its body heaved. He felt a flutter of alarm. Had he harmed it? He uncovered its head; the piglet was breathing hard. The little rogue was terrified. Mud clogged its nostrils. He touched its side and the skin was chill against his fingers.

He sat down in the mud, wedged the pig between his legs, and freed his shirt. He wadded it up and wiped the pig's face. The piglet struggled until he hit on stroking it as if it were a dog.

Once the piglet's face was clean, he figured he might as well finish the job. His tunic couldn't get any dirtier. He scrubbed the pig with rainwater, keeping it firmly between his knees, until it was pink and warm again.

Keeping his tunic around its chest, he marched it to the barn, cracked the door open, and shoved the piglet inside.

He stood, straightened his shoulders, and turned back toward the house. Bluebird stood at the window, laughing. When their eyes met, she covered her mouth with her hand and stepped away from the window.

Wonderful. Just wonderful. If they knew he couldn't catch a tiny pig, how would he convince them he could lead an army of Toilers to rescue Violet? He twisted his tunic to wring out some of the water and mud, put it back on and smoothed it out, and approached the door again.

He banged on it. Growling Dog opened the door. "Go away and leave us alone."

Celatu had never begged for anything in his life. He did now. He dropped to his knees in the mud. "Please. Please, for the Servant's sake and the Land's."

The door started to close. Then a large knee jutted between the door and its frame. "Let him in," Bluebird said. "Let's give him a chance to talk."

The rained poured down yet again, and winds blew it across Kassia's face so hard that some water went up her nose. Her horse and the others plodded steadily on, though, loyal to their king's wishes. She dabbed her nose with her handkerchief, reminding herself that by riding through the rain, they would reach the Seat that much faster. *I can bear this for Urushi's sake.*

Kassia looked back at Fila and clenched her fists. *After all the time I put into helping her last night—for which she did not even thank me!—she's a mess again.* The wind had torn away her hairpins, and her hair hung in heavy, cold, metallic coils that dripped water in her eyes and down Kassia's spare dress. Her hands, tied together and to the pommel of the saddle, were azurite blue. It made Kassia shiver just to look at them.

Their glances met. Fila looked … strange. Kassia would say angry, but that was impossible for a Goodborn. *Poor thing. The rains and earthquakes remind her every day that the Land regrets choosing her instead of me. I must be patient. I'll fix her hair again tonight.* She didn't know what else to do now to win back Fila's love.

Once everything was put to rights, when she was Servant and Fila was not, she would give her presents. Some pretty dresses. Maybe a position on the Servant's Council, or Servant and King's Council, or whatever it would be called. Then Fila would love her again.

"Hurry up, men," Hirtu ordered. "The sooner we get Fila to King Urushi, the sooner we get our reward." The other men cheered.

Kassia smiled, hearing her beloved called *King*. Her stomach warmed every time his loyal men used his new title or spoke of him with admiration.

Fila nudged her horse with her heels, and it trotted a few steps until it was next to Kassia's horse.

"You trust him, do you?" Fila asked Hirtu. "A man who killed his parents? A man who plans to kill his sister? Why do *you* expect more loyalty than he showed his own family?"

Shifting in his saddle, Hirtu clenched his jaw, and grief passed over his face. Quietly, he said, "Urushi owes me."

Kassia turned to face her cousin. "Urushi would never kill you, as you surely know, and your parents' death was an *accident*."

"That's right," Hirtu said somberly. "I was there."

"What? You should have told me that!" Kassia frowned at him and drummed her fingers on her saddle. "Was Urushi injured?"

"Yes, but his nurses healed him," Hirtu replied.

"I'm worried for you, Cousin," Fila said. "How do you plan to protect yourself against similar *accidents*?"

"Urushi would never hurt me." Kassia lifted her chin. "When I am Servant, I will heal him, and his magic will work properly."

Fila looked at her with pity.

Kassia fumbled under her blouse and pulled out her gold chain with Urushi's ring. "The king gave me his ring as a token," she said, her thumb hiding the growing black corruption as she displayed it for Fila. "*He loves me. He swore it on the Land itself!*"

"He loved our parents, too."

Fila knew she should feel ashamed of hurting Kassia's feelings, but she did not. In fact, as she had needled her, she had tingled with pleasure. Her cruelty had fulfilled some unfamiliar desire deep in her soul. The angrier Kassia had gotten, the more Fila wanted—no, needed—to goad her.

Her fingers and toes still vibrated, even now. Fila furrowed her forehead. She disliked more and more the person she had become since the assassins' attack. That she was trussed up like a game bird did not improve her mood.

Tears filled Fila's eyes as she remembered their childhood, when Urushi was just like any other boy who idolized his father and picked flowers for his mother. He had taught her to read; he had shown her the secret passages in the Servant's House. What had happened to that Urushi? When did he change?

The latter she could guess at. His body grew like the other boys', but the signs of his magic didn't. When she still lived at home, he had been grumpy about being a late bloomer.

What happened when his magic didn't bloom? When hair the color of a boy's was a constant reminder to him and everyone else that he was not a normal Guardian man?

Because she was Goodborn, she had not realized the effects his abnormal development would have on him. Now she had a glimmering: Anger. Bitterness. Loneliness.

This is the Urushi I will face at the Seat. Not the brother I remember, but the one warped by events out of his control.

She had to escape. She needed to meet Urushi on her own terms, not his. She needed a plan, but first she needed to take the measure of her captors. They sat their horses as if well trained, and they had wielded their weapons well and to deadly effect in the ambush.

But they were not the brightest of the Land's creatures. As she eavesdropped, they exchanged unimaginative insults, outrageous boasts, and an excessive number of fart jokes. But no one discussed politics or Urushi's plans. They were supposed to be guarding her but paid her little attention.

Urushi had not chosen his assassins well. They had skills and magic enough to carry off an ambush, but no more than that. If the right opportunity arose, she could trick them or fool them or perhaps even bribe them.

Her main obstacle to escape, then, was clever Kassia. Fila knew her cousin's strengths, and they were many.

But she knew her cousin's weaknesses, too. Fila would ponder how to use them to her advantage.

A drowsiness fell over her. Fila wiggled her numb fingers and toes, afraid she would fall off the horse if she drifted asleep. But her mind slowed and her head dropped.

She was back in the forest where she had camped with Celatu by the oak with the double knothole. As she wiggled her now-free hands and shrugged stiff shoulders, a shape formed and sparkled before her.

"Hello again, Servant."

"Hello, Shadow. I am surprised to see you now that the battle between my brother and me favors him."

Shadow wound around her and lost most of her transparency. Fila could see a white scar across her mahogany cheek that pulled her mouth into a permanent snarl, the detailed carvings on the beads woven into her long twists of black hair, the thick metal rings on the hauberk she wore over her gown, the massive muscles of a warrior. This, at last, must be Shadow's original appearance, how she looked when she was the Berserker.

Fila felt as small and inconsequential as a housefly.

"My offer remains open," Shadow said, looking down from her great height. "Invite me in; make my strength yours. You can defeat Urushi and restore the missing half of yourself. You won't be lonely anymore."

Fila raised her eyebrows. "I'm not lonely." But as she looked at Shadow, now so substantial, she saw the sorrow and longing in her eyes.

What would it be like to be split into two and to live alone, divided, for a millennium? Fila shuddered. Existence would be a prison sentence that never ended. *I could not bear it.*

Fila's chest tightened. Although Fila could not miss the Shadow half she had never known, she knew what it was like to have a void that would never be filled. She longed for her mother as Shadow longed for her other half.

"Oh, Mother!" The words escaped on their own, and her hands curled like a baby's. Tears burst from her eyes. Her diaphragm clenched painfully as it struggled to draw in more air to compensate for her sobs. Yet the enormity of her own loss was nothing compared with Shadow's.

Tentatively, Fila embraced the dark form. Shadow had no more substance than a wisp of gauzy fabric. Fila broke the embrace, but the gauze clung like spiderwebs to her skin. Gagging, she tried to peel it off, but it stretched like mucus, the ends grabbing her skin.

Shadow walked around her. The shroud of gauze fell off Fila. She looked now into a different face, one that seemed more like a creature from a dream.

"I ache that you suffer so. Let me help you. Is there some way I can set you free?"

The creature pulled away and shrieked with laughter; Fila's skin crawled as the pitch went higher and higher. "Dear Fila, you're the one who's a captive."

"Your existence must be torture. Please let me help you."

Shadow drifted further away and reshaped as a wavering image of Fila's mother.

Fila stretched a hand out, but Mother was too far away.

"Only merging will make me whole, Fila. We belong together. You feel the lack of me. I can tell."

She closed her eyes so that she could remember she spoke to Shadow. "What about Urushi?"

"He wants to merge with me, but I delay him. I prefer you. Your goodness smells so tantalizingly sweet."

"Because of your absence, I trusted people I should not have," Fila whispered. "But I am frightened of what I will become if I accept you."

"You'll become whole."

"I already am a whole person, Shadow. You cannot convince me otherwise."

Shadow looked taken back, then covered her surprise with a sweet smile that made Fila smile in return.

"I'll let you have one more chance to think, my good heart," Shadow said. "I'll give you this a symbol of my sincerity." Shadow handed her a crudely woven charm of sticks.

Fila puzzled over the pattern; she did not recognize it.

"What do I do with this?"

"It can shield your magic." The figure dissolved into motes of dust that sparkled in the moonlight.

Fila raised her eyebrows. "Wait! What use is that?"

But Shadow was gone.

Chapter 34

Growling Dog motioned Celatu into the kitchen. "A better name for you would be Celatu the Selfish. You hoarded your time and didn't give it to those you owed it to."

Despite the chill of the rain running in rivulets down his chest and back and legs, Celatu began to sweat. He had lost so much time already. Fila was still alive; the glowing copper strand told him that. But with every minute that passed she was a minute closer to Urushi and death.

"Yes, selfish. Also foolish. Several years ago I vowed I would never use magic because—" *No, no making excuses.* "I swore an oath that harmed your family and everyone else in your village. If I could take that oath back, I would. But even the Servant cannot make time run backwards.

"I came here to beg for your help. Violet needs you. The Land needs you. Please, help me. Do it for her, in spite of me."

"You haven't given any reason for us to break the Land's laws," Growling Dog said.

"Violet's death would hurt Guardians and Toilers alike. Urushi has no interest in the Land, and he looks down on the Toilers. He cares only for power."

"Like the old kings and queens?" asked Bluebird.

"Yes. His followers already call him *King Urushi.* He must be stopped," Celatu said.

"I agree," Growling Dog said. "But he's a Guardian. Your kind must stop him."

"We can't. He created magical creatures called firehounds and icedragons to kill Guardians who oppose him. Without the help of the Toilers, we who support the Servant will fail. Urushi will rule."

"Violet will set things right," Bluebird said. "Servants always have. If Fila can't do it, the next one will, or the one after that."

"How many Guardians and Toilers will die before then? As Urushi's actions throw the Land more and more out of balance, rivers will overflow their banks, and the very ground will shake and split apart. Perhaps right here, in this village.

"Violet is powerful, yes, but she is one person and she did not finish her training. She needs you."

Bluebird pursed her lips. "We are peaceful people. Conciliators." She stared at the swirling bubbles in her tea. "We can't go against the very nature the Land gave us."

"Perhaps this one time you can." He had hesitated to tell them of the prophecy. He had no idea whether Toilers believed in such things or considered them foolish nonsense. "There's an ancient Guardian prophecy you should hear." He took a breath and recited:

> *"A Servant dies by a loved one's hand;*
> *Dire storms spring from the grieving Land;*
> *The new Servant can a shadow withstand;*
> *If Toilers fight, and a coward makes a stand."*

"Shadows? Cowards? Fighting Toilers? What nonsense!" Growling Dog said.

But Bluebird turned pale, and her lavender eyes fixed on Celatu.

"An ancient evil spirit that calls itself Shadow appeared to Fila. It plans to ally itself with Urushi if Fila rejects its help."

"A version of that prophecy is known to the Toilers. My grandpapa made me learn it when I was little," Bluebird said slowly. "Urushi killed his parents, and we have had the storms. The Servant met a Shadow. Now, Celatu the Coward sits before us and wants to make a stand. We seem to live in the time prophesied."

Celatu nodded and leaned toward the couple. "All we lack are Toilers who fight. Will you help me form a Toiler army to rescue the Servant and defeat Urushi?" He gulped down the warming tea as he awaited their answer.

Growling Dog shook his head. "It is not who we are. The prophecy doesn't say we *will* fight. It only says that *if* we fight, the Servant will prevail."

"Why did someone make the prophecy then, if not to encourage Celatu to be brave and us to fight?" Bluebird asked.

"Perhaps it was to tempt us to fight, to lure us into breaking our compact with the Land. No, we are not fighters." Growling Dog thumped his mug on the table for emphasis.

Celatu's belly knotted. *If I had done my duty as a Guardian, I might have convinced them.*

The hair on the back of his neck rose and his heart beat faster as the copper connection came to life. Disappointment and exhaustion surged through him, leaving him breathless. Then the feelings were gone.

Violet needed him. Now. With slumped shoulders, he pushed back from the table and stood. "Thank you for hearing me out." He walked to the door and put his hand on the cross bar.

"I'm going with you. The Toilers will listen to me," Bluebird said matter-of-factly.

He whirled toward her in surprise.

She took off her apron. "Violet saved my niece Chipmunk's life and healed many other villagers when she was here. I owe her my help."

Growling Dog's face grew red. "What will I eat for dinner?"

She shrugged. "If what Celatu says about Urushi is true, sooner or later we'll have to get used to being hungry. You can start practicing now."

"You would go off to risk your life for a stranger and leave the little ones and me?"

Bluebird's mask of unconcern dropped. "I will risk my life for you and the younglings to make things right in the Land again. That how much I love you all."

"It's a fool's errand," Growling Dog muttered. "You'll realize that and come back."

"You know me better than that." She cupped his cheek with her hand.

Her husband turned away. "Do you have your knife? Take the sickle from the barn, too, hear?"

She leaned to kiss his head, but he shook her off.

"Let's go, then," she said, following Celatu out the door. Outside, she took the lead, walking briskly to a small one-story stone building with unusually wide doors and a bulky bell tower beside it. A thick rope hung to the left of the doors. Bluebird pulled on it several times, and bells clanged loudly. She threw open the doors and led him inside out of the rain. "The villagers will join us soon."

"In here? Ten Toilers would crowd this building."

"This is only a shell to protect the entrance to our most important resources, which are below."

Celatu saw no stairs; she led him to a wide gate with blackness beyond and turned a knob on a wall. Gears clicked; steam whistled; the gate shook. A room rose into place beyond. She opened the gate and stepped inside. "Toilers have had ascending rooms for centuries, but *our* village created the tech for a steam-power-assisted ascending room."

The ascending room descended jerkily for at least a minute. When it stopped, Bluebird opened the gate. The space beyond was huge, well lit without any scent of magic, and warm without any sign of fires. Dwarfed and a little cowed, Celatu jogged to keep up with Bluebird as she walked and told him what lay down halls and beyond doors: the communication facilities, libraries, study rooms for scholars, and laboratories for tech workers in all the sciences: chemistry, genetics, geology, mathematics. They ended at a room she called a *performance hall*, which looked something like a miniature version of the inside of the Seat.

"You'll speak standing on the raised platform in the middle; the villagers will sit in the seats around you. There's no need to shout. We have tech to make sure everyone can hear."

As Bluebird greeted the arriving Toilers, Celatu stood on the platform, his thoughts jumping all over the place. Too soon, the room filled and Bluebird stood beside him, speaking. "The Land is in danger, and we need to make some decisions about what we will do. Our Guardian, Celatu the Coward, will explain in more depth. Please listen without interrupting, no matter what you think of him. First, though, some of you may know my grandfather was a prophecy keeper, right here in this building, and he wanted me to be one too. I want to recite one of the prophecies he made me memorize. Please keep it in mind as our Guardian speaks.

> *"A Servant dies by belovèd one's hand;*
> *Sorrow wets the heaving Land;*
> *The new Servant can the shadow withstand;*
> *When Toilers fight, and a coward takes a stand."*

Celatu cleared his throat. "The Land designed our two species to help each other, each in a specific role." His mouth was so dry his tongue clicked against his teeth. "We have magic. You have strength and tech. Guardians need Toilers; Toilers need Guardians." He looked around his audience; bored and annoyed faces looked back.

"These are unusual times, times like never before. I think we are living in the time of the prophecy Bluebird recited. Who agrees with me?" A few hands wavered in the air.

"Servant Hyacinth was killed by her own son. Never before has such a thing happened. Yet the prophecy's first line is *A Servant dies by belovèd one's hand.*

"After Servant Hyacinth died, the Land raged with grief, sending torrents of rain and heaving with quakes. Never before has such a thing happened. Yet the prophecy's second line describes that, too: *Sorrow wets the heaving Land.*" The Toilers were sitting up straighter now, and some were nodding.

"Many of you met our new Servant Violet when we stayed here a few days ago. Some of you had injuries or illnesses healed by her. She's a Goodborn, daughter of Servant Hyacinth, and she is dedicated to her duty.

"However, the man who killed Servant Hyacinth plans to kill our new Servant as well. Why? He wants to rule as *king*." He paused to let his words sink in.

"Do your libraries tell of the ancient queens and kings? Ours do. Those times saw nearly constant warfare as people vied for the crown and the power it gave: the power to levy unbearable taxes, the power to take land from its owners, *the power to enslave the ancestors of the Toilers*." Now he had their attention.

He told them of the icedragons and firehounds, of Shadow, of the fulfillment of the third line of prophecy.

"Now it's time for the village to make a decision. I, Celatu the Coward, am taking a stand and backing the Servant.

"One event, and one event only, remains for the prophecy to be fulfilled in whole: In these unusual and unnatural times, Toilers must go against their very natures and against the law of the Land and fight for Violet and against Urushi.

"We are not under the rule of a king. Yet. So I can't order you to follow me into battle. You are free to decide for yourselves what to do. I urge you to consider what will be best for your village, for your children and grandchildren, for both Guardians and Toilers, and for the Land itself." He stepped off the dais, took a seat in the back ring, and promptly fell asleep.

Bluebird shook him awake. Of the crowd that had filled the performance hall before, only twenty Toilers remained, including his friend.

I failed. He tried to swallow the lump in his throat, but his mouth was too dry. His cheeks stuck to his teeth, and his mouth tasted defeat.

Yet Bluebird beamed at him. "You did it! We have the start of an army! Twenty people will break the Land's rules to help the Servant."

He rubbed the spot above his nose. Only twenty, yet they were twenty on whom Urushi could not sic firehounds or icedragons. Twenty who were all taller and stronger than any Guardian. Twenty who fought for the good of the Land rather than Urushi's favors. *Twenty is a good start after all.*

"Gather your hoes and shovels, your kitchen knives and marble pastry boards. We will meet outside the entrance above in an hour to go to other villages to find recruits."

He and Bluebird took the ascending room to the surface and stepped out into sunshine. Bluebird took his arm as she looked up at the blue sky. "I'm relieved. To go against both law and instinct is a hard decision. The Land is letting us know it is the right decision."

As the rest of his army returned over the next hour, most voiced the same opinion. They began their trek toward the road to the Seat with enthusiasm and shouts and singing. As they passed Bluebird's home, she looked over her shoulder, her lips pressed together and her eyes glistening.

The door swung open. Growling Dog stomped out carrying a stout stick and fell into step beside Bluebird.

Surprise stopped Celatu dead in his tracks.

The Toiler scowled down on him. "Some people in the next village owe me favors," he said roughly. "You'll get your Toiler army." He lay his hand protectively on Bluebird's shoulder.

He had done it! With one impossible thing down, the next impossible thing, defeating Urushi and his creatures, seemed slightly less daunting than before.

He felt for the copper thread in his mind, imagined himself grasping it with both hands, imagined tugging slightly so the Servant would notice. He focused on the thread. *Hold on, sweet Violet. I'm coming to help you.*

Chapter 35

O NCE AGAIN, Shadow had seemed as real as life. But Fila was still on the road with her kidnappers, and the rain still poured. The assassins nattered on as before.

Something unfamiliar bumped her wrist. She glanced down. Her hands were still tied in front of her, but she now clutched the wooden charm Shadow gave her. It was as solid as any other object in the real world, and her fingers wove through the gaping holes.

Clearly but faintly, as if he were far down the road, Celatu called. "Hold on, sweet Violet. I'm coming to help you."

The rain stopped.

Fila blinked and looked around. Celatu was nowhere in sight.

Of course he wasn't. He had deserted her. So why did she think about him so often?

"What's that?" Kassia demanded. Fila held her breath, fearing her cousin had seen the charm or heard Celatu. Then goosebumps rose on her arms.

Baying. Quite a distance off, yet so deep it resonated in her chest. The baying grew quickly louder, as if the source covered ground preternaturally fast.

The assassins stopped.

"What are firehounds doing out here?" one asked.

"Don't be stupid," another answered. "What do firehounds hunt and kill? Guardian women. Whom do we have with us? Guardian women."

"Ignore him," Hirtu ordered. "Protect Kassia."

"We left the Seat several days ago. Kassia could have fallen out of favor since then."

"You know how fickle Urushi can be."

"If firehounds are coming, our job is done. We can go home."

"Stay!" Hirtu roared.

"What are you all babbling about?" Kassia shouted.

The assassins, minus Hirtu, galloped off into the forest. From around the bend in the road far ahead bounded two flaming behemoths.

"Pus and blood," Hirtu swore.

The firehounds were pony-size, with muscles that bulged like those of lions. Their eyes glowed scarlet.

Fila's heart pounded. Waves of warmth from their fiery hides reached her from an impossible distance.

Kassia moved close to Fila. "What are they?"

"Firehounds. Untie me! Quickly!"

Kassia just stared.

"I'll protect you, Kassia." Hirtu kicked his horse to race toward the hounds.

The firehounds did not veer from their path; neither did Hirtu. The beasts passed on either side; flames licked Hirtu and his mount.

The horse screamed and reared. His clothes smoking, Hirtu hung on, low to the horse's neck. The terrified horse landed, bucked, and then threw Hirtu off.

He landed several yards away in a broken heap.

Kassia's mouth opened in a silent scream.

Hair rose on the back of Fila's neck: The firehounds' gaze had never left her and Kassia.

Time slowed as those unearthly eyes watched them, and Fila struggled against ropes that refused to yield. "Untie me!"

"Pus pus pus pus pus," Kassia muttered. She leaned over and yanked at the knots binding Fila's hands. The knot holding her hands to the pommel loosened and gave way.

The hounds crouched. The larger one tipped back its head and howled. Then both sprang.

Kassia screamed as the firehounds soared.

Her spooked horse stomped and snorted.

Shadow's charm jittered in Fila's hands.

The dogs landed and were on them in an instant.

Or rather, the firehounds were on Kassia, gnawing her boots and scorching her legs.

Kassia yanked her legs up, out of reach, and wobbled on the saddle on her tailbone.

The larger hound rose onto its hind legs, its head higher than the horse's back.

"There's a tree limb above you," Fila shouted.

Kassia stood and jumped for the limb.

She caught it and swung.

Her horse turned in circles, kicking the firehounds as they tried to scrabble up its sides to reach her.

Face blotchy with exertion, Kassia pulled herself onto the branch and then straddled it.

The firehounds leaped higher.

"Sleeping charms! In my bag!" Fila shouted.

Kassia yanked open the needlework bag and rummaged through it. The thief's knife fell out and skittered across the road.

The knife landed at the feet of Fila's horse, which danced, ears back, in fear. *If only I could reach it!* Shadow's charm touched her mind.

Guiding the horse with her knees and bound hands, Fila turned it eastward. Kassia tossed a sleeping charm on the closest firehound as the other one ripped out her horse's neck in frustration. Kassia's horse screamed—briefly—as Fila nudged her own into a canter and rode away.

"Fila!"

She turned. Kassia had fallen. A firehound had her in its massive jaws.

I have to go back!

Fila kept riding.

Fila ignored the screams behind her. "I have to stop Urushi," she muttered. "Only I can. Only I can. The Servant. Kassia's life is not as important as...."

The words blocked her throat, choked her. Fila pulled back on the reins. She tried to cough to free her words.

No. Those are not my words. They are Shadow's words. Shadow's thoughts. She is trying to change me, as she did my poor brother.

The good Dimidiata would not abandon a friend—or an enemy—to firehounds. Shadow had poisoned her soul.

A growl gathered in her throat. Fila pushed it out, spun her horse, and galloped back to help her betrayer.

"Kassia!" Her voice freed. "Kassia!"

Her cousin did not respond. She lay on the ground, unmoving, her leg in the maw of a firehound.

The other firehound, a charm on its forehead, sprawled across the road, its mouth opened in a huge yawn, its eyes closing.

"Hirtu!" He did not answer either. His spirit had left him.

She returned to Kassia. Her hands were still tied, so she swung her leg over the back of the horse and tumbled onto the packed dirt of the road.

When Fila came to, she did not know where she was, or why, or when, until the firehound's growling and slavering penetrated her cloudy mind. *I have to save Kassia!* She groaned, made sure she still had Shadow's protective charm, tried to sit up, and fell flat again. *I cannot do it.*

I must do it. She squirmed until some of her skin touched the ground and then sucked energy from the Land like an orphaned calf from a bottle. When she could sit, she lunged for the thief's knife.

She got it.

Holding the knife and the charm between her tied hands, she crawled toward the firehound that held Kassia. It ignored her as it had Hirtu. Its singlemindedness chilled her; it mirrored Urushi's own blindered efforts to be king.

She shot a quick glance at her cousin. Her leg was open from knee to ankle. Bone and blood and gristle glistened. Thank the Land, her wounds still bled; her chest still rose and fell.

She had to kill the firehound, but the thought of pressing the knife home through living flesh, of feeling the hound's warm blood spilling onto her hands, sickened and repelled her.

For the first time, she wished she were a man so she could kill the firehound cleanly from a distance. But women's magic offered only a few roundabout ways to kill, and the charms were complex. She had to use the knife.

The firehound opened its jaws, revealing a crimson tongue, pink-filmed teeth, and a gape large enough to swallow a natural dog whole.

Fila thrust the knife into its chest with all her might, gritting her teeth against the flames that swallowed her hands.

The firehound scratched the place with a hind leg, not even bothering to look at the minor irritation.

Horrified, Fila cried out. Where had Urushi put the creature's heart?

She yanked the knife out and chose another spot. Her hands refused to enter the flames again. *Kassia stood up for me many times when we were children.* She stabbed and stabbed and stabbed. At last, she pierced the tough hide and hit something important.

The firehound whined and whipped around, snapping. Despite Shadow's charm, she had its full attention.

She scrabbled backward. Steaming blood sprayed from the dog's wound, burning like acid every place it touched her. Inexorable, like a Toiler pup's mechanical toy, the firehound dragged itself toward her with its front legs.

Her head hit a tree. She could back up no farther. She lifted her knife toward the advancing firehound. It kept its red eyes fixed on her, never veering from a straight path toward her.

She braced her back against the tree, her elbows against her knees, and her heels against the ground, holding the knife straight forward. The dog's chest touched the point. Its powerful muscles impelled it forward. Even as it impaled itself, it opened its mouth and reached for her face. Then with a pitiful whine, the firehound collapsed onto its side.

Fila crawled painfully toward Kassia and let her copper hair puddle in Kassia's wounds. Huffing, she wrenched her needlework kit from Kassia's hand and tipped it over. She took inventory quickly. She had made so many healing charms lately that her remaining supplies were not enough to heal Kassia.

She fumbled to undo the ties of Kassia's needlework bag. Fila looked inside and trembled with anger. The bag was stuffed with charms of regrowth and of knitting together. While Kassia was pretending to be Fila's friend at Boraga's manor, she had been planning for violence.

Fila flung her hair back and crawled about Kassia, dropping charms over the mangled leg as best she could with her hands tied together. Then she sat down and wedged the knife, point up, between her knees, wincing when a near-boiling drop of blood ran down the blade and fell on her hand.

She held the ropes at her wrists to the knife and sawed. She expected it to be a long job, but the acidic blood ate at the rope. In minutes, her hands were free. She yanked the boots from her feet and threw them far away. Now she needed only to make certain the charms on Kassia's leg were working properly and kill the sleeping firehound.

She squatted next to Kassia. Beneath the knots of the charms, bone and tissue slowly filled in. Fingers of skin reached out from healthy areas to cover the injuries.

Kassia would be forever scarred, but she would live.

Now Fila needed to get far away before her cousin woke up. She repacked her needlework bag and added the knife after wiping it clean on the dead firehound's ashy fur. She did not want to foul the Land by cleaning it in the dirt. She tied the needlework bag to her belt, stood, and turned toward her horse.

A man with a bruised face leaned against her horse, chewing a cordgrass stem as he watched her. Another horse stood behind hers, its sides heaving like bellows.

"Stand aside."

He tossed away the stem. "The Land is on my side today. Urushi sent me with the firehounds to find you, and here you are."

She felt no fear—she had defeated a firehound, and the victory still thrilled in her veins—only a deep weariness that she had to face yet another enemy today.

"The Land is on your side?" she scoffed. "The firehounds almost killed Kassia. Urushi will not be pleased when he hears you allowed his bride to be injured."

The man paled and looked around. His gaze went to Kassia's body lying motionless on the ground, her pale hair undone and lying in the dirt, the many charms covering her leg. "Land preserve me! The firehounds were instructed to kill only the Servant."

"Unfortunately for Kassia, she was wearing my needlework kit." *While I was protected by Shadow's charm.*

The man narrowed his eyes and looked at her with suspicion. "Why did the hounds ignore you?"

"Either I am not as powerful as Urushi fears, or I am far more powerful than he can imagine. Now if you will move away from my horse, I will be on my way."

He thought, frowning. "No. King Urushi says Kassia is meant to be Servant. I think the firehounds just confirmed that by ignoring you." He stepped toward her. "You won't be leaving. I have my orders." Male magic tingled in the air.

From the corner of her eye she saw the sleeping firehound stir.

"Kassia is badly hurt," she told the man briskly. "You'll need my help to get her on a horse without reopening the wounds. First I must wrap her leg to keep the charms in place."

The man crossed his arms and watched her like a bird of prey as Fila pulled off Kassia's petticoat and tore it into strips. Her body hid the awakening firehound from view, and she knocked the sleeping charm from its head with her elbow. She wrapped Kassia's leg and other wounds slowly and thoroughly. Behind her, the firehound growled.

"You will have to help. She is too heavy for me to lift, and she is still senseless."

The man eyed her with suspicion.

She continued giving orders with the assured voice of a Servant. "Take her other arm. Be careful of her leg. The firehound did a lot of damage. She will not be completely healed for perhaps two days. Which horse should we put her on? The firehounds killed hers."

Fila took Kassia's right arm, and Urushi's man put his arms around Kassia's back and waist. Together, they put Kassia across the saddle of the man's horse.

The surviving firehound was now standing, wobbling a little but sniffing the air. The man did not notice; he was adjusting Kassia so she would not slip off. Fila moved behind him, pulled out clumps of her hair with both hands, and stuffed them down the back of his shirt.

"What stupid trick is this?" He whirled around and scratched at his back. She pulled out more hair, tossed it on him, and dashed for her horse.

"You'll be dead in seconds, you stupid girl," Urushi's man said. A bolt of male magic shot toward her, then veered crazily away. She threw herself on the horse and turned to look at Urushi's man.

His eyes were wide with fear as he faced a crouching firehound. Fila's hair in his shirt, no longer hidden by Shadow's charm, was like a lodestone to the beast. With a roar, it leapt and knocked him to the ground.

Fila rode over to Kassia, grabbed her horse's bridle, and rode for the Seat of Enchantment. She shook as if it were winter and she had no cloak. What she had done was not good, but she hoped at least it was right.

Once again, riding away, she heard a human scream.

This time, tears filled her eyes, but she did not turn back.

Chapter 36

KASSIA AWOKE to a throbbing headache and a buzzing ache deep in her leg, a sign of a serious wound healed by magic. She forced her eyelids open and looked about. It was morning, and she lay on the ground in the woods next to a small campfire. None of Urushi's men were in sight, and Fila walked about freely. Kassia's memories held no clues.

Kassia tried to sit up. She couldn't; her feet were tied together and her hands as well. She looked at her belt; both her needlework bag and Fila's were missing.

"Fila! Get over here right now."

"Ah, you're awake. What do you want?"

Fila was free, Urushi's men were gone.... Wary now, Kassia tempered her voice. "What's going on? I don't remember anything."

"Be glad you do not." Fila gazed at her with a flat expression, as if she had judged her and found her wanting. Again. "Urushi sent firehounds to kill me. Instead, they attacked you."

"He would never harm me."

"Perhaps not on purpose. The attack on you was an *accident*." Fila walked over and carefully picked up the edge of Kassia's skirt and peeled it back.

Kassia gasped at the sunken scar, wide and pink and jagged, that ran from above her knee to her ankle. The flesh nearby was deeply pitted. She had never seen anything uglier. A sob choked her, and tears puddled in her eyes. Her beautiful leg was beautiful no longer.

Fila continued in a calm voice. "Accidents seem to happen around Urushi, do they not?" The heightened color in her cheeks belied her tone.

"Where are my men?"

"My brother had at least one friend with some honor. Hirtu lost his life defending you from the firehounds. "

"Hirtu, dead?" She felt sick; her forehead burned as if with fever. "My poor Urushi." *Poor me, as well. I liked him the best of Urushi's friends.*

"The other assassins deserted you. They believed Urushi sent the firehounds for *both* of us."

"You think so poorly of Urushi, you probably believe that too," she said bitterly.

Fila's face softened. "When I was a youngling, he was a good brother to me. I want to believe some of that Urushi still survives."

"It does. Despite all he has suffered."

"I'm glad. In the stories you told me of your suitors, you never tolerated any who spoke down to you or liked you only for your beauty. After you betrayed me, I realized I never knew you as I thought I did. But I wanted to believe you still had your self-respect."

"You and Urushi are at odds, and I'm caught in the middle. That's not betrayal."

"What would you call it then? And it was not only me you betrayed. Amma is *dead*. My cousin Durio and the rest of my father's men are *dead*. Celatu almost died."

Kassia found herself at a rare loss for words.

"I'm struggling, Kassia. What did I—or Spotted Turtle or Cousin Durio— ever do to you to deserve such treatment?"

"It had nothing to do with you. I have a destiny. A destiny to be the Servant."

"You've dreamed since we were little girls of being Servant. That's not a destiny. You know I dreamed of living in a Toiler village and knowing with every stitch exactly who I was helping. Not all youngling dreams come true."

Fila sounds so bitter. She truly does not want to be Servant. "I do have a destiny," Kassia insisted. "I feel it deep inside me; I always have."

"If being Servant were your destiny, you would not have to do anything to bring it about. It would just happen. As it happened to me."

"You're wrong. You worked for it or paid for it somehow. Like good grades. Like love."

"If I did, it was by accident." One corner of her mouth quirked. "You should have stopped me."

"But … but … I have to admit that I never saw you trying to win the Land's favor. But you must have done something."

"Kassia, the Land is not a cat that will love you because you feed it, give it water, and let it sleep on your bed. The Land is so alien that the longer I am bound to It, the less I understand It."

"So all the things I did to please It, to make It love me, were wasted. It took my gifts and gave nothing back." Kassia's hands started shaking first, then the rest of her body. She was cold, not from the weather, but from the inside out.

Fila picked up her own blanket and wrapped it around her. "Do you need a charm to calm you?"

She shook her head. "I need to figure out what I did wrong."

"Nothing. You did nothing wrong." Fila sat and wrapped her arms about her. "The Land is fickle. Temperamental. Subject to melancholy. It often does not understand what I want or need. How could you—or anyone—ever hope to please It?"

Fila's words stunned her into silence. *The Land is like Mother. No matter what I do, it is too little or too late or too wild to win her love. But she refuses to tell the secret.*

The world was cracking. It had always been logical, predictable, sensible. Now she didn't understand how it worked anymore or what her place in it was. Everything had been held together by a single linchpin: her destiny to be Servant.

She was no longer special.

No, I cannot live with being ordinary.

I don't feel ordinary. I feel that I am meant to be Servant.

I am still young. I could still be Servant one day. The Land could have Its reasons. I will have to wait and trust.

Fila interrupted her thoughts. "Are you feeling well enough to travel? We need to get to the Seat as soon as possible. The firehound I did not kill is likely looking for us."

Kassia put her bound fists to her forehead and leaned on them. "Urushi said it would be a bloodless coup."

One of Fila's unplucked eyebrows lifted. "That may be what he wanted, but it is not what he did. Firehounds are not the only magical creatures Urushi created. There are also icedragons, which hunt Guardian men. Urushi sent one after your brother."

Kassia shook her head. She could not believe the things Fila was saying. Urushi would never harm her or her family.

Would he?

No. Two things she knew for true: She was destined to be Servant, and Urushi loved her desperately. "Tul is mistaken. Urushi would not risk losing me."

Fila's expression changed, not to disbelief, but to a closed-off face that revealed she was hiding something.

"You know something. What is it?"

She thought Fila wouldn't tell her. She said nothing as she untied Kassia's feet and hands, helped her up, and led her to a horse she didn't recognize. Fila did not give her needlework bag. Only when Kassia was mounted did Fila speak.

"I believe someone bad, someone evil with powerful magic, is influencing Urushi. I do not absolve Urushi from trying to kill me. He should have recognized bad counsel from an evil … person and not allowed her to get close. But perhaps her magic is so strong.…"

Kassia's insides turned to ice. "Tell me about this counselor and her magic."

Fila pressed her lips together and would say no more. She mounted Hirtu's horse. "Do not think to escape because I have not bound you while we ride. While you slept off your injuries, I rode both horses. I gave you the slower one. If you try to escape, I will catch you easily."

"I have no intentions of escaping you," she said with a purposeful hint of hurt in her voice. *Not until I have gotten more information from you about Urushi's evil counselor. Then I will go to him and send her off. I want my husband to be a beloved king, not a hated one.*

"I am so glad you are willing to be sensible." They had traveled about half a mile when Fila turned to her and asked, "Did I hear you refer to your brother as Tul?"

"Yes. When I was very little I couldn't make an *S* sound. I called him Tul instead. Even though we're grown, every so often, I still call him *Tul*. Why do you ask? Does it matter?"

Fila frowned. "A little bit."

Urushi squats by an anthill, using his magic to break several pieces of bread into tiny crumbs. A few ants wander by, find crumbs, and carry them to the nest. He laughs when a minute later, ants pour from the anthill and scurry in different directions toward the piles of crumbs. They work hard. Most ants carry crumbs bigger than they are.

"Urushi? Where is Fila? I thought she was with you," Mother calls from the picnic blanket on the bank of the stream.

I forgot all about Fila! He shouts her name and hears her call for help. He runs along the stream, continuing to shout.

He finds her waist deep in water, crying. "Don't be scared. I'm here. Just take four steps and you'll be with me."

"I can't," she wails.

"Why not?"

"The fishies. They're touching me."

"I'll rescue you," he says, pulling off his shoes and pants. But when he takes a step toward her, saplings sprout from the ground, blocking his way. He runs

upstream; he runs downstream; wherever he tries to get around them, more grow and block him.

He returns to the place four steps from her, determined to cut his way through. The roots resist his pocketknife. The trees are made of Toiler metal, not wood.

He sends bolts of magic at them, but they fizzle out before hitting the saplings. His skin tears open anyway.

Fila blubbers and screams, "Urushi! Urushi! Help me!"

He looks up from his attempts to get through the saplings to reassure her, only to see the stream is rising. Fast. The water is up to her shoulders.

He finds a pair of saplings with a gap between them and tries to wiggle through sideways. He gets stuck. He sends out magic to break one of the saplings, but it splits into waves that wobble off in various directions. He is helpless to do anything but watch as the stream closes over Fila's head.

The sound of his bedroom door opening woke him. He pulled up the sheet and wiped moisture from his forehead.

"Another nightmare?" Hooting Owl asked.

"Yes. I'm glad you came in when you did." He threw off the blanket and sat on the edge of the bed. The room air felt cold; he was sweating all over.

Hooting Owl frowned. "Was it about Fila again?"

He petted Wiggle. "What is on my schedule for today?"

"Your uncle will be here soon with some coronation robes for you to choose from."

"Pus and blood! I forgot! Please feed Wiggle and delay my uncle while I clean up." Hooting Owl carried Wiggle out. Urushi splashed water on his face and pulled on pants and a simple tunic, then shoved shoes on his feet. Soon, someone knocked at the door. A Toiler rolled in a rack hung with robes of every color, some ancient, some newer, one the robe Father wore when he was invested as Consort.

It seemed a frivolous waste of time; his desk was piled with urgent requests and reports from those who accepted his rule. But Hooting Owl had urged him to choose a coronation robe with care. Given the opposition to his rule, Appa said, he needed to look every inch a king, wise and strong and powerful.

He wanted a robe of red velvet, just as the ancient kings and queens had worn for their coronations. But heeding Appa's advice, he had ordered many robes brought from storage. He was still looking over robe details and trying to decide which looked most regal when Hooting Owl brought in Uncle Bifac.

"I am honored you called on me to help choose your coronation robe."

Bifac's obsequious tone pleased him and put him in a good mood. "Thank you for coming, Uncle. I am pleased to see you."

"What do you want to try on first?" Appa asked.

"The plain red velvet, the one without puffy shoulders or embroidery."

Appa helped him put it on. He turned this way and that in front of his chamber looking glass as Bifac stood with his hands clasped, the picture of a loyal courtier, and Hooting Owl adjusted the folds of the robe. His shoulders looked broad even without the prissy fuss of puffy shoulders, and it was not too big. Appa had warned him any man looked half-grown in a too-big robe.

"What do you think, Uncle? Would Kassia like to be crowned in red?" *I could have both crowns set with rubies from the ancient treasury, with opals in Kassia's to match the ring I gave her.*

"I suggest the green robe instead," Bifac replied. "More flattering."

"Kassia does look good in green. The red might be too bold for her pearly skin." He fingered the gold buttons, wondering how much ornament Kassia would think was tasteful. He had expected her here by now to help with these decisions.

"Bifac meant more flattering for you," Hooting Owl said.

Urushi's looked from his uncle to his appa and back.

Bifac glared at Hooting Owl, who said to him with Toiler calm, "You're not a good counselor if you give him only half the truth."

"Uncle?" Urushi growled. If Appa spoke so, he had good cause.

Bifac's jaw tightened briefly. "Your appa is quite old. Perhaps he should retire. He seems to be becoming senile."

"Hooting Owl?"

"Your father's green robe would be more flattering on you because it has a hood to cover your hair. Also...." Appa put his arm around Urushi's shoulders and led him closer to the looking glass.

Urushi saw the problem. His scars. From habit, he had looked only at his body when he studied his image in the robe. Now he squinted to see what his poor magic had done to him over the years. The newer scars stood out a vivid purple, sucking color from the red robe. His skin had a healthy flush from the red reflecting against it, but his old, white scars looked even whiter.

He wrinkled his brow. The scarring in his eyes continued to expand. Perhaps the heightened colors of his scars were another symptom of his failing vision.

"The green robe, please."

Appa brought it over and held it in front of him. Next to green, the scars were less noticeable. Appa was right—he should cover his hair, unless Shadow or the Toilers' cream turned it silver by his coronation.

The skin under his right eye spasmed; the eye shut and opened, shut and opened, in an annoying rhythm he could not control. Deep inside, he felt the pressure of his magic expanding. He swirled around, pushing Hooting Owl to the side and tearing off the red robe. He advanced on his uncle, who blanched and backed up a step.

"You would have let me take my place as king looking like a boy and a freak," Urushi shouted.

"I told you the green was more flattering," Bifac protested.

"But you did not tell me *why*!" The sentence ended as a roar. "What other good counsel are you keeping from me?"

Bifac studied him, then bowed his head. "Some rulers like their truth hidden behind honeyed words. Forgive me for thinking you one of them."

"So answer my question!"

Bifac licked his lips. "I've been thinking since we talked last. Your plan to kill Fila could turn on you. One Servant dead is shocking enough. A second one would be rather much."

"Too late. I already sent two firehounds for her."

"Land preserve us!" His eyes shone with tears.

"I promised you and Kassia she would be Servant. I keep my promises."

In a strangled voice, Bifac said, "Of course you do, Majesty."

"You are dismissed for today, Uncle. Hooting Owl can help me from here." Bifac bowed and rushed out, shutting the door hard after him.

Appa looked at Urushi with a sad frown.

"You think I was wrong to send someone to kill Fila. Believe me, Appa, I considered every option."

"You Guardians have your own ways, and we Toilers have ours. I shouldn't judge your *right* and *wrong* by Toiler standards." He took the green robe back to the rack and hung it up. He returned and wrapped his arms tight around Urushi, crushing the breath from him and lifting him off the floor. Hooting Owl's voice became vehement. "As your appa, I want you to flourish. I remember which boys mocked you when their hair turned silver and yours didn't. I want to see them kneel before you. I want your hair to silver and your magic to stabilize. What you choose to do, I will support." He dropped Urushi, and Urushi doubled over, coughing, as his lungs sucked back in air.

When he stood up, Appa was crying. "But I am really going to miss sweet Fila."

Appa left; Wiggle ran in through the door he left open.

I am really going to miss Fila too. He sank onto the bed, his body heavy as a sack of rocks. Wiggle jumped up beside him and stood on his hind legs to lick his face. Like Wiggle, Fila had adored him once, and he had loved her.

He wept.

Chapter 37

BY LATE AFTERNOON, Celatu and his army had taken tree-lined back roads to three other Toiler villages and persuaded nearly one hundred Toilers to join up. He had been careful to stay in the shade, and although twice he thought he saw the flash of icedragon wings, none had attacked.

Now, at the last village, a prosperous one with vast orchards of fruit trees, he looked at his makeshift army in amazement. A week ago, who would have thought that he, a simple scholar, would lead an army to depose a usurper king and rescue the Servant? Some part of him urged him to flee, told him he still had time to save himself, but he refused to listen to those self-preserving messages of his pre-Violet self.

He had dedicated himself to restoring harmony to the land. Veridia needed him; the prophecy confirmed it. Violet needed him.

And he needed her.

"We've got an army. Now what?" Growling Dog asked. Around and behind them, the air hummed with the deep voices of Toilers joking, questioning, and bragging about their coming brave exploits.

This was the moment Celatu had dreaded. He knew nothing of warcraft but what he had read in a few books on military history. He straightened his shoulders. He could bumble his way through this situation as semicompetently as he had every other one since he fled the city on Swallowtail.

He had deduced from the histories that every campaign should start with a speech to inspire and embolden. He faced his troops and bellowed "Friends!"

The excited murmuring quieted. The sun blazed, but the Toilers stood proudly with their weapons. Women's apron pockets bulged with steel kitchen knives as long as his arm. Although useless against magic, they would be more than a match for the iron weapons of Guardians. Hoes and sickles and shovels rested on brawny shoulders. Several hunters carried slings, bows, or crossbows. Behind the foot soldiers waited the wagons. Quick-thinking Toilers had loaded them with arrows, crossbow bolts, and barrels of water.

The hair stood up on Celatu's arms at their bravery. The Toilers knew they would have no protection against magic but himself and no Guardian woman to heal their wounds. But they came to the aid of the Land anyway.

He climbed onto a barrel so the Toilers could see him. "Urushi wishes to return Veridia to the days of tyrant kings and queens. He thinks no one can stop him." Celatu paused and let the silence hang. "But Urushi is wrong! You Toilers can stop him. Unlike any Toilers before, and perhaps any Toilers after us, *you* are the fulfillment of a prophecy. You will help the Servant take her Seat and save Veridia from the tyranny of kings and queens." He pulled the knife Bluebird had given him earlier that day out of his belt and held it aloft. "Will you Toilers fight for the Land and fulfill the prophecy?"

"Aye!" The Toilers' deep voices vibrated inside his ribs and in the barrel beneath his feet. They stomped their huge feet in unison, rocking the barrel and forcing him to grab onto Growling Dog's shoulder to steady himself.

"Then we go to rescue the Servant and depose a false king. For the Land!" *For you, Violet*, he thought, hoping the copper cord would carry his dedication and devotion to her.

"For the Land!" the Toilers roared in reply, their voices rustling the leaves of the trees. Celatu jumped off the barrel and strode down the shady, rutted path that led away from the village and through the forest, the last hope of Veridia behind him making the Land tremble.

When they reached the main road and emerged from the trees, Celatu turned east toward the Seat of Enchantment. The sky was bright, and the forest on either side of the road was unusually quiet. Wishing he had nictitating membranes as the Toilers did, Celatu shielded his eyes with his hands against the glare.

A female voice shouted, "Look!"

The Toilers murmured, and the sound of marching stopped.

Celatu whirled. The Toilers stood with heads tipped back. As he started to follow suit, Bluebird clapped her hands over his eyes. "Don't look! It's too bright for Guardian eyes."

But his brief glance had already taken in a second brilliant, blinding light in the sky. *How can I lead the army half-blind?*

"What is that circling?" someone called.

"Look at the long tail!" shouted Growling Dog. "It's a lizard."

The bottom fell out of Celatu's stomach. "No, it's an icedragon."

The word was repeated dozens of times in dozens of voices. Some in Celatu's army gasped or screamed. Metal clanged as others readied their weapons.

Celatu blinked several times to clear the glare-induced tears, but it didn't help. He licked his lips. "The icedragon comes for me, not you!" He took a deep breath so he could yell louder. "Kill it when it dives for me."

"Kill it when it dives!" Growling Dog's voice echoed.

"Where do we strike it?" cried Bluebird, her voice shrill.

"Its skin is thick and tough. Strike it anywhere you can, just strike it *hard*!" Celatu shouted. "But be sure not to touch it; it burns the skin like acid."

He focused on his core of magic and drew on it, shaping and honing a bolt strong enough to blast a boulder to smithereens. Would it be enough for an icedragon?

His magic thrummed in his chest, eager to fly, but he clenched his fists and doused the bolt's fire with his will. Because he could not look at the icedragon, he could not aim accurately, and he dared not chance hurting anyone in his army.

I will have to stand here, blind, as a lure to draw it in.

He wished the icedragon would stop its circling and do something. He grew more jittery by the moment, and he suspected many of the Toilers did too.

Oh, if only Fila could see him now. Her mouth would fall open in astonishment.

The thought made him smile, and he felt his tight muscles relax a little. It was just one icedragon. The Toilers towered over him, and they should be able to kill it before it reached him. Excitement and energy surged through him, crashing through all his niggling doubts and fears, and leaving behind a gift: He felt invincible.

He pulled out his knife, lifted his arms wide to the sky, and cried, "Come and get me!"

Wings flapped louder and louder. He was ready. The air whistled, and cold air burned his scalp. This was his moment of glory. He bent his knees to absorb the shock of its impact. He grinned with anticipation, feeling the increasing cold.

Then … nothing.

"What happened?" Celatu's voice sounded tight and small.

"It swooped over your head and up again." Growling Dog's voice was full of awe. "It's fast, faster than a Toiler can move. And it's huge. Each of its claws is bigger than your knife, and its neck is ringed with spikes." He dropped his voice and whispered in Celatu's ear. "We can't kill it."

Just as quickly as it had come, his joy in the confrontation fled. Celatu had believed he had been afraid before. No. *This* was true fear. Choking, panting, gasping, gut-wrenching fear. Struggling not to piss his britches fear. Wanting to scream for his mother fear.

He grabbed onto Growling Dog's beefy arm.

The Toiler, following his protective instincts, wrapped his arms tightly around Celatu and ran toward safety.

"No," Celatu rasped. "Put me down! You *can* kill it. Take me closer to the forest so I can see a little. Tree limbs will slow the icedragon down."

Growling Dog did as he requested. "Too bad we didn't bring a net," the Toiler grumbled, the strength back in his voice. "You should have thought of bringing a net."

"Forget the net we don't have," Bluebird chided. "We'll be ready." Her hand touched Celatu's arm. "You'll have me right beside you. If everyone else misses it, I'll get it."

"Too close. It might injure you by accident. Stand near Growling Dog. If the icedragon is as huge as he says, you'll still be able to reach it, but you won't get hurt."

Her hand let go, his hand-shielded eyes saw her feet move away, and then all fell silent.

"Here it comes," someone yelled. Celatu gripped his knife tighter.

A shriek pierced the air, and Celatu's hair stirred in the whirlwind the creature created as it plummeted. When metal clashed and a chill hit him, he dropped to a crouch, keeping his head down, and jabbed his knife upward.

The knife hit scales, ratcheted down the belly, and bit in.

The icedragon screamed, and the length of Celatu's arm burned as if a hot poker had raked him. He pulled his knife free and struck again blindly. He gasped as another line of fire crossed the first one.

"We've got it pinned!" Growling Dog shouted.

Celatu rolled away, hoping he was now out of reach of its burning scimitar claws. He struggled to his feet with Bluebird's help and, panting and shading his face with his uninjured arm, opened his eyes to a squint.

The huge creature lay spread-eagled; several Toilers stood on each wing and several more on each leg. It struggled and screamed and snapped, but to no avail. Missing scales revealed raw, oozing skin underneath, and the icedragon bled from several wounds where the Toilers had pierced its hard scales and hide.

Urushi had made it tough enough to withstand the strength of a Guardian. He had been shortsighted in not making it tough enough to withstand a group of Toilers.

Celatu stared at his enemy. Its scales glistened in the sunlight like polished slabs of stone. It was beautifully proportioned and had surprisingly delicate features. Its teeth gleamed like pearls, and its faceted eyes, like a mountain lake. He stared into those eyes, and they stared back, intelligent and cold with fury.

Intrigued, he watched expressions play across the icedragon's face. In movement, the reptilian face became strangely humanlike, even familiar. In fact, its magic, too, had a tinge of familiarity. It tasted something like … Urushi's.

He took a step back, disgusted. He did not even want to think about what Urushi had done to create these creatures, which somehow were creatures of his cousin's own flesh and spirit.

"Hurry up!" said a Toiler struggling to hold one of the icedragon's feet still.

Celatu inched closer to the icedragon, careful of its raking claws and snapping teeth, searching for a gap or soft spot between its belly scales, and he found its gaze instead. It heaved a breath and fell still. Resigned. Doomed.

He raised his knife.

The dragon winced.

Celatu lowered his arm. The icedragon quaked with fear and helplessness. Like the rabbit kits so many years ago.

He couldn't do it.

"What are you waiting for? Kill it," Growling Dog said.

"The icedragon is innocent. It behaves only as instinct dictates. Urushi is the true murderer who gave it an instinct to kill."

Growling Dog spat on the ground. "Land spare us Guardians who philosophize! Kill the monster."

Bluebird spoke softly to Celatu. "When you walk outside, ants and beetles die beneath your boots. When you helped Mosquito clear his plot, thousands of beings died. No one is innocent of death."

"No one is innocent of death," Celatu muttered. He stuck the knife in his belt. "I will kill it humanely. Unlike Urushi, I am no murderer."

He sent a strand of magic toward the icedragon, seeking the pulsing of blood. Other magic rose up in him of its own accord to strangle the seeking strand, recognizing kin magic in the beast. Sweat rolled down his forehead as he kept the strand safe.

The beast shielded itself.

Celatu set his strand of magic spinning. It bored through the shield and the icedragon's upper thigh into an artery. The strand followed the blood vessel to the heart.

Celatu crushed the heart. The icedragon fell limp, instantly dead.

Celatu staggered and fell as skin ripped all over him. Twinges of pain sparked inside him as well. Fighting both his own magic and the beast's had drained him, and he was sick and woozy from pain. Thank the Land only one icedragon had found him. He needed time to catch his breath and dress his injuries.

"The icedragons are mortal!" Growling Dog shouted.

The Toilers stomped their feet and cheered.

Bluebird tore pieces from her skirt and bound Celatu's wounds. He watched her hands, bemused as they became three, then four, and then two again. His head lolled, and he blinked his eyes hard several times to coax out soothing tears.

"You need to rest before we go further," Bluebird murmured.

Celatu nodded. He had to get his strength back, mind and body, before the next fight.

"What's that?" Growling Dog cocked his head, listening. Despite his mental haze, Celatu heard something too.

Dozens of wings.

Chapter 38

FOR A MOMENT Celatu thought the sun had exploded. He squeezed his eyes shut, but light pierced his eyelids as if they were but thin oiled paper. White-hot light glared, and his mind screamed at him to close eyes that were already shut. He pulled off his tunic, twisted it, and tied it around his head.

He exhaled with relief as the light dimmed to a bright reddish-pink. The damage had been done, though: Dozens of stars twinkled before him, and some rocketed across the insides of his eyelids. His tunic became damp as his seared eyes streamed.

Snow blindness. Or in this case, icedragon blindness. Land help him, he would not be able to see clearly for days. How could he fight a pod of icedragons blind?

A chill breeze kicked up. The Toilers shuffled and muttered, the sound muted by the beat of wings overhead. Celatu stood, and his hair pulled free of his blindfold, whipping in the wind, catching in his mouth, wrapping obscenely around his tongue. A lump of fear, cold and hard and heavy as iron, formed in his chest. "What's happening?"

"The sky is filled with icedragons," Bluebird said. "Some Toilers are running away. No prophecy can change that we are not designed for fighting."

"Come back, cowards!" Growling Dog shouted.

Cold air blasted him. An evil hiss echoed in the forest. Bluebird touched his arm. "One came down and poked the dead icedragon with its snout. Now the others are whipping their tails and snapping at each other."

The wind chilled and got stronger. Celatu had to lean into it to remain standing.

"They're forming a circle."

Celatu ached to tear off his blindfold. "Circle me!" he called. He dropped onto the matted leaves and spread his arms and legs wide. "They'll have to swoop low to reach me. You'll be able to attack them from all sides."

His voice cracked with fear. He was completely exposed, completely vulnerable, completely at the mercy of the Toilers' skills and bravery. He would not see the bearers of his doom approaching, only hear the beating of their scaly wings and feel the frigid caress of their breath.

He took a firm grip on his still-bloody knife. Drops of blood, colder than ice, colder than death, landed on his chest and sizzled as they ate away his skin.

He waited, fear a metallic presence in his nose.

"Bluebird, tell me what the icedragons are doing."

"They're circling above us. They pay attention to no one but you. Oh!" Bluebird exclaimed.

The air whined. Celatu fought the urge to curl into a ball. "What happened?"

"They're swooping."

"Make ready," Growling Dog shouted.

Screams and hisses pierced the air. Frigid drops hit Celatu's chest and ravaged his skin. More icedragon blood. He bit his lip to hold in his screams.

"They're whacking each other with their tails!" Bluebird exclaimed. "Each wants to be first."

"One's breaking away!" someone called. A crossbow snapped. A screech pierced the air, followed by a thud.

"This next one's faster! Shoot! Shoot!" A crossbow fired, but no screech or thud followed.

Burning claws skewered Celatu from either side. He cried out in pain and panic as his body lifted free of the ground. Celatu flailed about with his knife, trying to find the creature's belly.

"Hold still!" Growling Dog shouted from just below him.

The Toilers must be striking the icedragon. It twitched after each blow, and Celatu smelt the stink of its spilled blood. But still the icedragon rose. The skin and muscles of his sides stretched agonizingly as his weight pulled groundward.

He slid his right arm across his body to slice his knife above where claws gripped him on the left side. The knife connected. The icedragon bellowed. Its left feet opened.

Celatu dangled now from only the right feet, throwing the icedragon off balance. It lurched and fell a terrifying few armlengths before its rapidly beating wings stabilized it.

A Toiler screamed unintelligible words.

The icedragon dropped him.

As Celatu hit, a heavy thud set the ground vibrating. His left arm and leg screamed with pain.

"Got it with my sickle!" Bluebird puffed, triumph in her voice. "The others are finishing the beast off." Whimpers dwindled into silence. Toilers cheered and stamped.

While they celebrated, jaws snapped shut around Celatu's left ankle and his right arm. Celatu's knife fell from nerveless fingers. Wings churned the air. He was yanked skyward and pulled in opposite directions.

Celatu's mind detached, an island of calm.

Elsewhere, a roiling sea of pain. Screams. The metallic taste of blood. All outside his island.

In the days of kings and queens, criminals were ripped apart by horses running in different directions. His fear turned into swallows that dispersed over the sea. He reached for an apple, but the tree ran away as the sky melted into butterscotch pudding. Floating was nice. Floating was safe. Danger could not reach him here on this island.

Far away, twanging sounded, and Bluebird's voice called to him.

He did not, could not, answer.

That night was cold for early summer. Fila wrapped two blankets around Kassia and tied her to a tree. Then she curled up on the ground next to her under a single blanket, shivering despite their fire.

The oblivion of sleep will come soon. But though her every muscle ached with fatigue, she fretted about the next day and what it would bring. She lay wide awake.

She was again at the tree with the double knothole. Shadow rubbed against her arm like a welcoming cat. "My charm saved your life."

"I know. Thank you." Fila fiddled with her silver necklace, which had accompanied her into the dream. "The charm was not all you gave me, was it? Celatu believes you changed me during the assassin's attack."

"Did you enjoy what followed? Surely you did." Shadow wove around the tree. "You stood up to your cousin. You killed a firehound. You turned a firehound against a man and left him to be ripped apart. Ooh, that was particularly a fine move. All because I gave you a small piece of me. A slender little slice that could sit on the tip of a nail of a baby's pinky finger."

Shadow floated closer and whispered in her ear. "Just think what you could do if we merged and you had all my powers."

Cold breath tickled up her spine. Fila shuddered.

"I do not like the person I have been since your first gift. Sarcastic, angry, even cruel." Fila faced Shadow and spoke her next words slowly and clearly.

"What you've done to my brother is even worse. How could I possibly want more? I want to be myself again, myself only."

"Noooooooooooo!" Shadow twirled away, rocking from side to side and stroking her arms. "No! Take me in! Take me in!" Her pain lanced Fila's guts.

"I am the Servant. Take back whatever you gave me. I order it."

Fila felt something tug inside her mind, stretch thin, and then snap free. Her head snapped back.

She shook her head to clear the ringing in her ears. Free of the roiling, unpleasant emotions that had plagued her, she felt as if she had stepped out from under a crushing waterfall into a calm pool beyond. Empty, but at peace.

Shadow slumped against the tree, murmuring to herself and twisting her beaded hair.

Fila blinked away tears. *Poor, lonely half-soul!* "Shadow, I offer again. Is there some way I can ease your suffering? I will even end your existence if you wish."

Shadow shook her head. "The first Servant cursed me when she threw me out. I am doomed to live forever lonely in this dream form unless a Servant or Consort merges with me." She looked sadly at Fila, and her eyes shimmered with tears. "I love you. You are my true other half, so good, so pure. But your brother has offered me a home."

"He is not a good home," Fila said gently. "He is damaged."

"I will repair him."

Fila's breath caught. *I will have an even harder time defeating him then.*

Shadow stretched her hand out toward Fila and snapped her fingers. The charm she had given Fila, the one that had made her invisible to the fire-hounds, now sat on her palm.

"Farewell, Fila." Shadow faded into sparkles. "Nothing protects you from my hound younglings now. If you survive, we will be enemies when we meet again."

"So be it." Goosebumps rose on Fila's arms. "I will be Servant on my own terms or not at all."

Copper. Glowing copper wire, hot and cold at once, burst into existence and burned a path through Celatu's mind. The Servant was alive. The wire didn't flicker or dim, but glowed steady and true. *Violet, I'm coming,* he thought.

He struggled weakly to sit up, only to be pushed back down by many hands. The air smelled of healing herbs. He forced open his gritty, swollen eyes. Water seemed to float between him and the faces above, softening and distorting their features. Spots obscured some of his vision, and he turned his head back and forth, trying to get a good view. "Servant?" he croaked.

A giant hand engulfed his own. "Don't move," Growling Dog's voice ordered. "The icedragons are dead."

Celatu's memory returned. The blazing light in the sky. The rain of blood. The pain. Oh, the pain. How could flesh survive such agony? Even now, as he woke further, it strengthened and threatened to drown him. But he was alive! They had triumphed over Urushi's beasts, and next they would triumph over Urushi himself. Violet would be Servant. He would be Consort. Violet would be his to kiss to his heart's desire.

"I did not think I would survive." Celatu chuckled weakly, a poor reflection of the elation and relief he actually felt. The effort exhausted him, and his eyes closed.

"You won't, not unless we find the Servant soon," said a female Guardian's voice. "I did the best I could, but I only bought you a little time."

"Why? What's wrong with me?"

"The icedragon clawed through your skin and hit internal organs. Every place it touched eroded away as if the beast were made of acid. I healed you over and over, but the wounds returned. Its magic is stronger than mine."

His eyes and back. They, too, had been injured by the icedragon's claws. "Violet healed icedragon wounds before. She can do it again."

"If she still lives. Otherwise your wounds are mortal."

The news felt like a blow to the chest. Struggling to breathe, he watched the copper wire shimmer and thicken. It tugged on his mind, pulling east, toward the Seat of Enchantment.

"Fila lives," he whispered. "I can find her."

Although it was now late morning, the dew lingered in the forest, and Fila's and Kassia's wet skirts clung to their legs as they led their horses along a barely visible deer path. With each step, Fila's chest grew tighter. How could she defeat Urushi and Shadow together, united into one being? Even if she could, what then? She could not kill her own brother.

The ground vibrated against her feet in approval.

She reached a hand down to touch the Land more intimately, and to her surprise the cool earth warmed against her palm.

"You've returned to me?" Fila asked. "Why did you abandon me?"

The Land inundated her with emotions and thoughts vast and fleet.

She grasped nothing. She knelt to allow more of her skin to touch the Land. "Again, slower. Please." She held her breath, waiting for the Land to fall silent again.

But It poured ideas into her. They surged through her, making her hair stand on end, blowing joy through her heart. An image took shape in her mind.

Shadow.

"I blamed *You*. I thought that You hated me. That You abandoned me," she murmured. "I thought Shadow was my only friend. Please forgive me."

Forgiveness tickled her knees and hands and spread throughout her body, warming her chest like a beautiful sunlit day. Hope blossomed in her.

She drew a deep breath. "I need Your help to take my place as Servant." She waited. She still did not know the rules governing the relationship of Servant and Land. *Perhaps I must succeed or fail on my own.* As the moments passed, so did her expectations. She sat back on her heels and dusted the dirt from her hands.

Before her, a sprig of green burst from the ground. Two oval leaves unfolded. The stem stretched toward the sky, large serrated leaves popping out on alternating sides.

She watched, entranced, as unable to move as if she were a plant herself. When the stem reached the height of her face, it stopped growing; a large, spiky bud like an artichoke emerged. The bud turned to face east—toward her, toward the Seat of Enchantment—and the spikes peeled back. In twos and threes, brilliant yellow ray flowers popped open, framing a face nearly as large as her own. The unfurled disk flowers swirled in complex, overlapping patterns that mirrored the Land's thoughts and were just as dizzying.

Blissful and blithe, she laughed and clapped her hands.

"Fila! Stop playing around." Kassia's whisper was harsh. "I hear noises."

She imagined at first someone was sweeping the forest floor with a broom. Then the swishing became more familiar and more ominous. She and Kassia made the same sound moving through the forest: skirts rustling through underbrush. A whiff of smoke tickled her nose.

She exchanged glances with Kassia, whose faced was scrunched with worry. If this was another Urushi-instigated attack, her cousin didn't know about it.

"Do you hear an animal snuffling?" Kassia whispered. A deep growl set the larger trees humming in concert. The growl of a firehound.

Fila yanked her cousin toward the nearest tree with low branches. Leaning against it, she interlaced her fingers. "Quick! Step here and climb up."

Kassia stood frozen, eyes wide, turned toward the noises alien to the forest.

The firehound burst through the undergrowth, fur spitting sparks like a blacksmith's forge, and its fiendish copper-red eyes glowing. Leaves singed as it flew toward them.

Kassia screamed, a full-throated sound of outright terror.

Fila shoved her behind the tree. She scrabbled in her sewing bag for Boraga's charm while kicking leaf litter aside to dig her toes into the Land.

The firehound stopped in midair, snarled, and dropped to the ground. It sat, lifted a front paw, and washed between its toes. A leash of leather interwoven with pale blue yarn encircled its neck.

Only then did Fila realize her heart pounded a harsh staccato and her breath came in gasps. She leaned against a tree to catch her breath.

Several Guardian women emerged from the forest. Erudia the Melancholy strode in front, her bulbous-knuckled hands tight on the leash. The other women sank to their knees in front of Fila. "Honored Lady," one of them murmured.

"Thank Veridia we found you!" Erudia said. "This is not a safe place. Come. We must talk."

Chapter 39

F ILA STARED IN AMAZEMENT at the thin woven strand that wound from tree to tree, encircling the women's camp and, they said, making it invisible to firehounds. "Please teach me how to make such a strand."

"Later." Unsmiling, Erudia appraised her, the firehound next to her. "As a child, you ran through the library singing."

"I promise not to do that any more," she answered flippantly, then winced. *I spent too much time with Tul.*

"Good. You were a great nuisance."

Fila swallowed. *Why does she look at me so sternly?*

"What shall we call you now you are Servant?"

"Vio—" Fila started. *A violet does not survive long when trod upon. I must reconsider my Servant name.* "Call me Fila for now. I am not yet secure in my Seat."

Erudia nodded. "We aim to change that."

The other women joined them, staying well clear of the firehound's jaws. Erudia introduced them. Fila remembered Kriga of the caterpillar eyebrows and Daucina the Talent from when Mother made the tapestry. The others—Afissa and Elata—were strangers.

"We cannot complete the years of training you should have had before becoming Servant," Erudia said. "But if you will grant us a few days, we can teach you shortcuts to working magic faster and more powerfully. One or more may help when you face Urushi."

Kassia rushed into the group. "How is he? How is Urushi?"

"Mad, or close to it," Kriga said. "He tromps about the Seat proclaiming himself king. Be wary, Kassia. Rumor has it he wants you as his queen."

"With my full consent!" Kassia lifted her chin proudly, her fists on her hips. "Fila is not worthy of being Servant!"

"Yet I *am* Servant," Fila said.

Kriga's eyebrows arched. "The Land does not make mistakes."

Kassia crossed her arms defiantly. "It did this time."

"Queen you may or may not be, Kassia, but never Servant," Fila said. *She is too much like the Berserker; she has a sweet and loving side, but sometimes the darkness in her crowds it out.*

Erudia's forehead wrinkled as she looked between Fila and Kassia. "Urushi's magic is no more controlled than before, but it grows. These creatures he conjures—" she glanced at the harnessed firehound—"no one has written of the like before, even as legends."

Fila bit her lip. "I worry for my poor brother."

"Waste no pity on him," Erudia warned. "Harden your heart, because the only way to save Veridia is to kill him."

"You are wrong," Kassia said. "You underestimate the strength of my Talent, and you discount the bad counsel he receives."

"From the Servant's Council?" Erudia shook her head. "He does not listen to us."

"Another holds his ear, and I will replace … that person. When I get to the Seat, I will make him better. Once I am Servant, I'll heal him completely." She glared at each woman in turn, daring someone to contradict her.

Fila reached out and squeezed her hand. "We both long to see him healthy and complete." Her heart ached for them both, but especially for Kassia, who clutched false hope as if her will could make it true. "Kassia, could you tie our horses up with the others?"

Once she was out of earshot, Fila said, "Please tell me more about the skills you propose to teach me."

"Kriga has recently discovered that within the patterns we see in plants and fibers lie patterns within patterns, visible only with a sharpening lens. She can use these hidden patterns as catalysts. Magic forms more quickly and acts more strongly. She will teach you."

Erudia turned to Afissa, who had lively eyes and a quick smile. Fila liked her immediately. "Afissa's my daughter-in-law and a Goodborn. She was born with her fingers fused together and has always used her feet as hands. She will teach you to work magic with your toes."

Elata had elegant features and a stripe of gray in the hair over her left ear. "Elata trained with your mother and Boraga," Erudia said. "She has developed a technique for knitting thrice as fast as usual. The result is less powerful, but it reduces the speed advantage of men's magic.

"My cousin Daucina is a Talent. She studies how slight differences in color affect the strength of a pattern and how long its magic lasts."

Making a wide path around the firehound, Fila walked to each woman in turn and kissed her. "Thank you. Why have you risked your lives to help me?"

"Boraga asked me to aid you," Erudia said.

Fila recoiled from the blunt reply. The last time she visited her parents and walked in procession with them, the streets thronged with people. Hundreds had shouted her mother's name and tossed flowers in her path. She swallowed. "Are you five my only supporters? Are there no men with fast magic to help us?"

Erudia shrugged her shoulders and snorted dismissively.

"Erudia!" Kriga exclaimed. "Fila, many oppose Urushi. They will back you when you reach the Seat."

"Perhaps." Erudia shrugged again. "In the time of kings and queens, people sometimes preferred to live under the most terrible of conditions rather than risk their lives for freedom."

"There's a rumor Celatu the Coward escaped the icedragon Urushi sent to kill him. He certainly has no love for Urushi now," Elata said.

Fila gritted her teeth. "He helped me escape from Urushi's assassins, but afterward he betrayed me. He will make no effort on my behalf." The Land pricked her feet, reminding her Celatu had rescued her twice. *The Land also blessed our kiss.*

The memory of that kiss warmed Fila. She searched her mind for some sense of him, for the copper cord she was not sure was real. Faintly, so faintly it might have been her imagination, he called, "Fila!"

"Well," Erudia said. "Well, well. Celatu has always been a most uncommon young man. We shall see what he will do. In the meantime, will you let us teach you?"

Fila's first instinct was to go to the Seat immediately, rally the despairing Guardians, and defeat Urushi and Shadow before they grew stronger and did more harm to the Land and Its two peoples.

But without a Consort, without full training in magic, she was no match for the pair of them. Time with these women could mean the difference between a Veridia at peace and a broken Veridia under Urushi's tyranny.

She bowed her head. "Yes, I accept, with great appreciation for your bravery and loyalty."

Erudia nodded, and Kriga slit the firehound's throat with her sewing shears and jumped back. Red smoke coiled from the gushing blood, which killed plants wherever it landed.

Kassia rejoined the group. "Why didn't you kill that awful beast as soon as you found us?" she demanded, hands on her hips.

Erudia directed her answer to Fila. "Veridia is what matters, not you or any individual Servant. If you had been silly, or reckless, or faint-hearted, or otherwise unsuited to the task of defeating Urushi, I would have let the firehound have you and seen whether the Land made a better choice for Its next Servant."

The young Servant looked dazed after her lesson with Elata. Afissa smiled reassuringly at Fila, held out her hand, and led her away from the chatting women to a quiet place where running buffalo clover grew in soft mounds. *Such a relief to be with another Goodborn! I wish we could just talk and get to know each other.* But she must concentrate on teaching her as much as possible; later, if the Servant survived, perhaps they could be friends.

Afissa sat and gestured to the place next to her.

Fila sank into the spot with a sigh. "Do you always go barefoot?"

"Since I was born."

Fila stretched out her legs and set her bare feet next to Afissa's. "Do you draw power from the Land as I do?"

Afissa laughed. "I wish it were so. No, I don't have your powers. Sometimes, though, I sense the moods of the Land, and I can access my magic more easily than some."

"Why didn't your father destroy the webbing between your fingers when you were born?"

"He did. Twice. It grew back. The Consort—your father—destroyed it a third time. Again it regrew."

"The Land can be so cruel. How could It treat you so?"

"Your mother said the Land must need this sacrifice from me and in the fullness of time we would understand why." She looked into the distance. "I never believed your mother's words. But she was right. I have a useful skill to show you only because I have fused fingers."

"The Land is an alien thing. It loves the Guardians and the Toilers, yet its ruthlessness continues to shock and surprise me. I doubt I will ever understand It."

"You have thought about this?"

Fila bit her lip. "Yes. Recently, I have thought about it often."

Of course she has. The Land was cruel to her brother. Afissa put her arm around the young Servant. "If the Servant doesn't understand the Land, I suppose I should stop trying."

"I am so glad you were brave enough to come from the Seat to help me. Our destinies are now linked. Teach me, so together we can save Veridia."

They worked for an hour, taking breaks as Fila's weak toes needed, until her toes were no longer capable of any coordinated movement. She had learned only to tie thick yarn into two simple shapes.

Fila looked at them in disgust. "They give off but a few feeble tingles of magic. They're not good enough." She flung the charms to the side. "How can I continue with my toes locked up?"

"Lie on your stomach. Press the bottoms of your toes against the ground, and push your heels away. The muscles will release."

As Fila stretched her toes, Afissa took several colors of hair-fine strands of silk thread from her bag and knotted them into an intricate set of loops, like the cross section of a snail shell. "Here." Afissa passed the charm from her foot to Fila's. "Keep this close to your heart. It will keep your mind clear when panic or pain or tiredness threatens to overwhelm you."

Fila sighed. "As you've already seen happen. What a thoughtful gift. Thank you, Afissa." She traced the coil with her finger and then giggled behind her hand. "As the colors change, so does the taste of its power."

She picked up her tossed-aside work, set it beside the shell, and compared them. "Your work is exquisite. Perfect knotwork in such a brief time! No wonder Erudia brought you along."

Afissa's face warmed. "You'll get better quickly, and your feet will stop cramping."

Fila looked doubtful but nodded. Then she tucked the charm inside her dress.

Fila could not remember ever having been so exhausted. As twilight fell, Erudia lowered herself stiffly to the ground beside her and asked whether she had any questions about her lessons that afternoon.

"No. But I would like to know whether my library has any information on a creature called Shadow."

Erudia stiffened. "The what?"

"Shadow. The evil half of my ancestress, the first Servant."

"Shadow is just a legend."

Fila shook her head.

"A legend," Erudia insisted. "Think about it. The good Dimidiata died a thousand years ago. How long could a disembodied spirit survive?"

"At least a thousand years, because I have met her. She wanted to merge with me." Fila looked Erudia straight in the eyes, but the older woman did not even blush at her denial of Shadow's existence. "Mother once told me you had read every document in the library. Surely you can tell me more about Shadow."

Erudia remained silent for a long moment. "I have read much about the evil spirit." She stood and stretched.

Fila glanced away for only a moment, but that was enough time for Erudia to have a knife at her throat.

Fila breathed slowly, composing herself and pushing her feet deeper into the dirt. "I am the Servant! Put down your knife."

"I cannot. The Shadow came to you. Now you're a danger to Veridia."

"Because I know she exists?"

"Because you merged with it."

"No. I considered her offer and rejected it."

"No one could turn down such power."

"*I* did."

The knife bit sharper, nicking her skin.

Fila sucked power from the Land faster. "Listen to me. Shadow intends to merge with Urushi. We must pool our knowledge to figure out how to defeat them."

"You merged with it." Erudia grabbed her copper curls with her empty hand and pulled Fila's head back.

Fila's dry cheeks stuck to her teeth, and her legs cramped from the pressure with which she pushed into the ground. "I can prove I did not merge with her."

"How? Answer quickly."

"You know Shadow would prevent a link between the Land and me?"

Stillness. Then, grudgingly, Erudia said, "Some documents hint the Land and the Shadow cannot, or will not, share the same body."

"Watch." Fila stretched her arms out slowly and flattened her palms on the ground. Closing her eyes, she sent her request into the Land. *Please, please, understand what I need.* Nothing happened for a moment.

Then power exploded into her feet and immediately out her hands, so brightly she saw it as pink explosions on the insides of her eyelids. Despite her intentions, her body could not help but jerk.

As her head flew back, Erudia's blade skittered across her throat.

Then she heard a thud.

Erudia no longer held her hair. Her hand flew to her neck. Only a trickle of warmth dribbled from a wide scratch. She opened her eyes.

She sat in a circle of running buffalo clover. Runners headed out in all directions and took root. Meanwhile, the clovers around her formed buds and opened into perfect pink-striped flowers. She turned slowly. Erudia lay on her back several feet away, with the other women gathered around her.

"That's it, Erudia," Kriga said. "No more tests."

Erudia slowly sat up, rubbing her back. "No more tests. But I must talk to the Servant alone."

Afissa helped her mother-in-law stand, led her over to Fila, and remained.

"I promise not to hurt the Servant."

"I will watch to make sure you keep that promise," Afissa said coldly. She backed away, her eyes never leaving them.

"Is it true that the Shadow wants to merge with Urushi?" Erudia asked.

"Goodborn don't lie," Fila said, just as coldly.

Erudia blew out her breath. "The situation at the Seat is far more perilous than anyone imagined." She rose to her feet, joints cracking. "If you had joined with it, you could have defeated Urushi easily. Why did you turn it down?" Her voice held a curious yearning.

Fila's skin crawled. She weighed the question. Celatu would say she rejected Shadow because she was a Goodborn and had no choice. *I don't believe that. I had a choice, and it would have been easier to say* yes *than* no. She finally answered, "Because I will be a better Servant without her."

Erudia barked an unamused laugh. "Arrogance, then. You think you can defeat Urushi alone. I would not have expected you to have such a high regard of yourself under that meek and humble exterior."

Fila felt as if she had been slapped. She raised her head high and looked Erudia straight in the eye. "I am humble because I know my limitations. That does not mean I do not know my strengths—or the Land's."

Fila did not join the others for supper. She had no desire for company, especially Erudia's, and she wanted to fix everything she had learned into her mind for use in the upcoming battle with Urushi.

Kassia approached with a steaming bowl of soup, offered it to her, and sat on the ground next to her without an invitation, spreading out the ruin of her dress around her.

The aroma of leeks and lentils awakened Fila's sleeping taste buds, and she sipped the nourishing liquid—after first sending her senses through it looking for magic. "Thank you, Cousin. It was kind of you to bring me supper."

Kassia reached out and tucked a wayward strand of Fila's hair behind her ear. "I don't trust these women." She glanced toward the fire, where the older

Guardians were deep in conversation. "They probably all want seats on your council."

"Perhaps. But not everyone acts out of selfishness." Fila took another sip of soup. "At least they haven't betrayed me."

Kassia bent her knees up to her chin and wrapped her arms around them, showing no sign of shame. "You're Goodborn. You won't hold a grudge."

Fila's time with Shadow had changed her. "I can forgive you for what you did to me, but not for Amma's death. She never did you or Urushi any harm."

Kassia looked away. "I loved her too."

So did Urushi, or so I believed. Fila's hands tightened around her bowl.

"Please say something," Kassia begged. "You still love me, don't you?"

"Of course I love you. I always will. But I cannot trust you. Your selfishness rules you and blinds you."

"You talk about *my* selfishness, but listen to you! You want me to choose between you and the man I love."

Fila huffed in frustration. "The man you love wants me dead. How can we possibly be friends?"

"You're the Goodborn. Can't you see a way?" she pleaded.

Pity filled Fila's heart. *I'm partly to blame for her selfishness. I let her get her way too often, just as everyone else did.* "The ways lies in your making decisions based on what is right instead of on what you want."

Kassia sobbed. Fila finished her soup.

"One day you'll love someone. Then you'll understand," Kassia said.

Fila touched her lips where Celatu had kissed her. The memory still thrilled her. *The heart does not always make good choices.* "Kassia, I'm worried for you. My brother has changed in strange and terrifying ways. What will he do to you the first time you cross him?"

She took off the chain that held Urushi's ring and clutched it in her fist. "Despite what you think, Urushi is not evil. He would never hurt me."

"I hope that's true."

Kassia smoothed her skirt. "The women say you must kill Urushi." Her voice shook.

At last we come to the reason she brought me soup and begs for my friendship. "The Servant chooses her own course. I will not kill my own brother." Fila turned and put her hand on Kassia's. "But Urushi is not good for you." Fila said the words as kindly as she could. "Whether or not he loves you—"

"He does. I know it as surely as I know four clover stems tied in a bittergall knot will calm a ewe."

Oh. Fila hadn't known that. She started again. "Even though Urushi loves you, his magic is warped. He cannot stop himself from hurting you. His corrupted magic is a curse." Under her feet, Veridia rippled. "Do you want to go about wrapped in charms as Wiggle does? Do you dare carry the fruit of his seed in your womb?"

"Have you no compassion? He did not choose to be cursed by the Land, to be pitied and hated for what he cannot control. When I heal his body, then his soul can heal too. Why can't you understand?"

"I'm trying," Fila said softly. She, too, cared for a flawed man. Celatu had betrayed her, yet she still yearned to take his burden of cynicism from him and teach him one person *could* make a difference.

That he had made a difference to her.

Fila touched her lips with the back of her free hand, remembering their kiss, the need in the way he pressed against her, the delight of having the Land bless them and send Its soul through her and into him, uniting them in a way far more intimate than could even a marriage bed.

Kassia squeezed Fila's hand. They sat in silent camaraderie, knowing that any words would shatter their brief, fragile truce.

Chapter 40

KASSIA SWALLOWED BLOOD yet again. To keep herself awake, she had chewed on the insides of her cheeks and lips until they were raw. Now, snores, snorts, and loud, even breathing convinced her that Fila and the women from the Seat were asleep.

She stood and stretched the kinks from her joints. Erudia the Melancholy had thought it barbaric Fila had tied her up each night and had insisted that Kassia sleep in the middle of them. Thanks to the librarian, she could now go to the Seat to help Urushi.

First, though, she needed her needlework kit. Fila still wore it on her sash next to her own. Kassia knelt next to her. Fila slept with her sash tied tightly, and she had knotted the strings of the needlework bags around it. Kassia could not release it without banging her hands against Fila's ribs.

I'm cleverer than Fila. There's some way I can do this. Her mouth smiled before the idea was fully formed. She slowly, slowly eased the neck of Fila's bag open. Her hand wouldn't fit, but a couple of fingers would, and that would be enough, given how long and slender her fingers were. She reached in. The contents were an unorganized jumble—*Of course! I should have expected no better from Fila*—but as she gently sifted through, she hit several charms of the same size and shape.

She extricated one sleeping charm and placed it on Fila's forehead. She snorted and lifted her head as Kassia pressed down, but the charm took effect before she could fully wake.

It was an easy matter to untie her own needlework kit and retie it to her own sash. She sat back on her heels, her lips pressed together, and watched her cousin sleep. *Oh, Fila! I do love you, even though you're Servant instead of me, and I love Urushi too, even though he has done some bad things. I will not choose between you. I wish you weren't a Goodborn so you could understand. I wish you weren't going to wake up and think I betrayed you.* She stroked Fila's hair and kissed her face.

She took the charm from Fila's forehead and stood, watching. Her cousin didn't wake. She ran to the horses, found Durio's, and untied it. The horse agreeably followed her to the edge of the clearing. She had done it! Now to the Seat and the man who needed her.

Something caught at her waist, and she squeaked and jumped back, blood pounding in her ears. Trees, tall and sturdy, stood on either side of her. Who or what could have touched her? She held very still, waiting for it to touch her again or to hear it leave. Seconds passed, then a minute; neither happened. She was trapped between *it* and the sleeping women.

She glanced over her shoulder to make sure everyone still slept. They did, but she could not stand here all night holding the horse's bridle. She took a deep breath and with her free hand fumbled blindly in front of her, ready to jerk it back if she touched flesh or fur.

Instead she touched a thin strand of strong magic.

Land take me, I forgot about the cord protecting the camp! I can duck under, but the horse can't. Now what?

Urushi's future depended on her, and hers on him. She had to reach him as soon as possible … even if it meant putting Fila and the old women in danger. She had to cut the cord.

She pulled her sharpest snips from her bag and felt for the cord again. She held it with one hand and brought the snips close. It was too dark to position the snips by sight, so she used a finger. It was awkward, but after a few tries, she had the sharp blades on either side.

She didn't squeeze the snips.

She could get away and still protect Fila from firehounds. Leading the horse, she followed the cord to where it encircled a tree. She snipped the cord there and took one end in each hand. She wedged one end between the thick, jagged bark and the trunk, then led the horse out.

Once out of the circle, she walked back to the tree and wedged the other end of the cord into the bark, making sure the ends overlapped. Her cousin would be safe.

Fila had saved her from a firehound. Kassia had now paid her debt to Fila in full.

Fila woke when Erudia shook her shoulder. A lone barred owl called nearby. The other women still slept under a dark night sky. Erudia led her around the fire and to the edge of the clearing. She sat and signaled for Fila to do the same. "I have no special magic to share with you, but I am now willing to exchange information about the shadow. Our combined knowledge could be useful."

The air was cold; the ground was cold and damp. Shivering, Fila blew warmth onto her hands. "To Urushi as well. Why should I trust you? Yesterday you threatened me with a firehound and then you tried to cut my throat. I get the impression you do not much like me."

"I don't. I believe the Land made a mistake when It chose you. I still believe you have some alliance or agreement with the shadow. But by the Land and all I hold dear, I promise you that I oppose Urushi with every cell in my body."

At last Erudia's rudeness and actions made sense: She did not support Fila, but rather wanted to keep Urushi from taking over the Seat. "Why?"

"One of his creatures killed my only son. Afissa's husband."

The bottom dropped out of Fila's stomach, and her head sank into her hands. "I am truly sorry." *How many more people have to die before I stop Urushi and take my Seat?*

"I don't want your sympathy. I want you to save Veridia."

She straightened up. "I intend to." She took a breath. "I think an important key to fighting Shadow is to determine how the Berserker cast Shadow out." Her words sounded strange to her, and she realized she was talking in Celatu's scholarly way. He had rubbed off on her most annoyingly. "If we knew that, we might know how to cleave Shadow from Urushi."

"The Berserker? You surprise me with your knowledge," Erudia said. "You may already know, then, some of what I'm about to say. Before the good Dimidiata became Servant, there was no magic, and the Toilers were barely more than beasts we Guardians used like any other animal. I know of no record or legend of how the Berserker made her covenant with the Land. But the result was we Guardians were blessed with magic, and the Toilers gained speech and reason and became our equals in caring for the Land. Guardians adopted a simple way of life and gave up their technology to the Toilers. The price the good Dimidiata paid was half her soul."

"The Shadow half. Do you think the Berserker used ancient technology?"

"Perhaps."

"Why is Shadow back now?"

"Urushi comes to the library sometimes. He may have found an old book with instructions for retrieving her. Or perhaps, given his abnormal magic, he accidentally called her while trying to do something else."

"What will happen when Shadow bonds with Urushi? Will they be one unified person, as the Berserker was? Or will they be two entities sharing one body?"

"There's no way of telling—"

A chorus of howls made Fila's hair leap away from her scalp. Firehounds! The trees around the clearing became black silhouettes against red as the glowing dogs neared.

Fila's breath caught in her chest before she remembered the delicate yet powerful cord encircling the clearing. The firehounds could not see or smell them through the magic barrier.

But the firehounds could hear them. She put her finger to her lips to remind Erudia to remain silent, and together they padded over to the other women.

Fila pulled copper hair from her scalp, gave strands to each woman, and began knotting a protection charm based on what she had learned the previous day. But a feeling nagged at her, a feeling that she had seen something important but not realized it.

Mindful of Kriga's lesson, she broke off several stalks of squirrel corn—the most complex pattern she could see among the nearby vegetation—and encased the stems in copper, then went back to tie a knot on each leaf. In silence, the other women also knotted charms with their fingers or toes, no one daring to click a knitting needle or draw a thread through a cloth.

The pack of firehounds should have passed by, should continued its search. Instead, the creatures slowed. The leader, a monstrous hound the others deferred to, padded close to the barrier and sniffed along the ground, her nostrils flaring. She whined, and her sisters loped over. They snuffled in the decayed leaves and stuck their snouts between the trees.

Somehow, the beasts sensed the Guardian women.

Elata drew her breath in sharply and pointed at the cord.

Fila stifled a gasp with her hand. Yesterday, the cord had been taut around the tree trunks; today it drooped.

Afissa leaned over and whispered in her ear, "Where's Kassia?"

Fila looked around. Kassia was not among the women. Her fingernails cut into her palms. She leapt up, picked up her skirt so she could move quietly, and followed the cord around the clearing with her hand. Behind where the horses grazed, she found the reason the cord drooped.

Someone—Kassia?—had cut the cord. The two ends were held in place only by rough bark ... with a gap of several inches between them.

Shaking, Fila put her hand to her mouth. She counted the horses; one was missing. *She cut the cord to get a horse out.* She snatched up the ends to tie them together.

The knitted strands had unraveled and frayed. She could not get the ends to meet, let alone tie them.

I have to close the gap before the firehounds find it. She pulled a strand of yarn from her needlework bag.

Kriga sneezed. The firehounds' ears tilted forward. The largest paced purposefully around the edge of the clearing. She sniffed the air and trotted as she neared the gap. The other beasts followed.

No time to tie the strands together now. If only Celatu were here to use his male magic of destruction.

Fila dashed toward the others. "Quick! Gather around me!" She kicked leaves away as she tore off her clothes. She threw her naked body to the ground, ignoring the sticks, damp leaves, and prickly weeds. She pressed her flesh against the Land, keeping Afissa's charm of clearheadedness against her chest and Boraga's copper and silver charm in her hand. The Land received her eagerly. Inside her, Its power joined her own.

A horse screamed.

She hurled her thoughts outward toward the acorns, nuts, seeds, tubers, bulbs, and other plant life resting dormant under the ground the firehounds stood on. *Grow! Grow!*

A dog yowled.

Several women gasped. "Plants are springing up around the firehounds!" Daucina exclaimed.

"Not fast enough," Erudia barked. "Faster, Fila, faster!"

Fila dug her fingers and toes into the dirt and drew more power from the Land and directed more magic toward the growing thicket. The Land buckled under her as roots raced to seek space and water.

"Dig!" Erudia shouted at the women. "Cover her with the Land's own flesh."

Fila squeezed her eyes shut as damp, cold earth showered her. Firehounds growled and snarled and the women whispered tensely among themselves— "Hurry!" "Faster!" The blanket of earth grew heavier. Fila's thoughts mingled more thoroughly than ever before with the labyrinthine mind of the Land.

It did not think as Guardians or Toilers did, in words and concepts and pictures. But like people, It had goals. Its goal now was to use her as a conduit to defeat the firehounds, which It hated with fierce passion. Fila stopped her own efforts and allowed the Land to use her as It willed.

It sent a stream of pure energy through Boraga's charm and into her, magic beyond her comprehension, full of rage and sadness and disappointment, amplified by the charm she held so tightly.

Above and below her, seeds in the dirt sprouted and pierced her skin, a dozen places, a hundred places, a thousand places. She screamed as she and the

Land became one. The pain was beyond that of the day she became Servant, beyond unbearable.

"Break away, Fila!" Afisa cried. "Stop, or you'll die!"

But Fila could not. The Land controlled her and her magic now.

Chapter 41

Kassia rode hard and reached home shortly after dawn. She woke the stableboy and left the slathered, heaving horse with him, then she dashed to the house and ran inside, her shoes clattering on the floor and echoing in the long hall. At long last, she was home. By the time Fila and the old women arrived, she and Urushi would have the Seat in their hands.

"Father! Mother!" she called. A few Toilers were about their early morning tasks, but she saw no one else. She grabbed a Toiler by the arm. "I am Kassia, daughter of this house. I demand to know, where are my parents?"

"Breaking their fast in Bifac's study," was the reply.

"Bring a dish of berries with cream to me there. Bread, too. And a slice of pheasant." She walked down the hall to the oak door and knocked. "Father! Mother! I'm home!"

The door swung open, and Father, smelling of parchment and smoky tea, pulled her into a tight hug. "Thank the Land you are alive and safe! We were worried, so very worried."

"Why are you limping?" Mother asked, frowning. "What happened to your dress? I paid quite a bit of money for it."

Kassia pushed Father away, her feet dancing with excitement. "I don't have time to talk now. I must wash and dress and go to Urushi."

Mother pursed her lips and grasped her arm. "No, you cannot! Bifac, tell her she cannot."

Father put his arm around her, restraining her more gently, but restraining her nonetheless. "Urushi's wits are addled, Little One. He piles violence upon violence, and he no longer trusts me. You are not safe with him."

Kassia shook with anger and disbelief. She had come all this way only to face yet another hurdle? It was unbearable. "You do not want me to be queen? You want goody-goody Fila to rule over me? How can you do this to me?" Tears sprang to her eyes. "How *can* you?" She leaned against her father's side and sobbed, hoping he would melt as usual.

Instead he held her tighter.

"We want what is best for you," Mother said.

"What's best for me is Urushi!" Kassia sobbed harder, this time adding a tremble.

Father stroked her hair. "There, there, Little One."

"I want to be a queen," she whimpered. "I want to sit in the Seat of the Servant." Still they did not relent. "Urushi won't be pleased if you try to stop me from going to him."

She had hit home. Father stiffened, and Mother's eyes widened with alarm.

"Bifac, what should we do?" Mother said. "The family will be in danger whether we let her go or no."

The Toiler servant entered with Kassia's food, saw the argument, and backed out. Father's massive cherry Toiler-made clock ticked many seconds in the silence.

Father loosened his grip. "Don't cry. I will not stand in the way of your destiny. You will be queen. Go and pretty up now." He drew back and patted her on her head, and she sniffed back her tears. Father had circles under his eyes, and his skin had a gray tinge. She would have to ask him later whether he'd been sick.

Kassia dashed from the study and beckoned to the servant to follow her. Behind her, her parents continued their discussion. "Are we doing the right thing?" Mother asked. "Are we sending our daughter to her death? How will that look to society?"

"I will deliver her to Urushi personally. I will be back in his good graces, and the opposition will shrink when our charming Kassia is his wife and queen."

The rest of their conversation faded as Kassia ran up the curving staircase and down the hall toward her suite. She burst inside, causing a maid to shriek. Ignoring the maid, Kassia threw open the doors of her wardrobe and went through her dresses. Not queenly enough, not queenly enough, not queenly enough … she stopped at the purple silk with layers of lacy lavender petticoats. This was it! The matching purple stockings would hide her damaged leg from Urushi. She pulled the dress out and draped it over the bed on her way to her bathing room.

An hour later, after eating, bathing, dressing, and painting her face, she held her gold-rimmed looking glass away from her and admired her reflection. The purple looked resplendent, and the petticoats peeked out fetchingly above her ivory silk shoes with pearl buttons. She looked almost like a queen. She frowned at the *almost*. What was missing?

Jewels. A queen should wear jewels.

The flighty maid shrieked again as Kassia ran past her toward her mother's dressing room. She picked up the shell-inlaid chest on the dressing table and poured out the sparkling contents. What to choose, what to choose? Her fingers raked through the jewelry until she came upon a net of pearls, which she draped over her hair, fastening it with gold hairpins set with garnets cut en cabochon. Urushi's ring caught on the delicate netting, reminding her she should choose something with opals to match. She found a necklace of opal cabochons alternating with faceted garnets and fastened it about her neck.

She turned to leave. Mother stood in the doorway, her face tight, her arms crossed.

"Do I look like a queen?" Kassia waited, nervousness mixing with her excitement.

Mother looked her over, frowned, then moved into the room and picked up a pair of gold earrings with garnet drops.

"Put these on instead of pearls. You must so overwhelm Urushi with your beauty he won't dare hurt you and mar the perfection."

Kassia winced, thinking of her scarred leg. "Mother, he wouldn't hurt me. Why don't you believe he loves me?"

Mother sniffed. "Do not limp. The king will find it unattractive."

"I've mastered all you taught me about attracting and pleasing a man. Please, please, be happy for Urushi and me." Kassia waited for her mother's cold eyes to soften. They didn't. Deflated, she kissed her mother on the cheek and went downstairs.

Father was waiting, sporting a large yellow diamond in his ear and wearing his best coat over a white silk shirt. The coat hung on him like a potato sack; he had lost weight. Frowning, Kassia pulled at it, trying to make the drape a little more flattering.

"Ready?" he asked, his voice heavy, as if he accompanied her to the gallows instead of to her glorious destiny.

"Yes, I'm ready!" She took his arm and they walked outside and across the cobblestones to the coach. The coachman opened the door, and they climbed in, choosing seats opposite each other. Kassia tried to compose her face into a serious, queenly expression, but her smile kept forcing its way back onto her face.

"Father, I am so happy!"

Father leaned closed and whispered, as if the coachman were an enemy spy and had the ears of an owl. "Urushi has changed mightily since you last saw him, Little One. I beg you, do whatever he asks of you, no matter how odd. Do not make him angry. I would die if he harmed you."

She put her hands over his. "Dear Father, don't worry. My Talent is stronger than ever. I can make him better and stop him from sending those awful animals to kill people. Everything will work out once we are together."

Father's cold hands trembled.

Afissa screamed as the Land killed Its Servant. Thousands of plants thrust through Fila's head, back, buttocks, legs, feet. Her arms and her hands. Her blood poured onto the ground and was quickly absorbed.

Fila moaned.

Cold ran up Afissa's spine. She jumped back, hands over her mouth. The Servant still lived. What agony she must be in!

"Afissa!" Mother Erudia called. "Come help us make spears."

The Land had used the Servant's energy to save the five other women. Some firehounds had been skewered; the remaining ones were penned in by new trees. The women stripped bark and branchlings from long branches.

Afissa ignored the summons. If the Servant was still alive, her duty was here. She pulled the tools, yarns, and threads she needed from her bag.

Grimacing, she yanked a big hunk of hair from the Servant's head and set it beside her feet.

Fila didn't react.

Afissa's stomach turned over. She needed to work faster than ever before. She pulled out some of her own hair and set it next to the Servant's. Her toes picked up a few strands of each and then moved faster than she could watch as they knitted a simple charm—simple because she needed so many of them.

She squeezed and opened her useless hands. Then she saw the needlecase for her crewel needles. She used her hand as a scoop to bring the package close.

Her toes finished one healing charm, tossed it toward her hands, and started another one. She easily brought the charm close.

She knew what she had to do, but she couldn't bring herself to do it, not yet. She forced herself to stare at the Servant's wounds, watch her body pale as it emptied of blood, watch the labored breathing that made bubbling sounds. Now.

She maneuvered the needlecase in her paddle-like hands, getting it open and forcing the biggest crewel needle further out of the fabric. She drove her thumb down deep on the thick needle, wiggled it around, and shoved the charm underneath to catch the blood.

She nearly fainted, but forced herself to remain awake. When the charm was soaked, she pressed it against the Servant's back. Heart and lungs first.

She became like a Toiler machine: Make a charm. Punch a deep hole in a blood-rich fingertip. Soak the charm in blood. Place it on the Servant. Repeat. Repeat. Repeat.

She pulled more hair from the Servant's head, more from her own. She ran out of white yarn.

She substituted yellow.

Her fingers were as white as a corpse's. No more blood came out.

Efficiency. She slammed the pad of her big toe against the needle and started a new charm. By the time it was finished, it was ready to put on the Servant.

Repeat. Repeat. Repeat.

She fainted. When she came to, she kept her head down so she would remain conscious. As her feet continued to churn out charms, she took a deep breath and slammed her arm down on the pointiest of the branches that pierced the Servant.

Afissa's blood ran down the branch and spread over Fila's wounds and skin as well as the charms. Her feet continued on their own as she lingered in a half-daze.

Someone called her name. She was too weak to answer. Feet gathered around her, but her half-closed eyes could not identify them.

"Afissa, what have you done? Oh no. Oh no."

Her arm was torn from the spike; knitting needles were yanked from her toes. Something wet and warm was placed on her arm. Another one on her fingertips.

She forced her eyes half-open. Mother Erudia was taking the healing charms from the Servant for her! The other women ran toward them.

"No! Heal the Servant. For Veridia."

"She's right," Kriga said.

Mother Erudia cradled her in her arms, crying. Afissa let her eyelids close. The rapid clicking of knitting needles told her the other women were making healing charms.

"The firehounds are dead," Erudia whispered. "You must live."

Fila woke screaming, surrounded by hands. Reaching hands. Grasping hands. Pulling hands.

This time, the hands and the terror and the agony did not end when she woke. Her eyes poured tears; her muscles spasmed. She kicked and fought, even though it increased her anguish and had no effect on the hands. Her feet, slick with sweat, slid off whatever they touched.

How can a person suffer such pain and still live?

The Land.

Let me go. Please, she begged It.

It pulsed love through her. Strength. Healing energy.

The healing energy should have been first, she told It, half-delirious. To take her mind off her agony, she concentrated on her hallucinations. The hands. Now women's voices as well. Movements around her, although the sun shone so bright she could not see what those hallucinations were.

Blackness.

Light again, less bright. Her pain: less agonizing. The hands: Now she saw they were attached to the older women from the Seat who had come to help her. The women wore worried faces. Nearby, Afissa gasped harshly.

Fila rolled on her side. "Afissa?" She blinked away tears to clear her vision.

A few feet away, Afissa sprawled in Erudia's arms, gray as a corpse. Her chest barely rose.

"Afissa!" She summoned strength from the ground, dug her fingernails in, and tried to pull herself toward her.

Hands held her back.

"Let go. Let me help her. Let me help her," she whispered.

"You can't." Kriga loomed in her vision, eyebrows drooping along with the rest of her face.

Daucina's kinder voice added, "You were a Servant's hair away from death. You must rest and heal."

"But Afissa!"

"We've done all we can do for her. Now we wait."

"Help me ... lie next to her."

Hands lifted her and moved her. She moaned. She rested her hand on Afissa's. It took all her strength.

She and the Land were still connected. She tried to divert healing energy to Afissa.

The Land would not let her. It pulsed with sorrow.

Sorrow for Afissa.

She lay still then. She absorbed what the Land gave her, felt thousands of wounds healing, stayed with Afissa until she returned to the Land. When she was ready she sat up.

"What happened to me? What happened to Afissa?"

The women would not meet her gaze, none except Erudia, who returned it with eyes filled with hatred.

Fila swallowed. *I had something to do with Afissa's death.* She looked around and took everything in—the dead firehounds, the dense stand of plants where before none had been, the charms and thousands of healing wounds on her own body, Afissa's bloodless body and pierced toes and fingers. She closed her eyes against the horrific story they told.

She shook, and the Land quaked beneath her in sympathy. Her awareness joined Its awareness, and They were One. Together, they stretched up, down, and out, encompassing every bird in the sky, every worm in the dirt, every living thing within the magic border around Veridia.

She knew every creature, knew the wants and desires and hurts of each one as if they were her own, and she loved each anyway. She could no more fear or hate them than she could fear or hate herself.

All were part of the fabric of Veridia, she realized, and the fabric grew as each new creature was born. The world was one and it was many, all at once. The death of any creature left a hole in the tapstry no new creature could fill.

She and the Land expanded their awareness farther until she thought she could stretch no more. They were Veridia and everything and everyone in it. She knew each creature because each creature was part of her.

Too much to take in.

She rose and jumped onto a thick layer of leaves, jerking as her connection with the Land tore, leaving only a gossamer thread of contact. She was one person again, separate from other beings in her own sack of skin. Fila. Servant of Veridia.

But she was not the same Fila as before. She felt … larger, more porous. A new emotion filled her, one she had never experienced before, yet now it dominated her soul.

Compassion, the Land told her.

She looked at Erudia and understood her wounds and loved her. She thought of Kassia, who had brought today's trouble on them, and loved her fully, without reservations. She understood Urushi, and his pain became her pain, and she loved him too. Her Goodborn instincts remained, but they were tempered by acceptance of the flaws of the non-Goodborn.

The Land strenghtened the contact between them. *Now you know why I chose you as my Servant. Now you are almost complete.*

* * *

Urushi sat in the Servant's plain maple chair at the bottom of the amphitheater, clutching the ends of the unpadded arm rests and imagining the forty tiers of benches that encircled him filled with his new subjects. They would shout his and Kassia's names and throw rose petals. The petals would drift down like a light snow and carpet the dirt floor. He and Kassia would acknowledge the adulation with slight nods, careful not to lose their crowns.

The dirt floor had to go; Kassia could recharge her powers elsewhere. He would make the Seat suitable for royalty. Kings and queens deserved to sit on thrones, thrones carved from rare woods, thrones with padded velvet seats and arm rests, thrones gilded to reflect the light. He and Kassia would rest their feet on padded footstools. Kassia would love choosing beautiful things for this space. He would replace the dirt floor with a wood floor on which would sprawl colorful carpets of the finest wool.

He drummed his fingers on the armrests. Where was Kassia? He had hoped she would be here by now, glorious in long copper hair. With so many guards, he had assumed she would be safe. Could something have happened?

Footsteps sounded behind him. Hooting Owl entered from the Servant's secret door and walked toward him carrying his best vest. Appa's pebbled face smiled hugely. "Your bride is here."

"At last! Where is she?" Urushi jumped up and wrapped his scarf about his face. He shrugged his arms into the vest, his fingers trembling as he pushed the gold toggles through their loops.

"She and Bifac await you in your sitting room."

"Is Kassia the Servant?"

Appa's face fell. "I'm sorry, Urushi. Her hair is still blonde."

"Something has gone wrong. Station several people in the watchtowers. I want to know immediately if Fila arrives."

"Of course. Immediately."

Urushi's mouth twisted. Did Fila yet live? Or had the Land chosen someone else as Servant, someone else he would have to track down and kill? Bifac must have a hand in this somehow. His uncle was still playing both sides and hoping to come out a winner. "I need you to do something else for me, Appa. Kassia must not know."

"I understand."

"I don't want Bifac to leave the Servant's House." He would need to rename it soon; his eye twitched each time he called his home that. "I don't trust him. I want him kept in one of the underground rooms. Someplace comfortable, but secure. Kassia must not suspect."

"As you wish."

"Now let's go welcome my wife-to-be!" Urushi kept up as fast a pace through the tunnel as his mishealed injuries allowed, and they soon arrived at the House of the Servant and headed to the sitting room. A blur of purple flung itself at him with a shriek. Urushi buried his face and hands in Kassia's pearl-bedecked hair, which smelled of ginger and rose water. His crown fell off, and he heard it bang and roll across the floor and come to rest on the rug.

"Is this how a queen should behave?" he growled into her hair, and she giggled. He nuzzled her. "I didn't know whether you were safe. I should be angry at you, keeping me waiting so long." His hands tightened in her hair as his temper rose. "You've held up the coronation, kept everything in an uproar, knocked off my expensive crown."

Kassia squeaked and loosened her embrace. "You're hurting me!"

"You made me wait. I don't like waiting." His blood pounded in his temples. His fingers clenched as he fought back the magic. "I was so afraid you were hurt."

"Well, now I am!" She grabbed at his hands and tried to pull them out of her hair. A pearl hit the floor.

His chest heaving, he forced his hands to release his grip on her hair. She put her hands on her hips and glared at him, her cheeks flushed. She was so beautiful, so spirited. It was pure joy to be with someone who did not fear him.

She had come to him not in traveling clothes, but rather dressed as befit a queen, down to the smallest detail. His gaze caressed the curve of her body from head to breast to hip to foot. At this moment he did not care she was not Servant, only that she was *his*. Urushi stroked her smooth, unscarred face. "I'm sorry," he whispered. "I'm so sorry."

She struggled to maintain her glare, but her eyes and lips softened and soon she laughed again.

"Come." Urushi swept Kassia up in his arms, feeling his scars pull. "We have much to catch up on." She threw her arms around his neck and leaned her head against him as he carried her out of the room. He made sure she did not see Hooting Owl and two other Toilers waiting by the door. He nodded at them as he passed, and they headed into the sitting room toward Bifac.

As he carried her up the stairs, she pulled his scarf down slowly, letting it slide across his skin. Her fingers followed, relearning his face, discovering his new scars.

He searched her face. He found no disgust there, only joy.

She kissed him, then pulled back. "I'm never leaving you again. Boraga can come here to teach me the rest I need to know about magic. I am empty without you."

Her words inflamed him. He ran the rest of the way up the stairs and kissed her all the way down the hall and into his quarters.

Afissa was dead.

Fila had planned on giving her a seat on the Servant's Council. She had hoped once Urushi was defeated, the Land would allow Celatu or someone else with strong magic to separate her fingers.

It was not to be.

She wanted to curl in a ball in a hollowed-out oak and not come out for a long time. She wanted to cry until she craved salt. She forced herself to sit up in the sunset-lit space.

Around her, in a protective circle, sat the women of the Seat. Elata knitted slowly, but the other women slumped listlessly, their hands empty.

I've never seen Guardian women not working before.

The Land's energy, gentle and caressing for a change, coursed through her like a tonic. She would heal and live.

But Afissa was dead. The women had drained themselves in saving their Servant and would need days to recover. Meanwhile, more firehounds or more of Urushi's men could arrive.

She could not stay with the Guardian women and put them in more danger. She had to get to the Seat and stop Urushi.

She put her hand to her necklace and felt something strange under it.

She looked down. Over her heart, between her breasts, Afissa's charm of clearheadedness lay where she had placed it. But no longer was it a distinct entity. It had embedded in her flesh, held in place by semitransparent strands of scar tissue, delicate and pink-tinged like Afissa's webs.

Afissa was dead, but her magic would be part of Fila forever.

Not until sunset the following day did Fila have the strength to stand and dress. The other women slept the heavy sleep of the magic-depleted. Fila pulled out her hair and wrapped some around and between the fingers of each woman in case they needed it. She would leave the three surviving horses. She would heal faster if she walked and drew Power from the Land.

She gathered up the long cord that had protected the clearing and walked around and around the women, encircling them. They disappeared from sight. She tied and then braided the ends together and hoped for the best.

She had done all she could. It was time to go.

"Fila," Erudia whispered.

Fila turned from habit, but saw only the cord hanging in the air. She bowed her head. "Please again accept my deepest condolences." The words were so little compared with Erudia's losses.

"Afissa gave her life to save you and Veridia. I cannot understand her act. But I am proud."

"I will miss her grievously, though I barely knew her."

"She was like that. Her good humor and smile won over everyone. Now she is with my son. I am bereft. They are united. Together as they should be."

"I must stop Urushi before anyone else gets hurt."

"Wait till morning. Some of us may be well enough to join you."

Fila shook her head. "The sooner I get to the Seat, the better. Besides, you barely have the energy to talk. You still need much rest."

Erudia mumbled something. Fila knelt next to the cord.

Erudia spoke in gasps. "When we see you next. In your rightful place. Consort beside you. The way things should be."

"I doubt I'll find a Consort between here and the Seat."

"No time to be picky. If Urushi merges with Shadow. He may have powers of Servant and Consort both."

Fila rocked backward, too stunned to reply. If Erudia was right, Urushi might not need Kassia or her Talent once Shadow merged with him.

What would happen to her cousin then?

Fila took off at a brisk pace through the forest.

Eventually, the forest thinned, and fields began. The dark night softened. She wrapped her sash around her hair and trod the road at the normal speed of a traveler. It was not much of a disguise, but perhaps the early-morning workers would be too tired to give her more than a glance.

She topped a hill and stopped to draw her breath. The Greater Seat spread over an extinct volcano and across a plain, its streets and buildings sharp shapes of light and dark in the harsh dawn glare. The copper-covered tower at the caldera's peak shone too brightly to look at. Although everyone referred to the entire ancient city as "the Seat of Enchantment," the true Seat, the concentrated center of the Land's power and the place where the Servant sat on ceremonial occasions, lay at the bottom of the dead volcano's collapsed cone.

That was her goal, the true Seat of Enchantment itself, where she must take possession or give up her life.

The roads and fields in-between were strangely empty of both Guardians and Toilers. She had not passed any estates or villages in which to meet a potential Consort.

She would have to defeat Urushi by herself.

Chapter 43

KASSIA YAWNED AND STRETCHED. Wiggle bounced across the bed and slurped his tongue across her eyes. She held him away with a laugh and looked around. Urushi wasn't in the room.

"Where is your master, Wiggle?" He must have slipped out quietly so as not to disturb her. How thoughtful. He knew how tired she was from the trek from Boraga's manor—and from last night.

He had been shocked by the scar on her leg, and she had cried. Sweetly, he promised to buy her stockings of every color so she would never have to see it. She scratched Wiggle's neck, blissful that her life was so perfect.

She rose and dressed leisurely, stopping every few minutes to toss a ball for Wiggle to fetch. He truly earned his name each time he brought it back, growling as if to dare her to take the ball, his happy tail wagging hard enough to tip him over several times. Now that he was a royal dog, she thought, he would need a new sweater, one interwoven with gold thread and adorned with jewels.

After years of waiting, her life had finally begun: she was with the man who loved her and treated her as a queen. She would be both Servant and queen and rule over everything she could see and far beyond.

She picked up a comb from a stand and stroked the brown hairs caught in it with tenderness and pity. With all her heart, she hoped when they wed, his hair would silver completely. She would spend whatever time it took to heal his repulsive scars and restore the perfection of his previous beauty. No longer would she have to work quickly and secretly; now they were together, she could spend whatever time was needed, and she could drain her Talent without worrying someone would notice her fatigue.

She walked over to the looking glass with the comb, wanting to tame her bed-mussed hair before Urushi returned.

The blissful morning shattered. She was not alone.

The looking glass revealed someone behind her, a dark woman, her long black hair adorned with beads, her face haughty.

Kassia spun to confront the intruder. No one was there. She flung open the door to Urushi's sitting room, and she peeked in his wardrobe. *Where had the intruder gone so quickly?* She went again to the looking glass. Only her own face looked back, its beauty marred by her frightened eyes.

Shaken, she combed her hair quickly and moved away from the looking glass. She had never encountered such magic before. Wiggle barked once and picked up his ball.

She sat down next to him and pretended to try to wrestle it from him. Wiggle would alert her if a stranger entered these rooms. *Poor sleep and poor food has my imagination playing tricks on me.*

Today would be her first full day in the House of the Servant as Urushi's queen-to-be. What should she do first? Appa should bring her some breakfast, and then he should send someone to Boraga's to bring Two Sparrows to her. It was getting quite irksome doing her own hair and dressing herself.

The door flew open. Urushi strode into the room, fully dressed including a shawl to cover his dear scarred face. "Finally you're up. Come, we must hurry."

"I've not had my breakfast!" She tilted her head and stuck out her bottom lip in a way that had always before enticed him to give in to her wishes.

"There's no time. We must go to the Seat of Enchantment."

"Are we going to bond now?" she asked. Her body felt so light it might rise off the bed.

"We must wait until you are Servant. The bonding will be more powerful." He smiled at her. "It will not be long now. I have lookouts in the tower. They have seen Fila. She will be here soon."

"We can't wait until I am Servant. Fila said she tried to give up being Servant, but the Land didn't accept her request. It could be decades until I'm Servant."

"Do not worry. You'll be Servant soon, as you deserve." Urushi changed his jacket for one heavily embroidered with copper hair, one his father had worn for his official duties as Consort. He looked her up and down with a critical eye. "Put on something a little fancier, something suitable for your new status. I intend for the Burning of the Shoes to take place as soon as you are Servant and for our Bonding to follow."

"But I tell you, Fila either cannot or will not give up being Servant!"

Urushi hummed a little to himself as he replaced the silver hoop in his ear with a diamond stud. "Soon she will know better." He bent to kiss her forehead.

Kassia turned cold, and she gripped her dress to keep from shaking. *Urushi doesn't plan to wait for Fila to give up or die of natural causes. He intends to kill her, just as Fila said.*

"My darling, we can't kill Fila!" she said lightly. She forced herself to breathe as she waited for him to draw back in shock and tell her she had misunderstood.

Urushi paused while tying a silk sash around his waist to glance at her. "It's a regrettable necessity. She's all that stands between us and power."

"But she's my cousin! Your sister!"

"She deserted you when a wild beast attacked, leaving you a cripple."

Kassia flinched at the harsh word.

"Come, come, make yourself beautiful for the crowds."

"We should meet in private with Fila, give her another chance to renounce her title. She could help us with our plans, and you would win the good will of the people if she were your ally."

Someone spoke. "Urushi needs no support from her. He has a more powerful ally."

Kassia jumped at the unfamiliar voice with its antique accent and animal-like sibilants. Urushi looked toward the looking glass, and she followed his gaze.

A dark, sparkling mist spun in its depths. As a cold knot formed in Kassia's stomach, the mist assumed human form and became a woman, the woman she had glimpsed before, dressed like one of the ancient queens in a low-cut sleeveless gown of purple linen and a war vest of linked metal rings.

The woman's image enlarged as she approached them. She grasped the brass sides of the looking glass, stretched them apart with battle-hardened arms, and stepped through.

Cold sweat ran down Kassia's back and between her breasts, and she scooted as far back on the bed as she could. She looked toward the door, wondering whether she could run to it faster than Urushi.

The woman spared no glance for Kassia. Her brass bracelets jangled as she reached out an elegant hand to Urushi, who took it and brought it to his lips.

"At last you have substance, Shadow!" Urushi continued to hold the thing's hand, pressing it against his cheek. "Is it time?"

Kassia's perfect world cracked. "Time for what? What is this monster, this 'Shadow'?" Kassia's words came out in a nervous squeak instead of as a demand.

"It is time," Shadow said, ignoring her, smiling at Urushi, sliding her hand down his chest so intimately Kassia leaned forward to slap her.

But Shadow's body dissolved into an infinity of specks that encircled Urushi like a swarm of bees. His head tipped back and a scream ripped from his throat as the swarm invaded his body through his mouth, his nose, his ears, his penis, his anus, even his pores. In moments, the swarm had been absorbed. Urushi fell to his knees.

Kassia drew back, covering her mouth with her hands. "Should I call Hooting Owl? Your healers?"

Urushi pulled away and laughed. "Your feeble help is unneeded, *youngling*," he said in Shadow's voice and accent. "We are complete and invincible. We will have vengeance on Fila for rebuffing me." He stood.

"Get out of him, Shadow! He's mine. You can't have him. Get out!"

She waited for the sparkles to emerge, for Urushi's expression to returned to normal. Instead, his face changed.

She jumped back and covered her mouth with her hand. His eyes were no longer scarred and no longer human. They were dark, merciless pits, iris and pupil bleeding together into circles the color of peat smoke. He pulled the scarf from his face, hurled it to the floor, and stomped on it. His hair grayed and then silvered, and the raised scars on his face flattened and pinkened to match the healthy skin.

The hairs on Kassia's arms prickled. "No!" she shouted. "*I* am supposed to give him those gifts. *I* am supposed to heal him. Not a monster. Stop it! Stop it!"

The future was breaking. In the future she planned, she was going to fix him. He was going to love her forever. But instead, he had joined with some unnatural thing and let it give him Kassia's gifts.

"Let's not wait for Fila to reach us. Let us march out with an army and kill her on the road like a criminal," Shadow-Urushi said, their voice purring, their body swaying like a cat's tail.

"Absolutely not," Urushi-Shadow answered in his normal voice. "I want to defeat her with magic, one on one, at the Seat in front of all of the Guardians. Everyone must see me conquer her."

"She is stronger than you think." Shadow-Urushi brushed their hair back with a sinuous gesture. "She has twice escaped our firedaughters. Take no chances. Kill her now."

"No. I will fight her and I will win."

Kassia inched away, slid off the bed, and crouched low against the bed where it met the wall. She pressed hard against it, her chest heaving, wishing she were not so buxom. She would never fit under the bed. Her gaze darted from door to door. She could not get out unseen.

She was trapped.

She put her nose against the comforter to muffle the sound of her breathing. Perhaps he—they—whatever Urushi was now—would forget her and continue their argument elsewhere.

Shadow-Urushi swept around the bed, loomed over her, and extended a hand. "Come."

Kassia worked up her courage. "I would like to talk to Urushi, please." She held her breath. One second. Two seconds. Three seconds.

Urushi blinked and his face returned to its familiar lines and expression. "Kassia, please come with me." He knelt next to her and stroked her hair. "I still love you and need you."

His words stilled her jangling nerves and warmed the pit of her stomach. She steeled herself to reject him. *He's a monster now. Let him go.* "Let's be sensible, dear one. You don't need me now you have Shadow. I release you from all your promises."

"Of course we need you," Shadow-Urushi purred, stroking her hair. "At least at first. When you become Servant and name us your Consort, you legitimize us."

"Choose someone else. I agreed to marry Urushi, not you, Shadow."

Shadow-Urushi smirked. "I wondered whether this weak one would lose heart. We have a surprise for you. You will change your mind."

Chapter 44

URUSHI DRAGGED HER through the House of the Servant, taking dusty ancient passages Kassia had never seen, and forced her down several flights of stairs to a door concealed in a shadowy alcove. Hooting Owl opened the door, and a damp, musty smell rolled out from the darkness.

Kassia recoiled. *Urushi is going to shove me in a cave and leave me.* "No! Please, no!"

"Don't be afraid, my queen." Hooting Owl patted her shoulder. He took a step inside; the light from his torch bounced off polished black basalt walls. "This tunnel leads to the floor of the volcano and opens behind the chair of the Servant."

She pulled free of Urushi's grip and followed Hooting Owl on her own with eager steps. The Servant's chair at last! She had coveted it for so long.

But where was the excited beating of her heart? The intoxicated feeling of floating above the tunnel floor? Her beaming smile of triumph? The love and admiration in Urushi's eyes? Her hands shook, as in her daydreams, but from fear, not anticipation. Nothing was as she had imagined it; all was wrong, twisted, spoiled.

Shadow had turned her dream into a nightmare.

She licked her dry lips. *I have to pretend. I have to go along with Urushi until he lets down his guard. Then I can escape.*

Soon they reached a massive door; trumpets blared on the other side. Hooting Owl threw open the door, and she and Urushi processed into the bottom of the huge amphitheater, heads high, steps measured, Urushi lifting his hand in benediction, Kassia wearing a rictus of a smile to hide her anger and humiliation.

The amphitheater seats were half full already. Toilers behind the benches moved methodically from lamp to lamp, lighting them. More Guardians and Toilers streamed down the staircases, looking for seats.

She had expected shouts of acclamation and cheers of praise. Some Guardians came to kneel before Urushi before taking their seats, but most people wore wary faces or gazed at the floor.

She shivered. Urushi would be angry at the lukewarm reception, and she no longer believed he would not take it out on her.

Kassia caught the glance of a long-time friend of her mother's. Relieved to see a familiar face, she took a step toward her and smiled.

The woman turned away, her gray sash fluttering.

Heat flared in Kassia's torso and climbed up her neck and head. She took two steps toward a stranger and forced out a greeting, pretending he was the intended recipient of her smile.

His eyes widened with fear; he fiddled with his gray sash.

She backed up, smiling, waving, looking at the audience's clothes. A full half of the Guardians wore a gray sash of personal mourning. Others wore an orange-yellow sash of mourning for Servant Hyacinth.

Someone called out, "Her hair's not copper. Where's our Servant?"

Nausea gripped her stomach. She froze in place, her arm sticking awkwardly out like a badly made doll's.

"Who said that?" Urushi shouted, shaking his fist and turning in a circle. "If you disdain my queen, you disdain me."

The crowd quieted. But no one fingered the perpetrator.

Urushi held out his arm toward Kassia in invitation. She took it, clutching the fabric of his coat tightly to keep from collapsing or fleeing. He walked her in a circle, as if displaying a prized horse, and then led her to the two steps up to the dais containing the seats of honor.

They climbed.

As soon as his back was turned, disapproval flared again and seethed around them. Murmurs and hisses, catcalls and jeers rose from her left and her right, from high in the galleries and close to the floor, swelling as she and Urushi stepped onto the dais. "False Servant!" someone nearby sneered.

Tears flooded Kassia's eyes. She stared blindly at the chairs of the Servant and Consort, her vision too blurred to see their details. Her shaking, sweaty hand fell from Urushi's arm and clutched the side of her gown.

She at last stood where she always wanted to be. But she was not here because the Land chose her or because Fila abdicated in recognition of Kassia's greater skills and suitability. She stood here as a usurper.

Ashes. Her achievement was ashes.

As she neared the outlying houses of the city, Fila stopped and bit her lip. She had expected a confrontation by now, had expected Urushi would come to challenge her or send an army to kill her. The trumpet fanfares suggested an invitation to meet him at the Seat of Enchantment itself.

She shaded her eyes and looked up at the tower atop the collapsed volcano. Urushi's spies would be up there, watching her.

She would give them something to see.

She drew a ragged breath, then let it out. This was her last chance to turn around, to run away, to let her brother win. From here on, she committed herself to fighting Urushi.

Nearby, a hole in the tuff opened into a cave. She had played in it as a girl and knew she could reach the House of the Servant through its tunnels. But the Land was pocked with other holes, leading to other caves, whose tunnels went nowhere. After years away, she had to find the right opening on first try.

She scanned the area. A cluster of familiar rocks caught her attention.

She walked toward them, testing each step carefully, not wanting to break through the soft tuff into a deep cave or hidden crevice.

She reached the hole she sought, its edges ragged, its depths dark, its diameter barely bigger than her adult self.

Her pulse pounded in her ears. She stood on her tiptoes and raised her arms as if beseeching the Land for a boon. Then she stepped sideways, onto emptiness, and dropped.

Pain.
Pain.
Pain.
Pain.

Each jolt of the cart sent agony shrieking through Celatu, scattering his thoughts, making him no more than an animal, an animal whose mind contained only fractured images and bursts of sound, an animal with a glowing copper cord that anchored it to a well of calmness and clarity. Between jolts, in the brief moments when he was lucid, he sent his thoughts through the cord. *Be strong, Violet. You are not alone, Violet.*

I am coming for you, Lady.

As Celatu's clarity slipped away again, the copper cord faded.

But his clutched palm still felt the imprint of his copper good-luck piece. It danced in his confused mind and multiplied into many disks, some bright, some dark, some alone, some overlapping.

One set of disks caught his attention. He knew this set was more important than the others. But why? *Why? Why?*

He started, and the movement made him whimper. His coin was more than a coin.

And he now knew its meaning.

Chapter 45

"I CAN'T CONTINUE with this mockery," Kassia whispered. "Please, Urushi, let me go."

"No. I still need you."

Her stomach still twisted, and stars danced in the darkening in front of her eyes. "I'm going to faint. Or vomit. Or both."

"Get control of yourself! Act grateful! I'm giving you everything I promised you."

Her knees wobbled and banged into each other. She swayed. *I'm going to fall in front of all these people.* She didn't care. The oblivion of unconsciousness would be worth any humiliation.

Urushi grabbed her elbow and steadied her. His other hand touched her sweating forehead, her cold hands, her tight, throbbing abdomen.

He swore under his breath, then paraded her around the dais and back down the stairs as if that was his plan from the beginning. "Your father will convince you to get your nerves under control and to go along with everything I say." He nodded at a stiff figure in the lowest ring of seats.

She squinted. The encroaching blackness and the stars blotted out the man's features. Urushi held out his arm, and she rested her hand on it, seeing no choice but to play out the charade of loving couple. He led her toward the figure.

It was indeed Father. She pulled away from Urushi and lurched the last few steps on her own. She threw her arms about Father, embracing him tightly, so tightly the toggles on his jacket dented her skin. Then she kissed his face and whispered a frenzied appeal in his ear. "Daddy, help me! I don't know what to do."

He did not respond.

She released her embrace and took a step back.

Father's eyes blinked wildly, his gaze fixed, a tear in the corner of his eye.

"What's wrong?" she asked, panicked.

His nostrils flared, and he worked his mouth, but no words emerged. Some spell held him, yet she saw no charms. They must be hidden within his clothes.

Or perhaps it was a more sophisticated and dangerous magic. The magic of Shadow.

Staggering, she turned on Urushi-Shadow, hands on her hips, anger making her rash. "Set my father free!"

"He betrayed us. He helped Fila and Celatu escape us. Whoever is not fully for us is our enemy."

"I won't be your puppet. Let us go."

"Behave, or your father dies." Urushi casually extended his hand and magic shot out, perfect and pure, smelling clean and of caramel.

Father's ear fell cleanly off, without a single drop of blood.

Coldness pummeled her stomach, and she choked back a scream. She dropped to the floor, heedless of her dress, and snatched up the ear ... but she did not have her needlework kit with her, and the caldera contained no healing plants. She had no way to work magic to reattach the ear.

She stood up slowly. Father's tears dripped faster now. She caressed his cheek and then bent to kiss it, whispering, "I'll save you. Somehow."

She had loved Urushi with her whole heart for years.

That love had stopped between one heartbeat and the next.

Now she loathed him. But to keep Father safe, she had to play along with her murderous betrothed—a dangerous game, but she was skilled at games.

She forced herself to smile ingratiatingly at Urushi. "Please, don't hurt him. I'll do as you ask."

He beamed and held out his arm to her. They proceeded yet again to the center of the amphitheater, pretending all was well.

Urushi lifted his hands for silence. "My people, let me present my future queen, Kassia, daughter of Bifac and Gratia, niece of Servant Hyacinth. Love her as I do, and welcome her into your hearts."

Kassia forced a regal smile that promised beneficence and wisdom. A few people clapped half-heartedly.

Hooting Owl waved his arms at the crowd and bellowed, "Hail, Queen Kassia, most beautiful of women, most noble of bearing!"

No one echoed the chant. A few in the crowd tittered.

Kassia wished she could melt into the floor. *They are laughing at me. At me!*

"Land swallow them. Land swallow them all!" Urushi cursed.

Kassia moved numbly to the Servant's Seat.

But even that consolation was denied her. Urushi nudged her to the side and plunked himself on the uncushioned pine. Biting her lip, Kassia sat in the Consort's chair.

A boy ran down the stone stairs and stopped by Urushi's chair, panting heavily, his face red with exertion. "The Servant disappeared!"

Urushi slapped him. Kassia jumped at the sound, and the voices of the crowd cut off in shock. "You mean *Fila* has disappeared, don't you?" Urushi glared at the boy.

"Yes, your highness." The boy's cheek glowed red. "One moment all the guards could see her, and the next moment, she was gone!"

"So she's in the tunnels." Urushi mused out loud. He turned toward Kassia, his inhuman eyes narrowed. "Tell us what her plan is." Magic hummed from him, threatening, growing.

Kassia shrank into her chair and shook her head. "I don't know. Truly. She knew I was loyal to you."

He thrust his face into hers and bared his teeth. "I'll believe you ... for now."

Fila made it from the cave to the Servant's House without encountering anyone, friend or enemy. The house would never be empty unless Urushi ordered it so. More than ever, she believed he wanted their confrontation to take place in the Seat, before as many eyes as possible, so that no one could question who won and how.

She headed for her own room, then checked herself and climbed another flight of stairs to the Servant's private floor. She stared at the door to Mother's room, then pushed it open at last and stepped in.

It was not the bright, happy room she remembered. The Toilers had shut the curtains and draped some furniture with sheets. She went to her mother's wardrobes and looked for her state gown. Her hand trailed across the fabrics, seeking the smooth silk, but it kept stopping at other remembered textures and colors. Mother wore this blue-and-white checked dress to garden. She insisted on the impractical pale colors to stay cooler in the sun.

And this red nubby silk dress: She wore it every year on Fila's birthday because Fila liked it so much.

She forced her hand to move on, and it found the state gown. She pulled it from the wardrobe and slammed the door shut before more memories snagged her heart.

How magnificent and mighty Mother had looked in the yellow gown! The last time Fila had tried it on, the shoulders drooped and the sleeves hid her hands.

She tore off her filthy clothes, setting aside Boraga's charm so she would not forget it. She rushed through her ablutions, not bothering to smooth oil on her face after washing it. She slipped into the dress and stood in front of the looking glass.

The Servant's state gown fit. She had grown into it.

Fila tucked packets of her hair and Boraga's charm into her needlework bag. She would need every aid to her magic when she confronted Urushi and Shadow.

She went to her mother's jewelry box and again hesitated before violating the sacred object. Solemnly, she put on the heavy yellow sapphire earrings and the silver and copper rings on her fingers, one the ring of the Servant, one that of the Consort. She touched the circular pendant, a long-ago gift from Mother, that she always wore. She pulled it out and let it rest on the bodice.

One thing remained. She sat in her Mother's chair and pulled out knitting needles and yarn from the knitting caddy. As Elata had taught her, she knitted a cord of invisibility.

It was time.

She glanced in the looking glass. In the dim room, wearing her mother's clothes and jewelry, she seemed to see Mother's reflection, not her own. *Can I ever live up to her example?* Sighing, she bound the cord of invisibility around her waist and slipped into one of the secret passages to head toward the amphitheater.

Her feet remembered the way. She kept her steps slow; being completely surrounded by the Land magnified her senses and strengthened her powers. When she reached the large door, she nudged it open. She slipped between the door and its jamb, entering the amphitheater behind the chairs of the Servant and Consort, and sat, invisible, on the nearest bench. She scanned the vast space.

The restless crowd muttered and shifted; most gazes focused on a single spot. She stood to see, and her hand flew to her mouth. A Guardian sprawled at the bottom of a stairway, his neck at an odd angle, his silver hair fanned out like lacy fronds of catnip, his mouth trickling blood.

The scent of the magic that had killed him lingered, at once familiar and strange. The caramel she tasted belonged to Shadow; the spirit had been here, in this room, moments ago. But the other....

She forgot to breathe.

The other scent was Urushi's, but the hint of decay was gone.

His magic was no longer broken.

Her chest tightened. She could think of only one explanation: Urushi and Shadow had merged. She would have to fight the combined force of their magic.

She scrabbled in her needlework bag for Servant hair. She pulled out all of it: seven coils of her own hair. *Not enough. Why didn't I think to look for Mother's hairbrush?* Thank the Land she had Boraga's charm! *But where is it?* Her fingers searched the bag again, without success.

She emptied the contents on her lap, looking for flashes of silver and copper. It was not there. She patted herself over urgently, then again, her stomach twisting.

Somewhere between Mother's room and here, she had lost the charm.

Run! Run! Now! She knew the strength of Shadow's magic; she could guess at Urushi's. Her own magic was no match.

She leapt up and turned toward the door.

Afissa's charm, buried forever in Fila's chest, warmed. Afissa's gifts of calm and acceptance rippled in waves from the charm.

Afissa died for this moment. I cannot let her down.

Fila dug her bare toes into the hard-packed ground. The Land sent her encouragement and strength.

She strode around the dais and until she stood in a sunlit spot in front of the seats of honor. Fila almost did not recognize the woman in the Consort's chair. Kassia's eyes were puffy and red from crying. She gripped the chair's arms with such force that her knuckles shone bone-white. Beside her, Urushi lounged in the Servant's Seat, a crown on his head.

"How dare you sit in *my* Seat?" Fila roared.

Urushi jumped up, looking for the source of the challenge. The murmur of the audience increased.

Urushi regained his bearing and sat again, slouching self-assuredly. "Who are you to demand the Seat? Show yourself, imposter!"

Fila yanked the cord of invisibility free and tucked it in her sash. The sun shone hot on her head; her hair and yellow dress must be blazing.

"I am Thistle." Said aloud, the words were solid and satisfying. She was not, like a violet, pretty or sweet or easily crushed. She said it again, louder.

"I am Thistle!"

Whispers and gasps swept the amphitheater.

"Fila!"

"The *true* Servant."

"Hyacinth's daughter."

"Land help her!"

"Someone stop her!"

The shouts rang like bells in Fila's ears, but Kassia's trembling voice rang above them all. "Escape while you can! Urushi wants you dead!"

Fila and Urushi stared at each other. No scarf masked her brother's hair and face. His hair was fully silver, the skin of his face smooth and unscarred, his body upright. *At last, he is who he was meant to be.* Then his face hardened cruelly, and she realized his soul still bore scars.

"I have come to claim my seat."

Urushi threw back his head and laughed, and goosebumps rose on her arms. The high-pitched tinkle held more Shadow than Urushi.

"I have already claimed it, dear sister." Whiplike magic shot from him.

She shielded herself with a coil of hair barely in time. When his magic hit, shock waves vibrated up her arm and into her shoulder. Her arm twitched uncontrollably, and the copper hair fell from her nerveless fingers. It disintegrated into tarnished bits as it hit the earth.

Fila stepped forward. "The Seat is not yours to claim."

This time when he loosed his magic, she was faster, dropping and flattening her palms against the Land, willing It to send up climbing vines of poison ivy to ensnare Urushi.

Urushi's magic whizzed over her head.

On the dais, hairy vines sprouted, thick and ropey and writhing like snakes. They coiled around Urushi's ankles and climbed upward.

Urushi's magic flared, and the vines fell away, charred. He lobbed a ball of fire at her.

Her palms still on the ground, she sent a plea to the Land to compress, to rot, to collapse. It obliged, sucking downward the dais of the Servant and Consort.

Urushi countered by crumbling off earth all around the cavity; dirt spilled in and doused the fire.

Fila scooted backward to avoid falling in the opening chasm. She stood and lifted her dirty hands high, turning around so everyone in the amphitheater could see her. "I am your new Servant, Thistle. Those who support me, come to my aid!"

As one, the crowd stood. Some were not her allies; they blocked the stairways, penning people in.

The earth groaned.

She turned. The ground grew pregnant, elevating Urushi and Kassia, now standing upright, on its growing belly. It cracked, and steam blasted forth.

Fila jumped out of the way, but not soon enough to keep her bare feet from burning.

Urushi bore no wounds from the massive magic he had wrought; he didn't even look tired.

Fila puffed like a bellows.

"No more playing around, little *Fila*." Urushi gripped Kassia's arm with one hand and held his copper and silver crown on with the other. "I've melted the rock under the Seat. It boils and bubbles. Surrender, or I will free it. It will destroy you and the amphitheater."

He has to be bluffing. The thought calmed her. "You and Kassia will die as well. You will not be be king. History will remember you as a usurper and murderer of two Servants and a queen."

Urushi released Kassia. She gasped and wobbled on the rising earth and rock, grabbing the back of the Consort's chair just before she fell. Urushi ignored her struggle. Bending his knees, he sprang from the rock into the seats ten rows up, then leapt back to his original place. Screaming, moaning, and pushing each other, Guardians and Toilers alike bolted for the exits.

"What will it be, Fila?" Urushi taunted, his eyes black, hard, dancing with specks of light that reminded her of Shadow. "Will you let these people die?"

Chapter 46

Pain. Pain.

Pain. Pain. Pain. Pain.

Pain. Pain.

Pain. Pain.

THE AGONY WAS THE SAME; the rhythm was different. Celatu forced his lids open and groaned when the bright glare of copper scalded his burned eyes. The dome of the tower at the Seat? It must be. The cart no longer jounced beneath him; instead, Toilers carried him against the pull of gravity.

We must be climbing the staircase up the side of the caldera.

He clutched his copper good-luck piece and sought the copper cord that connected him to Fila. It wavered into view.

The effort of summoning it exhausted him. He closed his eyes and let in all the cord transmitted. Wariness and weariness. Determination and despair. An all-encompassing love. A growing, paralyzing terror.

He took time to form a message. It had to be just right, the exact words she needed to hear.

He sent the thought through the copper, making it blaze.

You can defeat him.

The color washed from the room, and Fila's faith in herself shriveled. *I didn't believe Urushi would threaten to kill thousands of people to keep me from claiming the Servant's Seat. What sense does it make to murder his own followers and Toilers?*

Celatu, of course, would have predicted it.

The thread that sometimes connected them flared to life, brighter than before. His voice, heavy with weariness, spoke in her mind: *You can defeat him.*

Her doubts fled. Buoyed by Celatu's words, her spirit revived, and she pulled energy and strength and encouragement from the Land. She was Goodborn and Servant; she would behave accordingly.

She straightened to her tallest, stretching her hands out in appeal to the fleeing crowd. "Men of Veridia! Harden your courage and help me with your magic of destruction!"

Most continued their panicked retreat. A few stepped aside, but kept their magic damped. They were too few to counter her brother's magic.

Urushi threw his head back and laughed. "You stand alone, Sister. I have won."

Her palms sweated, and her mouth seemed stuffed with cotton. She touched the cord of invisibility, her escape, then let it be. If she fled, she was conceding her right to the Seat. The brutal reign of kings would begin again. But if she stayed and died, a new Servant would arise, perhaps one who could defeat Urushi.

She could not breathe as she waited for the death blow. *Will he kill me quickly, perhaps crushing my heart, or will he drag my death out, perhaps burning me slowly from the feet up?*

Grinning, Urushi held his arm up, keeping her in suspense.

A sparkle on the ground caught her eye. The mote drifted about like dust, but its drift was purposeful, always closer toward her. She held still as it climbed her dress and neck and tickled her ear.

"I love you so much better than Urushi." The whisper was soft and seductive. "Invite me in, Thistle, merge with me, and we can defeat Urushi. He contains little good. I am still so cold when I am in him."

If she took Shadow's offer, Veridia would have a Servant, not a mad tyrant king.

Her duty as Servant was clear. "No." She spoke in a strong voice, her head tilted back, so everyone still in the amphitheater could hear her and draw courage. "I will not merge with you, Shadow. Go back to Urushi, your *second* choice. My brother will take you in."

A dark mink formed on her shoulder, heavy and scratching. The amphitheater echoed with its hisses.

Urushi balled his fists. "You offered yourself to *Fila*? Traitor!"

The mink's weight disappeared from her shoulder. Urushi's expression changed.

Shadow was again in him.

"She tries to deceive you, divide us, my sweet, my dearest."

"I should cast you out, Betrayer!"

In horrified fascination, Fila watched Urushi's face alter as the personality in charge switched—first the haughty expression and hard warrior eyes of

Shadow; then the tight lips and grief-riven eyes of a man shattered by too many losses; then Shadow again.

"Only I decide when I leave you. Now kill Fila."

"No!" Kassia reached her hand toward Fila. "Quick, give up being Servant! I don't want you to die."

"I cannot."

With a moue of distaste, Kassia stroked Urushi's arm and gazed up at him with the wide eyes of a baby animal. "Urushi, do not do this. I beg you."

Urushi's face switched from expression to expression, finally settling into something in-between himself and Shadow.

Fila stood straight. She was Servant and she would die bravely and with dignity.

Magic built in Urushi, magic so powerful that the magic in her, as well as her bones and tendons and muscles, vibrated in sympathy. Her nose was so filled with its scent she could barely breathe.

"Goodbye, Sister." For the briefest instant, Urushi's face flickered with regret.

Chapter 47

"**P**LEASE, YOUR MAJESTY, STOP! We beg you!"

"Who dares give his king orders?" Urushi demanded. His face flushed with anger, but the scent of his and Shadow's magic continued to build.

"We beg pardon, but we bring you an ally who needs the Servant's healing skills."

Fila's heart jolted. *Growling Dog?* Her stomach twisted. *Could there be a worse indignity than healing an enemy before my execution? I will not do it!*

Without waiting for Urushi's permission, Growling Dog and Bluebird led a large group of Toilers down the steps, sweeping with them those trying to escape. Metal clattered: they had brought their farm tools.

Fila squinted. Several Toilers bore a litter with a limp body covered by a sheet. An arm dangled over the edge like a wilted vine. The copper cord in her mind flared even brighter. For a moment, it stretched all the way from her to the litter.

Urushi strode forward to meet the Toilers. "Who is this?"

"Your loyal cousin Celatu. He regrets his earlier indecision and now wishes to offer his services to you."

Loyal? Offer his services? Meanwhile, the copper cord sent her waves of agony, affection, and … amusement? Celatu and the Toilers were up to something.

"Toiler, why do you speak for my cousin? Why does Celatu not tell me himself?"

"He is on the verge of death. No Guardian woman's magic has been strong enough to heal him. We request, King Urushi, that you allow the Servant to heal him before you execute her."

"I knew you would come around, Celatu. Why did you wait so long?" Urushi turned to Fila and grinned, showing his teeth like a wolf. "Do it. Heal this man who has just declared himself your enemy."

"No!" *I wish I knew what Growling Dog and Celatu are planning, what they hope I will do.*

"Please, Fila? For me?" Kassia's voice trembled. "If not for me, do it because you're the Servant and it's your duty. You know it is."

Celatu knows I always do my duty. He would expect me to agree.

"Dear Kassia, your words move me." Fila walked toward the stretcher. The copper cord confirmed Celatu indeed lay near death, a death caused by icedragon magic. Her heart ached for him … and for herself. She fingered her silver medallion, but its comfort weighed little against the burden of his nearing death.

If she healed him of such serious injuries, she would be drained as Afissa was drained. Afissa had died; Fila might too. Perhaps that was Celatu's plan: to try to succeed where she had failed.

She would do her best to help him. "Urushi, I have been humbled. Our entire family supports you instead of me. It is time for me to go along to get along. If I survive the healing, I will join my cousin in equal loyalty to you."

Urushi grinned. "You will bow to me? Serve me?"

"Whatever obeisance Celatu gives you, I will give you the same twice over."

His face twitched. The suspicious eyes of Shadow peered at her. "She lies. Don't believe her."

Urushi's face. "Goodborn can't lie." His smile broadened, and he licked his lips. "I agree to your terms."

"Thank you for your mercy, dear brother. Now please, step back and give me room to work."

Fila pulled back the sheet covering Celatu and gasped. Now, half of his hair had reverted to black. His body, clad in nothing but underdrawers, lay pale and bloodless except for angry red burns and long, deep gouges. Shaking with fear for him, she placed her remaining coils of hair on the largest wounds. She pulled out a hairpin and dug it deep into her arm, leaned over him, and squeezed her blood on his injuries.

The angry red skin paled. At every burn and slash, fibers of skin snaked out from the margins and knitted together. She placed her bleeding arm on the largest burn. As if her hand did not belong to her, it found his stubbled cheek and caressed it. *I am more afraid of his death than I was of my own.*

"What foolish, cowardly thing have you done now, to get yourself in such trouble?" she scolded.

"I love you, too," he mumbled. "Hide what I do."

Growling Dog stepped closer.

She put her arms on either side of him and shook her head.

Now that one hairpin was gone, others flew out. She tipped her head and a fountain of copper hair cascaded. Her silver pendant dropped onto his chest and glowed.

His trembling fingers took the pendant and fumbled with his annoying "lucky" coin, pushing them together.

His coin snapped into place in the middle of her pendant with a roar that shook the ground. The silver circle and copper disk glowed like a full moon in the countryside, growing steadily brighter. Celatu grabbed her hands.

The copper cord binding them glowed red hot, and burning thoughts and images flooded her mind like magma. A prophecy. An army of Toilers. A sky brilliant with icedragons. Love flowed into her, not from the Land, but from him.

Despite his still-healing injuries, Celatu shouted loud enough for everyone in the amphitheater to hear. "Servant, I offer myself as your Consort, to serve Veridia at your side, to merge our magic for the greater good, to aide you in good times and bad."

"No!" Urushi roared. He lunged toward them and grabbed Fila, pulling at her with superhuman strength, trying to break her connection with Celatu. Then his magic hammered at her fingers and hands, and they spasmed with agony.

Celatu's hands tightened painfully around hers, and Growling Dog wrapped his arms around them both, holding them together.

Other Toilers beat at Urushi's arms with their massive fists and struck him with their improvised weapons.

Urushi's magic wavered under the onslaught and his hold broke. He shouted in an unknown language as a Toiler picked him up and hurled him across the space.

"I, Thistle, accept you as my Consort. Together we will serve Veridia and Its two peoples." The Ritual was done.

No one, not even the Land, could separate them now. Her head spun and her legs trembled from loss of blood and power. She would have fallen to the floor without Growling Dog to support her. Instead, she collapsed on Celatu's chest.

His lips were enticingly close. It took all her strength, but she leaned forward and kissed them. The rest of her magic drained into him, but she drew more from the Land, pumping it into him as fast as she could, feeling his strength build and his mind clear, then her own.

Celatu pushed her away. "I'm healed enough to fight," he gasped, lurching to his feet.

Guardian men gathered around Urushi, and magic buzzed and perfumed the air like a hundred scented candles.

Near the dais, Urushi's supporters righted him. Others joined them. The fragrance of their magic rose, too, with Shadow's cinnamon scent stronger than any other.

Thistle took Celatu's hand. He shouted to the undecided and frightened people who remained high in the amphitheater. "Those who support the Servant, come forward. The Toilers will protect you and fight alongside you."

"You fool," Urushi sneered. "Toilers don't fight."

A Toiler launched herself at Urushi and closed her massive hands around his neck.

Her body exploded, splattering Urushi with gore from head to foot. He thrust his arms toward the sky and threw his head back, howling with laughter.

Roaring, the other Toilers thundered forward. Guardians who had held back now followed the Toilers down the steps, shouting, "For the Servant!"

Celatu squeezed her hand, and the cord that bound them transmitted the sense of his intention: "Together now."

She pictured a finely woven fabric; he nodded.

Magic shot every which way through the amphitheater. Toilers crushed Urushi's supporters with their bare hands. Amidst the high-pitched screams and deep grunts, Thistle and Celatu stood protected behind Growling Dog's wide back and mixed their magics of creation and destruction. They hurled their creation at Urushi.

As it rolled toward him, plants sprouted, only to be ripped by unseen hands from the ground. Vines and stalks rose toward the sky. Fine fibers peeled off, layer by layer. When the vines and stalks were no more, the spiderweb-thin fibers wove together into a diaphanous fabric impervious to magic. It drifted down toward Urushi.

Breathless, Thistle bit her lip, fretting that any moment one of her enemies would blast it apart. Celatu's hand tightened on hers.

The gauzy sheet stopped and hovered over Urushi. Her brother never glanced at the danger above or its slight shadow around his feet; he laughed and danced as he exchanged bolts of fire with two Guardian men.

The fabric dropped. Urushi's supporters jumped out of the way.

Just before the fabric touched the ground and sealed Urushi in, streams of sparkling liquid gushed from Urushi's orifices and flowed away. The tributaries joined. The liquid rose into the air, coalescing into the shape of a woman before dissolving into sparkling dust.

Fila's gaze followed the dust as it wafted up, up, up, and out of the caldera.

"Come back, Shadow!" Urushi pleaded.

But Shadow was gone.

"I love you, Urushi," Fila said, holding out her hand. "Give up your foolish plans. Let us be loving brother and sister once again and for all time."

"You have not won," he shouted through the nearly invisible fabric.

She took a step toward him, her hand of forgiveness still out. Urushi's eyes rolled back; his body twitched and jerked.

Her blood ran cold, and she backed into Celatu's arms. He gripped her shoulders as together they watched Urushi's convulsions. His silver hair returned to brown. Scars rippled into being across his face, tugging and twisting his features into a horrific mask of skin, a parody of a face. His pupils faded to a white-on-white patchwork.

Fila gasped. *So many scars! He's blind or close to it.*

Moaning, Urushi flailed against the fabric. His magic could not puncture it. His hands could neither rip it nor pull it off.

Fila's eyes rained tears.

At last, Urushi dropped his head and arms. "Kassia, help me! Please!"

Kassia had abandoned him. She stripped clothes from a man who had sat unmoving on a bench in the first row through all the tumult. Toggles popped off and cloth tore as she undressed him in a frenzy.

Uncle Bifac!

"Fila!" Kassia screamed. "Father's been charmed. I'll give you anything—everything—I have if you save him."

"In a moment!" Fila called. Urushi's supporters were still fighting, now striking Toilers as well as Guardians with their magic, trying to get to her and Celatu. If they killed either of them, the fabric confining Urushi would dissolve.

Celatu gestured toward some Toilers being driven up the stairs. Through their connected hands, Fila lent him power.

Celatu crushed the hearts of seven of Urushi's supporters.

Through the cord, she suffered his overwhelming sorrow and remorse with him.

Fila countered with soothing thoughts of cool, quiet forests and bubbling springs. "We must end this."

He nodded; four more of Urushi's men collapsed.

Urushi shouted to his supporters, "Kill Fila and Celatu!"

Urushi's assassins and other supporters gathered into a knot, their faces eerily alike in their expressions of determination and hostility. The air sizzled and perfumed with rising male magic.

"Stand in front of me," Fila told Celatu, yanking the cord of invisibility from her sash. She threw the cord around his waist and tied it.

He vanished.

Urushi's men looked around for Celatu and muttered to each other.

"You're invisible now." Fila whispered.

"You too?"

"No."

"What's the point?"

"You can sneak up behind them."

"Leave you unprotected? Not on—"

An assassin aimed his hand at Fila. Magic dribbled out and formed a smoky glob that rolled lazily through the air.

"Their magic is running low," Celatu shouted. "Toilers! Friends! Attack now!" He picked Fila up and carried her out of the path of the magic.

The ball of magic changed direction.

"Corroded copper! It's still coming right at you," Celatu said. "Now what?"

"Get behind his supporters and … take care of them." She didn't wait for his protest. She wiggled free of his hold and ran, zigzagging, toward Urushi, her body low. She slammed to a stop behind him, with his body between her and the ball of magic.

The ball of magic halted, quivering.

"It's waiting for you," Urushi taunted. "Will you hide behind me for the rest of your life?"

She ignored him and waited for Celatu to act.

One of Urushi's men collapsed without a sound. Several feet away so did another. Urushi's men panicked.

"Where is the Coward?"

"Never mind him. Kill Fila."

"How do we catch her?"

Celatu's voice rang out. "Surrender to the Servant's mercy, or more of you die."

A man laughed. "Trust the Coward to say that while hiding."

More bodies hit the floor.

"I surrender!"

"Me too!"

Men's voices argued. In front of Urushi, something exploded.

Fila peeked around him. The smoky glob that had chased her lay on the ground in pieces.

Take advantage of the confusion. She stepped out and shouted to Urushi's men. "Suppress your magic. Lay down your weapons. Urushi has lost."

They did as she ordered.

She heaved a huge sigh and ran to Celatu. She tugged on his hand. "Now to help your father."

"Not yet. Urushi still lives."

"Together we can heal him."

Celatu shook his head slowly. "When Shadow fixed his body, she didn't fix his mind. Maybe he can't be healed."

"Maybe she knew he wouldn't cooperate once he was in his right wits again."

Celatu looked at her with pity that echoed through their connection.

"We must try to heal all of him," she insisted. "The Servant does not kill. She preserves and nourishes life."

Celatu stroked her hair. "This is why the Servant needs a Consort."

She pushed his hand off.

The ground warmed and trembled under her feet. Her nose caught a whiff of Urushi's magic, the old smell, fetid and wrong. *It's not possible! The fabric completely covers him.*

"Oh, no!" she exclaimed. "We made a mistake. The fabric—it doesn't go under his feet! He's sending magic into the ground. We have to get everyone out."

"Too late, Fila." Urushi's face split open in a dozen places from the magic he was expending. "Now everyone will die because of you."

The ground heated quickly, rising like bread dough. Its crust cracked; steam burst out, followed by a trickle of magma.

Celatu whirled. "Toilers! Get yourselves and the Guardians out as fast as you can!"

Toilers threw Guardians from both sides over their shoulders and bounded up the benches toward the exits at the caldera's rim.

Celatu and Fila both ran to Bifac. With a pained grunt, Celatu lifted his father and draped him over his broad shoulders. "Get out, Kassia!"

Celatu lurched toward the stairs, but Fila called to him and Kassia. "Use the tunnel to the Servant's House. Follow me."

She and Kassia linked arms to help each other stay upright. The land bulged higher, and they struggled to climb over. Celatu's breath heaved behind them.

At the top, Kassia stopped and whimpered at the drop. "It's too steep. I'll fall and catch on fire."

Fila tugged, with no success.

Celatu topped the growing land, dropped to his backside, and slid. Fila followed his example, pulling Kassia with her.

Kassia screamed the whole way. At the bottom, she and Fila ran to the heavy door and yanked on the metal handle, now hot from the steam.

The bulging ground acted as a doorstop. Kassia squeezed through the opening, but Celatu, carrying his father, was too wide.

He eased his father off his shoulders. Fila helped him maneuver Uncle Bifac into the tunnel. Then Celatu squeezed sideways through the opening.

Once the others were safe inside, Fila slammed the door shut.

Chapter 48

GUTS CHURNING, Celatu dropped to his knees beside the too-still body of his father. "What happened to him?"

Tears ran down Kassia's face, smearing her cosmetics as she searched Father's clothes. She was dressed in finery but wore a ring set with what appeared to be a rounded lump of charcoal. "He's under a charm."

Their voices echoed in the tunnel, and the ground trembled. The tunnel wall cracked open.

I can't carry Father any farther. Where could the tarnished charm be?

"His shoe! That's where I'd hide a charm." A loud crack sounded; behind Father, the black basalt split open a finger's width.

Celatu yanked off Father's right boot. "Fila, get the other boot and sock."

"Fila's in the amphitheater." Kassia pulled on Father's left boot, but could not shift it.

"What!" Celatu sent an angry thought through the copper cord, now thickened into a rope. He looked at the crack; it widened.

"Stand back, Kassia. Far back."

Celatu shaped his magic and sent it to disintegrate every bit of nonliving organic matter around Father.

His shoes and clothes crumbled into dust. So did his hair and eyebrows. Silvery flakes showered from his body, leaving all his skin the shiny pink of a newly healed wound.

Father groaned and opened his eyes.

"Praise the Land!" Celatu exclaimed. Kassia pulled off her skirt and draped it across Father's naked lap and then embraced him. Celatu put his arms around both of them, kissing Father's face repeatedly.

"My dear children! You're safe!" Father touched the tears on each of their faces. "You're safe!"

Celatu helped him stand, gritting his teeth against the pain from his magic-making wounds. "Lead him to safety before the tunnel collapses," he told Kassia. "I must help my wife."

Breathing hard, he shaped more magic against dead organic matter and shot it at the door to the amphitheater.

The thick, huge door rotted and turned to clouds of tan dust.

Sneezing, Celatu limped into an inferno.

* * *

Fila ignored Celatu's mental reprimand. She couldn't leave until everyone was safe. It should be soon: The last of the Guardians and Toilers were pouring out the exits. Only Hooting Owl and Urushi remained.

Hooting Owl perched on the arm of the Consort's chair as its feet charred, pleading with Urushi, shaking his head as Urushi begged him to leave.

"Urushi!" Fila called up. He twisted in the fabric that trapped him and his magic. It had frayed in several places. He could hurt her now if his fingers found a hole. She kept her voice confident. "Surrender!"

"*I* should be giving orders to *you*." His voice, defiant, revealed neither fear nor repentance. The fabric clinging to his legs, he plodded to the Servant's chair and sat.

"Please surrender. I don't want you to die." She moved a little closer; her bare feet singed.

"I'll be a laughingstock. Again. Always."

"No. Celatu and I together can help you."

Urushi snorted. "From king to commoner? And blind to boot? I think not."

The mound under him turned red. The chairs of the Servant and Consort burst into flames.

Hooting Owl yanked up his feet and balanced on the back of the Consort's chair. Dancing flames kisssed the bottoms of his feet.

Lifting her arms, Fila sent her consciousness down into the ground and up into the sky.

Her copper hair rose, sending out sparks that sizzled in the heated air. Agony and rapture shot through her and out of her. Her body vibrated as she called for rain, a drenching downpour that would cool the Land and put out the fires, torrents of rain that would show Urushi just how powerful she was.

Flames reached Urushi and Hooting Owl.

"Run, Appa!" Fila called.

"No," Hooting Owl's voice boomed. He stepped down onto the burning chair seat, picked Urushi up, and held him above the flames. His face contorted in agony.

A raindrop fell on Fila's forehead. Another sizzled on the mound. Her magic was working, but too slowly.

Someone grabbed her waist. She shrieked even as his touch assured her. *Celatu.* He came back for her. Fila felt his body convulse as the full force of the magic tearing through her entered him, but he hung on and reinforced her draining magic with his own.

A thunderclap sounded, and a moment later lightning split the sky. Rain poured in torrents. The first drops hit the ground and sizzled into vapor. But so much cool rain came down that it puddled faster than it could evaporate.

The Land cooled, and Its redness faded.

Fila slumped back into Celatu's supporting arms. "You have lost, Brother. Let me release you and heal you."

With noble, gentle tenderness, Hooting Owl placed Urushi back in the Servant's chair and arranged his limbs as best he could through the fabric.

Urushi crumpled, no magic flowing from him. His expression held the gray bleakness of a landscape obliterated by a flood. He folded his hands in his lap and studied them. "Dearest Appa, have Fila treat your burns."

"I'm staying with you." Hooting Owl panted from pain. Large blisters pustulated his skin from the knees down.

"Go." Urushi's voice was heavy with defeat. "I need to catch my breath."

"No. I must make sure you are safe first."

Urushi smiled so sweetly and beautifully that Fila's eyes could not bear to look. Her stomach pulsed in time with her heart. She longed to run to him and embrace him.

"Go, Appa. That's an order."

"Yes, my dear lad."

Celatu rushed up to help the injured Toiler limp down the mound.

Fila pulled clumps of hair from her head, sat, and tied crown knots with both hands and feet.

Celatu helped Hooting Owl sit down next to her and steadied him.

She gagged at the charred smell of his skin and worked faster. As she finished each charm, she placed it on a burn, starting with his feet. The Toiler sat with his gaze unfocused and his head bowed, not even wincing as she hurt him against her will.

The muscles and tendons of his feet repaired themselves, and skin recovered them.

Fila grimaced: His feet remained misshaped. When she had more time and supplies, she would need to make stronger charms to finish today's emergency repair. His ankles healed next.

Yet the smell of char grew stronger instead of weaker. She and Hooting Owl sniffed the air at the same time.

Appa's eyes widened, and he shouted, "No! No!"

"Take good care of Wiggle." Urushi's voice resonated with despair and desolation. Alone on the sinking dais, he looked as forlorn as a Toiler cemetery in a long-deserted village.

As Urushi's head sank from view, Appa wailed. The top of the mound glowed like coals, and waves of heat battered Fila's face.

Fila lunged, but Celatu grabbed her around the waist; Hooting Owl as well. Fila and Appa struggled, but Celatu was as stone.

The Consort's chair tipped, balanced for a moment on two blackened legs, and then perished in the same fiery hole.

Fila waited for screams that did not come.

Hooting Owl pulled free and sank to the ground, his head bowed, his hands picking at his tunic.

Celatu wrapped both arms around Fila's waist, and she wearily leaned against him. At last she was safe, but at a price she did not want to pay.

"He made his choice," Celatu said. "It isn't your fault."

Fila turned and buried her face in his chest. His arms tightened about her. She should cry. She should cry for all of the dead—for Urushi, for her parents, for Amma, for Afissa, for everyone killed by firehounds and icedragons. She should cry for those who loved Urushi: Hooting Owl, Kassia, Wiggle. She should cry for the innocent person she would never be again.

The tears did not come.

"He made his choice," Celatu repeated.

She wrapped her arms around his waist. "And I've made mine."

Chapter 49

I T WAS UNUSUAL to wait two months to seat a new Servant, but these were unusual times. Celatu, Thistle, and Hooting Owl all needed to heal. Those mourning lost loved ones needed time to grieve and accept. Carpenters had to build new chairs for the Servant and the Consort. Stonemasons had to level the floor of the amphitheater and test the lower tiers of stone benches for heat damage. Thistle called in her mother's seamstress to repair the yellow ceremonial dress, but in the end a new one had to be made. Celatu's wardrobe contained no formal clothes, so he hired a tailor known for his speed.

At last, on a late summer morning of breathtaking beauty, the sky a brilliant sapphire, the clouds soft puffs as white as combed wool, the leaves rich and bright as malachite, the wind a soft breeze that carried the impossible scent of spring flowers, it was time.

Thistle chewed her thumbnail as they waited inside a new hidden door for the trumpet fanfare. A subdued Wiggle sat on her bare feet. He had not let her out of his sight since Urushi's death.

Celatu reached over and adjusted the glowing pendant-and-disk so it hung straight above Thistle's bosom. He still marveled that Servant Hyacinth had chosen him for her daughter all those years ago.

"You clean up nicely," he teased. "You know, if it weren't for your copper hair, I wouldn't have recognized you the day the Toilers carried me into the Seat to be healed. It was the first time I had seen you with clean clothes and an unbruised face."

"As if my looks mattered to you." Thistle sniffed. "All you wanted was to defeat Urushi and Shadow so you could return to your studies."

"I did hope you would be pretty and have a pleasing personality."

"Instead you are stuck with me."

He grabbed her close and kissed the top of her head. "You'll do."

She giggled. "If you dishevel my hair, my cabinet minister for fashion will scold you."

He shook his head. "I still can't believe you gave Kassia and my father positions on your council. I would have exiled them to our farthest estates."

"I'll keep them busy, and we can keep an eye on them."

He cocked an eyebrow. "Now who's the cynical one?"

"You have been a bad influence."

Trumpets sounded. Thistle shook out her stiff yellow skirt so it hung straight. Gently, she lifted Wiggle from her feet and set him beside her. He pressed against her legs. She picked up the pair of shoes to be burned. Her vice-chamberlain, Bluebird, resplendent in a white dress and white hair wrap, opened the new door from the tunnel into the caldera. They strode out and into view.

Cheers erupted.

Taking Celatu's hand, Wiggle trotting along beside, Thistle-who-had-been-Fila stepped into their future.

Acknowledgments

I am very grateful to the people who read early drafts of this manuscript and commented: my wonderful critique group: Laurie Bolaños, Rosalind Green, Margaret Nichols, and Farrah Rochon; and my former agent, Alaina Grayson Tucker.

Useful comments on the beginning chapter(s) also came from "Deep Edits Critiquer" Margie Lawson and judges of various contests, including judges of the Southern Louisiana Chapter of the Romance Writers of America Dixie Kane contest 2007, the Charter Oaks Romance Writers Golden Acorn contest 2008, and Laurel Anne Hill (San Mateo County Fair 2010). I thank them all.

Many, many thanks to Tom Vandenberg for a glorious cover. I loved working with you.

Huge thanks to my editor Terri-Lynne DeFino, who labored long and mightily over this book and greatly improved it. I appreciate your not coming to my house in the midst of editing to whack me over the head for taking up so much of your time.

Publisher Eric T. Reynolds of Hadley Rille Books was a joy to work with, as always. I especially appreciate his patience with my emergencies and many prior commitments during the production of this book.

Much appreciation to Laura Reynolds, who did the final edit, and to Tina Black for copyediting the book.

More thanks than I could ever express go to my supportive husband, David Malueg, who would win a blue ribbon in the "Best Husband of a Writer" category, if there were such an award for the long-suffering spouses of authors.

Thanks to structure maven Claire Merriam Hoffman for many interesting and useful conversations on motivation-response units and other aspects of story microstructure.

Renee Smith acted as my "typical reader" soundboard, providing feedback on clarity and believability.

Last but certainly not least, huge thanks to the valiant heroes who read through part or all of the final revisions at the last minute: sisters of the heart Laurie Bolaños, Rosalind Green, and Farrah Rochon; sister-for-real Renee Smith; niece Cassandra Smith; and Patti Lyon, Michelle McDaniel-Natale, and Jeremy Natale, who stepped up to help at Renee's request even though they did not know me.

About the Author

Photo credit: Vicki Stanwycks,
Stanwycks Photography, New Orleans

Shauna Roberts grew up in Beavercreek, Ohio, and started writing stories in elementary school. Her love of reading was fostered by her father, Edward Arthur Roberts, who took her to the library weekly to check out books; and by her aunt, Janet Louise Roberts, a research librarian and successful romance novelist, who gifted her with many books and encouraged her to read widely and dream large.

From 1986 to 2010, she worked as a science and medical writer and editor, first at scientific magazines and later (after 1989) as a freelancer.

She now writes science fiction, fantasy, romance, and historical fiction. She is a 2009 graduate of the Clarion Science Fiction and Fantasy Writers' Workshop, and she won the 2011 Speculative Literature Foundation's Older Writers Grant. Her past fiction publications include two novels, two novelettes, and many short stories.

Hadley Rille Books was also the publisher of her novel *Like Mayflies in a Stream*, the story of a priestess who is sent into the wilderness by her king to tame a wild man … and what happens after. Inspired by the "Epic of Gilgamesh," the historical novel takes place in the exotic land of ancient Mesopotamia, where civilization began.

She currently lives in southern California, where she listens nightly to the songs of coyotes but still longs for the steamy bayous of southeastern Louisiana.

Her website: http://www.ShaunaRoberts.com

She loves to hear from readers, and free signed bookplates are available on request. Write to her at ShaunaRoberts@ShaunaRoberts.com

You can sign up for her author newsletter at http://eepurl.com/Fr3Hf